Lovesick

MONTRA ALDRIDGE

Editing by Makenna Albert www.onthesamepageediting.com
Book cover design and formatting by Anna Volkin, https://coverfling.com

ISBN: 978-0-578-25112-7

This book is dedicated to my husband…

~

Eric, thanks for pushing me towards publishing. Your belief in me is empowering. I'm a lucky woman and I love you more with each day. Without you, I wouldn't know how to write happy endings. I wouldn't be able to bring swoon worthy men to life. You are the true muse to all my writings. Writing a love story is the easiest thing in the world to do when I live in one every day.

TABLE OF CONTENTS

~

Lovesick

CHAPTER 1

~

Today marks five years since he died, though it still feels like yesterday. How is it possible that one thousand eight hundred twenty-five days have passed without hearing his laugh? Seeing his smile?

The loss consumed me last night. Guilt, anger, and pain all surged through me, making it impossible not to toss and turn as I tried to escape the onslaught of chaos in my mind.

It hurts every time I think about our last moments together. I wish I would have told him I loved him before he walked out the door. Did he know what he meant to me? I wish I could go back, just have one more conversation with him...

We met our first year of college. He was handsome, fun, and a little bit of a trouble maker. Not enough to actually get in trouble, but he goofed off all the time and had that bad boy charm. On an awful date freshman year, he got sloppy drunk and tried to kiss me at the most inopportune time.

He playfully stalked me after the date, waiting outside my dorm after school or coming to the burger joint I worked at on campus. It went on briefly until I relayed my message that I clearly wasn't interested. I got home from school one day, and he was sitting on the steps of my building, looking sober and annoyingly cute.

"Hey Lily," he said with a giant smile and a twinkle in his

mischievous blue eyes.

"Dexter," I bit back and kept walking right by him to the entrance.

"That mini golf place opens tonight and I bought us tickets," he said, entirely confident in himself.

I turned around and laughed. "Our date was awful. You got drunk and puked on my shoes. I'm not very attracted to you anymore." *Amused, yes...*

"You are the one that wanted to do shots. You set the tone." He took a step forward. "One more chance. No drinking. Just mini golf and pizza at a place that checks IDs. I like you so much that I have resorted to making a complete jackass out of myself."

"Something you seem very comfortable with," I quickly pointed out.

He arrived for our first date looking immaculate. When I opened the door and saw his soft blonde hair illuminated in the shining sun, a little squeal erupted silently in me. He looked too good to be true. I was almost intimidated by him because he came from New York and I grew up here in this blip of a town. He seemed worldly and posh, more so than anyone I had ever been around. At dinner, the server never carded us when he slyly ordered a beer with his burger.

Both inebriated, he pushed me home in a shopping cart while we kicked down mailboxes and TP'd houses. By the end of the night, he got rather sloppy. He puked on my brand new pair of white sneakers. Then he tried to kiss me with a chunk of barf on his chin that then dribbled down his shirt.

"True...I'm okay with humiliation," he laughed.

"Listen Dexter, you seem like a nice guy, but I'm not interested." I figured our backgrounds were too different to work.

He gave up after that. We remained friends, though, and saw each other around for the next two years while engaging in other relationships. And then Lawrence came along in the summer before my fourth year.

My worst nightmare.

He was handsome and charming at first, but he was a control freak and never wanted me to leave him. Everyone called him Law and, in my head, everything he told me to do was the *law*. I only saw my parents for one week that summer when he allowed me to go. When he said we needed to move in together off campus, I obeyed, though I didn't want to live with him.

One night soon after school started, he didn't come home. He was with another girl—again. I asked him why he hadn't come home, and he said he had gotten drunk with his buddy, Tyler.

A lie, of course, since Tyler had been drinking beer with me and a few other people the night before and slept on our couch. I pointed this out to him, and he punched me right in the eye. I flew back and hit the floor. He rushed to me and helped me to my feet. His babble of apologies and promises meant nothing to me. I had heard them before. All I did from then on was plan my escape.

The next day, I had to go to the library to do research for a paper. I kept my head down, wearing oversized sunglasses to cover the shiner on my right eye. I ran into Dexter there.

"What's with the shades?" Dexter asked, amused, squinting and looking at the ceiling as though searching for the sun in the darkened library.

"Hungover," I lied.

"Must have been some night." His baby blue eyes twinkled. "You single? Veronica dumped my ass."

"About to be," I said, trying to hold in the tears, but they streamed down my cheeks at an unprecedented rate.

"Hey now, I'm not even this broken up about her dumping me." He sat down in front of me, and I hung my head a bit further to hide. "What's this?" He brushed a finger over the top of the bruise that the glasses must have missed. He pulled them off, and his eyes opened wide, and I snatched my shades back while he shook his head in disbelief.

He closed his hands into fists. "This is from him?"

I saw no reason to lie. Maybe I should've, like I had the other times.

"I'm trying to break up with him but, damn, his temper really scares me," I said, wiping my eyes on my shirt sleeves.

"He still working over at the grill?"

I sighed and nodded. "Yeah, he's there now. You should go order a bunch of food and stiff him."

"No, I'll give him a matching black eye."

He stood and marched out of the building while I followed, pulling on his arm and begging him not to get involved. He didn't pay any attention and zoomed right past the busy hostess and up to Lawrence, jotting down orders from the group of professors at the table. Dexter tapped him on the shoulder.

"Dude," Lawrence huffed, annoyed that he was being bothered mid-order.

"Dude, that black eye you gave Lily is super impressive. You must have really given her all you had," Dexter said, looking him up and down. "What do you weigh?"

Lawrence sighed and rolled his eyes, putting on a front for the teachers as though he had no idea what Dexter was referring to.

"I heard you brag once that you benched 225, so you are strong." Then he turned to me. "Lily, do you bench press?"

I stared dumbfounded at him. At this point, patrons and workers had stopped in the middle of lunch rush to watch the show.

"You don't, do you?" he asked me and I shook my head. "I figured. You are very petite. Can't weigh more than…one hundred twenty pounds soaking wet."

He was almost right on the dot.

Dexter smiled at me and it calmed my nerves right away, dispelling all anxiety from the crowd, Lawrence's death glare, my English lit professor's sad eyes. In Dexter's downright chivalrous presence, I had nothing to worry about. And looking back on it, maybe that's why I didn't lie. As scared as I was, I knew he'd save me from Law.

Dexter pulled back and slugged him right in the nose. "You touch her again and I will do more than that."

Only later did we find out that Dexter broke his perfect, stupid nose.

Dexter took me to his house right after that. The next day, he moved me in with my old roommate, Aubrey, who was looking for a new roommate anyhow.

Lawrence harassed me and stalked me after the incident but every time he did, Dexter would stand up for me. In the process of him becoming my knight in shining armor, I fell for him in a way I had never fallen for anyone. Even the chemistry and passion between us just as friends had been undeniable.

Despite my desire for him, I was still reluctant because of the things with Lawrence. We tried to go slow, but we fell desperately in love. He never puked on my shoes again. We got a place together the last semester of school. Moved to my hometown after graduation. Got married when we were twenty-four.

He died when we were twenty-six, right before our second wedding anniversary. Five days after we found out I was pregnant.

His death still haunts me. It paralyzes me when I think about how awful his last moments of life must have been.

He came home from work and went for a run. Dexter followed his normal running route that day over the little old bridge, the lake beneath churning with all the rain we'd been getting. A drunk driver collided with him, breaking both of his legs and catapulting him off the side of the bridge. He was still alive when he landed in the water, but he couldn't get himself out. I imagine drowning is awful...and lonely...and scary.

I jumped in the lake and held my breath for as long as I could after Drew was born, wanting to see how it felt. I couldn't even stay underwater for a full minute. I've often wondered how long it took him to die once under the water. How long did he suffer? It's not an easy thought.

I sit up in my empty bed and take several deep breaths. "Just get through the day," I whisper to myself.

CHAPTER 2

~

I turn my head and look at my sleeping beauty, resting peacefully on the baby monitor I still rely on. At what point is it considered creepy to watch her sleep? Drew is four years old, and she looks so much like Dexter. She's even named after him from Dexter's last name. I never changed my maiden name from Moore to Drew, so her full name is Drew Moore. My in-laws didn't love the name choice, but I wanted us to have the same last name. Lots of women keep their maiden names when they marry, so I never thought it was a big deal.

Drew and I still live in the house that Dexter's parents bought us as a wedding gift. Dexter's family moved out here after Drew was born to be part of her daily life. They have their own house, which is about a ten-minute walk from mine, and conveniently, my parents live seven minutes in the opposite direction. Our house is three bedrooms and very cute. It backs to the golf course with a gorgeous view.

We live in a gated community in a small town called Whimsy. Within the gates are a golf course, a country club, and a charming, fun little pier that has a restaurant, shops, and an ice cream parlor. The houses either frame the golf course or the lake. Whimsy is about an hour west of Yosemite National Park, and the town is as cute as it sounds. It takes three minutes to drive through the main strip of town. There are no chain restaurants or stores. Every shop is owned by a local resident. Driving in feels like taking a step back in time. It is pristine, and most houses have a white picket fence. The whole town is nestled into a cove on a gorgeous lake in the mountains. The air is fresh, the trees are tall, and I never want to live anywhere else.

Today is Thursday, my one day a week to work at my parents' liquor store, and the five-year anniversary of my beautiful, fun, super loving husband's death in Whimsy Lake on an ordinary day in May. It is still a tough pill to swallow, the way he died, raising our daughter as a thirty-one-year-old single mom and widow. My life kind of sucks, being a widow really sucks, and being a single mom totally sucks. That's not to say I don't love Drew with my whole heart. Like a mad woman I love her. She consumes my every thought, and everything I do in life is with her in mind. I don't know what I'm doing though. She's a handful, my house is a mess, my hair is always unkempt, and I'm constantly digging out clothes from the bottom of my hamper to re-wear.

I used to be so proud of the way I looked before this all happened. Yesterday, the shirt I wore to the grocery store smelled like mold and had a ketchup stain on the front of it. My mom comes over and does my laundry, delivering new clothes she bought me at TJ Maxx in Davenridge, which is the closest city to us. It's a bigger small town with major stores and a mall. That is where we drive to see newly released movies.

Our theater here in Whimsy is old, small, smells a little like mildew, and plays old movies. We still go, though. The theater owners just sold to a new couple who plan on renovating. They want to keep the charm and the cushy red velvet love seats, but they would like to get rid of the smell. Funnily enough, that mildew smell has grown on me. When I told them as much, they laughed.

"Lily, how is the scent of mold charming?"

It just is.

I get out of bed and walk to the window to look at the sky. I'm old school so I pull the window open and stick my hand out to check the weather. I could grab my *phone*, but this is my morning ritual. People are already on the lake water skiing. It's going to be warm today, so I lay out a pair of jean shorts and a pink t-shirt my mom delivered for me last night from her most recent shopping trip.

I climb in the shower, remembering all the times Dexter and I showered in here together. Feels like yesterday and so long ago at the same time. I wash my hair with the shampoo and conditioner my mom put in here last night. I even shave and consider donating what comes off my legs to Locks of Love.

While drying off and brushing my hair absently, I stare at his medicine cabinet. I open it, and pain shoots through my heart. It still feels so sad to see it empty. I throw open my drawer and pull out Drew's *My Little Pony* bandages and Neosporin, putting it in his empty space. Then I start adding more first aid stuff. I'm always searching for this crap and now it will all have a designated spot. Maybe it will make my life easier?

I walk back in my closet with some optimism and a sense of accomplishment that I didn't have yesterday. Never knowing where the bandages are with a dramatic toddler is something I imagine one could parallel to the feeling one might feel in the last few minutes of your life waiting for a nuclear bomb to hit.

Two nights prior, she was screaming about a non-existent cut while I tore through the house like a crazed psycho looking for those *My Little Pony* bandages. I found them in a kitchen drawer. I moved them into the bathroom and swore I would always keep them there until yesterday morning when I found them in her room after another dramatic moment. Every time I go to the store from this point forward, I'm buying some and hiding them all over the house.

I dig around on my messy closet floor for a bra. I have two bras. One nude-colored one with underwire bending its way into my heart for a fatal incision and a black one in decent shape. I need the nude one for the pink t-shirt. After a good thirty minutes, I find it. I put on my new outfit and look in the mirror. "Holy hell, Mom," I say softly to myself. I walk back out into my room, grabbing my phone off the bedside table, and call her.

"These are very short shorts," I say once she picks up, inspecting my butt in the mirror. "I think you got the wrong size."

"Send me a pic and I will tell you honestly how they look. Maybe we could go together next week and get you a new wardrobe?" It's what she always says.

"I'll send you my butt. Tell me if they are too short." I hang up and send her several pictures.

Not too small you look beautiful, she texts.

I turn a few more times and decide I don't even have time to care. I need to pay the electricity bill before they shut me off. I walk out to the living room and open my laptop and send the payment. Then there is a gentle knock on my front door. I look through the peep hole and find Sammy, the garbage man. I swing open the unlocked door with delight.

"Sammy! What on earth would I do without you?"

"Not sure," he says, reciprocating with his warm smile. Sammy is older than my parents and has been the garbage man for decades. "Your gate is locked."

I always forget to wheel my trash up to the curb. Sammy, being the world's greatest garbage man, stops his route, gets out of the truck, and wheels my trash can up to the curb when I forget. Which, in all honesty, is every single Thursday.

I motion for him to come in so he can go through the back door into the yard and get the trash. I used to insist I would bring it up on my own, but he's chivalrous and old school. Being a single mom has quickly made me abandon all feminism I searched for in my youth. All grandiose thoughts or beliefs snuffed out by tantrums and long sleepless nights. In the trenches of single parenting there is no room for feminism. I worry I'm taking advantage of Sammy's kind nature and big heart, but he always assures me I'm not.

"Can I make you a sandwich for lunch?" I ask. *Man on trash duty woman in kitchen. Given up.*

"Sure, extra cheese if you have it." Apparently I'm buying his support with deli meat and cheese.

"Have a seat and I'll fix it right up." He follows me to the kitchen and sits at the island.

We chat about his grandkids and his wife for twenty minutes before he leaves. I give him a big hug and put a shiny red apple in his lunch bag. I love living in a small town in these instances. The saying "It takes a village…" is so true, and Sammy is a part of mine.

On my walk back to Drew's room I hit the thermostat a few times to cool it off. It's unseasonably hot right now. I take a deep breath at the sight of her angelic cheeks, her pursed pink lips. She holds my heart in a way nobody has. I gently sit and rub her back. "Hey Drew…Let's go see Mimi." Mimi is Dexter's mom. She preferred it over Grandma, insisting the name made her sound old.

She bats her big innocent eyes slowly, trying to wake up. After they focus on me, I feel my chest tighten because she looks just like Dexter.

"Mommy, are you crying again?" Her adorable face is etched in such worry. Her saying *again* makes my heart sink in a wretched way, I am always in a state of heartbreak.

"No, sweetie. I just had a tiny bug fly in my eye when I was outside talking to Sammy." I quickly compose myself and fling open her closet. "What are we wearing today, Boo?"

"My sparkly *red* tutu." I giggle at her emphasis. Drew loves tutus and has about a million, so she must specify.

I pull her red sparkly tutu off the hanger and set it on the bed. I lay down next to her, pulling her into my arms.

"Tell me about your dreams last night." Another portion of my morning routine.

"I was married to Captain Underpants and we had a puppy named…" She pauses and looks at me with her giant clear eyes. It's so adorable when she doesn't know what to say next. "I don't know her name." She laughs and my heart soars at that sweet sound.

"Was it a girl puppy?" Her hair tickles my nose, still smelling fresh from her bath last night.

"Yes, and she cuddled and played," Drew says with her cute

small baby teeth exposed in a broad smile.

"I want to be a puppy and cuddle and play all day," I admit.

"That would be awesome," she says like a sassy teen and that makes a rumble of a laugh escape me.

"You want Mommy to help you get dressed?"

"I can do it. Will you please make sausage?" Sassy or not, my baby has manners.

"Deal." I walk out to start breakfast for my sweet girl.

After breakfast, we climb into my car and make the short drive to Mimi's. Drew bursts through her front door and yells, "Mimi...I'm here!" She stands in the entry way with her sparkly red tutu, one pink boot on her right foot and a brown one on her left. Her round belly hangs out the bottom of her small shirt. The front says "Trouble" in flaking hot pink sparkles. She also has a green boa around her neck.

The girl looks wild. She usually does, but I go with it since she loves to dress herself. Mimi hates that I let her "Parade around town looking like a homeless child."

If Dexter was still here, we would likely laugh for hours at her style attempts. Dexter was very humorous which is interesting because Lucille, his mom, is not. She rounds the corner in a sleek black pencil skirt and a crisp white blouse tucked in and the collar up. Red heels pop off her dainty feet and a huge pearl necklace hangs on her thin neck. She looks annoyed the minute she sees Drew's outfit. She closes the distance between us as she brushes her short blonde locks out of her makeup-caked face.

"Lily, we are going to lunch at the clubhouse in an hour with John," she bites. John is Dexter's stepfather. Dexter also grew up without his biological father, John raised Dexter from the age of three and Dexter called him Dad.

"She is exploring her style," I say. "She could be the next Vera Wang." Lucille loves Vera Wang. Being from New York City, Lucille is not suited for small town country living. She's too posh for Whimsy. The outfit alone will have her standing out like a sore thumb at the clubhouse. It's always too much. She tucks her hair behind her ears, revealing the biggest diamond earrings I have ever seen. The fact she's able to hold her head up is impressive; they're boulders!

"I wonder if Vera's mother let her *parade* around town in two different shoes," Lucille says with a look of utter distaste. If I had a nickel for every time she said *that* word…

"Mimi, this one lights up and this one has glitter." Drew stomps her pink boot to make the lights flash. Lucille's face drips with disgust.

"Why does she never wear the real UGG boots I bought her?" She glares at me, completely ignoring Drew. This is the glare that lets me know she thinks I'm a terrible mother. She doesn't have to repeat the way she feels about Drew wearing knockoff items.

I shrug. "Drew prefers these, I guess."

"Why can't you help her make better choices? Honestly, parenting is not this difficult." She looks as though she might be sick. Drew's face falls, her feelings clearly hurt. She was so proud of this ensemble how could anyone dull her sparkle like that?

"Let's get your hair brushed," she says this as if it is a fun reward, knowing full well Drew hates to have her hair brushed. I don't generally fight her, unless she is going somewhere special. Or maybe it's just when I forget to wake her and spend the morning with the 80-year-old garbage man? Or maybe I just don't brush it before she goes to Lucille's?

"Bye Boo, I love you more than I love Red Vines," I say as they walk away. Her tiny giggle echoes down from the hallway, which fills my heart with such joy. Red Vines are my favorite candy, and she likes when I let her know she means more to me than candy. *So cute.*

Lucille stops and turns to me with a disappointed look on her fake face. "Those shorts are way too short for a mother to wear. Honestly." I swallow the lump in my throat and feel ashamed. *Is she right?*

CHAPTER 3

~

I get in my car feeling the weight of Lucille's words. Why does she care what I wear? Thank goodness she didn't see me yesterday with the ketchup stain. She would have had me committed. I shake off her words and think of my mom saying I looked nice. She would never let me wear something unflattering. Lucille sure knows how to make me feel awful about myself though. I drive down to the gate and unroll my window to say hello to Tony, the gate attendant.

"Morning Lils!" he beams.

"Hi Tony!"

Tony lives in the community and is retired, so he volunteers his time at the gate. I adore him and his wife Shelly. Sometimes they bring Drew and I dinner or we go to them. Last week, she invited us over for the most amazing soft tacos with homemade flour tortillas.

"Your hair looks so pretty today." My eyes go big and I drop my sunglasses down the slope of my nose.

"Tony, I brushed it!" I tease.

"Whatever you did, it looks lovely." His easy nature is always welcome.

A car honks behind me, and I look in my rearview mirror to see grouchy Dee-Dee, who is not pleased that I'm having a chat with Tony. Her husband died many years ago, and her three kids moved away and never visit. I'm always nice to her, or try to be, and my mom invites her to every family gathering. She honks again, throwing her arms up in frustration. She's annoyed every time Tony chats with anyone. We exchange knowing glances about Dee-Dee.

She sticks her head out her window and screams, "Any day Lily!"

"You have a wonderful day!" I say to Tony.

"I have a great feeling about your day." When he says it, a shooting pain stabs my heart.

"It was five years ago today," I sigh.

"Make it really good. Change what today means," Tony says as Dee-Dee honks again. I blow him a kiss and drive off. I don't know why Dee-Dee is in such a hurry. We are going to sit at this road construction debacle right outside the gate for at least five minutes.

They are widening the road to accommodate all the new homes going in. Whimsy is growing. I sit outside the gate and wait for the go ahead from the construction workers. One of them is Johnny Johnson, which is just a silly name. What were his parents thinking? He smiles and waves and I force a smile back. He's had a thing for me ever since Dexter died. He's nice, a few years older than me. He graduated with my brother, Cameron. I'm not interested in Johnny, or anyone for that matter. He walks over to my car and I suck in a deep breath.

Just my luck. God, I hope he doesn't ask me out again.

"Hi Lily," he says once I roll down my window.

"Hey Johnny."

"You look beautiful today," he's pointedly staring at my boobs. *Rude. Puke. Rude.*

"Thanks...orange is your color." I gesture to his bright orange construction vest. The happy nature on his face gives way to that look in his eyes. I hold my breath because he's going to do it.

"Can I take you to the country club dance tomorrow night?" he asks. "Just as friends."

"Aw, that is awfully sweet, but I'll have to pass this year." I reject him every year. I want him to stop asking me out more than I want this underwire in my bra to go away. A shopping trip to Davenridge to buy new bras is calling my name.

"Come on...it will be fun!"

I'm sure people could argue that crack is fun, Johnny.

"Nah, Dexter died five years ago today." He looks away and goes silent.

"Okay, well, if you change your mind, you know where to find me."

Unfortunately for me, I do.

He stays and chats until he gets called away from Howard. Howard is a newer resident in Whimsy. Howard looks and even sounds like Dexter. He waves and I wave back while my hair stands up on my arms the way it always does when I see Dexter's doppelgänger. It takes my breath away every time I see him. Him and his wife have a little boy Drew's age, and they are always trying to set up play dates, but I refuse every time. He walks away and my heart breaks. Dexter was so young. So bright. Drew deserves a daddy.

My phone rings and I smile when I see Kylie's name on the caller ID. We met in preschool and have been attached at the hip ever since. Kylie is like a sister to me. We're synced and speak our own language. Not literally. I usually know what she is going to say before she says it and vice versa.

"Hi," I say when I pick up the phone.

"Hi, just wanted to call and let you know I'm thinking of you. I'm working a double, but I will be sending you peaceful vibes all day," she says. "Can you feel them?"

"I can. You're the best." My eyes sting and I blink back the tears. "I filled his medicine cabinet this morning. And I washed, brushed, and styled my hair. Tony noticed."

"Yay! Try to have a good day and I will call you on my break." She pauses for a moment. "Here's Tater."

Tater is another lifelong friend I met in preschool. He's part of my village and I count on him for so much. He owns a restaurant on the other side of the lake where Kylie works.

"Morning!" he beams. "How are you?"

"I'm okay. I'll be fine," I say. "This is the best I've ever felt on this day."

"Good. Call me tomorrow morning. I'm busy on a wait all morning. Nonstop."

"That's exciting, Tater."

"Your parents came in bright and early. I have a great feeling about your day," he almost sings.

"So does Tony!" I exclaim at the coincidence.

"I gotta run...I love you Lils!"

Lucille calls right after to say she'll be swinging by my house to get a new outfit for Drew because she didn't want her *parading* through the country club looking like a *street urchin*. Everybody in town knows my daughter is well loved. How can she care so much what Drew is wearing? It's adorable that she wants to dress herself, and she takes a lot of time putting together those outfits. Mimi making her change seems like a little too much tough love.

Does she even know what today is? She never talks about him, at least not to me. When they moved here, they left behind a posh, swanky life on the upper east side of Manhattan. They kept their penthouse and go back to visit about once a month. Drew and I have gone with them several times. It was awful for me, but I did it for Drew and Dexter. Drew will be going without me next month. I can't think about her being gone for nine whole days because it physically hurts. We don't spend a lot of time apart.

A construction worker finally waves me through, and I make the drive down from the golf course houses into our tiny tourist town. Many people come here for the food, the woodsy feel, and the lake. Whimsy has great food. Every restaurant makes their food from scratch. Whimsy is on one of the main roads to get into Yosemite, so we have a lot of traffic most of the time. Everyone is gearing up for summer, which is when we have the most activity. It's 11 AM and the traffic is heavy on the main road.

Tourists are standing outside Ma's Diner, which has been featured on *Diners, Drive-Ins and Dives*. Ma, the owner, is ninety years old and has passed it down to her two daughters, but she still goes in every day to bake her award-winning apple pies, visit with her regulars, and meet the tourists. She is a Whimsy legend and still sharp as a whip. Last time we talked, I questioned whether or not she had found the fountain of youth. She credits her love of apple pie for her youthful appearance. It made me laugh. Ma has five kids and sixteen grandkids...but it's her love of a sweet pastry that keeps her going?

I park behind my parents' liquor store adequately named Moore Liquor. I climb out of my car but don't bother locking it because Whimsy is as innocent as it comes.

"Hey Lily!" yells Mr. Buckets, who owns Cluck Yo' Mama right next door. It's a delicious fried chicken kitchen that has been open for about eight years. Mr. Buckets was livid he didn't get featured on *Diners, Drive-Ins and Dives*. I think it's better food than Ma's, but Ma's has been open for so long it's like the spirit of Whimsy. I bring home his fried chicken every Thursday for Drew and I.

"Mornin'!" I call. "Will you add a few more biscuits to my standing order tonight?"

"You bet! You havin' company?" he asks. Very nosy. Everyone in this town is on pins and needles for a big comeback for me. "A major romance for the young attractive widow" is what I have heard people say. This town is small. We have a population of 1200 people and yes, I know them all.

"Drew is off chicken and only eats the biscuits, which leaves me none for my morning tea the next day." His face falls that there is no juicy gossip to report.

"Don't let her tell you what to feed her!" Mr. Buckets scolds. I laugh. What does he suggest I do? Hold her down and shove a fried drumstick down her throat? Ground my four-year-old daughter for life because she doesn't like his chicken? I hate unsolicited parenting advice and between Mr. Buckets and Lucille, I have had my fill for the day.

"Have a great day, Mr. Buckets!" I bite my tongue with a big smile.

"You too, sweetie. See ya later," he waves.

I walk through the back door of the liquor store and see my dad. He's got a clipboard, checking the inventory list. His graying blond hair is coiffed into a nice little wave.

"Good morning beautiful!" He's a very handsome fifty-eight-year-old man with a gentle smile and soft blue eyes. His black t-shirt with the store name on it is tucked nicely into some old Levi's.

"Morning!" I turn my cheek so he can give me a kiss.

"I told you to spend the day with Drew." He had suggested that I take the day off with Drew, but my mom was up my booty to get to work today. She basically yelled at me last night when she dropped off my new clothes.

I wrap my arms around him. "This is where I want to be, with you and Mom," I say, earning me a warm smile. My parents are my life. Though my dad is sensitive and gentle, my mom is meddlesome and bossy, I need them both for everything.

He kisses my forehead. "Rose flies in tomorrow. Plans to stay a week," he warns.

Rose is my younger and spoiled rotten sister. She treats everyone like crap, including my parents, who give her so much money it is sickening. My brother and I both worked our way through college and took out student loans. Rose refuses to get a job. Her apartment is insane, and she gets an allowance for beauty *upkeep* alone. My parents give her a couple grand a month on top of housing and school. Last year, she threw an epic tantrum and they paid over ten grand for new boobs.

"Does Cameron know?" He's my older brother, the charming and beloved town doctor. He is married with three kids. His wife Jeanie grew up here in Whimsy. Using the word *hate* when it comes to family doesn't sit right with me, so I'll just mention that Cameron is not a huge fan of Rose. They don't do well in the same room together.

"Yes he does. Now Lily, your mom is so excited to have her home. Please try and bite your tongue."

I giggle at his face. "I always do. Don't I?"

"You're better at it than Cameron." *That's an understatement.*

I walk to the front of the store to say hi to my mom. She is at the cash register chatting with Darla. Darla is her best friend since elementary school here in Whimsy. Darla is like an aunt to me. She is loud, disrespectful, funny as hell, and has made a name as the town gossip. Which means my mom knows everything about everyone in this tiny town. My dad ignores everything he is told by either of them. He knows nothing but spends the most time with them. I often tease him and ask if he has cotton in his ears to avoid hearing them talk. He argues everyone should put cotton in their ears when the two of them are together. It always cracks me up.

They both smile and greet me brightly.

"You look skinny. I'll run next door and make sure Mr. Buckets adds more chicken and mac and cheese to tonight's order," Darla says, blinking at me with those big dramatic brown eyes. Darla is always concerned about my weight.

"Today marks five years, Darla. My baby girl needs hugs and extra love." My mom is fifty-seven but still looks forty. She has a great figure and is, I think, smoking hot for her age. Her ample chest offsets her slender, petite frame. She has a pretty floral top tucked into simple chino pants that brush the tips of her loafers. Her shoulder length blonde hair is adorned with soft curls, and her beautiful green eyes are showcased in the perfect amount of makeup. She always looks so put together.

Everyone says I am her clone. I used to hate it when I was younger, but now, I hope and pray I end up aging as well as her.

I smile at her and let her squeeze me with all her might. *I need it.*

"You look beautiful...was I right?" my mom asks while she fusses with my hair.

"Right about what?" Darla asks as she adjusts her apron.

"I told her if she got ready today and looked beautiful, it would help her feel better." My mom swipes some lip stick on my lips and then makes me rub them together. "Dress up and cheer up. Can't feel good in a shirt with ketchup stains."

"Yes, Mom, you were right," I say and then kiss her cheek, leaving a bright pink lip imprint on her cheek. She howls in laughter while Darla takes a picture and posts it on Facebook with lightning speed.

Darla starts right in on the gossip. Tater had *relations* with a tourist last night. Sounds typical.

Dee-Dee made a *scene* at Ma's last night when she got the wrong order. Also typical.

"Oh dear. That poor woman," my mom says, grasping her heart. "I should stop by and bring her dinner or something."

"Why do you try with that cow? She's rude to you," Darla says, annoyed. Darla isn't wrong. Dee-Dee is awful to everyone, the only exception being my dad.

"Because underneath all that anger is an abandoned woman." My mom is meddlesome but has a giant heart. Darla looks more annoyed by this answer.

"I for one am sick of her, and next time she snaps at me, I'm gonna stick my foot in her big ass." My mom cracks up again. Big heart with a great sense of humor.

"I gotta run back to the shop and make sure everything is good to go for Mr. Beazer." Darla is the town florist and covering Mr. Beazer's funeral today. He was the original country club owner. He sold it last year and recently lost a gruesome battle with cancer. "I'll pop in and add a red velvet cake slice to your order, Lily. Have you tried it?" she asks. "You're just too thin."

"Nope, only that death by chocolate cake," I reply, ignoring her comment.

"I ate so much red velvet cake one night I shit red for a week." My mom and I erupt into laughter at her admission. "I'm not kidding!"

Darla kisses my mom on the cheek and then grabs me in a

big hug, fluffing my hair. "You have a good day sweetness. You look beautiful. You always do, even with ketchup stains and ratty hair."

"Aw, you're a good liar," I tease.

"Not lying, but this is a better look than what you had going on last week when I brought—"

"You could have given a girl some warning." Her face is etched in amusement. They ambushed me with a stranger for a blind date, I didn't look good.

"You would have called in sick," Darla protests.

"That's what I meant. I needed a warning so I could call in sick. I'm still mad at you both for that." Darla looks at the clock and bolts without any more delay.

"Sweetie, your dad and I should go to the funeral. You want to go?" my mom asks. Going to a funeral on this day would be unbearable for me.

"I don't, but I sent flowers and made Mrs. Beazer a casserole. I dropped it off last night," I say. "We had a nice visit. She was so grateful and understands my absence today." I take a deep breath to try and steady the further cracking of my heart.

"Will you watch the store? We should be busy. Did you see that traffic?" She points out the window that faces the main road.

"Of course," I say, happy to help. We are the only liquor store and we sell sandwiches too. The store sees a steady stream of customers every day.

I settle in the office and get busy cooking the books. Not really. We are running a clean shop here, but that is what we call it. At 2:00, my dad peeks his head in to call me up to the register so they can leave.

"Don't close up like you did last time," my mom says and I roll my eyes.

"Kylie and I ran and got takeout. I was closed for five minutes. You do it all the time." I push her away as she starts fussing with my hair.

"Maybe the new conditioner is a bit heavy for your natural

waves," she says, pulling a brush out of her Mary Poppins bag. Trying to save my apparently flat, lifeless hair.

"Lily, don't listen to your mom. You can close up." She turns and instantly starts in on my dad, waving her tiny brush in his face. I sit down behind the cash register and prop my feet on the old wooden counter. I grab my book while they fight about me.

"I'm not going to leave. You have my word. Now go before Mr. Beazer gets reincarnated." I bat my eyes at my annoyed mom.

A whole hour goes by without much activity. I'm so bored and about to close-up to get an iced tea when in walks Ace Lancaster. I have replayed this moment over and over in my head for years.

What will I say? How will he be around me? Does he hate me?

His head is down. He hasn't seen me yet. *Oh god.* My pulse races while sweat clamps my palms, and I feel this intense urge to run. *Yep, you should run!*

I bolt up out of my stool, but my erratic movement knocks it over. It crashes to the floor, which of course draws his attention to me. *Oops!* His smile instantly spreads, and even though I'm nervous as hell, I can't help but smile like I haven't smiled in years. He looks good! *Too good.*

CHAPTER 4

~

Ace Lancaster was my high school sweetheart. My first everything was with him. He was there my first day of school, the first time I stood on a jet ski, and we shared our first kiss when we were twelve at Justin Watson's party. We had sex for the first time in this store on Fourth of July during the firework show when we were sixteen. We always said we would get married, have a dozen kids, die in Whimsy, and be buried together holding hands. After high school, he moved to Texas for college and then was drafted as the Cowboys quarterback. He has been married for years to a pretty country singer named Trina Zimms.

Still, him being married, I feel something I shouldn't feel with this one look he's giving me. I go to set my book on the counter but miss it completely and it drops on my foot. *Ouch!*

"Hey Sprinkles." Ace beams and struts his stuff over to the cash register. Sprinkles is what he always called me because of the freckles that I get on my nose during the summer.

He doesn't sound or look mad. I let go of the breath I've been choking on since he walked in.

"Ace Magoo...where has all that adorable acne gone?" I ask with a huge smile. His older brothers gave him that nickname. He never had acne, only a few zits during two yearbook pictures, but of course I had to tease him about it.

He laughs. Oh, that laugh. I've missed it. It's like sweet music to my ears.

"You going to come give me a hug or what? Last time I saw you, you were crying...saying goodbye to me at the bus station. Right before I left for college." His smile hasn't wavered. His deep blue eyes haven't changed.

"I believe you cried. I skipped off and made out with Justin," I tease. His contagious laugh reaches my ears again and uncontrollable giggles escape me. Justin is his best friend, and the biggest flirt in the world. "That wasn't the last time we saw each other though."

He shrugs. "Not supposed to talk about those times." He puts his finger to his lips to protect our secrets. I feel a little spark of excitement as I remember those times. Coming home for Christmas while in college and having quick flings, not to mention the summers at home. Skinny dipping in the lake, hiking in Yosemite, and late nights just the two of us.

"Get out here!" he insists with a huge intoxicating smile.

I walk around the counter, giddy as I watch his face. He's happy to see me, and my face alights as relief washes over me. *He doesn't hate me?* His caramel brown hair and tan skin make his deep blue eyes sparkle even more. They alone reveal that his excitement to run into me is nothing he expected today. Nor was I. I take in all of his facial features, and he seems to do the same to mine. The dimple in his right cheek, only visible when you're close, is just as tiny and cute. It looks as though he hasn't shaved in a few days, which just makes him even sexier.

Stop.

We wrap our arms around each other and I melt into his warm, sculpted chest. We hug for so long I could fall asleep. Man have I missed him!

"You never returned any of my phone calls," he says gently while still holding me.

"I suck," I admit. He called me many times after Dexter died. He sent flowers and cards. I couldn't bring myself to call him.

"How are you?"

"Great." *Overwhelmed.* Tears prick the back of my eyes. My emotions are all over the place right now. "What about you?" How can he be here today of all days?

"I'm good," he sighs while I'm still encased in his arms. His warm hand on the back of my neck feels so comforting. He smells the same as he did years ago: a mild and attractive male scent mixed with fresh laundry and lemons. He should bottle this scent. I always did like his subtle yet distinctive fragrance.

"Why do you have an accent? Are you a bona fide Texan now?" I turn my head up and smile at his gorgeous face.

"Nope...Whimsy all the way!" The easy laughter surrounds us both. "Soon as I'm retired, I'm moving home."

"Yay," I say in a small but excited voice. "Does Trina like Whimsy?"

He takes a deep breath and lets go of me. "Sure," he says, but he looks sad. Maybe he doesn't want to gloat about his beautiful famous wife because of my situation. I would feel awkward gloating about my love for someone else to him.

I retreat from the hug, and my hands land on his arms. "You are much bigger...this is all bigger." I motion around his chest and arm region, then squeeze just to be sure.

"You seem smaller." He bites down on his lower lip as a small laugh escapes him.

"Maybe only cause you're bigger. What are they feeding you out there? Straight steroids?"

"I don't do steroids," he playfully warns. "I miss you Lily!"

My insides churn with things I haven't felt in years. Must be nostalgia.

"What brings you in?" I ask, finally removing my hands from his sculpted physique. Only now do I realize how long I had them there and mortification creeps in. He just feels like he always did. Familiar, loyal, trustworthy.

Mine.

"Mom was tired of me sitting on her couch drinking beer and eating so she sent me to run errands. I finished her list and now I'm here to stock up for the rest of the week." He looks a little restless suddenly.

"Sounds magical," I tease and turn around to lead him to our new walk-in beer fridge. "When did you get here?"

"A few days ago."

"How did I not know this?" I ask, flummoxed.

"I've been hiding," There is so much sadness on his face. I don't like it.

"Me too. Last week, Darla was trying to set me up with this single mortgage broker from Davenridge. She brought him here to the liquor store without any warning. Made me so mad, so I've been locked in my house for the last week avoiding her and my mom." I want to fix his sadness. Make him smile and laugh.

"They're still meddling?" he asks with a warm smile back on his handsome face. "Was he ugly?"

"He was handsome and very nice." We both can't help but laugh. "I hadn't brushed my hair in a week and was wearing a Tater's t-shirt and workout leggings. I looked like a zombie." I sigh. "It's their personal mission to find me a new husband."

"Did you let him down gently?" he asks, still smiling. *Yay.*

"I'm sure he got one look at me and was just as annoyed as I was. He drove forty-five minutes. I'm not worth the gas money."

"I'm sure that was not the case. I've seen you at your worst and it's still quite adorable," he's still a gentleman.

"How many concussions have you had?" I tease as I pull the heavy door to the walk-in fridge. His resounding laugh makes my heart scream with joy, reminding me again how much I have missed him. He grabs the handle from behind me and pulls it open like nothing. I squeeze his bicep. "Maybe I should get some steroids."

I hold the door open with my body while he walks several cases of beer and a whole case of wine to the cash register. I watch and smile the whole time. My face begins to hurt.

He wasn't kidding about stocking up.

"You really know how to party! Where's Justin?" I ask, teasing him the way I used to when it came to his steamy, hot best friend.

"Happily married in Berkeley," His blues eyes lit up and lips still upturned into pure magic. Any sign of sadness has gone.

"I heard not so happy."

"Darla?" he asks, amused. Ace Lancaster can find the amusement in everything.

"And Kylie," I say pointedly.

He shakes his head. "He looks like every day is rainbows and daisies on Facebook."

I roll my eyes.

"I've been waiting for years for you to join so I can stalk you." He winks.

"It won't happen. I just stalk you through Kylie." My admission is easy in this playful banter.

"I stalk you through Kylie too. She posts pictures of you. I love the one of you two nerds in matching bathing suits on the beach."

"The two of us took Drew last summer. She's my daughter."

"Yeah, I know who she is." He picks up a cigar and a deck of cards and throws it in with his beer. "She looks like you..."

"No," I say. "She looks like him." I pull out my phone and show him the side by side of them I keep on hand.

"I won't fight you because I know how stubborn you are"— he raises his eyebrows at me with a noticeable pause—"but she looks like you."

I busy myself making him a sandwich and we sit behind the counter to catch up.

"This is the best sandwich!" he says halfway through.

"It's the bread. Have you met the new couple who run the bakery? Young couple from Arizona. Last name is Mackabee. They make these rolls specifically for our sandwiches. They don't sell them to anybody else."

"Haven't had the pleasure. Are they nice?"

"Yeah...she's swell," He grimaces at my thick sarcasm.

"What about him?"

"I have never had a conversation with him. He's too busy talking to my girls." I motion to my breasts.

"Does Tater like him?" he asks.

"Tolerates. He was at Willy's one night, absolutely drunk and being very obnoxious toward me. Tater almost punched him. Kylie and I stopped it from happening." Willy's is the local dive bar. It's dingy and something about being surrounded by old wood-paneled walls brings out the worst in people. Every time I go, some kind of small-town drama unfolds, leaving the whole town to talk about it until the next one.

"Does he treat Kylie that way?" Ace asks.

"Yep! All women. He's made it very clear to Kylie and I that he is open to an affair."

"Sounds irresistible," Ace says through a raucous laugh before shoving the last bite in his mouth. "Make me another."

I jump up. "You got it!" He grabs my hand before I walk away. It takes me a second to look into his eyes because I am startled by my body's reaction to this small and innocent gesture.

"Please make me another," he says, and he looks so cute that I have a flash of impure thoughts.

He talks about football and his success while he eats a second sandwich. I watch his face and his muscles. Ace was always a specimen, but this is on a new level. His arms are like steel cannons. His Dallas Cowboys t-shirt strains from his bulky chest. He is surreal, god-like even. He pats my knee as he tells me about his coach. I could unravel under his casual touch.

My parents walk in when he is in the middle of a story about his house in Dallas. My mom lights up and squeals and hits my dad when she sees Ace. Then she runs forward and squeezes him tight. My dad and Ace shake hands.

"I heard you were in town!" she exclaims. *She did?* "You look good!" She flashes bulgy dramatic eyes at me, pleading with me to agree that he looks good. *Not subtle at all, Mom.*

I give her an exhausted look and she mouths, *He looks so good.* I roll my eyes and then smile at Ace who catches me mid eye roll. Amusement crosses his face before he looks back to my dad, who asked him a question. *Doesn't he?* my mom presses. I bend down to pick up the book I dropped earlier when his good looks made me lose all my senses. So yeah, Mom, he looks better than good. Anybody with eyes would think he looks good.

My mom and dad badger him with questions for at least a half an hour while I ring up customers. At 4:50 on the nose, my dinner arrives from next door delivered by Mr. Buckets himself, which is a first. He must have heard Ace was here. He hugs Ace and asks a million questions too. Everyone is so starstruck by *this* Ace, and I can't help but laugh. It's like nobody remembers the nerdy little boy called Mr. Magoo by his two older brothers when he was a permanent resident here. I watch him, elated that he hasn't changed at all. Well-mannered, sweet, and patient, even with Mr. Buckets, who is super annoying. Mr. Buckets leaves and I beckon my dad to take my spot behind the cash register.

"I have to grab Drew," I remind them.

"Sweetie, our car broke down. We need your car," my mom says, pulling me away from my dad and the tourist he's ringing up.

"Fine, just drop me at home and then come back and get Dad," I say.

"I have so much to do..." She trails off. "Oh Ace, be a doll and run her around for me."

"Sure." Ace smiles at me. "We can continue to catch up." I nod eagerly.

"Lily can repay you by sharing her dinner," my mom says. I assess her through squinted eyes. What is she up to? He is married, and so am I for that matter. Regardless of how everyone else thinks I should feel, I feel married.

My phone rings. Lucille.

"Hello?"

"Lily, you okay with Drew sleeping over and me taking her

to San Francisco for the weekend? I want to take her to the zoo." A lump lodges in my throat. Drew sleeps over at her house all the time, but San Francisco is far.

"Uh...how many nights?" I manage to ask instead of telling her I hate her and this dumb idea.

"We will leave in the morning and have her back Sunday afternoon. Just the two nights," she says casually. Like it's no big deal. She's four!

"And tonight? So, three nights?" I ask as I look around for something to kick.

"What?" my mom asks, looking terrified that she may be the target of my anger.

"Lucille wants to take Drew to San Francisco for three nights," I say with my hand covering the speaker. I grab a fork out of my to-go order and stab a container.

There's nothing to kick.

Lucille is begging on one end while my mom is telling me it will be fine on the other. My dad tells her to butt out. After my dad and mom quit bickering, she grabs the phone out of my hand to talk to Lucille. I watch her facial expressions and continue to stab the container.

"Oh sweetie." She extends the phone away from her mouth. "We all understand your protection, but this will be good for you and her. If you hate it too much, she will bring her back Saturday. This will help prepare you for her New York trip."

I drive down the fork again, but Ace swiftly moves the food. I stare at him in disbelief.

I forgot he was here! This is embarrassing.

"Lily." My mom hands the phone back to me. "Talk to Lucille."

I grab the phone reluctantly from my mom. I turn my back away from all the eyes.

"Will you just call me a lot?" I ask as tears pool in my eyes. "It was five years ago today." Then they slide down my face.

"Lily, I know what today is," Lucille says in her snooty voice, reminding me that she is better than me at everything.

"Then you know that I really wanted to do what Drew and I always do on Thursday," I say. "I don't want to be alone."

She sighs and an awkward silence falls between us for a minute. "Come get her and we will do it another time. She is all I have left of my son." Emotion laces her voice, something she never shows. "You aren't the only one that lost him, Lily. We moved here so she could know him through us."

I take a deep breath. She is right. I hate that's she's right, but she is.

"Okay, Lucille. I'm going to come give her a hug and a kiss goodbye. Thank you for loving her the way you do," I take a deep breath after we hang up.

Everyone is silent, even the regular customers in the store.

"Ace, get her home," my mom says and basically pushes us out the door. "I'll see you both tomorrow for the country club annual dance-off. You both always said when you were twenty-one and could enter you were going to win." She flashes me with her over-the-top Maggie Moore smile.

I stare at her blankly.

"I'm not going. I'm sure Trina is a more suitable choice for Ace," I say incredulously. She is ludicrous for even mentioning we do that together when he is married.

"I doubt that will happen if she is in Maui making out all over the place with Brent Brave," she says, and then her face drops like she said too much. Ace looks mortified. Brent Brave is the Hollywood heart throb starring in every new movie.

"Give Drew a kiss for me." My mom turns away quickly after dropping the huge bomb of an affair.

CHAPTER 5

~

I give Ace directions to Lucille's. Neither one of us speak after that. I think we both are embarrassed by what happened in the liquor store. He got to see firsthand what a psycho I am, and now I know his perfect, pretty wife is banging a Hollywood A-lister. His problem sounds worse than my adorable daughter going to a fun-filled San Francisco trip with her rich grandparents.

"I can walk home from here," I say when he pulls in her driveway. I smile wanly at him. "It was so good to see you." My voice is small.

He laughs. "No way...I'll wait as long as it takes. I'm getting my share of that chicken and an explanation on your hatred for food containers." He rubs his hand through his hair. His uneasy nature is starting to fade.

"Fine, but I get an explanation about—"

"Don't say her name." He cuts me off with an outstretched palm.

"Okay Magoo, I'll share my dinner with you." I smirk. "I need a biscuit for my tea in the morning though and, judging by your size and the way you took down those sandwiches you don't look like you'll share."

His warm laughter feels just like the thing I have been missing for years. His casual, charming smile is alarmingly eye opening for me.

I'm lonely.

I walk through Lucille's front door.

"Mommy!" Drew screams. "I'm going to the zoo! And the American Girl doll store! Mimi said I could have whatever I want."

I laugh at her excitement and scoop her up. "Oh Boo! You're going to have so much fun! I'm so excited for you!" I don't want her to get a hint of my anxiety. Lucille steps out of the entryway with a nod in my direction. I guess we aren't speaking now. I shake off my frustration and give Drew another kiss.

"I'm going to pick a doll just like you, with long blonde hair and green eyes," she says and rubs my cheek softly. "Mommy, did you cry again?"

"No, I actually had such a fun day. One of my long-lost friends came home. My heart is so happy to see him," I reply with reassurance, very aware that my four-year-old daughter is submerged in my sad, pathetic grief. I have to do better, which makes me think Lucille may be right on the money calling me a terrible mom.

"Where did he get lost to?" she asks, her eyes big and innocent.

"I don't know exactly, but I will find out, and when you get back you can meet Ace."

I play a game of Old Maid with her and we kiss and cuddle for twenty more minutes before I peel myself off the floor and leave. Lucille walks me to the door while John and Drew settle down for a movie he put on for them.

"I will always keep her safe, Lily. She is my life," Lucille chides in her ever-growing distasteful tone. Distaste for my shorts, distaste for pretty much everything about me.

"Mine too." I walk down the porch steps. My heart is heavy knowing she will be gone for three whole nights. Despite me feeling inadequate in Lucille's presence, I spin around and walk back up the steps. "Thank you for loving her so much. I hope she brings you peace on this day." I wrap her in a tight hug.

She drives me nuts but she is important to Drew and Dexter.

Drew is lucky she moved here. She helps a lot despite driving me crazy. She finally relaxes into the hug and returns it. "I love you," I add. The lump in my throat softens. Forgiveness is always the best for my sanity.

I pull away and smile at her. She looks uncomfortable. Of course, the Ice queen and I have shared maybe five hugs since I met her nine years ago. She returns my smile; it's less frigid than normal.

"Your hair looks nice today, Lily," she says with a splash of sincerity that almost knocks the wind out of me. I take a deep breath. That's as far as that needs to go with our awkward bonding. I walk away self-conscious while she watches me. Probably critiquing my shorts in her head.

I climb in Ace's car.

"It's the bright blue house with the white shutters on the corner of Whimsy Court and Lake View Drive," I say without looking at him.

"I know which one...My mom points it out every time I'm home."

He drives slowly in silence, which is just what I need. He pulls into my driveway and turns the car off. We both carry the food in. I set it all on the table and excuse myself to use the restroom. When I come out, I point him in the right direction to do the same. I press play on the answering machine. A reminder for preschool sign-ups next week from Whimsy Tots Preschool. My brother complaining about Rose coming for at least two minutes, which makes me laugh.

"Call me. Darla was in and she said Ace is in town. She has an elaborate plan about setting you two up," he says and I roll my eyes. Figures. Mom's car is probably fine. Also explains her orders for me not to close the store while she was at the funeral. She did not want me to miss Ace. Bernie, Ace's mom, was in on it for sure. This all makes sense. Those old hens need to mind their own business.

Next up is Kylie, who I must have just missed. She always calls my landline on Thursdays when I get home between her double shift at Tater's.

"Lily, Darla was telling everyone about Ace being back and how she is going to set you two up. The whole funeral didn't give one shit about poor Mr. Beazer, only the pretty widow and the NFL star that is being shamelessly humiliated in the media. Trina is straddling this guy on the beach in a thong bikini. Honestly, she has a fat ass and shouldn't be *parading* around in a thong." She puts emphasis on the word because she knows how I feel about it. I giggle while she continues. "Brent Brave is so hot and his hands are in places I'm sure Ace would not approve of..." She gets cut off when Ace turns off the machine.

"I adore Kylie, but she has never known when to quit talking." He opens my fridge. "Got any booze?"

"Everywhere," I say. "Occupational hazard."

"I think the only hazard in this room is us," he teases. "I can't decide who I feel more sorry for, myself or you."

"I hear you...I decided you win." I take the cold IPA he hands me.

"I'm pretty sure you have me beat being the *pretty widow* and all," Ace says with a huge smile.

"You heard all the messages?" I cringe.

"Yes, and your brother is still hilarious. When he said he was going to *cunt punt* Rose I almost died laughing."

"I didn't hear you."

"Because your laugh has always been way too loud!" he taunts.

I push his stomach, flashing him a sneaky smirk. "Well...it's not. Your ears are just too tiny for your inflated NFL head."

We sit down at my little table and catch up. We talk about old times in this small town, it's both invigorating and gleeful being in his presence.

"I have missed you...all these years apart and it feels like we never parted," he says. "I haven't laughed in weeks."

"Is that when all this started?"

"Lily, do you not watch the news?" he asks, stunned. "It's been everywhere all week."

"Nope. It's only ever bad news and I can't take it." I pause and let out a dramatic breath. "We have been on the craziest bender of *The Greatest Showman* in this house for a couple weeks. I mean, it's a good movie, but I need to reintroduce *Frozen* or something," he looks amused. "So, is that when it started? A week ago?"

"Yep. I found out and then twenty-four hours later, there's a sex tape of them released. Now they are on the beach half naked groping each other. I want to die," he hangs his head in such defeat.

"Were you happy together before all this?" I ask.

"Nah. We had already decided to get a divorce. We both got lawyers. Nobody knew though. She has been pretty awful through this whole thing," he says. "I will never date anyone again."

"Me neither." I start to pull the label off my beer, not meeting his eyes. "Everyone is pushing me and clearly the whole town is trying to shove us together, but I still feel married. Even though my mind knows he is never coming back, my heart hasn't accepted it." I look up at him and shift my eyes away from his sad look. *He feels sorry for me.* "Please don't look at me like that."

His gaze is tender. Empathetic. "Don't you want to be happy again?"

"I am. I have my little Drew, a nice house. My friends and family are so intrusive and tell me how to live my life. It's like a dream come true," I say, a little sarcastic.

"Seriously Sprinkles, what is holding you back from finding love again?" he asks gently.

I take a deep breath. "It could never happen again...Anything less than what I had with Dexter would be settling. You know me...I don't settle." He looks so sympathetic and understanding. "Now, if Justin would just hurry up and get divorced, I may change my mind," I poke earning me an irresistible grin.

"You both never did more than hold hands and kiss a handful of times." He tosses his greasy napkin at my face.

"True...because of you...but I had the serious hots for him," I say, my eyes wide and a ridiculous smile on my face. He presses his palm into his heart.

"I can't believe how much this still hurts...more than Trina even." I laugh at the ridiculousness of that statement.

"Puppy love."

"Aw...we were more than puppy love. At least in my eyes. You are like my soulmate or a kindred spirit. Puppy love is something you outgrow. When I saw your face today for the first time in ten years, it was like no time had gone by. I didn't outgrow you, my love for you just grew." He sounds so sincere.

"I felt my heart float and a rainbow exploded out of my body when I saw you," I smile at how cheesy I sound. "I have missed you like crazy!"

"See, don't refer to me as puppy love. We are more like best friends." He winks before taking a sip of his beer.

"Alright, bestie. Should we go win that trophy tomorrow night? Keep me distracted from Drew being gone?" I ask, delighted at the thought. "And you distracted about...you know."

"You bet! Let's check that off our bucket list. We're only about ten years late, but my faith in you is unshakeable," he says. "Now run me through how you developed such a massive hatred for food containers."

"I honestly don't know what that was earlier." I peel the remaining wrapper off my bottle. "Drew is my whole world...I already know what loss feels like. I try not to think about losing her, but I do. Almost every time I close my eyes, I think of losing her. I made my parents fence their whole house from their lake entry. Lucille's house came with a pool and I had her fill that in."

"Do you two get along?" he asks, referring to Lucille.

"She's all up in my grill." I toss my head back in exhaustion. "Nothing I ever do is good enough. She thinks I'm lazy. She pushes her opinion on me all the time about how I could be raising her better. I just ignore it because she did move here from a place she loves to be with Drew. Drew loves her. Dexter loved her."

"What was he like?" he asks with genuine curiosity.

"He was funny, warm, compassionate, crazy. You would have loved him. Everyone did. I was his everything. Have you ever been someone's everything?" I watch his face intently because I've always wanted to know about the women after me.

"No. Trina and I had a steamy relationship, steam doesn't last forever. It turned to hate, our hate turned to boredom, and our boredom turned her to the arms of another man," he says. "I don't blame her. I just wish she wasn't so open about her new love."

There's a long stretch of silence. He looks sad. I want to find out about one girlfriend in particular he had after college, but I can't come right out and ask without giving my crazy self away.

"How long are you here for?" I finally break the silence.

"Until my coach makes me come back. He would hate to see me wallowing in fried chicken and beer so close to pre-season." His handsome smirk breaks into a hearty laugh. "He'd be pissed."

At 2 AM, I tuck a drunk Ace up in the guest room and then I climb into bed. I loved catching up with him. He wants to take me to breakfast in the morning. I have all these mixed and conflicted feelings inside my pained heart. Man, I am a serious mess. It's breakfast, not a steamy love affair. We're both married and despite this burning attraction, he seems completely unfazed by my presence.

We're just friends.

But I fall asleep fantasizing about having a steamy love affair with that friend.

CHAPTER 6

~

I have the same repetitive dream.

Dexter and I dance at our wedding to "Unchained Melody." His smile is a little off, but his grey suit fits him perfectly, his royal blue pocket square accentuating the brilliance of his soft blue eyes. His blonde hair is perfectly shaped and molded to accentuate every one of his glorious facial features. His sun-kissed skin illuminates his bright white grin. His voice sings the song slowly to me, and then he's gone in a puff. I spin around frantically, calling his name.

When I finally see him, he's in a glass box that fills with water, and I pound on the glass while he dies in front of me. I scream and cry, and my hands hurt from hitting the glass box with such determination. I can't save him...

I bolt up. Ace is standing in my doorway, looking almost as anxious as I feel. I open and close my hands to see if they truly hurt but they don't, which always stumps me as to how realistic that dream still feels after five years. I'm a thirty-one-year-old woman with regular nightmares.

"Lily...you okay? Your screaming woke me." He attentively crosses the room.

"Yes, just a nightmare...a familiar one." I grab the water glass on the nightstand and take a small sip.

He sits beside me. His soft smile makes me feel crazy. "Hug?" he asks. I open my arms so he knows I'm okay with it. "What happens in this familiar dream?"

I tell him about the dream and I don't even know why. I'm sure he thinks I'm nuts.

"Sometimes it's Drew in the glass box...or my brother...or my parents...Tater and Kylie," I say. "Mostly Dexter and Drew though."

"That really sucks," he says sincerely. I lay down and scoot over so he can lay beside me.

"Yeah...it does," I admit. "Drew sometimes hears and it scares her. I feel like a total failure when it happens because she tries so hard to make me feel better about it." I rub my face, frustrated for being such an emotional mess when it comes to my poor Drew. "She doesn't even speak like a four-year-old. It's like she's a twelve-year-old with her vocabulary. Doesn't mispronounce words...has a keen fashion sense as well." I tell him about her epic outfits and how Lucille hates the way I let her dress. We both laugh at my pathetic existence which may sound weird, but it makes me feel better.

I yawn and he grabs my hand. "Close those pretty eyes of yours. I'll stay awake and fight off the dream monsters for you." When we were little, we believed there were dream monsters that caused nightmares.

"You close your pretty eyes too," I whisper, and it only takes me a few minutes to find sleep again.

The next morning, Kylie's chipper voice wakes us.

"What do we have here?" She has a devious smile on her adorable face as she stands in my doorway. She looks as though she just walked in on us both naked.

"Good morning," I rub my eyes.

"Why do I feel like I'm eighteen? You can't steal my best friend again!" she yells at Ace in a teasing manner.

"Great to see you too Kylie...and thanks for asking...I'm doing great. Your best friend here has a nightmare every night that can wake a 230-pound man out of a drunken sleep,"

"I know that!" she boasts. Incredulous at him thinking he

knows something about me that she doesn't. "Now get up and let's go to Ma's Diner for pie like we used to when we were seventeen and hungover." She beams and then frolics over to place a kiss on Ace's cheek. "Then we can really analyze her crazy dream."

"Sounds good. I need a chicken-fried steak," Ace pats his belly and I can't help but notice his chiseled abs sneaking out of his wrinkled tee.

"You look good for a guy being publicly, I mean nationally, no, I mean internationally humiliated," she mocks with a devilish glint in her eyes. Ace flicks his chin with the tips of his fingers to politely say *fuck you*. I can't stifle the laugh that escapes me.

"What about you? My mom says you are still waiting for Stan to grow up and marry you."

"What else is there to do in this small dismal town?" Kylie wears that same tired look she has in regards to Whimsy.

"Get out...see the world. Let me send you on a vacation," he's beaming with a sincere smile. I bet he is completely generous with his fortune.

"Please...send me to Bora Bora and I can stay in one of those charming huts over the ocean." I adoringly watch their back-and-forth exchange like a tennis match. After several minutes of them catching up, we pile in Kylie's car and head to town.

The whole drive, Kylie and Ace make good on their promise to analyze my dream.

"It simply means she is trapped in a state of fear," Kylie says.

"Could be...or maybe she wishes she could have saved him or blames herself for not being there to save him." I can see him pondering as he turns to me in the back seat, looking for an answer.

I shrug. "Maybe?"

"What if he still died and you lost Drew?" Ace asks.

"No good answers." I am getting tired of this conversation.

"I had a dream last night that Stan and I got married and had a deformed daughter that kind of looked like a russet potato in a pink bonnet," Kylie says with a small smile. "What do you think that means?"

"This town is so small you two could be cousins. Hence you gave birth to a child of incest?" I tease. Kylie lets out her signature tiny snort that is always the cutest. It's never loud, just soft, like an adorable baby pig. It's one of my favorite things about her.

"Or simply, he ain't the right guy for you," Ace says. "Does he still crush the beer can on his forehead?"

"Still drops my panties every time," Kylie snorts and I howl in laughter.

"You need a vacation more than I originally thought," Ace says, bewildered. Honestly, the whole town is baffled she still dates Stan. I certainly am.

~

Breakfast was good. With our nonstop chatter, it's starting to roll into lunch. It's great to catch up, but it still feels like he never left.

"All we're missing is Justin and Tater," Kylie says, high on the nostalgia. "Tater will be at the dance tonight."

Growing up, Tater was chubby and hilarious. When he was in seventh grade, this bully kid named Keith pushed him and called him a "fat tater." Lewis decided to embrace the name to show everyone he didn't care. Tater isn't chubby anymore. Tater is kind of hot in a small-town way. He started two successful business ventures and does very well for himself. Next to his restaurant called Tater's, he has a boat rental shop. He rents many different lake toys and stays busy all year. Tater's is known for having a vast menu of potatoes cooked many different ways. And true to Darla's gossip yesterday, Tater has many flings or one-night stands with the vacationers.

"Last time he came to visit me, he was getting all the ladies," Ace says. "Who knew?"

"He's a total slut. However, he is such a good uncle to Drew and he practically supports Kylie here." I can't help but tease her about their relationship.

"I never ask." She shrugs. "He just takes care of me."

"What does he do?" Ace seems amused.

"He pays her more than any other employee and monitors her checking account because we all know how bad she sucks at math." I roll my eyes at her and she returns the gesture. "I don't understand it, but I wish he'd manage my checking account for me."

"Really...you don't understand?" Ace chuckles and pats the top of my head. "You two are still clueless."

"Why?" He turns his head and stares at me. After a long gaze, the light switch in my head flips on. "Oh..." I laugh. "Kylie and Tater sitting in a tree..."

"Tater?" Kylie whispers and looks over her shoulder to make sure no one is listening.

Ace nods. "Ever since I can remember."

"Oh my god...makes total sense." I smack my forehead with the palm of my hand as I think back to every nice thing he has done for her over the years. "I can't believe I didn't see it!"

All the color has drained out of her flawless face. She tucks strands of her coppery hair behind each ear. She appears as though she can't accept this.

"I hope I don't get in trouble with Tater but seriously...you two dipshits didn't know?" The incredulous look on his face sends me into a laughing fit. He's right...we are dipshits.

"Is it too early to start drinking?" Kylie is your typical country girl. Doesn't bother with too much makeup or primping, and she doesn't need any of it. Complete natural beauty. She has an adorable figure that makes her a total knockout. She's the town catch. It's more than unfortunate that the only one she has wanted to catch her was Stan.

She leans back into the booth and I study her stunned face. She places her hand on her belly like she may be sick. Ace leans forward against the table and I do the same. She looks at me and her pained expression makes me giggle.

"Kylie, if you have another option other than that dumbass

Stan, it's not a hard choice." She looks like she may vomit in his face. "One is the coolest guy I've ever met and the other is a pill pusher."

"Tater has my vote," I have to agree with Ace and earns me glare from her silver eyes.

"Guys, stop. He's like my brother." Her face is priceless. Like we delivered life-threatening news.

Kylie drops Ace off at his parents and comes home with me. We're going to get ready together here for the dance, and I have some bills to pay. I open my laptop and log into my bank account.

"You will never have to work a day in your life," Kylie says over my shoulder, snooping as always. Dexter left me a hefty life insurance settlement, not to mention he was a trust fund baby.

"Eventually I'll take over the liquor store. I want most of this to go to Drew's future." I write the check to the country club for our membership and the HOA fees. I promised them I would drop it off yesterday. In true fashion I forgot, so I need to drop it off tonight.

"You want to get high and message with Justin on Facebook? He likes to do that with me."

"Uh...I haven't been high in forever. Do you think my fragile crazy mind could handle that?"

The last time may have been before I married Dexter.

"All I know is the last time you and I got high together, you sat in the backyard talking to a family of bunnies and I wet my pants because I laughed so hard." She snorts while I think about that over-the-top afternoon. I really thought they understood me. Staring at me with their vibrating noses looking all bunny intense, I knew they were in danger from something. Yeah, I was out of my mind.

"They were so stinking cute!" She is silently pleading with me to give it a try, and I know this because we are mind readers. "Okay. I'll do it." I clench my lips and do a nervous squeal as she pulls the joint from her purse. She lights it while I grab an ashtray and an extra chair for her to sit at the desk with me. "Bring on the bunnies."

I really hope I don't do anything crazy. Talking to bunnies is a little weird, but I have a distant memory of getting so high with Ace and Kylie one time that I went skinny dipping by myself on his parent's dock. The lake was full of people, but in my super-high head they couldn't see me. But they could...and they did.

Ace jumped in to cover me while Kylie almost snorted to death on the dock. I don't even know what happened. One minute I was laughing and the next I threw up and became deathly feverish. Some people are cool on weed and some are like me.

CHAPTER 7

~

I decided to only take two hits. In the past, I've gone all in, and I should just aim for cool. Kylie is always cool when she's high and so is Tater, but I never join in because I'm afraid I won't be. We are in a full fit of laughter about our new revelation with Tater being in love with her.

"In the movies the best friend always knows. You have a stupid best friend, Kylie. I should have known." She throws her head back in a big laugh and slaps my shoulder.

"I guess it's pretty obvious," she screeches and we both lean into each other. It's tiring to laugh this hard. "Why has nobody ever said anything until today? I've known him since we were in the womb."

Tater and Kylie grew up as neighbors. Not in this gated community but on the other side of the lake. Their moms were great friends, and there are pictures in his mom's house of Kylie and Tater both naked at the age of two in a bathtub.

Kylie's parents both died. Her dad when we were seventeen and her mom about two years ago. Her mom had ovarian cancer, leaving Kylie with a huge hospital bill. She has no siblings to share the burden, as her sister died at a very young age. Tater and his family organized a huge fundraiser to assist her with the bills before and after she died. Tater's family is her family now. She spends Christmas and Thanksgiving with them. They are practically married.

"Are you going to say anything to him?" I ask through a giggle.

Kylie shrugs. "Probably."

"What will you say?" I ask, amused at her brave disposition.

"Maybe I should tell him what happened and then kiss him to see if there's anything there," Kylie says. "He is my best friend after you. I have no secrets from him...I can't deny my curiosity."

"What about him being your brother?" I remind her of what she said this morning with air quotes and a giggle.

"Eh...worked for Cersei and Jamie."

"Not really," I point out and we both crack up. We are obsessed with *Game of Thrones* and have watched the whole show many times.

She logs into Facebook from my computer and goes straight to Justin's page.

"He's so hot," Kylie says. "Why does he have to be married? I feel like you guys would be so good together. He has two boys. It could be a modern-day *Brady Bunch*."

"I may just come out of celibacy for Justin. I can't believe I never did more than kiss him." I shake my head in remorse, but I'm not at all remorseful. It's just fun to be a silly girl right now, and Justin Watson exudes so much sexual prowess.

"So...." she says and bites her lip. "I hooked up with Justin after senior prom and once when he was visiting from college." She looks so scared.

"What? Why did you never tell me?" I ask. The bubble of laughter in me is about to explode.

"I thought you'd hate me. You hooked up first," she says, looking ashamed. "Plus you two had this weird dynamic."

"He wasn't mine. We only ever kissed. Not even make-out kissing. Just a kiss." It takes a few minutes of reassuring her I'm not mad, sad, or any emotion except curious. I grin. "What do you mean *hooked up*?"

"On prom, I let him finger me in the girls restroom. The next time we did *it!*" she screams and I drop my jaw.

"It? Like...sex?" I'm so high and this is blowing my mind. How did I never know this?

"Weiner in me, Lily." Her eyes are red and big. I throw my head back and laugh.

"Oh my GOSH! Tell me every single last detail. Was he good? Was he big?"

Her eyes roll back into her head. "So good! I still fantasize about him. And yes, he's big."

"Shit!" I say. "I'm super high and feeling a world of regret for never rounding home base with Justin Watson. Probably because I spent too much time talking to bunnies."

"It's not too late," Kylie says, her smile mischievous.

"To talk to bunnies? Do you see any?" I ask, standing and peering out the window with my head swiveling back and forth like a lunatic.

"To sleep with Justin. Your poor vagina must be lonely." I turn and look at her with my nose scrunched.

"I could never sleep with him. For many reasons but also because we're friends and we can't all sleep together." Her lips purse and I can see she disagrees. I roll my eyes.

"But Ace is back, and you two are so cute together!" she exclaims. "Are there any sparks?"

"Nah, I love my husband."

"He's dead," Kylie says, her eyes serious. "You are very much alive, and Ace is single." She pats my cheek as if she is snapping me out of something. "Hot and rich."

"Ask Justin what he's doing," I say, distracting her. I don't want to engage in a conversation about dating. I'm too high.

"I need a snack first. Whatcha got?" *We literally just ate.*

"Go-Gurt?" I offer, and she springs up into my kitchen. I follow her when she announces she's making ramen and grilled cheese sandwiches.

I look through my pantry for bread, and I find an old giant

russet potato, the ones the size of a newborn baby. I smile to myself and walk to Drew's room, pulling out one of her little bonnets I saved. I tie it around the potato and laugh hysterically while I draw a face on it.

"The dream means you and Tater are going to have babies!" I say as I walk back into the kitchen. She's ramming slices of cheddar cheese into her mouth. She looks up with chipmunk cheeks and laughs with her signature snort.

"Oh my god! I love her," she mumbles with a block of cheese in her mouth and takes her *Tater* baby from me, looking down on it adoringly.

After our lunch, we finally sit down to talk to Justin. I'm holding the Tater baby while she controls the keyboard.

While we wait for him to respond, we look at pictures of him, his gorgeous wife, and their two cute kids. Justin isn't conventionally good-looking like Ace. He is more like a Girard Butler versus Chris Hemsworth. Ace's face is perfection, and he has the matching too-good-to-be-true manners. Justin is just hot! All the time. He is not so much a gentleman. He was always a bit slutty when we were growing up. He has swagger and charisma, and that makes it easy for every woman on this earth to be attracted to him. When Ace picked me up for homecoming, he told me I looked beautiful. That same night, Justin told me he would fantasize about me in that dress for the rest of his life.

Justin always appealed to me on such a dangerous level. He used to say naughty things to all the girls. He could get away with it and not sound creepy. One night when we were in college, he called me while he was drunk and wanted to have phone sex. Dexter was sleeping next to me, and I had never done anything like that. I almost hid in the closet and had phone sex with him because Justin is the kind of guy that can turn a good girl bad.

Justin: *Working. You?*

Kylie and I both squeal like we're twelve again because we're high, and there is something about Justin that feels exciting and deliciously scandalous.

"Should I tell him you have been fantasizing about him for years?" Kylie asks.

"Should I tell him you've been fantasizing about him since his big torpedo entered your body?" I shoot back.

"I think everyone, even Ace and Tater, fantasize about Justin," Kylie says and I nod. She could be onto something. His sexuality is so powerful he could turn a straight man gay.

Kylie: *Sitting here with Lily. She misses you.*

Justin: *LILY! I miss you. How are you?*

I give Kylie a mischievous look out the corner of my eyes, then push her hands away from the keyboard.

Me: *I'm good, Justin. Why don't you ever come home? Ace is here, and Kylie and I just found out Tater is and always has been in love with her.*

Justin: *I'm calling you.*

Within a minute, my phone rings. We both squeal, and I feel like we're back in eighth grade, staying up all night to talk with him on the phone.

"Hello!" A giggle builds in my throat while my eyes fill with happy mist from laughter.

"Hey, it's Ace."

"Hi Ace." Kylie's huge smile falls. This makes me laugh.

"What's so funny?" Ace asks.

"Kylie and I got high." The confession makes me feel weird. "I haven't done it in years and we are waiting for Justin to call. We are chatting with him on Facebook," I fidget in my chair all the sudden I'm very uncomfortable. "I don't get high."

Be cool.

"Justin Watson?" He sounds off.

"I know two Justins and one is only seven years old. So yeah, Justin Watson." Kylie motions for me to wrap up the call with Ace.

He sighs. I'm suddenly hit with déjà vu of talking to Justin on the phone when Ace and I were dating and he would sigh. Is he jealous?

"Tater is picking me up at seven tonight. We will come get the both of you. Sound good?" Ace asks. He seems hurt. Or maybe I'm just high as heck?

"Yeah," I say right before my other line beeps.

"I'll let you go. That has to be prince charming now." He sounds indifferent.

"See ya at seven. I'm excited." I feel a little surge of adrenaline to win this dance contest.

"Yeah, that's why I will let you get to it," he says, referring to Justin. He hangs up before I can correct him that my excitement stems from seeing him tonight and dancing with him. Now I find myself sighing.

I click the line and say hello.

"Hey gorgeous." Justin's cool voice comes through and my heart skips a beat at the sound of it.

CHAPTER 8

～

We talk on speaker phone with Justin for over an hour. I'm so high and we still have the Tater baby with us, lying between us on my bed with a baby blanket over it. It's safe to say we have both lost our minds. I hadn't talked to Justin in over a year, and it's refreshing to catch up with him. He is *unhappily* married and open about it. They have both cheated but are staying together for the kids.

"Okay, the kids and I will come next weekend. Can I stay with you, Lily?" Justin asks in such a naughty way I think I may be blushing.

"No, Tater would be devastated," I say and Justin sighs. "Not to mention your wife may find it odd."

"She doesn't have to know," he says. For the first time, I feel disgusted by his playboy behavior. *Plus, he has slept with Kylie! What is going on?*

Be cool, I remind myself.

"Just get out here already!" Kylie screams in the phone with pure enthusiasm. *She doesn't seem to care. She's cool.*

"I can't wait to get on that boat with you two girls!" He sounds seven years old again.

"I don't go on the lake since Dexter died and Drew doesn't know how to swim. I don't allow it," I say. *I'm so not cool.* A vortex of anxiety coils around all my organs, making me sweat.

He sighs heavily. "Lily, that's crazy. If she can't swim, she will certainly drown." I wipe my sweaty forehead, wanting to vomit at the truth.

"I know...I just can't bring myself to let her get in there." I close my eyes and take a deep breath, waiting for his reaction.

"I'm coming and we're all going boating," Justin says in a spirted tone and it annoys me deep down inside.

We hang up because he has a meeting to get to and Kylie and I should start to get ready. I get off my bed and remove my clothes, throwing them in my overly full hamper in the bathroom before turning on the shower. Kylie walks in the bathroom and takes one look at my hamper.

"I'm going to put a load of clothes in for you. The amount of dirty clothes you have is insane," she yells.

"I love you forever," I say with a big smile. Helping with laundry is basically the nicest thing one can do for a single mama. "I'm so high and I think I may start freaking out soon." I bore my eyes into her giant steel-blue ones, so she knows about the brewing anxiety grabbing hold of her best friend. Threatening to pull me under.

"Is it because of Justin and I sleeping together?" she asks and again looks so ashamed of herself. "I shouldn't have told you! It's too weird."

"Kylie...I so don't care about that. It's all my other stuff. Like Drew and the lake and my dreams about Dexter. I'm crazy and scared to death that I may start talking to the intense nose twitchers again and never stop." I grab her free hand and she squeezes mine back.

"Lily, you aren't crazy. I won't let you freak out. Are you positive this has nothing to do with Justin and I? I've been so stressed out to tell you." Her intense eyes cut into me, and I can't help but feel guilty. He was never mine. I can't believe she's been feeling guilty about it all these years...and now her guilt is making me feel guilty. It's a downward spiral of unnecessary guilt.

Be cool.

"Kylie, I could never be mad at you. Hoes before bros." That earns me a cute giggle. "You are my very best friend. I can't survive one day without hearing your voice or laughing with you. I'm actually excited because now you can describe his naked body to me in great detail while I shower." Her laughter bounces off the bathroom walls.

We get ready slowly and I listen to Kylie talk in great, elaborate detail about Justin and their hot night together. It sounds like some kind of epic romance novel, not a one-night stand. I am so high I can't decide if the buzzing noise I am hearing is in my ear or if it's vibrating out of Kylie's throat. We get high one more time with her medical-grade marijuana. We also manage to drink a bottle and a half of wine. At 7 PM on the dot, Tater lets himself and Ace into my house.

"You girls aren't even dressed," Tater says amused when he catches me in the kitchen in hot rollers and a robe, holding Kylie's *baby* in my left arm and pouring more wine with my right hand. They both eye the Tater baby in my arms.

"What is that?" Ace asks. He looks upset. Is he upset about me not being ready? Smoking pot? The time I got so high I peed in the corner of our tent in the middle of the night?

Be cool, my mind whispers while the anxiety and paranoia start to wind themselves around my sanity.

"This is Tater and Kylie's baby." I look up into his cool blue eyes. It takes a minute before he registers her dream and we both laugh. "Here Tater. She just ate and she is ready to be rocked to sleep."

Tater is amused and also completely confused. "Ace will fill you in. I'm gonna go take these hot rollers out. This is Kylie's second attempt at my hair tonight. I looked like Cindy Lauper from the eighties with her first one. Fingers crossed boys. I'd hate to embarrass you." I squish my eyes closed, willing the anxiety coil to release itself. "Also, don't worry about me being cool on the *weed* tonight. I so got this." I give a big wink.

"As long as you don't eat out of any trash cans tonight...I'm not worried." Tater sniggers as Ace's face lights up with recognition. "Dumpster diving Lil's isn't welcome."

"That corndog was in perfect uneaten condition," I defend myself.

"Still...the vision of you going through a trash bin for food is..." Tater closes one eye while bobbing his head trying to find the right word.

"Weird?" Ace quips, and they both explode in laughter at my expense.

"Remember when she full-on wailed in your living room because your dad was hunting like he did millions of times before? Then she claimed to go vegetarian," Tater points out. I don't have a problem with responsible hunting, but when I do think deeply about it, it makes me sad. It is a loss of life.

"I can't be cool if you both point out all the uncool things I've done while being high. Like lock myself in the bathroom because I thought everyone was talking about me on prom night. I'm a single mom and I'm really trying to be super cool tonight."

They both look like they're going to bust up laughing at me. I try to scorn their souls with my eyes so they know I am serious.

"Lils, you are the coolest woman in all the world," Tater says and bends down to kiss my cheek.

"I know. I know," I almost whisper as if it's my *mantra*.

"Let's go boating tomorrow," Tater says with his warm grin. *I'm not that high.*

"I'm going to put on my dress." Ace is eye level with me, closer than normal, as he is sitting on the bar stool. I lean over and kiss his cheek without really thinking it through. His head slowly turns and I hold my breath. Our eyes meet. His usual deep blue orbs look more of an icy blue mixed with what can only be disgust.

I wince, quickly turning away while my pulse races through my veins. *Am I just paranoid? You've got to be cool!*

Once Kylie and I are both dressed, the boys compliment us, and I have a very rational moment when I realize I was being paranoid about Ace. He seemed genuinely sincere about me looking nice tonight. Honestly, the dress is a little sexier than I feel comfortable in, but Kylie sold me on it. Not like I have a ton of dresses that fit me correctly. It's a vivacious red with a plunging neckline, a fitted bodice and a twirly skirt. The back also plunges with a criss cross detail that I needed assistance figuring out how to get on my body. Kylie and I nearly wet ourselves getting me in it.

"I heard Justin is coming next weekend," Ace says from the front seat of Tater's truck as it climbs up Lakeview Drive to the country club. I'm behind him, and I can smell his signature scent that delights my nose and every part of my senses.

"Will you still be here?" I hold my breath, waiting for his reply. *Please don't leave, don't ever leave.*

"Now I have to be. How can I miss this reunion?" he replies with his charming accent. It's slight, but I can distinguish the Texan drawl.

"Justin has the hots for Lily," Kylie says while she hits Ace's arm. He sighs and turns away from her gaze. I gape at her and she winks at me.

"Always has. Still the same old Justin I see," Ace says, looking out his window.

"Stop," I say to Kylie. "He's married."

"He hates Maria!" she screeches. "I hate her too. She cheated on him."

"He cheated on her first," I blurt out in defense of poor Maria. Kylie's loyalty to Justin is in full control of her thought process.

"She isn't a nice human." Tater says and slaps Ace. "Remember the wedding?"

The three of them reminisce about Maria and Justin's wedding and now I have a pretty yucky taste in my mouth at how awful she was to Kylie. No wonder she hates her.

We pull up to the country club and the boys hold our doors open. Ace sticks his hand in and helps me out of the tall truck. When I place my hand in his, the familiar sensation of *joy* floods my body.

"Come on Sprinkles, let's go win this thang." My heart beats a little faster when our eyes meet. It feels like he's escorting me to prom again.

The country club sits on top of a hill overlooking all of Whimsy. The view is unrivaled up here, waves of green trees as far as the eyes can see. The sun is low and painting the expansive sky in shades of peach and hot pink. The glow coming off of Ace's tanned skin feels warm and intoxicating.

I watch in amazement as Ace looks all around him at the scenery as if it is his lost love. Studying his profile was always my favorite past time when he was *mine*. The hard line of his jaw, his tiny dimple with his ear-to-ear grin, the way his nose scrunches up when he is deep in thought. It's hard to pinpoint the origin of his brilliant blue eyes, but they are uniquely exquisite.

He looks down at me with a brilliant smile. "Whatcha looking at, Sprinkles?" *Your gorgeous profile.* "Do I have a boogie or something?" His eyebrows pique in interest.

"Oh, I was about to ask you something when your face morphed into a deer, and I panicked thinking your dad might come out in full hunting gear and shoot you," I tease. The warmth of his smile is almost too much for me to bear. "Imagine his devastation of mounting his own dead son on the wall."

"Sprinkles, remember to be cool. You're so close." He winks. "What were you really thinking?"

"When's the last time you've been up here? Have you been here since the remodel?" His eyes study me as if to point out that is not what I was thinking. He would be right.

"No. My gosh, they really stepped up their game. How's the gym?"

I reach out and squeeze his bicep. "Not big enough for these things." He rolls his eyes, still carrying his brilliant smile. "It is actually nice, and they have a lot of fun classes that I like to take. Pilates, yoga, spin, and even Zumba."

"We tear that shit up in Zumba!" Kylie exclaims as she sticks her hands in the top of her dress and scoops her boobs to increase her cleavage, sending us all into hysterics.

Tater and Kylie bound up the steps, eager for cocktails. I follow a curious Ace around the country club grounds. I walk behind so I can stare at him. Mostly what I notice is his butt. That is one shapely, firm tushy. His broad shoulders tautly stretch his white button-up shirt across his expansive back. Does he work out twenty-four hours a day?

He stops when we arrive at the huge terrace.

"I miss the way it smells here. Like pine, clean and untouched." He looks so serene and filled with appreciation. "It's so gorgeous!"

"This is where George Balor got married last year," I say as I motion to the huge travertine patio that extends out over the hill. It looks like something you would see in Tuscany.

"Nice wedding?"

"Stan got so drunk he fell down those steps during the reception, but not before he tried to stop the wedding, claiming that George had been unfaithful to Sabrina." I pause. "So, yeah, it was awesome!"

"Whimsy weddings are always the best. Did George cheat on Sabrina?" he asks.

I shrug. "It's George so I wouldn't be surprised." Our laughter intertwines to make one harmonic sound.

"Where did you get married?" he asks me gently.

"It was before the remodel. We had arranged to get married on the golf course but it rained that day, so we had to move it into the ballroom."

"Raining on the wedding day is supposed to bring good luck, but it also rained on my wedding day and we both know how that turned out."

The silence seems suffocating right now, and I don't want to talk about wedding day luck with him. Dexter and I had no luck.

"I bet your wedding was beautiful. The ballroom has always served well for Whimsy weddings."

"It was pretty. If I had to do it again, this is where I'd do it," I say, motioning to the stunning view.

"Would you invite Stan?" he teases.

"Wouldn't matter. You know Whimsy. They all come to the weddings regardless of invites. George or Sabrina didn't invite him to theirs," I point out and he nods. We talk as we watch the sunset. I am being super cool right now. Now that we're not talking about our weddings, that is.

"It's funny how it feels like no time has passed between us," Ace says with a huge smile. "That is the sign of true friendship."

"I'm so glad you said that because I don't want to lock myself in the bathroom being paranoid you don't like me," I say sheepishly and he shakes his head in amusement.

"I wouldn't want to be with anyone else tonight, no matter what happens in there, just remember that. If you get hungry, I'll get you food. You need a drink, I'll get it. Someone makes you uncomfortable, I'll be able to read you and I can make it right. Don't do anything crazy before consulting me." My mouth falls open to say something, but I can't form a straight thought when I watch him rise to his full height. Okay, so maybe I'm gawking, not watching. My protest on being an independent woman takes a back seat while I drink in his magnificence. He can mock me all he wants with his cowboy boots and those fitted Wranglers he is wearing all too well.

He puts out his hand for me to grab. I hesitate briefly before placing it in his giant bear paw. He helps me to my feet and then we walk back down toward the country club entrance.

"I can take care of myself. It's actually quite—"

"Sexist?" he interrupts, as though he looked into my brain and plucked the word right out. "We're having this conversation again?"

Once I register what he means, I giggle awkwardly. One time when I was high, I burned all my bras in my parent's fireplace while ranting and raving about Ace, Justin, and Tater all being sexist. They were just trying to steer me from eating peyote at the party we were at earlier that night. They claimed I needed to be watched when I was high, and I took offense to it. I tried to turn myself into a women's rights activist. It was pretty wild, and my mom was furious the next day when she had to buy me new bras. Keeping me from peyote was a good idea, not sexist. When Ace tried to stop me by pointing out how seeing the outline of nipples through t-shirts always made me uncomfortable, I pinched his poor nipple and called him a Neanderthal.

I'm never getting high again.

"Holy shit," I think I may have yelled once we step inside the packed country club. The room has gone quiet, staring right at us. "Is it me or you?"

Of course it's him. Unless I've had a nip slip.

I glance down at my chest and relief washes over me.

"It's always you, Sprinkles," he teases and a loud laugh escapes me. Of course it's Mr. Big Shot!

The first person I notice is my sister Rose talking to Stan and his band of merry men. I point her out to Ace.

"Oh my god...that's Rose?"

"Yeah...you can pick your jaw up off the ground," I say. I try to giggle but it bothers me that he thinks she's hot. I realize this is irrational and immature, but I can't stomach the idea of my high school sweetheart having the hots for my bitchy kid sister.

I'm so jealous. Like I could punch her.

"She looks...." He pauses and scrunches his nose, deep in thought. Adorably deep in thought. "Gorgeous."

I will murder them both. Can I take on a lengthy murder trial right now?

CHAPTER 9

~

I can feel Ace looking down at me as I plot his double murder with Rose. *How dare he?*

"Did you just call her gorgeous?" I ask as I ponder where I can buy a black-market gun at this hour.

"Are you hearing things? Like on prom night when you heard Kylie say she *wanted me?*" He laughs.

"Ha ha," I say through clenched teeth.

"No, I didn't call her gorgeous. She looks so different." He pulls me a little closer. "Nobody I'd rather be with," he hums, reminding me of what he told me moments ago outside.

"Okay...I know...I know," I whisper. His warm lips kiss the top of my head, and warmth spreads through my whole body. My toes wiggle in excitement. I turn and stand right in front of him with a big smile. "I'm super cool." He nods his head while he bites the side of his bottom lip. *So cute.*

"Behind you coming this way is Johnny Johnson," he whispers as though we are in a covert operation.

"Oh god," I say as the weed really kicks in. "Don't let me faint or tell him to fuck off."

"Lily, you said you weren't coming," Johnny says as he taps my shoulder. I close my eyes tight to pray he vanishes through a wardrobe entrance to Narnia or something. *Get lost.*

I turn around and smile. "Hey Johnny. I wasn't planning to

but then I ran into Ace. We've had this planned since we were like seven. The first time my parents won and brought home the pretty trophy, we made a pact," I say as he kisses my cheek. "I lost my virginity to him." I look up at Ace, who smiles awkwardly.

Okay, that was a weird thing to say. Be cool, dang it.

Johnny sniggers. "Lucky guy." He's staring at my chest. This makes me very uncomfortable when men do this. Makes me second guess this dress. I shift uncomfortably and feel Ace put his hand on my shoulder.

"Hey Johnny," Ace says and reaches out his other hand for Johnny to shake. They talk for a minute before Johnny is pulled aside. He glances back at me over his shoulder as he walks away.

"Weird speech you gave him but overall, I'd say you're still *so cool*, Lily Moore." I throw my head back and laugh, which makes him laugh with me.

"It just came out." I shrug as I wipe my damp eyes with the tip of my finger. He reaches behind him and grabs a napkin off the table. I look up at him with a sweet smile. "Aw. Thanks."

He sticks his arm out for me with his ridiculously handsome and charming smile. I slide my arm through it, and I let him escort me around the room. Everyone seems to be vibrating with the excitement of having Ace home. He looks nothing but gracious as he takes a pen and football out of Mr. Buckets's hands and signs it. "Let's do a few pictures?" Ace agrees. There is no denying he is such a good sport.

Rose walks up to us. "Hi..." I start, but she ignores me and looks right at Ace.

"Ace Lancaster. How have you been?" She smiles with her dazzling bleached teeth. Maybe I should buy some teeth whitener? Her hair is shorter and has the perfect tousled wave. It's dyed to a dark caramel blonde color, making it look magnificent with her blue eyes. Her fake boobs push out of her black tank top. A skin-tight floral mini skirt shows off her lengthy toned legs, ending in sexy hot pink high heels.

"Good. How about you?" Ace asks with a giant smile on his

face. *Gross.*

I'll cut them both. Can I afford a good enough lawyer for a double murder? That's the weed talking.

"Better now that you're here. Can I have the first dance?" she asks in such a flirtatious way I can feel some of my wine start to come up.

"We actually are here to win...Been a goal since childhood," I say. *I will end her.*

She looks at me as if she hasn't even seen me yet.

"Hi Lily, you look like you actually brushed your hair today." I don't miss the venom in her voice trying to make me look bad in front of Ace. *How dare she?* I'm doing just fine on my own, Rose! Carrying around potatoes in bonnets, talking about losing my virginity to him, plotting a double homicide...

"And you look like you got twenty more CCs added to those suckers." Cameron comes up behind me and swings his arm across my shoulders. *Yay, back up!* I smile up at him while Rose sighs. I don't know whether he is talking about her inflated boobs or her swollen lips.

"You two are the worst! How can we be related?" Rose snips and runs her hands over her hips. She then sends a seductive gaze Ace's way, biting her bottom lip like some kind of porn star.

"I don't know. We are both good people and you are horrible," Cameron says and takes a swig of his beer. He then looks to Ace. "Hey buddy, how ya been?" He sticks his hand out and they shake hands and do a manly one-arm hug. Rose scampers off when she doesn't receive more attention from Ace. Cameron and Ace catch up for a few minutes before we take our seats to eat.

It's barbecue ribs, a baked potato, garlic bread, chili, and salad. Ace and I are at a big round table with my family. Kylie is eating with Tater and Stan all the way across the room. I wish we were eating with them. Now that she knows Tater's true feelings for him, it must be awkward.

Cameron introduces Ace to his three kids: Devyn, his angelic nine-year-old daughter; Oscar, his ornery five-year-old son; and

Delilah, his adorable two-year-old who is covered in chocolate. While everyone is chatting away, Rose comes and plops down on the other side of Ace and starts flirting with him. Asking him what he thinks of her short hair. If he likes her in black. What he thinks of her boob job. Cameron and I exchange knowing looks. Who in their right mind asks a guy if they like their boobs? Of course he does! Every man in this room is fantasizing about licking this award-winning barbecue sauce right off them. Dimwit.

"Th-they look great, you look great," Ace stutters, looking uncomfortable. She is rubbing his leg under the table. I try to stay calm and cool, but my mind is silently doing a roll call as to who at this shindig can get me a gun. *Stan?*

I look at my fork and imagine sticking it in her boob. *Would she deflate just like a balloon?*

"Rose, hand jobs aren't permitted around your nieces and nephew," Cameron says. Ace bolts up and excuses himself to go to the restroom.

"I swear, Cameron, I wish you would die," Rose says, shooting daggers at Cameron.

Die?

"Nice," Cameron bites, full of sarcasm and a deep loathing.

"Don't you two start," my mom protests.

"Mom, Rose is trying to bone Lily's high school sweetheart. The whole town is vying for them to get back together and your slutty hard-boobed daughter is trying to undo everything you have been working on for the past few months," Cameron says.

"Months?" I ask through a slur.

"Oh, he's exaggerating," she says dismissively while she holds her wine glass up to her pursed lips.

"Well..." my dad starts, and my mom hits him in the stomach. He winces forward in pain.

"My dad doesn't like you," little Oscar yells at Rose. His loathing almost matches his daddy's.

I look at Jeanie and we both silently laugh. When Ace returns, he sits on the other side of me. Jeanie is thrilled to scoot over and make room.

"Lily, you haven't touched your food," Mom says, monitoring me like she always does.

Dad rushes to my rescue. "Leave her alone. Maybe she had a big lunch."

"No, I smoked weed all day," I say to my mom. Cameron laughs so hard he almost falls off the bench which sends me, Ace, and Jeanie over the edge.

"Oh Lily, you have a daughter to think of." Her voice is laced in disappointment.

"I am trying not to obsess over her. She is so far away." I quickly chug half my wine in one gulp.

"Oh Lily!" my mom says with a teensy weensy bit of sympathy. "Ace is here. He hasn't seen you in so long." I glare at her. "Lily doesn't drink much and she never smokes weed," she tells Ace as if putting him at ease.

"Mom, I am going to eat a rib just for you," I say, picking up my rib, "but I am on weed right now." Cameron shoots beer across the table out of his nose. I give up on my rib and howl in laughter right alongside him.

"She is probably still stuffed from the big brunch we ate this morning. She must have eaten five pancakes," Ace says with a big smile.

No I didn't. He's a liar, but I love a good liar when it benefits me.

"Breakfast?" my mom asks with hope.

"You mean you hadn't heard? Ace slept over and we went to breakfast together."

Mom looks thrilled. Dad, on the other hand, looks...*stressed?*

"Just as friends. He did wake up to comfort me when I had my nightmare," I say directly to my dad. His stress gives way to relief.

"Still with this boring dream?" Rose shouts. "This is why I never come home! Lily and her grief have ruined this family."

"Shut your lips!" Cameron yells. "Or can you not anymore

with all the lip plumper in those sad suckers?" He tries to do the duck lips. I want to laugh, but when I see Ace's pained expression, I snap out of it.

"Sorry...Let's go say hi to your mom," I suggest.

"Yes please," he says, all too eager to get away from this family. They're a lot.

As soon as we are a couple feet away from my family, a look of mortification crosses his face. "I can't believe you told your dad I slept over."

"You think that is what he is thinking about while his youngest and oldest are about to kill each other? Rose said during dinner she hoped Cameron Moore, the town doctor, adored by all, would die," I point out and he grimaces.

We wander over to the snack table, and I grab a few grapes. "I'm sorry Rose was molesting you! Makes me wonder if she's on weed too?" I pop one of the grapes in my mouth and hear him laugh, a soft whisper of a noise. I glance up into his gorgeous blue eyes.

"Only cool people say *on weed*." He air quotes the term. When I laugh, the whole grape I had put in my mouth shoots down my throat. My eyes widen, like they want to jump out of my skull. I start pounding my own chest trying to get it out. Ace's eyes get big as he registers what's happening. He steps closer to me.

"Are you choking?" he asks calmly, and I move my hand to his chest and pat it a couple of times to let him know I'm taking my last breaths. He mentions the Heimlich. I start to panic as I realize a Heimlich is so *not cool*. I came here for a trophy, not a Heimlich. Why is my life such a series of misfortunes?

I feel a firm pat on my back that can't be Ace because he's still standing in front of me. The second hit comes harder before I am grabbed firmly by someone who shoves their fist into my diaphragm. My feet lift off the ground. The fist grounds deeper into my diaphragm, my feet swing in the air, and the grape releases itself. I gasp for the welcomed breath and watch with horror as the grape soars across the room in slow motion. It makes its decent down into Kylie's wine glass. We all let out a large sigh of breath. Then when she picks up her glass, we all grimace as she takes an unsuspecting sip. *Oops.*

"You've never been cool *on weed.*" Cameron, my heroic doctor and brother, mocks me too before he takes the rest of the grapes out of my hand and tosses them in the trash bin. "Grapes are one of the biggest choking hazards for toddlers, Ace. You gotta do a better job tonight."

"You're right. I will make sure she doesn't jump into that trash to pull out those perfectly *uneaten* grapes." Cameron roars and slaps Ace's back as if that is the funniest thing he's ever heard.

"Yeah guys, I'm feeling okay. Thanks for asking," I say, still gulping down sweet air. "I think you broke a rib." Ace grabs a cold bottle of water out of the ice bin, twists the lid, and puts it in my hand. I smile wanly at him. As hard as I tried, I've really not been cool tonight.

"I know you're fine because I didn't have to work that hard to get the grape out," Cameron gloats. I grab a napkin to dab at my watery eyes before excusing myself to the restroom.

〜

"Hey Bernie!" I beam at Ace's sweet mom when I come out of the restroom. Her and Ace are at the snack station, and I glower at the grapes.

"Oh, Lily you look beautiful!" she gushes. "So glad to see you here this year."

I love Bernie Lancaster. She is one of my life heroes and has always gone above and beyond for me. Now she does the same for Drew.

We all face the stage when the owner of the country club greets us with the dance contest rules. The dance contest is five dance styles, and the couple who wins gets the one-thousand-dollar grand prize, a picture on the wall of fame with the thirty-five other couples that have won over the years, and of course the coveted trophy. It's gold plated with a dancing couple on the top. Mr. Beazer made them originally, and the new owner has learned the art as well. The romantic-looking trophy will look nice in the liquor store next to my parents' trophies. Nobody has won twice except my parents. Ace's parents have won once.

"You two going to win this thing?" Bernie asks us with a big smile.

"Yeah," we both say in unison. Our easy laugh makes me feel very aware of how much I am enjoying him and his cute tushy being back home.

First up is an Elvis song that we dance to like a true fifties couple. Ace has always had natural dance skills. Kylie and I took dance lessons every summer at the YMCA when we were younger. We aren't great, but nobody in this room is. This is like the town get-together as adults and choosing the most popular couple. The next song is "Macarena" and we give it our all. We have lost several couples already who have been tapped on the shoulder. The next song is "I Gotta Feeling" by The Black Eyed Peas, and we are in our element for sure. We both slide right up against each other when it switches to "Somebody Like You" by Keith Urban. We do a two-step, smiling and laughing the whole time. At this point, there are only eight couples left on the dance floor. The next and final song is "Unchained Melody" by The Righteous Brothers. *Why?*

My chest and throat constrict. This was the song Dexter chose for our first dance as husband and wife at our wedding. I hear it most nights in my dream. I used to think it was beautiful like every other person in the world, but now I just find it haunting. Debilitating. Awful.

"Are you okay?" Ace asks. "You're very stiff. Relax, Sprinkles." His voice feels like warm syrup.

"This was..." I stop myself and take a deep breath. I close my eyes. "I'll relax." I take another huge breath, inhaling his lovely smell, relaxing into his warm body as he effortlessly spins me around.

"Have you seen who Kylie is dancing with?" he whispers. I open my eyes and smile because she is in the contest with Tater... not Stan.

"Stan looks peeved," Ace says. "Maybe the next song should be Beyonce's 'Single Ladies' so he gets the hint to *put a ring on it*."

I laugh and look up at Ace. "I'm so glad you're home," I say before pressing my cheek back into his chest. "You smell nice. I've always loved the way you smell."

I'm really trying to be cool, but he does smell and look amazing. I can't shake this recurring sensation I keep getting. *He's still mine.*

But he's not.

"You smell like pot and booze." I smile into his chest while inhaling him like a crazy stalker. The music stops but we don't let go of one another. I finally pull away when it hits me that I shouldn't stalk my ex-boyfriend. I smile up at him while he looks around the room. My eyes trail around the room to find a trans-fixed group of Whimsy residents, all focused on us.

They look like they are about to cry happy tears, and that makes me feel wholly self-conscious. Ace grabs my hand so we can face the stage to hear their choice for this year's winner.

"Tough decision for us this year with our three final couples," Bill says, looking torn. One of the other final couples is Rose and Mike Hampton her friend from high school. He's very well-liked and owns a coffee shop down by the grocery store. Then with Kylie and Tater, we have some stiff competition for sure.

He announces Kylie and Tater as third place. They get a free oil change and a tire rotation at Red's Automotive Shop. I scream so loud for them and jump up and down. Ace is whistling with two fingers in his mouth.

"The next two girl competitors are sisters, which just adds to the drama," Bill says. Ace puts his arm around me and squeezes me tight. "Whimsy's 2018 annual dance contest winners are Ace Lancaster and Lily Moore!" he announces in a booming game contestant kind of way.

"We won!" I scream as I turn to face Ace. I jump up in his arms as he spins me around.

We walk up the stairs that lead to the stage, and Bill hands me the microphone. I don't want to say anything. I look at the sea of adoring eyes and internally laugh. It's a big moment, something I have dreamed of with Ace so many times.

"Thank you. Maybe it's silly, but Ace and I always said we'd win this trophy, and I am so proud right now." I blow everyone a kiss before stepping aside for Ace to say something. He's the big star after all.

"Isn't she beautiful?" he says and motions to me, making me feel like a blushing teen. I press my palms to my cheeks. "Lily and I met in Whimsy Tots Preschool when we were three years old. She lived down the street from me and we grew up best friends, high school sweethearts, and now we have been reunited after ten years. She feels like home to me...I'm so glad to be here with y'all. I don't ever want to leave." My heart leaps and my eyes sting with tears. I don't know what that emotion is, but it sure feels nice. "We decided to donate the money to the animal shelter. I also plan on adding to that," he adds and everyone claps and cheers.

"Well look at them!" the country club owner shouts after Ace hands him back the microphone. "Whimsy's most adored have won tonight, no doubt about that. Please, tell us what song you would like to dance to as winners."

I stare at Ace because I have no idea what song to pick. There are too many options.

"'She Will Be Loved' by Maroon 5!" Ace says and again it's an onslaught of wild emotions. We danced to it at prom after being crowned king and queen.

We walk back down to the dance floor as the music starts, hand in hand. I feel adored and on top of the world, just like I did as prom queen.

~

We get caught up in a photo frenzy by my mom when we stop to take our picture for the wall of fame.

"Just one more of Ace lifting you the way he did when they announced you winners. Just hold the trophy out nice and far, Lily, so I can see it." She beams and I can't help but laugh. I look at Ace to gauge if he can humor one last ridiculous reenactment photo for my mom. He smiles and grabs me around my waist and lifts me up exactly the way before. I throw my drunk head back and push the trophy toward her with a giant smile. She takes several more before my dad intervenes.

"Maggie, enough already," my dad says with a great deal of amusement. "Our daughter is high as a kite." I channel Kylie and snort while laughing.

"Earl, let me have my proud mommy moment." She instructs Ace to spin me a little to the left.

My dad rolls his eyes and grabs the camera out of her hands and tells her to back off. She plants her hands on her hips and lets him have it, which makes me laugh. I love my parents even when they fight...because it's not fighting. It's two people who have built an amazing life together getting irritated with the person they love more than anything in this world. It's adorable.

Ace gets into a conversation with Tony, the gate guard, while I stand and yawn for what feels like a solid fifteen minutes. My mom was right on the money earlier when she told Ace I don't drink or smoke pot. Occasional glass of wine or two but not to this extreme since college.

"You two looked pretty cute. Mom may be onto something with all of her plotting the last two months," Cameron says quietly while Ace signs more footballs and pictures for the small-town residents. They all adore their local legend.

"Mom is drunk twenty-three hours a day," I say as I sip on some water. She nudges me and laughs, accepting my joke.

"Yes, but your brother is not," Cameron says. "Aren't you kind of attracted to him?"

Yes.

"What?" I ask, annoyed. "No...Cameron...I-I-I'm married."

He holds his hands up to stop me. "I'm still attracted to Kelly. We have both been happily married for years, but when I see her, I can't help but dig her." Cameron is one of those people that can say anything and make it funny. The animated dramatization on his face is enough proof.

"Well, you two were the absolute power couple in sixth grade, so it makes sense."

"If you were attracted to him, it wouldn't be bad." I grab his hand because he is trying to make me feel better about something he thinks I'm struggling with.

"I know...I'm not though. I still love my husband." I bore my eyes into his, hoping he will, for once, get it.

He sighs. His pretty blue eyes mold into two hard stones before removing his gaze from mine. He takes a deep breath, preparing to hold back what he really wants to say, and I smile in appreciation. "Alright, well, Tater says he's gotten you to agree to boating tomorrow. We are all meeting at Tater's at 11 AM. I can't wait to boat with you again. Dad is so elated he almost cried when Tater told him."

"I never agreed to that," I say and shake my head vigorously. The aggressive movement and the fear make me want to vomit. Mock amusement etches his face, and I roll my eyes at his ridiculous lopsided smirk.

Kylie walks over, a look of exhaustion on her face. "Let's go smoke more weed and go to bed. I've had a weird night and need to talk about it till all my weed is gone."

"Weird night?" Tater asks as he places his arm over her shoulder and she shifts a little awkwardly. He waits for her to tell him about it, but after a long silence, he moves on. "I'm too drunk to drive home, so I'm coming to your house."

Tater is like a lab puppy. Always happy, very loyal, and overall adorable. He has light blonde hair with light blue eyes. His face still looks like he is sixteen, and he gets carded when he is outside of Whimsy.

"Well...let's go!" Kylie says with adamance. "I'm done with

this place."

"Come on, Blue. Let's steal a golf cart to drive home," Tater coos, using the nickname only he calls her. It's cute and now it means more to me. I can see by the look on her face she feels the same.

"Race ya!" she exclaims and runs away from us, Tater chasing after her.

Ace and I follow them to the front of the building where we find them in a stolen golf cart. I jump in the back with Ace. Kylie takes off with the pedal to the medal, spinning on the turf of the golf course.

"Kylie, slow down and stop spinning. Remember Coda? She got a compound fracture doing this same shit," Tater yells in full panic. Kylie laughs like a drunk, high maniac.

"Compound fracture!" she screams repeatedly while doing donuts. I grip the seat for dear life while Ace holds me in the cart. I laugh so hard it hurts.

I feel like I'm sixteen again. Not a care in the world. I can barely fit the key in the front door when we get to my house. I finally get it open, and we all spill through the front door in a drunken stupor.

"I'll open more wine. Ace, you find food, and you two are in charge of the music," Tater says.

"Aye aye captain," I say with a salute. "I gotta get this stupid dress off first!" I motion for Kylie to join.

"Nope, I'm staying put. I love the way my tits look in this dress." She scoops them up. I burst into giggles.

I hang my dress up and put on a tank top with a built-in bra and some leggings. I slide into slippers and twist my hair into a bun. Feels so good to be home in pajamas.

When I walk out in the living room, Ace is messing with the stereo while Kylie and Tater are lighting a joint outside. He hands me my glass of wine.

"You look adorable," Ace says and I roll my eyes playfully. "I'm serious...you do."

"Thank you," I say and take a sip of my favorite rosé.

He grabs me and spins me around the living room to a slow song I don't recognize. We dance and chat until our two high friends come in. Kylie claps and cheers for our dancing. She scoops her boobs back into place again which kills me.

CHAPTER 10

❝Lils...Lils." I try to open my heavy eyelids but it's as though somebody has super glued them shut. "Lily, you need to wake up. Drew is on the phone." I roll on my side and force my lids to open before they quickly shut themselves. "Drew is waiting." I bolt upright as I finally recognize the voice, who I am, and who Drew is. I rub my face and squint at Tater with one eye, painfully trying to register the light. He passes me the phone.

"Hi Boo!" I beam.

"Mommy! I ate clam chowder and the Golden Gate Bridge is red, not gold!" she says in her little sweet voice, melting my guilt-stricken heart.

"Oh my gosh! I miss you so much," I manage to say before my eyes fill with tears.

I am so hungover.

I listen to her excitement for the zoo. They are getting ready to head there for the day. The American Girl doll shopping spree is tomorrow morning before they head out. I wish her energy was contagious. All I feel is guilt. Guilt for having fun when she is gone. For getting so drunk and smoking weed. I'm not a rebellious teen trying to find my way. I'm a mother of a precocious little life. My mom was right last night...

When we get off the phone, I smile wanly at Tater, feeling like a deadbeat mama.

"She sounds like she is having fun." I watch him buzz around my house cleaning up. We stayed up until the wee hours of the morning, and I think we may have all slept on the couch. At least I did.

"She is," I say, my tears building.

"Why isn't Mommy happy then?" he says in a baby voice with a flipped lip, mocking my sensitivity.

"I feel like such a loser. I got high and drunk and wore a slutty dress to a dance and if I'm being honest, I didn't think about her much." I pause and wipe my tears. "I mean, I didn't think about her as much as I should have."

"Oh, Lils, you look good slutty," he mocks and I attempt a feeble laugh. His empathetic smile makes me feel a little better. "You are a wonderful mom and you are entitled to cut loose."

I sink back into the couch and pull the blanket up to my chin. "You really think that? My mom was guilting me last night about being high in front of Ace."

"Maggie has ulterior motives if you haven't caught on," his pretty eyes glittering with amusement.

"I'm gonna die." My head is pounding. Tater is in the kitchen putting glasses away while whistling. Radiating joy. "Why are you so chipper?"

"Because last night was awesome...wasn't it? It's like he never left. Man, I've missed him."

"Me too. But my head hurts," I whine and pull a pillow over my head.

"I know what will make you feel better." I stay hidden under the pillow until he nudges me and puts a mimosa in a fancy champagne flute into my face.

"Oh god...no way. I'm going to throw up." I push it away. "I haven't partied in years. Sure, wine with dinner or a beer but this..."

"Just try one," he says, gently cutting me off. His pleading eyes make me reach for the glass and take a small sip. It does taste nice. I put it back to my lips when he says that it will cure my headache. He does own a bar, he would know.

"Where are Kylie and Ace?" I yawn.

"Getting bagels," he says while wiping down my coffee table.

"What do I look like right now? Be totally honest."

He rises to his full height and studies me. "Like a professional dancer." I beam as that awesome memory makes its way back into my heart. "Also like a homicidal maniac."

"I feel like both of those things are accurate," I admit and close my eyes, trying to syphon the painful thumping in my brain out of my body.

Kylie and Ace come flying through the front door laughing. It's infectious. After they tell us about their bagel run and all the people they ran into, Kylie plops down next to me and grabs my mimosa and takes a hefty sip.

"Wanna get high?" Her makeup smeared while her hair resembles a tuft of tumbleweed. She looks like I feel.

"I think it's best if I get *off the weed* for life." Acceptance is key here.

"No!" Kylie protests with sad eyes. She plows forward to plead her case. "Guys, isn't she so much fun when she's high?" I watch her glance from Tater to Ace. Neither of them agrees with her.

"Cameron had to give me the Heimlich. It brings out all my insecurities...I say weird things. I'm not cool on it like you and Tater are," I point out while releasing a sigh.

"I never thought you'd give up on this Lils," Kylie says with exaggerated heartbreak.

"It's not what any of us want, but Lily has a point," Ace says, dripping in sarcasm. "She's going to need our support to get *off the weed* once and for all." Kylie snorts and I lay my cheek on her shoulder. "I can send you to the best *weed* rehab there is." He pats my knee, sending little waves of anticipation through my body.

"The first twenty-four hours are the hardest. Usually mimosas help to ebb the withdrawals that being *on weed* cause," Tater says.

When Kylie goes to the restroom, she nudges me over to Ace. I allow it, as my body is experiencing a case of Bernie from *Weekend at Bernie's*. I rest my head on his arm.

"So, what do we need to get ready to go boatin'?'" Ace asks Tater in his southern drawl.

"Just get these two purdy ladies in my truck and we're off."

"Oh no...." I start but Ace stops me.

"Oh yes. You're coming, and we're going to have a blast."

I shake my head. "I can't go on that lake."

"Lily, we grew up on that lake. That lake is part of you. Don't you miss it?" he asks.

I shake my head again.

"Liar. You tell me all the time you do," Kylie says.

"Traitor," I spit before slamming back my mimosa. But another realization makes me pause. Kylie isn't the only traitor. "Tater...you got me drunk so you could get me on the boat."

"Yes, I did. Now go get a suit on or I will put one on you myself. Which sounds weird but I am a good friend and I will do it." His smirk is adorable. "I never push you. I have never given you my opinion about all your phobias or fears. I just listen. I have been there with you every single step of this journey." He laughs. "Don't you ever forget I held your boob for you when you were having trouble nursing."

We tell the story to Ace between fits of laughter. I had just gotten Drew latched right, and the lactation consultant told me to keep my thumb pressed into the side of my breast so it wouldn't block her nose. For the duration of her feeding, I had to use both hands in the beginning. She would nurse for so long it was debilitating. My mom, Kylie, and Tater took turns feeding me the first few weeks. On this particular time, it was a juicy, greasy barbecue burger from Ed's BBQ Shack. They are so messy, so you really need two hands. It was just Tater and I, and he couldn't get the giant burger in my mouth, so we switched jobs. I held the burger with one hand, and he pushed my boob away from her nose. It was hysterical. I was so hungry and tired I had to get it in my mouth right away, so I didn't care. Boobs are tools in which to feed your child, not to be drooled or fantasized about by grubby men.

"You are a true friend," I admit to Tater. "But...I'm still not going."

"Some of the best times in my life have been with you on a boat," Tater argues. "Lils, you're so good on those water skis."

"Tater..." I start but he interrupts me.

"Like I said, go get your suit on." He stares at me for a long time, our eyes locked in what appears to be a battle. A staring battle that I won't let him win. After about a full minute of silence, Ace starts laughing.

"Lily, please, let's go. Everyone you love most in the world will be there. We'll all be safe." His hand traces small circles on my arm since I am still propped up against him. I look up at his face which is a giant mistake because I can't say no to that adorable puppy dog look. His eyes are filled with so much warmth. Gah, and that dang adorable dimple.

"Fine." I shrug and he squeezes me tight. Tater and Kylie look stunned that he got me to agree. "My mom happened to buy me a new black bikini." An alarm goes off in my brain. *This is part of her plan...*

"I stopped and got mine when we ran out for bagels." Kylie flashes me her bathing suit strap under her tank top.

"Did you go in her chicken shack?" I ask Ace. Kylie laughs while rolling her eyes. She rents a tiny studio above Cluck Yo' Mama and her studio smells like fried chicken.

"It's awful. She should move in with you," Ace says, I watch Kylie shift uncomfortably. "What did I miss?"

"Lily depended on Kylie too much," Tater chimes in. I squint my eyes at him.

"I still do. It would be more convenient if she lived here," I am reading from her telling expression that Kylie is considering it. I look at Ace and then to Tater. "See, I knew it! She wants to, but you made her promise she won't. Because of Daddy Tater, my best friend lives like a chicken."

Tater feigns surprise and Kylie admits, "I did promise him."

I shake my head while staring at Tater. I'm hurt.

"Lily, you would beg her every day to call in sick. You had her lying to me. Hiding, going on secret trips. Ace, it was bad. You know how these two slip into their own little world."

"Oh, I remember," Ace says, taking Tater's side in the argument. "Nobody can join in your conversations most of the time. I sometimes don't even know what you two are laughing or talking about."

Kylie and I both lock eyes. "I didn't have a dime to my name," she admits sheepishly to me.

I take a deep breath. "I was your sugar mama...we had so much fun, I still could be." I grin at her and her face falls.

I know she thinks it's unrealistic and maybe it is, but I'd prefer her here than in the chicken shack.

~

"I'm gonna have to do a quick bikini shave," I say to Kylie as I throw my clothes in the hamper and turn the shower on.

"Amber went to this place in Davenridge and got a bikini wax and says it's amazing. We should go together before Justin comes to town."

"I'm not spiffing up my *who- ha* for a married man." I laugh at her idea to wax her beaver for Justin.

I shave and get in my new black bikini and look in the mirror. It is a cute bathing suit but awfully tiny.

"Kylie, is it possible that my mother is trying to sex traffic me to Ace? This suit is absolutely ridiculous." When she looks up from her phone, her jaw drops.

"Maggie Moore is feisty. That suit is insane...turn around." She whistles as I spin and I roll my eyes. "I know I made him jealous last night when I mentioned Justin liking you, which was on purpose, by the way."

"I hadn't noticed. You're so sly." My sarcasm can't be missed. "You ready?"

That two-word question floods me with anxiety. It's wrapping around my lungs the way it always does, and I try to take a few deep breaths. Kylie looks at me with sympathy. She knows I don't want to go. She knows every time I see that lake it reminds me of how my young healthy husband drowned in it. Water terrifies me. It haunts me in my nightmares and usually kills everyone I love.

"Lily, nothing is going to happen. I promise we will have the safest and slowest day on the lake." She stands up and walks to my closet while I stare at the waify woman before me in the mirror. I guess my curves are still there despite my extra slender state. Kylie tugs a dress over my head. I push my arms through, feeling wholly defeated at the prospect of boating.

We drive to Tater's house to get his boat before heading down to his restaurant to launch it with everyone else in Whimsy. Ace and Tater get out at his house to ready the boat while Kylie and I stay in the truck.

"Lily, stop pouting," she says while I stare out the window.

"I know you all want me to forget...to move on and just be the same, but I can't. I see the lake as my enemy. I don't see it as a place to let loose and have fun anymore." Tears fill my eyes. "I wish I could be like everyone else. I wish I could be the same carefree girl I used to be. I lost my life partner, and I'm frozen in fear and pain."

"Lily...nobody wants you to forget. We just want to help you conquer the fear." She wraps me in a hug.

"What about all the pain?" The soft whimpers escaping me are pitiful.

"I guess we have to conquer that too. I won't let you go through any of it alone. None of us will," Kylie says. "I also know you look stupid hot in that bikini!" I smile at her compliment.

"I want to hear all about your night with Tater. Why didn't Stan enter with you?"

"I couldn't tell Tater I knew about his feelings. I did, however, tell Stan. He was jealous and acting like a jackass, so I entered the dance contest with Tater. He stormed out and called me a cock tease."

"Why a cock tease?" I ask, amused at his choice of words.

"Who knows? He's such an idiot." *Yeah, Kylie, we've all been telling you this for years.* "I don't know how to act around Tater now. One minute I feel normal and then the next he's staring at me and I feel self-conscious," she says, completely defeated and full of remorse. Like everything she knows and loves in life is ruined with this revelation. "Like, does he think about sticking his schlong-a-long-a-ding-dong in me?" We both erupt into a wild laughter that I fear may crack Tater's truck window.

"Do you think you could ever have feelings for him that way?" I ask once we calm down from Tater's schlong-a-long-a-ding-dong.

"No," she protests. "That much is clear to me." She gets distracted and stops, pointing out the window at a shirtless guy walking down by the lake. "I do like him though...who in the fudge is that?"

"Probably just a vacationer," I say as we both watch the sexy man. "You gonna confront him or just let it go?"

She shrugs, defeat hanging on her shoulders and covering her beautiful features. "Tell me what to do."

"Kiss him. Kiss him once, for me. You owe me after today."

She slowly smiles. "Fine...one kiss when the time is right."

Maybe she could have the same feelings?

"Promise?" I ask her.

"I promise," she says with her beautiful smile. Kylie never breaks a promise.

When the boys get back in the truck adorned with carefree smiles, we fall into an easy banter. They drop us at the restaurant so they can get in the line to launch the boat. My parents are here with Rose eating breakfast.

"Hi guys."

"Lily...you look so happy," my dad says. "I'm so happy to get out on the water with you today."

He looks adorable and I don't want to let him down.

"Oh god...you treat her like she is fucking five," Rose says with hostility.

"Rose, watch your mouth." My dad turns to Rose with a stern face, then looks back at me. "You girls want some coffee or something to eat before we head out?"

I smile brightly and kiss his cheek. "I love you, Dad. I ate a bagel before we left, and I'll eat a sandwich on the boat."

"You look tired," my mom says with a disapproving *tsk*.

"That will happen when you stay up all night long laughing with your best friends." My mood is too happy to get annoyed with her. She's hyper focused trying to pimp me out to Ace.

"We are delirious," Kylie admits. "Lils here is really hungover."

"Oh Lily...please get it together," my mom says. "What will Ace think?"

"Oh, I don't care." I can see the worry etched on her face. "That is an odd thing to say considering Ace was up all night long with me."

"The only odd thing is your behavior." My mom purses her lips to sip her coffee. Dead silence hangs in the air while we stare at one another. *Another hostile stare down?* I'm on a roll today.

"Let her be. Her daughter is gone and her best friend, who she hasn't seen in years, is home. She deserves to have fun," my dad says, coming to my rescue yet again.

I smile at him. "That's what Tater said when my guilt was suffocating me this morning."

"See, Maggie? Don't make her feel more guilty."

My mom shifts uncomfortably. "I want her to show her true character to a man she hasn't seen since she was a kid." My eyes roll far back.

"We will see you out there in a few," Kylie says, rescuing my dad and I from my mom. "Earl, Tater had them pack your favorite sandwich." She motions to the big bag of sandwiches in her hand. Tater named his hot pastrami sandwich after my dad. Earl the Great is his best-selling sandwich.

"I sure do appreciate Tater doing that. He always takes care of everyone, especially you girls."

Kylie and I erupt into laughter because no doubt we are both thinking about Tater's schlong-a-long-a-ding-dong *taking care* of Kylie.

CHAPTER 11

~

I stand on the shore of Whimsy Lake, watching the active scene before me. The smells of sunscreen and gas fill the air, while echoes of harmonic laughter ring in my ears. People load up boats to various songs blaring out of several trucks. Garth Brooks, AC/DC, and Lizzo all compete for lake song of the year.

So many emotions swarm through me. I want to go out and enjoy the day, but I'm scared. There are always boating accidents out here on our pretty lake. Last summer, a boat crash claimed the lives of three adults and two kids. It was tragic and didn't sit well with me. My nightmares increased so much I thought I was losing my mind with the lack of sleep. Cameron was so sick of it after several months that he prescribed me a sleeping pill for a few nights and after a few restful nights of sleep, the nightmares subsided back to their normal amount.

A warm arm drapes over my shoulder. "Do you need to be carried onto the boat?" Ace teases.

"I don't know." I smile up to him. "Do you think I'm crazy?"

"No, I would be just as fearful if it had happened to me," he reassures. "Nobody thinks you're crazy; we just want to help you. Five years of living with this fear has made it bigger than any of us can comprehend."

"You're right. I'm having a hard time comprehending it my-self. I should have done this sooner," I admit. "I know I'm holding back my daughter with my own fear."

I'm so pitiful and I'm sick of it.

"Don't beat yourself up...she's only four years old. I can't wait to meet her." Ace's warm smile sends a little shiver through me.

He wants to meet my daughter?

"She'll love you." The thought of them meeting, something I never thought would happen, makes me feel giddy. "Let's go before I lose all my nerve."

I'm going to be cool and not pitiful today.

He grabs my hand and leads me down the dock to Tater's boat. The four of us are going on his boat, as well as my parents and sister. Cameron has Jeanie, their three kids, his assistant, her husband, and their two kids on his fancy boat. When I climb aboard, Kylie hands me a mimosa.

I smile at her. "Thanks." My mom shakes her head in disapproval as she sips her mimosa. She's the one who brought many bottles of champagne for us and many, many beers. Such a hypocrite...but then again, aren't we all? This is a huge step for me. A few mimosas to calm the nerves are much deserved and appreciated.

"Cheers Mom," I say and hit her red solo cup with mine. I turn to my little sister. "Rose, tell us about school." *May as well try.*

She smiles because she loves to talk about herself.

"It's good. Arizona is a blast. So many parties and Mill Ave is so much fun now that I'm twenty-one." She tosses her head back, making a complete spectacle of herself.

"Any boys you're serious about?" I ask.

"There is kind of one...but we aren't committed." She shrugs.

"What does that mean?" Kylie asks with a big mimosa-induced grin.

"That I can date while I'm here," Rose says, pointedly looking at Ace. Oh brother. To say Ace looks uncomfortable would be an understatement. He may jump ship! Does she not get how weird that would be to date guys I have dated? Especially Ace. At one point, I believed that I would marry him. I bet most people in this town thought that.

"There is a boat of hot guys on vacation on the lake today... your fake boobies could catch their attention," Kylie says to my sister and I laugh. "Let me do the talking though." Her way of saying Rose has the personality of an avocado.

"Kylie, my daughter does not need to be helping you land guys," my mom says sharply. This will be such an awesome day, I'll need twenty-four mimosas to make it to lunch.

"No, she doesn't...I have done just fine on my own all these years. Just trying to cut her in." Everyone laughs, including my mom, who truly adores Kylie.

When we leave the dock, the wind glides through my hair. Something I have truly missed. I wave to my brother as he drives his big new fancy boat past us.

Once the jet skiing starts, I find myself holding my breath every time somebody falls. When Oscar and Devyn tube behind my brother's boat, I have several heart attacks when their little bodies fly off. Kylie and my mom keep reassuring me that everything is okay. I drink many mimosas to help steady my nerves per Dr. Cameron's recommendation. "Doctor's orders." I smile brightly at my disapproving mother as she matches me mimosa for mimosa.

When we stop on the lake and pull out the sandwiches, it feels nice not to watch people I love be pulled around by a boat in dark murky water. The two boats are tied together. We hear some cat calling coming from the boat speeding by us. It's Stan, yelling for Kylie to come with him. I stare at her, waiting to see what she'll do.

"I'm not going," she says and I smile brightly.

"How do you two do that?" Rose asks.

Kylie shrugs. "We are like conjoined twins separated at birth."

It's true.

"Sisters," I say. My mom glares at me and I catch Rose's face in a full pout. She folds her arms under her boobs and sighs. I look away. Awkward but true. Kylie is my actual sister. Rose feels like a stranger to me, even when we lived together at my parents. We don't sync the way Kylie and I do.

"Tater, these sandwiches are so good," I say, changing the subject.

Tater laughs. "I'd believe ya, if you had taken a bite first." I look down at my sandwich as we all laugh at what a bad liar I am.

Stan pulls up with a boatload of other Whimsy derelicts.

"Come on Kylie! Let's party," he says with a big I-love-you-so-much Stan smile. Which can easily, after one too many beers, switch to you-are-the-most-annoying-girl-in-the-world glare.

We all stare at her. Waiting for her reply.

"I'm gonna stay put. Lily is on a boat, Stan!" She beams at him.

"Oh, for fuck's sake. Who cares! Get your cute ass over here. Your man misses you," he says like the complete sexist idiot he is. I bulge my eyes at Tater and he returns with a grimace. We both are tired of this relationship.

"I miss you too babe but not today. Come to Tater's tonight."

"Nope, last chance," he says like a baby. She shifts uncomfortably like she wants to go. She looks at me with sad eyes, and I take a deep breath, readying myself to say goodbye to her. Pretty typical for Kylie. She can't resist this dipshit, though none of us have ever understood the appeal.

"I guess I blew my last chance."

Stan throws his beer can in the lake, and my brother yells at him for being a jerk.

"Fuck you Cam!" Stan shouts, and my brother looks pissed.

My dad jumps in the lake and throws the beer can in Stan's boat. "You seemed to have dropped this. Don't want to litter our beautiful lake."

"Sorry, Mr. Moore," Stan says like a *busted* little kid. I smile at my dad with pride.

Stan motions to his friend driving and they speed off. Stan pulls his pants down and moons us with his gleaming white tooshy.

"Nobody can say he doesn't have class," I say, and Cameron laughs out loud with me while everyone else stays silent.

"Next time he gets kidney stones, I'm totally billing him."

"You don't charge him?" I ask Cameron with my jaw on the boat deck. Stan doesn't deserve any good nature from anyone.

"He charges no one! There is no way we can have that fourth kid he wants unless he starts," Jeanie says, rubbing a hand through Cameron's hair.

"Only if they don't have insurance. It's expensive to get healthcare." His small smile lets me know he's never going to change this.

"Oh my god Cameron, you are the sweetest," I say. "Mom, Dad...you did so good with this one."

They both agree with pride.

The rest of lunch is nice and relaxing, and everyone is ready to get going again. Speed around on a boat with other boats speeding too. So reckless.

"You wanna go next? I could pull you and Ace in the tube," Tater asks, dripping in hope.

"No. I'm having a hard enough time watching," I admit.

"Come on Sprinkles...I won't let anything happen to you," Ace says sweetly. I quickly look away so that ridiculous charm and warmth doesn't win me over and make me do something stupid.

Having Drew grow up with two dead parents that drowned in the same lake would be a pretty dismal life.

"I'll go with you, Ace," Rose says like such a hoebag it pisses me off. *I will end her!*

"No, I'll go," I smile at Ace. Right after I say it, I lean back in the chair and feel my heart pounding out of my chest. Jealousy and pride are going to kill me.

"Great! No backing out!" Tater yells. "Jump in!"

Ace grabs my hand to pull me up while I look at Kylie for help. She is all smiles though.

"You'll love it! Think of all the times you've done this...This is our lake," Kylie says. "Respect her, don't fear her."

I walk to the back of the boat and reluctantly jump in. *Man, this feels so good.*

The water is crisp and on the verge of being too cold to tolerate, but it wakes me up in a way I haven't been able to today after my wild night. The goosebumps and chilly temperature make me breathe deeply, trying to steady the overwhelming feeling of adrenaline. I dip under again and wipe my hands over the front of my hair. Ace smiles at me while we both acclimate.

"Now there's your true smile, Sprinkles." His fingertips brush over my belly to tickle me. I bat his hand away.

"It feels so good. Thanks for making me get in."

We get settled onto the raft side by side.

"Remember when we cut school senior year and stole your parents' boat?" Ace asks me as we bob around the water when a boat speeds by, causing huge wakes.

"Yes, I believe we went skinny dippin' over by Whimsy rock?" I inquire, making sure we are talking about the same day. We always jumped off Whimsy rock into a great big swimming hole, then sat under the spray of the waterfall. Boats can't get to it, so you have to park and then hike for an hour, but it's worth it. Especially when you're young and in love and you have sex there while ditching school. My pulse quickens at the memory.

"We did more than skinny dip that day," Ace says in a proud tone.

Oh, I remember, big guy.

"You, Ace Lancaster, got very emotional that day. You were leaving me in a few months for college and you didn't want to." Should I open this can of worms?

"I loved you like crazy.

"He squeezes my hand. His sweet, intoxicating smile kind of makes my head spin. *I loved you so much too.* Our eyes remain locked as the silence encapsulates us. It's not uncomfortable, but it feels like he's waiting for me to respond. Our moment is broken when Tater calls out to us from the boat.

"Go slow and be gentle," Ace shouts over the screams of the rowdy boat passing us. His voice is stern, which makes Tater laugh and dismissively wave his hand in the air.

"Kylie is driving!" Tater yells. "She didn't trust me."

I smile at how protective she is. We give the thumbs up and Kylie eases into a cruising speed. It is slow enough we can still talk.

"How much longer do you think you will stay?" I ask Ace, hoping he says "always."

"I dunno...I probably have to go back after Justin leaves. You and Drew wanna come? You could bring Kylie and hang in the big city of Dallas for a bit."

"Okay," I feel so excited by this opportunity to spend more time with him. "I've never been to Dallas. Would we stay with you?"

Please say yes.

"Yep. I have a massive house and a chef. Trina should be all moved out when I get back so it would be nice to have company for a few days," Ace says. "We may have had a bad marriage, but I did love her once."

"Oh Ace, I'm sorry you are going through all this. You do not deserve this, and I will never buy an album of hers again."

I'm such a loser for fantasizing about him when he is clearly mourning his marriage. *What's wrong with me?*

"Did you ever?" he asks, amused. I pique my eyebrow up in confusion. "Buy any of her music?"

"No...I have never been a fan." We both laugh softly. He looks relieved and I hope my face doesn't reveal my true feelings towards Trina.

Kylie speeds up a little, and we are going fast enough that talking is out. I panic, white knuckling the handles on the tube. Ace gets Tater's attention and puts his thumb down, and Kylie slows to a fun speed. Not too fast and not too slow.

"Thank you, Ace." He is the best. All these years I have missed him, even though I may not have known it. I think about our dancing and his speech. He said I felt like home. I have never heard that before, but man does it feel like the perfect way to describe it. He feels like home to me, too.

"Look at Kylie manning this boat. I feel strangely proud, but then she's such a hoot it's hard to take her serious." Ace scrunches his nose, signaling his deep thoughts.

"A hoot? What are you, a ninety-five-year-old lady?" I ask, studying his adorable expression. "What do you two chat about on Facebook?"

"Mostly you since you've been ignoring me for all these years. The last few times I have been in town, you have been suspiciously out of town," he says with a questioning raise of his perfect eyebrows.

"All coincidences," I say but I can see on his face he doesn't believe me. He would be right. When Bernie would tell me he was coming, I would take Drew away on a vacation and drag someone with me. Last year was Southern California, the time before that was Seattle. I was worried he hated me, and I didn't want to meet Trina. It was an awkward situation I wanted to avoid. This doesn't feel awkward though—it feels like home. Like a lazy Sunday afternoon waiting for a berry cobbler to come out of the oven while watching a movie.

After twenty minutes of tubing, Kylie stops the boat and I jump in the water to pee. My brother pulls up beside us.

"Lily, can I get on the tube with you?" he asks. If anybody has missed boating with me most, it's Cameron.

"Yes, I would love that." He jumps overboard that instant and I laugh at his enthusiasm.

Everyone, even my niece and nephew, wanted to ride in the tube with me after Cameron. By the time we pull back around to the boat launch, I have a permanent smile on my sun-kissed face. I promise to bring Drew next weekend when Justin is home.

At 7 PM, we pull up at Tater's packed restaurant for dinner. We all sit outside and watch the kids run around on the playground he recently had installed. My idea. All restaurants should have playgrounds. Ace is next to me on the picnic table, and he grabs my hand under the table.

"You did it. You conquered your fear," he says.

"Uh, I think I have a ways to go. I still have to bring Drew." I take a deep breath. "That's the true test."

"You will." His eyes scan my face with adoration. His faith and confidence have my heart fluttering at the speed of light.

"Can I take you and Drew to Yosemite on Monday? I got a room at one of the hotels. I'd love the company." His smile is faint, almost bashful.

No.

"Sure, Drew loves Yosemite," I say quickly, ignoring the voice in the far corner of my mind. I've always wanted to stay in the hotel there. I can't very well turn my back on my bucket list. "I can book us a room...I don't want to put you out."

"Silly, I have stayed at your house two nights in a row." His warm and comforting smile reaches his baby blue eyes and sends a tiny shiver up my spine.

"Drew is loud and always comes with a typhoon of snacks and toys," I protest, shaking my head. There is no way he's ready for that.

"I got a suite with two rooms. She can bring whatever she wants." My heart is pounding out of my chest at the way he is looking at me. I know we are here with a huge group, but under his gaze and the twinkling of fairy lights above us, it feels like it's just us.

Tater invites us to walk down by the lake and go to his house after dinner. I have stayed with him many times over the years, so I walk down with him, Kylie, Ace, and my sister. She was partying with Tater and doing shots.

As soon as we get to Tater's, I shower and put on some of Kylie's shorts and a big t-shirt. Rose is past wasted and hitting on Ace so forcefully I can't take it. She keeps rubbing him and pressing her body up against his. He looks even more annoyed than me.

I climb into Tater's guest bed. I call Lucille to check on Drew, who is already fast asleep. She sends over an angelic picture of her in a big poofy dress sleeping on her side with a tiara crookedly placed on her head. Her perfect blonde curls cascade around her like a princess. My lids are heavy after a day in the sun and little sleep the night before.

~

I wake screaming, which is completely normal. The strong warm arms wrapped around me aren't. The anxiety and terror from the recurring torture I face most nights has coiled around me so tightly my breathing is erratic.

"Same dream?" It's Ace. I try to relax as he strokes my hair gently, making me feel safe.

"Yeah...tonight it was Drew in the glass box," I admit. "I miss her. This is the longest I've been away from her." I pause as I release the suffocating breath I was holding on to. "You must think I'm pathetic."

"What?" he whispers. "I don't think that at all. Look at you kicking weed with no problem today." His teasing makes me laugh softly. His hand moves down to the top of mine. My hand stiffens for a brief moment while his giant bear paw wraps around my smaller one, engulfing it in a warmth that shoots through my whole body.

Please don't ever let go...

"Go back to sleep...I'm here if you need me."

I haven't been alone since Dexter died. My parents, Cameron, and my friends have been a good support team, but the way he said he's here for me takes my breath away. Despite having all these people to help me, I still feel alone, but Ace makes me feel a little less lonely. He makes me feel hopeful.

CHAPTER 12

~

I wake up in Ace's arms, warm and surprisingly well-rested after that awful nightmare. My lips turn up in a full smile as excitement floods me. Drew comes home today, and Ace asked us to go to Yosemite with him. It feels so good to have a giant warm body next to me. I shouldn't get too attached to his presence, no matter how good this feels.

I rub his arm and gently climb out from under it, tiptoeing to the kitchen to start a huge breakfast. I put bacon in the oven, cut potatoes, and mix some pancake batter. Kylie comes strolling out in her own pajamas from Tater's room and I'm flooded with merriment.

"You two," I say and point to her pajamas.

"What?"

"Married couple who doesn't have sex is what you two are." I shake my head in total amusement. They should just do it already. "Maybe you should look into that schlong-a-long-a-ding-dong after all." I can't stifle my laughter when she throws her perfect little upturned nose into the air, ignoring me as she starts to crack eggs in a big bowl.

She changes the subject as she whisks the eggs around in the bowl. "Your sister puked everywhere last night, and I had to call your dad to come get her."

"Tits McGee is a lightweight, eh?" I ask.

"I guess...She tried really hard to get Ace to have sex with her, but he declined in a sweet way as we all knew he would. Still the best guy I know," she says as she turns the stove on for the eggs.

"I'm so glad he's home. He invited me, you, and Drew to come back to Dallas with him."

"He told me...I'm gonna land an NFL player!" she squeals in delight. "Finally leave this small town and have some babies. Gonna get the old vajay waxed before we leave"

"Sounds torturous." I raise an eyebrow and we both giggle.

"So.." she says with her little nose upturned again. "Ace slept with you last night. Anything you want to confess?"

"No," I say and mimic her. "As you and Tater clearly know, two friends can share a bed without crossing lines."

"Sure...can be done, but you two have never had a platonic relationship since your first kiss when you were twelve," she points out as she grates cheese for her and Tater's eggs.

"Things change," I say, still being aloof as she was to me.

"Lils...just talk to me," she begs. "He broke your heart and you broke his. Have you two even talked about it?"

"No. I think we both just feel like the past is the past. He's only looking for friendship and that's all I want." I drop my nose back to a normal position. "Should I not go to Yosemite with him? I don't want to get too attached..."

"I think you should go. Sounds like he could really use a friend right now. Plus, he's easy on the eyes, so I doubt it will be terrible," she says and bumps my hip with hers.

Very easy on the eyes indeed.

I smile when I hear Tater gleefully whistling in his room. I turn my head and give her a knowing look.

"Did you kiss him?" I ask.

"No. Drunk kissing could lead to sex. I will do it, but it will be one kiss...when I feel it's a good time." She pours the eggs into a pan and starts scrambling.

Ace walks out with a sleepy smile and tousled hair, which

makes me giggle. He grabs some bread and butter to toast. Tater joins us moments later and puts hot sauce on the table, along with syrup and butter.

We have a laugh-filled breakfast, and then I call Lucille on her cell phone and speak with Drew before she goes to the American Girl doll store.

"Mimi and Papa said I could get two. One that looks like you and one that looks like me." She is practically singing, which makes me so happy. "Can we get a puppy?"

"Maybe one day," I say. "I will see you in a few hours, Boo. I miss you so much my heart hurts."

"I miss you more," she says. I say goodbye with a good kind of anxiety…and that's to see my baby very soon.

"Kylie, I'm going to take your bike home. I need to go clean and make a pasta salad for my parents' dinner tonight. You are all more than welcome to come," I say to the three of them.

"I could drive you," Tater offers.

"No, I want some fresh air." I walk into the bedroom to put on my clothes from yesterday. I grab a baseball hat out of Tater's closet. Back in the living room, Kylie is on the couch between the two guys looking at yearbooks.

"Here you two are as prom king and queen." Kylie looks from me to Ace. "Man Ace, look at your acne."

"Shut up!" he yells. "That is two zits…hardly considered acne."

"So sensitive," Kylie teases.

"Look at your head gear," Ace quips back, and I cuddle up next to him so I can see Kylie.

"You look like the girl from *Sixteen Candles* with the neck brace," I tease.

"You look the same, Sprinkles," Ace says gently. "Still just as pretty."

I rest my cheek on his shoulder. "You're sweet." I look carefree, brave, and excited in this picture. Now my face shows age, worry, and heartbreak.

I leave them after two yearbooks and head home on Tater's bike. I stop at the store to buy the few ingredients I need for a pasta salad. The store is always like a happy hour of socializing, Ace and I winning Friday night is the talk of the town. "He is so handsome," "You two looked so good," "He is single which must thrill you" are a few things I hear in the store.

When I get home, I start the pasta salad and listen to the radio. As I'm chopping a handful of parsley, Trina's annoying voice fills the room. I roll my eyes and mock the whole song. After the song finally finishes, it cuts to an interview with her. I can't listen to her irritating southern twang, so I set my chopping knife down and walk toward the stereo to change it. I stop dead in my tracks when the radio host asks, "You've been hinting that things with Ace fell apart first in the bedroom. Can you elaborate?"

"He was a terrible husband who didn't know how to satisfy a lady like me," she says cruelly. "Which is why I had to find a passionate lover like Brent."

Oh, that is awful and downright hurtful. "He also couldn't perform without Viagra." She is evil. I grab the phone and dial his Mom's number to warn him. I'm sure it will be aired everywhere today.

"I've heard it. I hate her," he says. "Actually, hate isn't even a strong enough word."

"I bet," I say with empathy.

"Can I come over?"

"Of course. Come help me chop veggies for my pasta salad," I say, excited for the company.

Too excited.

Ten minutes later he is on my front porch, looking downtrodden. I let him in with a sympathetic smile and then try to squish his hard form in a tight hug. I can't imagine how he feels. On the inside, that is. On the outside, he feels epic.

"What can I do for you?" I ask, my arms still lingering on his firm back. "Anything?"

"Well...I mean, was I that bad?" he asks reluctantly. "I'm feeling pretty emasculated at the moment."

"I only remember loving you and thinking the world of you, Ace. You will always be amazing in my eyes." I smile at him with sincerity.

More than amazing, actually.

"Thank god...You sure you aren't just saying that?" He looks humiliated.

"Nope. I feel like you've got to be even better now. We were so young." I gulp when his eyes flicker with something unknown to me.

"Why does she want to humiliate me in such a way? I haven't done anything to her."

"Whose idea was it for the divorce?"

He looks thoughtful as he stares straight ahead. I realize I'm still in an embrace with the married stallion and force myself to step away, even though my body doesn't want to. If he had a door into his chest, I'd let myself in and throw away the key.

"I guess it was me," he finally says, his eyes finding mine.

"So, she's hurt," I point out. "Not that it's justified, but maybe she didn't want a divorce?"

"I guess it could be her pride. She wanted a divorce though." He's adamant. I shrug because I have no idea how Trina feels. I know that I'd never want to lose the guy.

But you did.

We spend all day at my house together and it all felt so carefree and effortless. At 4:00, we walk to my parents' house. They still have my car after theirs 'broke down' Thursday, which I know never happened because my dad said as much yesterday on the boat. Mom is a total liar. I walk in and kiss both my parents and a hungover Rose. Ace does the same. My brother is skipping rocks on the lake with Oscar and Devyn. Little Delilah is sleeping on the sofa in the living room and Jeanie is in the kitchen helping my mom.

"Boo should be here in about 30 minutes," I say to my dad.

"You made it." My dad beams at me with a mixture of pride and amusement.

"You all provided great distractions," I say while grabbing a few grapes off Jeanie's cutting board. Ace's eyebrows shoot up as a giant smirk graces his gorgeous face.

"Careful there, Sprinkles." I howl in laughter.

My dad leads Ace and I to the backyard so he can start the barbecue. They mostly talk about the NFL and Ace's career and I listen without much to add to the conversation. Not that I mind just watching Ace. His golden light brown hair is crumpled into perfection and looks incredible in this light. He looks like something out of a dessert window, like a decadent caramel cake, drizzled with honey, then sprinkled with bronze glitter and topped with two of the brightest blue eyes imaginable. His tiny dimple is on display as he gleams about his career to my dad, who looks like he's in heaven with this conversation.

Ace turns and looks at me with a warm smile. Amusement flickers in his eyes because he's caught me ogling him. I straighten up quickly, smoothing my hair to busy myself. My dad's question gets his attention back, leaving me to my sneaky observations.

I shoot up out of the chair when I hear Drew's little voice and make a beeline for the door. She's talking to my mom, who is listening intently in a squat position to be eye level with her. I rush over and squat down next to my mom and listen to everything she says. I laugh and watch her animated little face while she introduces us to her two new dolls named Erica and Layla. Erica has blonde hair and green eyes like me, and Layla has blonde hair and blue eyes like Drew. She tells us all about the polar bear at the zoo and asks if we can get one. I wish we could.

"We had tea, and this is my new dress," she says as she twirls around to show us her ornate, no doubt expensive dress. After several minutes of her talking nonstop, I look above me and see everyone listening to my excited Drew.

"Can I have a hug?" I ask her. She flies in my outstretched arms, and my whole body relaxes. I hadn't realized I was this tense all weekend. My eyes sting at the revelation of how much she truly is my everything. My mom rubs my head and I turn and look at her. We both share a smile between two understanding mothers.

"Who is this?" Drew asks and points to Ace.

I stand up with her in my arms. "This is my long-lost friend I told you about before you left," I say and smile at her pinched-up face as she studies Ace.

"Ace Lancaster, nice to meet you, Drew." He reaches his hand out and she puts her tiny hand in his and he lifts hers up to his lips and kisses it gently. "I have heard so much about you."

"How did you get lost?" Drew asks.

"I wasn't lost. It does feel good to be home though," he says, looking adorably captivated by her. "My mom is your Aunt Bernie."

"Bernie is your mom?" Drew asks, blown away. She looks at me with big eyes. After a few minutes of getting to know each other, she begs to go skip rocks down by the lake with Uncle Cameron. I take a deep breath. Her by the lake makes me nervous.

Ace smiles at me. "I can teach her." His offer makes me feel all sorts of warm things. He wants to get to know her and it twists my mind into mush, but also makes my heart kind of race. I'm such a mom.

"Okay, let's go...Just be a really good listener," I say to Drew and set her down.

"I promise," Drew says.

After throwing open the sliding glass door, she runs down to the lake, screaming to her Uncle Cameron. He turns around and scoops her up. Cameron is the closest thing she has to a dad. He is amazing to her and so are her older cousins.

I walk down and we start teaching her how to skip rocks, offering all sorts of advice. She tries with no success. It just makes a plopping sound and a slow gurgle as it sinks. Her frustrated face is scrunched after her first few attempts. Ace squats down and slowly explains again how it's done. She listens and then watches him intently a few times before she does it again.

"That was close." I squat down on the other side of her. "It's just something you have to practice."

"Okay." She giggles, and that plus her fancy dress makes Ace and I laugh in unison. "It's fun to watch them go down. I love the sound." She starts tossing them in and I join her.

"Guess what I get to do next weekend?" Cameron asks all the kids.

"What?" they all ask. He picks Drew up so her face is close to his and both their eyes are level.

"I get to take Drew on a boat for the first time." Drew's eyes get huge and Devyn and Oscar scream in delight. "I get to teach you how to be safe on the lake and how to drive a boat. I can put you on a tube and pull you behind the boat." I involuntarily shudder. *We didn't talk about that part.* Her face lights up.

I know it has to happen, but anxiety binds all my vital organs again, making it hard to breathe normally. I watch her giggle with Cameron and take a few calming breaths. When he hands her to me, I snap out of it.

"Come on Boo, let's go get washed up for dinner with your cousins," I say as I kiss her soft velvet cheek. I take the kids up to the house so they can wash their hands before we eat.

We have a nice dinner, even with Rose and Cameron bickering the whole time. Lucille and John are starstruck with Ace at the table. When dinner is over and all the dishes have been cleaned, Bernie walks in with Ace's dad, Tim. They bring two apple pies and ice cream. They couldn't make dinner but wanted to join the fun. Drew is on Bernie's lap and won't stop talking, making me laugh and swell with love. Darla comes a few minutes later with a big bottle of bubbles for the kids and takes them in the front. I watch the whole time out the window as Drew jumps around popping the bubbles.

"She is very cute. Only been one other girl in Whimsy that came close," Ace says.

"I was never that cute," I say with an amused smile.

"Oh, I know...I was talking about May Appleton." May Appleton was my *frenemy* all through high school. My competition. She beat me for class president, I beat her for head cheerleader, but she graduated first in our class, leaving me in the dust. We get along but have never been friends.

"I think she won. She's a successful lawyer in San Francisco now. I'm a crazed, sleepless widow who can't handle weed."

He laughs heartily. "No competition between you two... There never was. You were the best in most eyes."

"Just not yours," I say, teasing him. I tickle his side and he flinches but laughs.

"Yeah right," he says with sarcasm and a dreamy smile. *I love his smile.*

I force myself to look away from his delicious form and glance out the window, watching Drew jump around with her cousins. They will be the closest things to siblings she has. She falls on her knees and begins to cry, and I run out the front door as quick as I can. I pick her up while Darla is checking her out.

"Let's get you home, Boo," I say after looking her over.

"I'm okay Mommy. See, no tears," Drew says.

"I still want to go. Don't you want to set up all your new American Girl doll stuff?" Truth be told, I've had enough change in these past few days to last a lifetime. Boating, separation, knee scrapes...The whole world is spiraling out of my control and I want to sleep with Drew and never let her go.

We head inside and start the goodbyes. It takes way too long because when you are four years old, this cute, and people feel sorry for you because your Dad died before you ever got the chance to know him, you get an awful lot of attention everywhere you go.

"You wanna pick me up at about 10 AM tomorrow and head out?" Ace asks with a big infectious smile.

You shouldn't go.

"Yes, call me tonight and we will finalize our details," I say, ignoring that buzzkill of a voice again. I give him a big hug. Again, we don't let each other go right away. I can feel everyone staring, so I pull away even though I'm not ready. *I could hug him all day.*

I get my car loaded with all Drew's swag from her big first-class trip without me. Everyone walks us out, and my dad buckles her up and gives her many more kisses while I patiently wait behind the wheel.

"Lily, I love you. Come see us before you head out tomorrow," he says after whispering with Drew.

"Of course. I love you more, Dad. Thank you for always being the gentlest person I know." I lean through the window and kiss his cheek. He places his hand on his chest and strums his fingers on his heart with a warm smile on his handsome face, the way he always does when we say goodbye. Like his heart is mine. Or he loves me so much it hurts him to say goodbye. The motion could be interpreted so many ways, each one cuter than the last. All I know is it's something he only does with me.

I drive away, waving to everyone as if they are saying goodbye forever, which makes me laugh at how much we are loved. Rose looks pissed with her arms folded under her hard boobs like she has had enough of Drew hour. Not enough attention on her when the kids are around. All I want is *Drew hour* and nothing else.

"Hey Boo, you want to go to Yosemite tomorrow and stay in a lodge?" I ask and she sucks in all the air out of the car.

"Yes! Will we see a bear?"

"Well...I sure hope not, but it is possible," I say and take a moment to giggle with her. "Wanna pop popcorn and watch a movie tonight?" She gasps, her eyes like saucers.

"Yes! Can we watch *Frozen*?"

"Yes! Can we take Mommy's long-lost friend to Yosemite too?" I ask.

"Ace?"

I nod and look at her in the rearview mirror.

"Okay, can I skim rocks with him again?" she asks full of whimsy.

"Yes," I say and then tell her a hundred times before we pull in our driveway how much I love her. We carry all her stuff in and set up her American Girl bunk beds and wardrobe full of clothes in her toy-filled room. I can't even imagine what this all cost. Lucille lost her mind in there, which I understand. I blacked out in the Build-A-Bear we drove to for Drew's fourth birthday. Her four-legged unicorn cost over a hundred dollars. I don't even think she asked for any of it...It was just me blown away at the possibilities. Having grown up without Build-A-Bear, I questioned my childhood happiness. It's just so much fun.

I lay next to Drew on her floor and flip through the American Girl doll catalog and then before I can stop myself, I get online and order her and her dolls matching pajamas. By the time I have paid, I feel feverish at my $250 cart. How is it possible? I smile at Drew while she sings a song from *Moana* and brushes her doll's hair. Who cares, she will love it all, and I had fun.

I throw myself back on the plush, newly installed carpet and brush her other doll's hair. We dress them in their pajamas and sing them to sleep before I put Drew in the bath and wash her and sing to her. We play until she is pruned. We both put on our favorite pajamas before we pop a giant bowl of popcorn. We climb in my big bed and watch *Frozen* for the millionth time. I still cry every time she sings "Let it Go."

"Mommy, why do you always cry when Elsa sings this?" Drew asks, concerned.

"One day when you are older, you will cry too. It's just a beautiful song," I say. "No rush though...Just be young, Boo."

"Mommy, I don't even know what that means," she says with her innocent smile and perfect eyes.

"I'm not sad. Sometimes people cry when they're happy."

"Whoa." I laugh at her confused face and pull her closer and kiss her face over and over.

The phone rings and I grab it and say "Hello" very quietly.

"Is it too late to be calling?" Ace says.

"No. We are watching *Frozen*," I whisper. I scoot away from

Drew and sit on the chair across the room and put my feet on the cushy ottoman. "How was dessert?" I bolted out of there before the pie was served.

"Interesting," Ace says.

"How so?" I can't help giggling because he sounds stressed about something.

"Your sister was all over me and it was so uncomfortable. When does she leave?" he asks.

"Ask me tomorrow morning on the drive. The number will be lower." I giggle. Drew smiles at me and bounces her sweet eyes back to the TV.

"You don't mind driving? I could rent a car," he says.

"Don't be silly, of course I don't mind. Drew is very excited and hopes to see some bears." I can't stop giggling. Something about talking to this man makes me so giddy.

"I hope we don't," he almost grunts, which makes me smile at his vulnerability, "but I can't wait to spend some time with you two."

That is sweet, but I don't know what to say back. I feel so aware of my past relationship with him all the sudden.

Maybe I shouldn't go.

"I will be there at 10 AM. Sound good, Magoo?" I ask.

Shut up, voice of reason.

"Yep."

"Thank you, Ace. Let me know what I owe you for the room and I can write you a check?" I wink at Drew and she giggles.

"No," he says and laughs. I can't help but join in.

"Why is that so funny?" I ask.

"I play for the NFL and have many endorsements. Nobody ever offers to go *Dutch* with me."

"I don't ever want to take advantage of your generosity."

"That is the last thing I'm worried about with you." There is something in his voice that wasn't there before, he's worried about something.

"What are you worried about?" I just have to know.

"Uh..." He pauses. "Nothing I guess."

Not convinced.

We say goodbye when he gets a call from his coach on the other line.

"Mommy, who was that?" Drew says, not taking her eyes off the TV while I crawl back next to her.

"Ace." She turns her face and smiles at me.

"I love your laugh, Mommy." Her voice is so angelic I could squeal in delight listening to it and her carefree giggles. "Makes me laugh when I hear it."

"Yours makes me laugh too," I say and hold her tighter.

"I like Ace because he makes you laugh." A little pang twinges in my chest. Like a bolt of lightning, reminding me that he doesn't live in Whimsy anymore. This is only temporary.

My poor heart.

CHAPTER 13

~

The next morning when I wake, I feel so refreshed. I slept well and didn't have the nightmare. I'm sure it's because Drew is home and she comforts me when she sleeps with me. We sleep together a lot, even though I do try to maintain a structure and put her in her bed. Sometimes after she falls asleep, I don't want to let her go so I sleep in her L.O.L. doll bed with her. She is heaven and I thank my lucky stars for her every day. She is my everything.

We get up full of excitement and giggles. I quickly pack my suitcase while she eats a piece of avocado toast and apple slices. When I finish, we go to her bedroom to get her stuff. She unzips her suitcase from San Francisco and pulls out a swimsuit and hands it to me. I look at it and feel a rush of anger. Lucille bought her this.

"We went swimming!" she says. "Mimi told me not to tell you, but Mommy, it was so fun I have to tell you."

I force a fake smile, but I want to call Lucille. No, I want to drive to her house and punch her in the face. How dare she tell my daughter not to tell me something. That is what a sexual predator tells kids, not your grandmother, whom I trusted.

"Can we swim on this trip?" she asks with big hopeful eyes.

"Yes, Boo we can," I say and put it in her new suitcase. We have to bring her dolls and their very own suitcase. I'm too lazy to unpack this one. She also packs a backpack full of L.O.L. dolls and her iPad for the car.

At 10:15, we pull into Bernie's driveway, ten minutes late. I could blame it on Drew but it's just me. I'm not punctual. She is outside watering the plants and puts her head in my window.

"Mornin' you two," she says, a big smile on her face. "Ace is ready. He's just helping Tim in the backyard. He will be out in a minute."

"Okay. How was dessert last night?"

"Oh, ya know, same ol'...same ol'..." she hums.

I know already it wasn't, but she doesn't want to tell me, which is strange. I wonder why? So many reasons pop in my head. Maybe she wants to spare my feelings, she is embarrassed by Rose advancing on her son like that, or maybe she doesn't want to say in front of Drew. Ace walks out and he looks so handsome. His warm smile makes my stomach flip. He rounds the back of my car to load his luggage in my trunk. I watch his biceps flex with wide eyes through my side mirror. Those things are so impressive. I wonder how it would feel to...

"Sprinkles, I gotta take these bags out," Ace says and lifts his head to meet my gaze in the rearview mirror. It's like he knows what I'm thinking when he makes eye contact with me, his smile airing toward arrogance. Tim and Bernie have their heads in the back seat with Drew making her laugh. I try to focus on them and not the hot man playing around in my trunk.

Playing around in my trunk? Criminy!

He closes the hatchback and walks to the passenger side. He opens the door and climbs in, and I gulp at how fitted his plain black tee is. Did he iron that sucker onto his perfect body?

"Sprinkles!" I resentfully draw my eyes away from his exquisite body and giggle when I see how cheerful he looks. "You look well-rested and beautiful as ever."

I beam back. "So do you! Well-rested, that is...not beautiful. Well, shoot, it's not that you don't look beautiful." He looks amused with raised eyebrows as I trip over my words. I look away as I feel a little flustered, almost like a bashful schoolgirl or something. I get a grip and look back at him. "You look well-rested too."

There.

"Nothing like sleeping in a twin-size bed purchased in the late eighties," he moans in defeat. "I gotta get on Amazon right now and order a Tuft & Needle. That way when I get back, I have a nicer bed to sleep in."

I can't help but laugh at his predicament. "What is a Tuft & Needle?" I ask.

"Only the best mattress ever," he says with his adorable smile and my heart leaps.

"How are those Star Wars sheets holding up?" I arch my eyebrows.

"I don't have those anymore." I know he does. About a month ago, we came here to have dinner and Drew fell asleep, so Bernie laid her in Ace's Star Wars bed.

"Drew loves them." He pokes my belly when he realizes I know he still has them.

"I wish I could use them on my new Tuft & Needle." He looks a little flushed and it's adorable. "Better?"

"They say honesty is the best policy," I tease and he rolls his eyes.

"They're just so soft."

We say goodbye to his parents and start our journey. He orders his bed that will be there when he gets back.

"That is fast." I flash him a quick smile while we glide down the road.

"That's why they're the best."

"Mommy, can I get a Tuft & Needle?" Drew asks.

"Why do you want one?" I ask, amused, watching her in the rearview mirror.

"Ace said they're the best," My laugh mingles with Ace's.

"Your bed is only two years old," I point out catching her

angelic eyes in the mirror.

"Sometimes my back hurts in the morning," she says. It's quite funny, she has no idea what back pain is.

"I'll buy you one for all the birthdays I have missed. Queen or full?" Ace asks Drew, and she stares at him blankly.

"Queen?" she asks, confused.

"It's a full," I interject, "but you do not have to buy her a mattress. Just buy her a balloon."

"She wants a mattress. Let me do it."

I look at his face and I light up on the inside at how silly this is. "Please, Sprinkles! I would have bought her a pony had you ever invited me to her birthdays." He is begging and I can't help but agree to him buying her a new mattress.

Ace and Drew talk the whole drive about all the wildlife we can see in Yosemite. He is very sweet with her, and she is fascinated by him the whole time. Once we get to the hotel, her breath catches at the sight of its exquisite beauty.

"It's beautiful," she says. I love seeing the world through her eyes.

We valet the car, and the bellhop disappears with all our stuff. Drew drops my hand and runs and grabs her American Girl dolls off the cart.

"You can't run off like that," I say when I reach her to pick her up.

She starts crying as the bellhop gets in the elevator. She arches her back and screams like a banshee. After the elevator door closes, I realize why. It's her L.O.L. dolls; she thinks they're gone forever.

"Boo, don't worry, they will be up in the room shortly. That man is going to take them to our room. They're safe." I smile to reassure her. She settles down to a light sob, resting her cheek on my shoulder. I smile up at Ace, who looks completely unphased by her tantrum.

"You want your own room now?" I ask him.

"Reminded me of the time you cried when your parents wouldn't buy you a puppy," Ace grabs the American Girl Doll stuff, walking toward the gorgeous hotel. "Only you were older so the tantrum wasn't quite as cute."

"Well, I got my way," I say.

"You always do."

"Not always." I follow him through the doors. He turns and smiles at me and stops.

"You can have your way the whole time we're here." I laugh, but he fixes me with his gaze. "I'm serious. You both can." He turns around and I stand still, watching his finely sculpted tush walk away. He is truly gorgeous.

"Mommy, can I walk?" Drew asks as she presses my cheeks in her warm tiny palms.

"You must pay the toll." I turn my cheek towards her and she kisses it. "I love you more than Red Vines."

"I love you more than Goldfish," she squeezes my cheeks into a fish face. I flutter my lips like one causing her to giggle.

I put her back on the ground and we hold hands. Her eyes bulge and her mouth gapes as we walk through the lobby. High ceilings made of dark wood beams, etched with intricate carvings, arch overhead. There are two huge fireplaces on opposing walls that have to be seven feet tall. Giant sliders let the outdoors in, allowing a light breeze to roll through the expansive lobby. The piano, being played by an older woman, echoes brilliantly around the room, filling the whole space with ambience and joy. The opulent lodge, though high end and sophisticated, still feels casual, where any minute kids might run through with fish dangling off their poles and covered in mud.

"Wow!" I say as I glance around.

"You want a cabin or a big suite that overlooks the pool?" Ace squats down and asks Drew.

"I want to see the pool."

"Too cute," he says and I nod. She is so delightful that she makes everything better for everyone.

"Good thing you got the suite already. This place is busy...All the cabins are likely full," I say.

"I would have used the NFL card for her," Ace says and I roll my eyes, making sure he sees it.

"Big shot, don't make me remind you about Mr. Magoo." His eyes crinkle with laughter.

"What's an NFL card and who is Mr. Magoo?" Drew asks with big innocent eyes. Ace and I laugh so she laughs too. Drew and I walk around while Mr. Big Shot Magoo checks us in.

When we get into the elevator, Drew is excited to push the buttons, and Ace seems happy to oblige her curiosity and lets her stop at every floor. He's very patient for a guy who doesn't have kids. I'm trying not to swoon, but he's sweet and his tushy looks really good in his jeans. Ace lets her open the door with the room key, which also elates her. I feel the same as I stand behind, watching him bend over to help her. I scold myself internally for being such a depraved pervert. If I was Catholic, I'd find myself a confessional and admit all my sinful thoughts about Ace Lancaster.

She runs into the room, squealing when she sees her L.O.L. dolls and I sigh with relief. I was worried they wouldn't be up here yet, which would surely cause a meltdown. The room is exactly the same as the lobby. Perfectly decorated in whites and creams for a modern, clean look but still maintains a certain rustic charm.

"Man, this place," I say as I open the big sliding glass door to our private balcony. The view is exquisite and looks like a picture from a postcard. Almost unreal.

"Remember all of our hikes in this place? I have so many pictures of us here." He leans on the railing and looks out at Yosemite's amazing beauty.

I'm certainly depraved because he's thinking of the hikes and I'm thinking of all the things we did on those hikes...after the hikes... before the hikes...

"Yep, and our camping trip with one sleeping bag," I say, turning his thoughts. His eyebrows raise in surprise. His gaze makes my belly do a quick somersault. I giggle when I realize he looks a little bashful about me bringing it up. He puts his arm around me and squeezes me to his side. *What we managed to do in that one sleeping bag is still an epic feat.*

"Man, we were so young." He turns his focus to the scenery before us.

And limber...

"I imagine you need a sleeping bag for each arm now." I squeeze his bicep and he smirks.

"Sprinkles, I'm not that much bigger. I'm telling you, you've shrunk."

I hold my head high. "I'm tiny but mighty."

I look in the living room and Drew is already on the floor with her toys and a bag of Goldfish.

"You hungry?" he asks. "We could go eat at the pool or get room service."

"Room service on this amazing balcony." I motion to the table and chairs they have out here. "We can do the pool later?" I suggest with a big smile.

"Whatever you want, anything you want." He smiles while handing me the menu. My stomach flips at how cute he is.

You on the menu? I scold myself again for being such a perv.

After we order, we tour the rest of this massive suite that has two separate bedrooms. One with a big fluffy king size bed and a room with two queen-sized beds. Each room has their own bathroom.

"Drew, you want one big bed or two smaller beds?" Ace asks her.

"One big bed!"

"No, Ace gets the big bed. He is bigger than both of us combined," I say to her.

"I don't mind," he says, but I adamantly shake my head. He protests about giving us whatever we want on this trip as he said in the lobby.

"Ace, she is four and very irrational. We sleep in a full size bed together most nights. A queen is like a huge upgrade for us Moore girls." I giggle when I look in his eyes and see how disappointed he is. "Your poor biceps need a king, Magoo."

"Okay...I do really like a king," he admits in the most adorable way with his tiny dimple tucked so perfectly into his pretty smile. His eyes almost dance with adoration for me making him take the king.

We get in our swimsuits and apply sunscreen so after lunch we can get her in the pool because she won't stop talking about it. I can see out our window how busy it is in the pool. It makes me nervous.

"It is important you listen to Mommy in the pool. We need to stay together," I say calmly.

"Can we go to the store and buy toys for the pool...the ones we saw?" she asks, referring to the souvenir shop in the lobby.

"Yeah Boo, just promise you will listen to me in the pool," I say again. She nods eagerly with wild eyes.

When we walk out of our bedroom, the waiter is wheeling room service onto the balcony. Ace hands the guy a fifty-dollar bill as a tip. After the guy shuts the door behind him, I say in a low voice, "Wow, Mr. Big Shot."

"When the whole world thinks you are a bad lover you must make up for it where you can," he says in a whisper with his left hand cupped around the side of his mouth so Drew can't hear or see. A smile tugs at my lips and a little bubble of laughter escapes me. I'm glad he can make jokes about what Trina did yesterday. *Horrible!*

He pulls the lids off all the plates as I put Drew in her seat. Ace pulls my chair out for me and scoots me in. "Thank you," I say and feel my heart race when he touches my shoulder as he sits down.

Ace eats his grilled chicken sandwich, fries, over half my salad, and most of Drew's kid meal.

"That is why your arms are so big. It's not muscle, it's fat." He leans over to tickle my belly and I jerk away. Drew giggles and tickles me too. "No," I squeal and bolt out of my chair. Drew jumps quickly out of hers.

"Let's get her!" Drew yells, and I bark out a nervous laugh as Ace stands to his full intimidating height and takes off running into the room. Both of them are at my heels. It's a ruckus of high energy and loud squeals as they both chase me around the hotel room for a couple minutes.

I yell out, "Let's go to the pool!" Drew sucks in a lungful of air and just like that, tickling Mommy is forgotten. Ace laughs and applauds me for my mothering skills.

"You moms are always ahead of the game," he says with admiration etched all over his strong facial features. "I love it."

I get goosebumps looking up at him.

The three of us head to the store in the lobby and buy all the overpriced garbage you could get at the dollar store, but we are paying ten to fifteen dollars an item at this high falootin' resort. Ace puts it all on the room.

"Ace, you don't need to do that," I say. "I honestly am well taken care of financially. Dexter was very smart about finances."

He stares at me with the sweetest look. "Sprinkles, just agree this is my treat. I've got so much and It means nothing if I can't share it."

"But..." I start, and he puts his hand over my mouth. Our resounding laughter makes me feel like I'm floating.

"You save it for her college," he winks while his tiny dimple gleams at me.

"What if she asks for everything?" I ask after he drops his hand away from my mouth.

"She can have it within reason."

"Oh yeah? Where does Mr. Big Shot Magoo draw the line?" I ask with sarcasm.

"A bear."

"Mommy, can I get this bear?" Drew asks, tugging on my shorts. I look down at her and can't help but smile at her adorable obsession with bears. Ace grabs the cute stuffed brown bear out of her little hands and then scoops her up.

"What will you name it?" he asks.

"Big Shot," Drew beams.

When we get to the pool, I want to go back to the room and cuddle Drew. This seems like total chaos with kids running and cannonballing over each other's heads. I walk her in the pool on my hip and sit on the step. *Now what?*

"Farther, Mommy," she whines, unimpressed with my caution. I look across the pool and see Ace on the diving board. Drew watches with big eyes. When he springs in the air and executes a perfect dive, she claps with great enthusiasm.

"That was so good," she says, just mesmerized. After more begging, I stand up to walk her toward Ace. She asks me to set her on the step, so I do, but she keeps telling me to go further and then jumps from the step into me like she was trying to dive.

"Drew, you need to warn me," I say firmly with maybe too much anger. My nerves are shot. Kids drown all the time. I know I have to teach her to swim, but I have issues after Dexter drowning. I know they're irrational. Like Justin said, she'll surely drown if she can't swim.

"Let me show you what Poppa taught me," she says with eyes as wide as silver dollar pancakes. Ace swims over and stands a few feet in front of me. "Let me show you, Mommy."

Then she squirms out of my arms and into the water toward Ace. She rolls over on her back and floats. It happened so fast I can't even make sense of it.

Her eyes are closed, and she is totally relaxed. "If I ever get scared in the water or get tired, then I need to roll on my back," she says with calm assurance. "Poppa showed me this too." She rolls over and swims under the water and grabs Ace. He lifts her up and smiles at her.

"Whoa! You're a little fish," Ace says, confused. No way he is more confused than me. Did she learn that by swimming once in San Francisco? If she did, then she must be the next Michael

Phelps.

"When did Poppa teach you that?" I ask.

"Thursdays...and we swam a lot in San Francisco," she says and shrugs her shoulders.

Thursdays? As in recurring?

"At the club?" I ask and feel my eyes sting with tears. She nods her head. "Did they tell you not to tell me?"

"Yes, but I don't like keeping secrets from you." Drew reaches for me. "Are you mad at me?"

"No, Boo! In fact, I am so proud of you! Show me again." She has me put her on the edge of the pool and she jumps in the water, swimming a minute before rolling onto her back. She flips back over and glides toward me.

"Poppa says next summer I can join the minnows swim team at the country club!" Drew says with excitement.

I smile at her but inside my blood is boiling at what a horrible thing to do. Not the teaching her to swim part. That is cool. No, the part about teaching my sweet daughter to lie to me. I am so mad I could scream.

"Why don't you go have a glass of wine and Drew and I will play. Take a minute so you can enjoy the rest of the day," Ace says. I absorb his words before I agree.

"Please don't let her out of your sight."

"Never," He says. I trust Ace Lancaster with my life. More importantly, I realize in this moment that blind trust also extends to my child.

I sit at the bar and drink a Moscow mule, then ask the bartender for a phone.

"Everything okay?" Lucille asks on the other end.

"Not really. See, we're at the pool and it has been brought to my attention that Drew swims, John taught her, and you both told her not to tell me—"

"We can explain," she defends.

"Let me explain to you that if you ever tell my daughter to

lie to me again, you will never ever see her again. Is that clear, Lucille?" My veins are on fire. I can't think or see straight.

"Now wait a minute...She can't grow up on a lake and not know how to swim," Lucille spits.

"I get it, Lucille. I even understand why you did it. Her learning how to swim so efficiently is really cool. I am so proud of her. I am not excited about it being done behind my back. Do you understand that?" I ask in a steady and calm voice.

"We wouldn't had to have done that if you weren't so overprotective." She sounds condescending as though she is talking to a child. "I swear sometimes I could just smack you."

Smack me? Am I gonna have to brawl with my baby g-ma? This is wild.

"It is my job to be overprotective of her. It is my job to teach her right from wrong. Lying is wrong, I don't lie, and I don't want my daughter being told it is ever okay to lie to me to protect an adult," I say. "If you don't get that, then we are done. I can make other arrangements for Drew on Thursdays."

"I get it...You're right. Can we please get on the same page with her? I understand you. I understand your fear of water... your dreams. If she doesn't know how to swim and be respectful of the water, then she is at a higher risk. Can I please enroll her in swim lessons at the YMCA for the rest of the summer?" she asks. "Or hire a private instructor at the club?"

"Yes, Lucille, you may. Just promise the lying stops here," I say and close my eyes. I am so hurt by this.

I motion to the bartender to make me another one, mouthing *A double* at him. We hang up after her apology. My body is pulsing with anger and hatred. I can't decide if I hate her or myself for not getting her in swim lessons myself. That was one confident little minnow in the pool. But I am also confused as to how she knows about my nightmares. Who told her? I hate that she knows.

I finish my drink and head back to Drew and Ace, who are having the time of their lives with the super soakers over in the zero-entry part of the pool. I grab one and join them. The day at the pool tuckers Drew out, and after I tuck her in for the night, Ace and I sit on the balcony and have a glass of wine together. I tell him all about my conversation with Lucille.

"I'm proud of you," he says sincerely.

"Why, because I had vodka in order to deal with my over-bearing, snooty mother-in-law?"

"No, because she is in swim lessons and she is such a re-markable little girl. You do know that part, right?" His smile is so rewarding.

"Yes." I beam with pride. "I hope I don't mess it up too much...I am the only parent to blame if I do. She could end up hating me."

"Never. You two are so close. I love watching you two to-gether." His hand reaches for mine, and my stomach flips when he grabs it. I stare at my hand in his for a minute. When we were younger, he would hold my hand and I would always point out how my hand felt so perfect in his. It feels like it belongs in his hand. He smiles widely when I look at him.

"Are you thinking about how perfect your hand feels in mine?" he asks, and I see a look in his eyes I haven't seen since we were eighteen. Is it longing?

"Yes, was it me that said it or you?" I ask with a small smile, amazed he knew what I was thinking.

"Both," he hums through a soft smile. We sit in silence for a minute looking deeply into one another's eyes. A little sparkle of electricity comes to life in the air between us. "Still feels the same to me."

Me too.

I turn my gaze away when I hear loud bursts of excitement from the pool below us. Sounds like a group of people are party-ing down there. We end up drinking the whole bottle of wine and laughing hysterically until about midnight. I yawn and stand. "I should go to bed if we're going hiking tomorrow."

"Yeah," he agrees and stands too. "Night, Sprinkles. I had a great day with you." He gently pulls me in his embrace. I sigh in relief because it feels so good. Neither one of us make any attempt to let go for what feels like several minutes. I turn my head up and melt even more when I see the adoring look in his pretty eyes.

"See ya in the mornin', Mr. Magoo," I whisper and he smirks. I reluctantly pull myself away from him. "Night." I turn to leave. He walks in behind me, clicking the door shut.

"Alright, Sprinkles...sweet dreams." I smile at him. This feels so awkward for some reason. We walk away but keep looking back at each other, prolonging our night ending. I let one last lingering gaze transpire between us while we both stand at our bedroom doors on opposite sides of the living room. I let loose a breath that is filled with tension.

"Sweet dreams, Big Shot." His mouth crooks into a sleepy little smile before I twist my door handle and step inside. I close the door and lean up against it, trying to steady my thoughts and feelings. How is it even possible after all these years that I still feel the exact same way about him? *Like nothing else matters. Like I'm floating. Like I'm smiling nonstop...*

I climb into bed and have a hard time relaxing because I'm so giddy from the fun I had with Ace. I talk myself out of crossing the living room to see if he's still awake. That seems an odd thing to do, to go knock on his bedroom door in the middle of the night and say...*what*? What on earth would I say? You have amazing biceps? Your smile melts my heart? I can't stop smiling? I take a deep breath and roll over and stare at the moon.

We'd never work.

CHAPTER 14

~

It's Thursday morning and we are on our way back to Whimsy after such a fun trip. We went hiking and swimming every day. Drew had such an awesome time and was a trooper on the long hikes. When she would get tired of walking, Ace would put her on his shoulders. She asked if he was her uncle like Tater and Cameron. It was quite adorable, and Ace had such a perfect response. "Yep...sorry we are meeting so late. I have four years of spoiling to make up for." My heart beat like a drum and, if I'm being honest, it gave me butterflies. I'm such a mom. Who gets butterflies over a hot guy having a conversation with a toddler?

Ace and I ended all three nights with a bottle of wine on the balcony, laughing and reminiscing. On this drive home, I'm trying to grasp that soon we will be saying goodbye to him. I wish he lived here because I sure don't want to see him leave. The last two nights were like the first night, with lingering hugs that felt like he was still mine, that his heart still belonged to me. And every night, I went to bed giddy and wanting to wake him up. Last night I realized it is because I miss him when he isn't with me. I know it's silly because I have lived without him all these years. I should be able to sleep across the hotel room without him. My heart beat unsteady and anxious that I feel all these emotions and he's leaving soon. *I'm too attached.*

We pull into Lucille's at 12:30 PM. "Bye, Boo." Ace gives her a hug before I walk Drew in the house. She turns and waves to him one last time before I let myself in.

"Bye, Big Shot!" she yells with an exaggerated wave that makes me laugh. She has been calling him that and it has kept us in great humor the whole trip. Ace smiles with pure amusement. I twist the handle and Drew flies in, screaming for Mimi. She runs into her arms and hugs her tight before Lucille pinches her face up in pure disgust at her outfit. This is absolutely ridiculous! Drew has a brand-new pink t-shirt on that has a brown bear and says "Yosemite" on it. She's also wearing a pink tutu with some pink sparkly jelly sandals. She looks cute with her hair pulled up into pigtails. I want to roll my eyes right now but instead...

"Hi Lucille. How are you?" I ask with a warm smile. Well, as warm as it can be at the moment.

"Lily," she says and stands to her full height. She has on black slacks with a baby blue collared shirt tucked in with a gray sweater tied around her neck. She looks like her name should be Hildegard or something uptight like that. We are in Whimsy, not the Hamptons. "I've asked you to dress her in club attire when you bring her on Thursdays. She looks..."

"Like a four-year-old?" I ask. *Give me a break...*

"No, like she is being raised on welfare." She looks like somebody has shoved a corncob up her derriere. *Snooty!*

"Perhaps you could keep some stuff here that could bring her socio-economic appearance up a few notches," I say as neutral as I can. My eyes wander over to where Drew has pulled out her toys in the living room.

"Perhaps," she says as though I am being unreasonable.

I think she looks adorable with her little round belly showcased above her low-hanging tutu. Her little pigtails in one ringlet on each side. She is perfection whatever she wears. Drew looks at me and waves and I blow her a kiss goodbye.

"Can she stay about thirty minutes late tonight? I'm getting a late start," I ask, despite her look of utter disgust for me as she scans my outfit. It's a pair of black jeans and a black tee with the Moore Liquor store logo on the right breast. It's completely appropriate for my job.

"Yeah," Lucille says as she follows me onto the porch. "So, are you two dating?" She motions to my car where Ace sits.

"No," I say, stunned. "Just friends."

"Friends that stay the night with each other?" she asks. I want to punch her. It isn't really her business.

"Do you have a problem with it?" I am at my wits' end with her.

"As a matter of fact, I do. I don't want her scared by all his media coverage," she bites.

He signed a few autographs in Yosemite but was unrecognized for the most part. He had a nice four o'clock shadow and wore a ball cap to throw people off.

"Bye, Lucille. Have her ready. I will text on my way. I don't want to have to come in," I say and walk away pissed off at her. This feels like she's pointing this out to even the score because she got caught having Drew lie to me.

"This conversation isn't over," she insists.

"Yeah it is." She can't have a say in my personal life. *Can she?* I get in the car and look at Ace. "I totally hate her."

I vent the short drive to his parent's house.

"She has a point...something I haven't thought of. If you three are serious about coming with me next Tuesday, they will find me and it will be vicious," he says. "We can be careful and take separate cars but there *are no* guarantees."

"I trust you. We'll be fine. Drew wants to go so bad and Kylie is in full preparation, getting a bikini wax and everything. She plans to marry one of your teammates." We both laugh at how determined she is.

"I'll see you tonight to come set up her mattress. Can I bring y'all dinner?" he asks when I put my car in park.

"Nah, we have a standing order at Cluck Yo' Mama." His gorgeous blue eyes are swirling with warmth. "I'll add more to the order for you. So, I guess I'm buying you dinner."

"Can you afford to feed me, Sprinkles?" he teases and for some reason, the look on his face sends a little bolt of electricity through me.

I clear my throat while turning my gaze to my steering wheel. "I sure can," I reply. His gaze is on me, but I feel awkward right now and don't know why.

In my peripheral, I see him lean in to, I think, kiss my cheek. In a complete panic, I turn my head toward him. His soft warm lips land on mine and apply gentle pressure that makes my toes curl with the adrenaline I feel pulsing through my body. I jump back in my seat while releasing an uncomfortable giggle. Not meeting his gaze, I say, "I have to go." *Awkward.*

"Are you embarrassed, Sprinkles?" His teasing tone makes me cringe.

"No," I say and hear his snarky laugh.

"Well, you're very forward. I just wanted to give you a hug and you basically assaulted me with your mouth. Are you trying to get to second base with me?" Teasing me more. A humorous twinkle glows in his eyes, letting me know he's completely kidding.

I want to die.

"No...I'm trying to get you out of my car," I say and push his shoulder. "Go Magoo!"

He laughs at me, which doesn't do much on behalf of my dignity. He opens his door and when he doesn't get out right away, I reluctantly meet his gaze, which makes my lips tug upward into a huge smile to match his. He winks before climbing out and pulling out his suitcase from the trunk while I watch the glorious show that is Ace Lancaster. He is gorgeous! I try to make myself calm down and steady my thoughts as he walks to my side of the car. I unroll the window when he taps on the glass. I smile up at his sincerely happy face. He leans in through my window. "For the record Sprinkles, I liked the kiss." I flinch.

My heart thuds in my ears. My cheeks welcome a strong flush that seems to make its way into my equilibrium. I should say something, but my mouth is frozen as my mind tries to process his words. I pull my sunglasses down over my eyes, sheltering myself from his intense gaze. He laughs, which unfortunately does nothing to slow down my racing heart or cool my warm cheeks. "Have a good day, Sprinkles. I'm going to miss you." His flirtatious smile makes me feel even more flustered.

"You can quit teasing me," I yell before I roll my window up.

"I'm not teasing you."

Yes, he is. I put my car in reverse, ignoring his smile. He waves at me. He sure enjoys me making a fool of myself. Did I mean to kiss him? The short drive to the liquor store has me in deep thought as I try to make sense of what just happened. Mr. Buckets, who is accepting a delivery in the back parking lot he shares with my parents, greets me again as I pull in.

"How was Yosemite?" he asks. I can't suppress a giggle that he knows I was in Yosemite. And no doubt he knows I was with Ace, just like I'm sure the rest of the town knows.

"Beautiful and very relaxing. Drew loved it," I say. "Can you add enough chicken and biscuits to my order for one more?" Ace eats more than a normal serving. "Ace is coming to dinner and he's a hearty eater." I tell him this bit of juicy gossip. He would have asked who was coming anyway. Also, it's a little fun to toy with him. His eyes gleam with scandal, and I know he can't wait to tell everyone in this tiny, nosy town.

"Of course! Ace loves my red beans and rice...and my mac and cheese." He is a small business owner who prides himself on remembering everyone's orders. It is quite comforting.

"Yes, make sure there is plenty of things for him. Have a good day!" I beam at him while heading into the store. My dad is off fishing, but my mom and Darla are eager to hear about my whole trip.

"So, did anything happen between the two of you?" Darla pries.

I think I kissed him this morning...

"No. I still love and miss Dexter." I watch their faces drop before stepping into the office. I have to get busy cooking the books if I want to get out of here on time.

I work diligently, taking no breaks. My focus is on seeing Ace again. That simple closed mouth kiss is on the forefront of my mind. At 5:30, my food arrives from one of Mr. Buckets's employees. I hurry with my last two tasks, bubbling with an overwhelming excitement.

"Oh honey, you look so happy. Kiss him," my mom says as I'm heading out the door.

"Mom, we're just friends. He's married and so am I," I remind her before kissing her on her cheek. Then I float over to my dad, who came back late this afternoon, and kiss him on the cheek. "Bye. I love you both more than Red Vines."

I bounce to my car, elated to eat dinner with Drew and Ace.

I honk my horn when I pull up at Lucille's. John walks Drew out and buckles her up before focusing his attention on me.

"We got her private lessons at the club. We will take her Thursdays. Can you take her Mondays? The instructor is flexible and said she will call you to set up a time that works for you."

"Thank you," I say and smile cordially at the man that told my daughter to lie to me. How can they think they have a right to tell me who and who not to be friends with? "Have a great night." I pull out of their driveway as soon as he shuts the door. When we get home, Ace is just coming down the hill on his old skateboard.

"That looks fun," Drew says with fresh excitement.

"It is fun. We used to sit on them and ride down the hill and launch ourselves into the lake off of Grandma and Grandpa's dock," I say absently, watching my high school sweetheart. The way he makes that look so effortless is incredibly sexy. Then I remember how dangerous it is and how I shouldn't give her ideas like that, but I'm lost in nostalgic memories seeing Ace on his skateboard, remembering my young love with the sweetest guy in town. He is the reason I believe in forever loves, and he is the reason that I am sitting here thinking about getting back out there. Maybe I should get back out there with him? I feel something I haven't felt in a very long time: curiosity about someone of the opposite sex. As fast as it comes, it is replaced with guilt and the sudden tightness of my wedding ring.

"Hey girls. I missed you both!" He shouts at us when he reaches my car. I climb out and he kisses my cheek before I open the door to unbuckle Drew. As soon as I pull her out, Ace grabs her and hugs her tightly, making her squeal. "How was your day, little lady?"

"Good. Mimi gave me this." She holds up *The Wizard of Oz* on Blu-ray.

"Oh, that's a classic," Ace says.

"Can you show me how to ride that?" she asks him, pointing her newly painted pink fingernail at his skateboard. I'm guessing Lucille did that. Ace looks at me to see how I want him to answer this.

"You need a helmet for that," I say and grab her from Ace. "So, you will have to wait to learn."

Ace laughs at me and my quick thinking. *Slow down world, I don't want her skateboarding.* He grabs the food while I carry Drew into the house. I send her straight back to use the bathroom and wash her hands.

We all sit at the table and talk about our days while we eat. Ace gets my picky toddler to try the mac and cheese and the red beans and rice. *Miraculous.*

"I like them both!" She even asks for more.

After dinner, Ace sets up her new Tuft & Needle. She thanks him a hundred times as she tries to jump on her new memory foam mattress.

"It's not bouncy like my old one," she says and looks disappointed.

"You're not supposed to bounce on it, silly. You're supposed to sleep on it," Ace says, throwing her on her new bed and tickling her.

After I get her settled down, with no help from Ace who keeps making her laugh, I kick Ace out and read her a book.

Takes her so long to fall asleep because she is so riled up from Ace but when she does drift off, I can't move because I just want to stare at her perfect button nose, her round rosy cheeks, and her sculpted full pink lips. I made her. She lived in my belly, which is a true miracle. I kiss her warm smooth cheek and tuck her under the covers before tiptoeing out of her room.

When I walk out, all the food and dishes have been cleaned. I look around and feel so relaxed. *My house is clean and my kid is asleep?* Usually, I come out after she's asleep, overwhelmed and exhausted. Then I wake to a dirty house. This feels like some kind of magic has transpired here tonight.

"Whoa," I say as Ace glides across the room with a glass of red wine for me. "I don't even know what to say." I take the wine and smile up at him with so much gratitude. "Can I hire you?"

"Yes!" He grins. "You want to watch a movie?"

"Okay," I say, dazed as I look at my empty dish rack. He must have put all the dishes away too. I can't even remember the last time it was empty.

We get situated on the couch and start looking for movies. "This is a star-studded cast and I have been wanting to watch it," I say. "You okay with it?" He nods, agreeing with my movie selection. "Yay!" I whisper-yell.

His gaze rests on me as a husky laugh rings in my ear.

"What?" I ask through my own laughter brought on by contagion.

"You're so cute, Lily." His charming smile and warm southern drawl make my pulse race. He scoots closer, and I unintentionally gulp when I whiff his intoxicating smell. His arm goes over my shoulder. I hold onto my breath in alarm.

Is this a date?

~

What I learn over the next two hours is just because it has a star-studded cast doesn't mean it will be good. It was awful, but

I had to watch the whole thing hoping there had to be a point to it, which there wasn't. Just two hours of my life gone forever on the world's worst movie.

"That was so stupid!" I exclaim when the credits finally roll.

"Tell me about it. It would have been more fun if we had stuck a few toothpicks in our eyeballs," Ace says.

"We still have time. Ugh...I hate it when you think it's gonna be good and then bam, it's rubbish." When I look at him, he is staring at me in a way I can't make out. "What?" I giggle awkwardly. Then I rub my forehead, confused. Maybe I have food smudged on it. "*What?*" I exclaim when he laughs.

"You haven't changed. Like today when you said you hated Lucille. You try and be angry, but it seems so out of place with you. It just comes off as adorable," Ace says and I roll my eyes.

"I hated that movie," I say with wide eyes. He squeezes my hand, staring at our perfectly entwined fingers. He looks so lost in thought. His gaze meets mine, and he smiles at me so I smile back.

"You wanna give me a ride to Tater's tomorrow night for the big reunion celebration?" He looks uncomfortable as he shifts his gaze away from mine. Justin comes tomorrow afternoon for the weekend.

"Sure. Pick you up at 7 PM?" I ask, hoping he will look back to me. He finally does and my heart skips a beat.

"I could ride my skateboard over earlier and we could take Drew to see the *Incredibles 2* movie she keeps talking about."

My face lights up. "Okay." He is staring at me with that same look he keeps getting. What is he thinking?

"You know..." Ace starts and then he stops and turns away.

"What?" I ask because I want him to kiss me and I feel he wants the same. I think so at least. He shifts uncomfortably and lets go of my hand, which I don't like. It felt so good in his warm strong hands. It felt like I mattered, being special and desirable. Something I truly miss...*intimacy.*

"I think I left this back door unlocked." He stands suddenly and walks to the door that leads to the back yard. *Don't go.* I feel abandoned at his sudden movement. I realize I felt abandoned by Dexter too when he died. The strong emotion coils around my insides and makes me want to scream out at Ace. I watch him with sad eyes as he makes his way to the back door. He twists the handle. "Nope, it's locked. I better go and sleep in my new Tuft & Needle." It sounds so rushed. He's leaving so quickly.

He doesn't want to kiss.

"Or we could watch another movie and eat that red velvet cake?" I suggest, trying to sound completely cool, when really, I want to fall to my knees and beg him not to go.

He runs his hand through his hair. "I am so beat...I should get home," he says, looking like I am the last person he wants to be with.

Despite my feeling of rejection, I choke out, "Thank you for coming over and for the mattress. She will love it." I stand, trying not to show how disappointed I am that he is leaving. We stand awkwardly in front of each other for at least a full minute, looking at the floor.

"I'll call in the morning and we can pick a movie time," Ace says. I nod before I wrap my arms around him. We hug for a long time, not saying anything. It's hard for me to stay silent because I want to say so much to him. I want to know what is behind his empty look, and I want to know if he has thought about kissing me. I want to thank him for loving me so sweetly all those years ago. I want to say so much more...

"You okay, Lily?" he asks in such a hushed voice. Like he is afraid to ask.

I let him go and smile at him. "Sorry...I just hate saying goodbye to you. I always have...Probably always will," I say while blinking back unshed tears. "I don't want to bog you down with my crazy head." I wipe the lone tear off my cheek that, despite my best efforts, escaped.

"Saying goodbye to me has brought you to tears?" he asks.

I shrug and look away. Is he making fun of me?

The silence between us is deafening. I did it—I got too attached to him. It's evident that I am looking for more with him than he is with me. It's so silly because of our past, and I know he doesn't feel the same. Not to mention the guilt I would feel over Dexter would likely kill me.

"I have always hated saying goodbye to you." *He has?* My elated eyes pop up to meet his sincere baby blues that penetrate my heart with pure adrenaline. "You keep teasing me about how emotional I got at the bus station when we said goodbye before college. You made me feel like it was one-sided." *Because I'm horrible.* His face twitches and his irises swirl with confusion. "I was a wreck on the bus and that whole entire first year away from you. I missed you so much. Felt like I was missing part of myself." He sighs. "Then when we saw each other over holidays and the summer, I had that same empty feeling all over again each time we said goodbye."

I take a deep breath and slowly release a lot of tension I was holding.

"It was the same for me." I take another breath to try and decide how much I should reveal. *Not much.* "All those times you called me when I was in college with Dexter, I didn't take your calls. There was no way I could have had you in my life and been true to Dexter." His eyes are lit up and washed in relief. I bite my lip out of nerves. "You know that is the reason I didn't stay in touch, right?"

"Honestly, I didn't, but it does make me feel a little less rejected." We both kind of laugh before looking away from each other. "I never loved anyone else the way I loved you." I flick my eyes to his and see a flurry of emotions inside his crystal blue eyes. I know mine are holding a lot of emotions too. *I really want to kiss him.* His gaze is smoldering. Should I do it? He said he didn't want to date right now, and why would he want to get mixed up with a single mom? My life is not exactly glamorous or exciting.

"I could never reject you…" He cuts me off when he pushes his hand onto my neck and runs his fingers behind it, sending a wave of euphoria and adrenaline through my core. "I would have..." I stop myself because I can't bring myself to say these words out loud and betray Dexter. When his thumb brushes my cheek, I bring my eyes back up to his.

His face is right in front of mine. His breath tickles my cheeks. There is no hesitation on my part as I tilt my face toward his and his lips eagerly take mine. His other hand grips my hip, while the one on my neck moves into my hair, creating heat everywhere his giant hands explore. I push myself closer into him, pursuing him further. My head is swimming with so many conflicted thoughts. I try to ignore the nagging voice within me. *You're a mom. NFL. Trina. Dexter. Drew.* All the reasons this shouldn't happen.

His fingers travel down my neck, slowly down my spine, making it vibrate in anticipation. His hand lands on my other hip, mirroring his opposite hand. I always loved the way he placed his hands on my hips. My hands are up the back of his shirt, placed against his silky and warm skin. When he pushes his hand under the back of my shirt, I pull away and look in his restless eyes.

"Ace..." I start to protest what is happening, but he quickly grabs me again and presses his fervent lips back onto mine. It is a very provoking kiss that turns my insides to lava. My whole body is screaming for more and when he starts to raise my shirt up to expose me in my hideous bra, I snap out of it by pushing his hands away. It doesn't do anything, except he pulls me closer and pins me to the door, making my head swoon again. I run my hands up into his soft hair, guiding his face to deepen the kiss.

But the voice in my head is too strong. So despite this amazing feeling and desire that has surfaced in me, I know this is wrong. I feel bad for Trina, which I know he'd say is silly. Then there is my dead husband. I pull away again, this time ducking under his arm to get enough distance from him.

"Okay...so call me when you wake up," I say. He runs his hand through his hair, looking flustered. He takes a few steps toward me, and I avoid him by walking around him to the door and opening it.

"Are you kicking me out, Sprinkles?" His facial expression is a mixture of amusement and disappointment, which seems hard to do, but that is for sure what he's doing.

"You said you were leaving and I'm tired," I say, not meeting his eyes. He steps in front of me, towering over me. His heat and my ardor mingle around us, and it is hard to ignore. If I look in his eyes, I will regret this more than I already do.

Regret what? Kissing him or stopping it?

"Sweet dreams, Lily." His warm hand cups my cheek. I unwillingly lift my gaze to his and smile wanly.

"Goodnight," I say, holding his gaze. Within his eyes I can see him begging for me to let him in my complicated life, but it's too much. When he turns to leave, relief washes over me. I lock the door behind him. I sink down onto the floor as tears spill down my cheeks, the guilt suffocating me. My hands run over my neck, trying to help release the foreboding feeling in which I am drowning. I go five years without a man and now I'm falling for a married one? What in the world is wrong with my head?

I peel myself off my floor after beating myself up for a great length of time. I absentmindedly walk through the house flipping off the lights before I open Drew's door. She is so full of peace and purity that I can't resist. I climb into bed with her. I need her peaceful nature to rub off on me. Plus, I'm super curious about her new Tuft & Needle. It feels weird at first but after a few minutes, I do find it very comfortable.

It takes me a long time to fall asleep because that kiss with Ace was mind blowing. I don't know if I have ever had a kiss that hot in my life. Did he say he never loved anyone the way he loved me? It's all such a jumble of unclear feelings.

I finally find sleep, but it isn't a restful one. I bolt upright screaming, waking up my sweet toddler.

"Mommy, I'm here...I'm here," she says in her gentle innocent voice. I lay back down and pull her into my chest, feeling apprehensive about subjecting her to this yet again.

"Sorry Boo, go back to sleep. I'm okay. I love you," I whisper.

That dream was different. I was trying to get myself out of

the glass box while it filled with water. Dexter was on the other side with a calm look on his face as he watched me scream and wither around in discomfort. Then he said with malice and loathing, "It serves you right."

He is right...

CHAPTER 15

~

I wake the next morning to Drew shaking me. "Mommy, Ace is at the door with donuts and flowers."

"What time is it?" I ask and look around her room for her iPad. I grab it at the foot of the bed and turn it on.

"12:00?" I yell and stumble out of bed half asleep, stepping on a Lego. I shout a string of curse words, making Drew scowl at me. Drew is the swearing police, always there to remind you not to say naughty words. Which she does while I hold my foot and consider calling 911. I sigh heavily as I decide to skip the ambulance and power through the sharp pain.

Before I complete the trek to the front door, I trip over my too-long pajama bottoms and fall in the hallway. Drew giggles when I yell "Snicker turds!" instead of a long string of offensive profanities. I take a deep breath, pick myself up, and try to remember who I am and what life is all about before opening the door to a smiling Ace. He looks like caramel dipped in honey and rolled in glitter. His little dimple is loud and proud, reminding me of that steamy kiss we had. His blue eyes sparkle with so much intensity it makes my head swim.

"Morning." His voice mingles with a hint of amusement. "Rough night?" His sarcasm doesn't do my ego much good when I realize he is referring to my appearance.

"Hey," I say and touch my hair. It seems to be rather high in the air in one solid form. It's a conundrum as what could have happened to it. *Is that a Lego in there?* I move to the side to let him in while I pull a teeny tiny microscopic toy purse out of my rat's nest of a head. *Must be the missing L.O.L. doll purse Drew has been whining about the last week?*

"Drew!" I look down at her and show her what I found. She squeals in delight. *One problem solved.*

I smile smugly back in Ace's direction as if to say, *I meant to look like this.*

"Come in. I was just trying some new things with my hair. Heard teasing is all the rage these days." He nods, self-satisfied. *Rude.*

"These are for you and these are for you," he says smoothly, handing me some beautiful lilies and giving the box of donuts to Drew.

"I just woke up...I don't know how long she has been awake. What day it is or who you are? I feel like the worst mom ever." *She's only four; is it that hard to get up with her?*

"You also have a toy smooshed on your cheek." He pries it off and shows me a pair of L.O.L. sunglasses and I release a giant breath. *Awesome!* It hurts where he removed it. I turn to the mirror and see a red indent in the shape of miniature sunglasses. *Why are all her toys so small and painful?*

"Wow...I slept hard," I say absently. Then it hits me. "On the Tuft & Needle. Maybe it's too comfortable?"

"Maybe," he says, amused. "Boo, how did you sleep?"

"Awful! First Mommy yelled and then my back hurt, so I had to wake up with the roosters. Can we put my old mattress back on my bed?" Ace and I crack up.

"What was Mommy screaming about?" Ace whispers.

"I was trying to get myself out of the glass box," I say while running my fingers through my hair. *Except they're stuck in this disaster. I should probably just shave it.* "Extra creepy."

"Not really...Maybe you're finally trying to save yourself," he says.

No, it's because Dexter hates me in the afterworld.

I shrug his comment off and look away from his penetrating gaze, I don't want to talk about my frantic dreams with Ace. "Sprinkles," he says as if he's pained and when I turn my face up to meet his expressive eyes, they tug at my fragile heart. "You need a hug?" I try to protest but before I know it, his arms are around me and I relax right into him. After a minute, Drew wraps herself around our legs and I smile. A few minutes pass before she lets go. I let go and plop down next to her and grab a donut out of the box she set on the coffee table. Ace joins us and picks out a donut. I look down at my hand and realize I'm still holding the flowers he brought me.

Thank him, idiot.

"Oh my god, I'm the worst," I exclaim. "These flowers are so beautiful! Thank you so much Ace!"

"Never been able to walk by a lily and not think of you," he says so sweetly that it makes my heart leap into my throat. I turn my head and smile with gratitude. How is it that I can feel so drawn to him but also feel guilty about Dexter? It's as though I can see Dexter shaking his finger at me from the cemetery across town.

"They're pretty," Drew says and rubs the petal gently, snapping me out of my depressive trance.

"They pale in comparison to your mom's beauty." That look in his eyes makes my body hum with a mixture of hysteria, confusion, and elation. It takes me a second, but I finally relocate my gaze onto Drew.

"Where should I put them, Drew?" I smooth her ratty hair. *Maybe I should shave hers too?*

"On the table by the front door, so they will be the first thing you see when you come home," she hums with a pristine smile on her faultless face. She is absolutely immaculate. *Aside from her hair...*

"You always have the best ideas, Boo." I stand and walk to the kitchen. Ace follows my every move with his eyes. It makes me feel vulnerable in a way I haven't felt in years. I pull out a vase and arrange them. A pretty pink vase that my dad gave me for my first Valentine's Day without Dexter. Makes me think of the last Valentine's Day Dexter and I shared together, right here in this very great room.

He made spaghetti and wanted us to share a plate like on *Lady and the Tramp*, inching our lips closer together on a shared noodle. He was a silly romantic who had a way of always making me laugh at his over-the-top gestures. He bought me red roses and a heart pendant necklace. While we shared a plate of spaghetti, he said, "Lily, I think we should try for a baby." I remember being stunned because when we had talked about starting a family in the past, he had wanted to wait a few years. I was so excited I jumped on his lap and kissed his face.

I can't fight the emotion that slithers around me like a boa constrictor, threatening to steal my last breaths. I take a few deep breaths, fighting with my lungs to accept the breaths. When I win that fight, I surrender to the next threat of unshed tears. My emotions are in a constant state of war, and I am quite sick of it. It takes a toll on me. I start weeping right in the kitchen while Ace and Drew watch cartoons. I'm a terrible wife, breaking my vows and kissing another man in our home with our daughter asleep in the next room.

"Go get cleaned up. There's a three o'clock showing and I heard it's packed," Ace says. Drew lights up when she turns to face him.

"Where are we going, Big Shot?" she asks him while jumping on the couch.

"The movies." She squeals in delight. "*Incredibles 2*! Do I need to see the first one to understand it?"

She sings in harmonious laughter, "I don't know." He laughs at her adorable response while he tickles her tiny belly. She jumps on his lap and wraps her arms around him. They have really become attached to one another. This can't be good. He's leaving... He's a famous NFL football player...We live in Whimsy. *What have I done?*

"Hey Sprinkles, go shower," Ace says while cuddling Drew.

"Why do you call Mommy Sprinkles?" Drew asks.

"Because when we were younger, she got very cute freckles on her face from the sun. Like she had extra radiance sprinkled into her." Ace turns back to look at me with his bright smile. His face falls when he sees I've been crying. He sets her on the couch and walks to the kitchen.

"You okay?" he asks, full of empathy for me and my crazy, pathetic life.

"No, I feel really guilty about last night," I admit and stare at the floor. "I can't let that happen again."

"Do you want that to happen again?" He avoids my protest. "Because I gotta tell you, I can't stop thinking about it."

"You have a wife. We have to just be friends or nothing at all." I wipe the tears away. "I hate myself right now."

"Oh Sprinkles! You have nothing to beat yourself up about. Please don't hate yourself. I won't kiss you again." He looks so sincere and sympathetic. I gaze into his bewitching eyes, ones I trust and long to see as a permanent fixture in my life. "It was just a kiss."

No, it wasn't. It was way more than a kiss. Feelings were revealed. Deep feelings that betray my loyalty to my husband. Ace gently rubs my arms. "I'm sorry. I don't want you to hate yourself." He tucks some stray hair behind my ear.

"You're not responsible for my feelings, Ace," I point out because I don't want him to feel guilty about anything. "It's my fault." I look at my toes. Gah, I need a pedicure so badly.

"I kind of am." His hands ram through his hair as he expels a long drawn-out breath, exposing how stressed he is.

"Big Shot, chill out," I tease and erupt into laughter at the look of betrayal on his face. I can't handle any more tension. He looks down at me with what can only be annoyance, so I poke his belly with my finger. A weary smile spreads on his face. I beam at him and he finally succumbs to a giant smile, rolling his eyes in the process. He grabs me in a big hug, and we stay put for a long time as we both relax.

I love him. Whoa...that is wild.

I love him as a friend, I remind myself.

In the shower, I pull myself together and think about how he'll be gone soon. I try to spin it as a positive thing, but it makes me feel empty inside just like he said last night. When he leaves, I'm sure I'll realize this was nothing more than pesky adolescent feelings that have resurfaced. That's all this is.

I blow dry my long wavy hair with care. I have good hair, once I remove the Legos and doll accessories. I also know that I'm attractive, but I feel like I have hit a wall. Nothing in my closet feels good enough for Ace. *Stop it!* I tell myself as I put on a pair of jean shorts and a fitted green tank top I bought at the tiny boutique in Whimsy. I feel lowly and not very pretty, so I put on a splash of makeup and some jewelry.

"Lily, you look stunning," Ace says when I walk out, and my smile widens.

"Ace, you are so sweet. It's just a tank top and shorts."

"Yep, but you always look magnificent in green." My smile is beaming. It's so nice to have someone who is attracted to me tell me I look pretty. I can't believe I became so self-conscious about myself. We're going to the movies in Davenridge, not the Oscars. I grab a worn-out flannel out of the coat closet in the foyer. The theater is always cold, and I will need it tonight at Tater's reunion party.

"Remember this?" I ask Ace, holding the flannel up.

"Yep. I bought this for you when we went to Reggae on the River from that old hippie. We were on shrooms and you said it was the world's most beautiful flannel." He looks happy and that's how I feel reliving the memory.

"You paid her twenty-five dollars and she took it right off her arms. Then you wrapped it around me." I couldn't get over how pretty it was. He offered her cash and she jumped right up and gave it to him. It is a navy blue and dark green plaid with little flecks of gold thread, and it is still pretty after all these years. I always get complimented when I wear it.

"As you can see, I still love it." I slide my arms into it and he laughs. "What?" I ask.

"See? You have shrunk. It's big on you," he says. "When your mom was monitoring your eating the other night, is it because you don't eat? I've noticed you don't eat, but why?"

I shrug. "Being a single mom is busy." *And lonely.* "I eat Goldfish and her crusts from peanut butter and honey sandwiches," I admit. "I expend a lot of energy on her." Momming ain't always easy. Sometimes this little human sucks the day right out from under my feet, leaving me exhausted and maybe even confused.

"You need someone to take care of you," he says with a big nod of his head and an evil little smile. "A man. You, Lily Moore, need a man."

"Why is that? I'm taking care of her. We have a house, clothes, American Girl dolls…" I say with my hands on my hips. As if having a man would just solve everything. "Besides, that's sexist, Ace."

"Sprinkles, we gonna do the whole sexist bit again?" he teases and I squint my eyes.

"Okay, so I may have been off before"—I look around for Drew—"when I was *on weed,* but you saying I *need* a man is demeaning. Makes me feel like you don't think I'm doing very well on my own and I'm fine." I rock back on my heels and hold my gaze on him.

So I have bad dreams and don't eat much. So I cry a lot. So my dirty laundry is out of hand. So what?

"Well….maybe *need* is the wrong word. How about *deserve* a loving, kind man? Maybe someone you know really well and has always thought the world of you," he says with charming arrogance.

If he means him, then yes please.

"Justin *is* coming tonight," I say with sarcasm.

"That still hurts." His gaze is steady on mine. Guilt twists around my insides.

"Aw," I say and give him a big hug. "You know I'm teasing." His hand cups the back of my head as he finally hugs me back. Took him a minute to reciprocate. He must really hate when I tease him about that.

"Do I look pretty?" I hear Drew ask as she rounds the corner into the entryway from the hall. She has on the best outfit I have ever seen. And when I say best, I'm being completely and totally sarcastic. It's awful!

"Oh Boo!" I exclaim. "I love it." I turn and look at Ace, who follows my lead and agrees. She has on tie-dye biker shorts that are so hideous and absolutely, without a shadow of a doubt, way too small. I don't even know how they ended up in this house. I sure as heck didn't bring them in. Over them, she has a 2T dress that I put in a bag to give Delilah. Drew was jealous I was giving it to her and must have dug it out. The dress is red with pink hearts all over it. It barely covers her butt, so I'm proud she had the good sense to put the hideous biker shorts on, even if they are *wayyy* too small. *She is such a lady!* She has brown cowboy boots pulled over her L.O.L. doll knee socks and a purple cowboy hat on her head.

I pull my phone out immediately to take a picture of her. She poses like a runway model and I take a video and ask her questions about how she feels in her glorious ensemble. Ace finally grabs my phone out of my hand with a huge smile.

"We have to go if we want to make this thing. I can drive so you can snap pictures of her in the car," Maybe I go overboard but come on!

In the car we talk about her outfit behind her back while she plays on her iPad.

"Those socks." He barks out a warranted laugh.

"Yeah, but she paired that small dress with biker shorts. For that, we must rejoice that I'm not raising Whimsy's next town hussy."

"I can't wait to see the next one." I'm distracted by my own thoughts as I look out the window. *He wants to see the next one?* He doesn't live here, and I absolutely can't get attached.

You're already attached.

I have to think of the negative things about Ace Lancaster. He isn't perfect after all. He did break my heart once before. He could be setting up for another heartbreak and this time, I have Drew to think about. Her mommy is already aching enough.

That kiss though...

CHAPTER 16

~

At the concession stand, the teen girl barely looks at us. She is too busy flirting with her coworker, and our presence seems to be putting her out. The teen boy is trying to keep her attention by catching popcorn with his mouth. Ace clears his throat, his eyes turned down to the counter.

"Uh....what can I get you?" she finally asks, still staring at the teen boy.

"A large popcorn, an order of nachos with extra jalapenos, a large root beer, let me try those sliders, two orders of fries and...." He pauses and stares at the menu. "A king size peanut M&M's." He drones on and on, and I watch his profile while he stares at the menu. He is so gorgeous and that kiss last night is making my head spin. I just want to jump on him and wrap my legs around his waist and never stop kissing him. Drew is singing in my ear, a song from *Moana*, while she plays with my hair. Ace smiles at me and then says something else to the girl, who has no idea who he is. He's cleverly disguised beneath a baseball cap and sunglasses. She just wants him gone so she can get back to flirting with her boyfriend.

"What do you guys want?" Ace turns to me and my jaw drops. That is all for him? *Piggy.*

"A bottle of water and a small popcorn," I say to the girl.

"Make theirs a large popcorn," Ace corrects.

When we get seated and he has made several trips to grab the rest of his food, I look at him. "You will be a *fat* old man if you eat this way after football," I say, munching on a piece of popcorn.

"Well Lily, you will waste away and float off into space if you keep eating that way," he says. "Plus, I was teasing out there. I got these for you and these for Drew." He hands me Red Vines and Drew some Life Savers Gummies. She lights up.

"These are my favorite!" Drew and I say at the exact same time.

He pats Drew's head affectionately before focusing his attention on me.

"I remember," he says with pride. "Every time I see them, I think of you."

He's still so sweet and thoughtful, which is problematic for my heart. Think of his negative qualities!

"When I was pregnant with Drew, I ate the big Costco one all by myself at my parents," I say as I take my first bite of Red Vines and smile at him with gratitude. "In one day."

"So you ate when you were pregnant?"

I roll my eyes. "Of course I did. You kinda have to if you want them to grow," I say like a bratty teen.

"Defensive?" He steals one of my Red Vines, and I pull the package safely out of his reach.

"Not defensive, it's just a stupid question."

"Miss Sanders used to say 'There are no stupid questions,'" he mocks as if we are still in elementary school.

"Whoever started that saying was probably painfully stupid." I shake my head. *Think negative thoughts.* "Was it you, Magoo?" I smugly stare him down.

"Remember when you asked Tater if I ever even loved you?" I flinch and see his proud smile. "Painfully stupid." He turns his head to the screen as the theater darkens.

Tater! He betrayed me?

I'm lost in thought during the previews because I am thinking of that conversation all those years ago with Tater. I did ask him that while sobbing on his shoulder when Ace moved in with a girl that he supposedly was so in love with he was able to forget all about me.

When the movie starts, Drew climbs on my lap like she always does. Ace slides into her empty seat and grabs my hand. It startles me and when I look up at him, he leans in and whispers, "It's okay. I won't kiss you anymore." *He has that look though.* "Also, you're not painfully stupid."

"Good thing one of us isn't," I say. He leans over and plants a big kiss on my cheek, sending ripples of warmth down to my belly, signaling the butterflies. My brain starts frantically searching for something negative about him.

He's gonna get fat one day...

I grab one of his sliders and steal a bite.

"Those are gross Ace." I spit it back out into a napkin.

He laughs and shoves a whole one in his mouth, looking so adorable doing so. Even when he's a fatass, he'll still be adorable. Think of something negative!

His dad is starting to go bald...

We hold hands the entire movie. Drew's asleep by the time it's over. I always hate this part. I want her to sleep, but she is heavy and the walk to the car is long and I have got to pee before our long drive back to Whimsy.

"Let me carry her for you," Ace says. I swear I almost cry while the butterflies that can't even think negatively about him swirl around my belly. *Just hate him!* It would be easier.

"Gah...you have no idea how bad I have to pee! You're like a painfully *stupid* hero." He hums a quiet laugh in my ear as he lifts her off me. His pleasant scent sends a wave of passionate heat through my entire body. *Think negative thoughts, darn you, Lily Moore.*

We are both quiet once we get in the car. He's driving and I stare out the window and text with Kylie, who is getting waxed in Davenridge right now. I keep laughing as she sends me selfies with exaggerated pained facial expressions. Every time I laugh, I show Ace her face while he drives.

"So on Facebook, I saw you two went to the Pink concert with Tater," he says.

"Yep, my parents went too and stayed in the hotel in San Jose with Drew. She was amazing."

"You looked so pretty I almost filed for a divorce right then."

I roll my eyes. "Ace...remember your promise."

He's broken promises before.

"I can't tell you how pretty you are?" he asks with a look of defeat on his face.

"It's the way you said it...*get a divorce*," I snap. "I don't have much respect for men that can't have the decency to stay faithful. Marriage is a *promise* to one another to always be there." Wonder if he'll catch my dig about *promises*?

"I just mean that it has pained me over the years when they post pictures of you. Makes me sad for all that I missed with you," he says. "You said you missed me, but why no calls? When I got married, did you think twice about it?"

Nope, he didn't catch it.

"I did miss you," I say, irritated. He's leaving, so why does he want to drag all these feelings up? I've had them tucked away nicely for years. Now they're flooding back.

"Why did you avoid all of my efforts? Even before I got married, I reached out so many times." He's also annoyed.

"I was a little busy being a single mom..." I bite back.

"This irritates you?".

I sigh because I don't want to fight with him.

"I don't want to dredge all this up...." His jaw clenches with frustration.

My phone rings and I rejoice in the interruption.

"It's Kylie, I have to take it." I realize this is so rude and insensitive, but I just want to be friends, and the direction of this conversation feels like something else. I spend the rest of the ride listening to Kylie talk about how painful waxing was. I don't even look his way the rest of the car ride.

He pulls the car right up to the back door of the liquor store, and him and my dad load up all the booze for tonight. I sit in the running car while my fashionable daughter sleeps. She was tired from her sleepless night on her Tuft & Needle. My mom comes out, beaming that I'm with Ace again today. While my dad and Ace talk at the back of the car, she whispers, "Anything happening between you two yet?"

"Yeah, I'm pregnant and moving to Dallas." I roll my eyes. "Give it a rest! What kind of mother encourages her widow daughter to have an affair with a married man?"

She pets my cheek in a very condescending way. "A really good one," she says gently. I take my sunglasses off and look in her eyes.

"I can't believe you really want me, a grieving widow and single mother, to get involved with a married man." I shake my head in annoyance. Everyone has lost their damn minds today.

"Just kiss him and if you hate it, then I'll leave you alone. You look the happiest I've seen you in years." I look away from her. I'm just about to give her a firm piece of my agitated mind when Ace climbs in the driver's seat.

"Drive careful, Ace," my mom says with a huge smile.

"Mom, we could throw the beer there. That's how far Ace is driving." She stares at me like she doesn't think I'm cute or funny. I am being a brat. Dexter died less than a mile from home.

We also stop at the butcher shop so Ace can supply all the meat for the barbecue.

"Send Henry and Sylvia my best," I say to Ace as he climbs out of the car. Henry and Sylvia are the butcher shop owners. Retirees from LA. They moved here a few years ago and opened this place. We didn't have a butcher shop before, and I don't know how we survived. Sylvia comes walking out, and I climb out to hug her.

"Oh, you look beautiful, Lily." Sylvia is, I think, my biggest fan in life. She laughs at everything I say, and she tells me how beautiful I look on my worst days.

"You are so nice. I love this dress," I say to her. She always looks so cute. She works with raw meat all day but when her blood-stained apron comes off, she has beautiful clothes underneath.

"Thank you. So, rumor has it you used to be Ace's high school sweetheart. Any sparks?" She looks so excited. I internally roll my eyes at everyone's nosiness in this town.

"Just friends." So what if my tone is on the defensive side? I am sick of all these questions about my married *friend*.

"Well girl, we need to order you an MRI to make sure your heads intact. He's so gorgeous I don't know how to even act around him." She's wildly giddy about Ace for a sixty year old married woman.

Ace walks out with Henry, who are both near collapsing at the mounds of meat in their arms.

"Did you leave any meat for the rest of the town?" I ask, stunned.

"I had to call your parents to come get the rest. It won't fit in your car." He looks so ridiculously sexy right now that my heart skips a beat and I'm starting to wonder if I have angina with the erratic behavior of my heart. He's giving me angina. I look over at Sylvia and notice she may also be experiencing angina.

"You two stop by when you close up," I say to the butchers.

"Oh, that sounds fun!" Sylvia beams. "Can we bring something?"

"Just yourselves." She howls in laughter and I can't help but reciprocate. *She is a nut! How was that funny?*

"Hey Howard!" Sylvia stares over my shoulder and my whole body stiffens. Dexter's doppelgänger today? After his loud and clear message last night from the afterworld that he hates me? *It's a sign!*

"Hi Sylvia," I hear him say. He greets Henry too, and they shake hands. Henry introduces him to Ace, and they make pleasantries while my palms sweat. "Hi Lily," Howard says, trying to get me to look at him. I hate this part. If I look at him, I'll have a mild panic attack but if I don't, then I look rude.

"Hey Howard," I say as brightly as I can before turning right around and climbing in the car. "Ace, we better go."

"We'll stop by," Sylvia squeals. I crane my head and accidentally make eye contact with Howard, who looks distracted by me as well.

"You going to Lily's?" Howard asks Sylvia. He's really settled into the small-town nosy snoop, hasn't he?

"Tater's," Ace says before shaking his hand one last time. "You should stop by."

What??

On the way to Tater's, Ace looks at me. "You okay? You look like you saw a ghost."

"You invited Howard!" I blurt out and he turns his head to look at me, confused. "What if he comes?" I rub my sweaty palms over the tops of my shorts, trying to steady my nerves.

"What's the big deal? You invited Sylvia. Howard was way cool, super down to earth. Didn't ask me for an autograph or a picture. Instead, he asked me how I like driving your car. He wants to buy his wife the same one," Ace says. I sigh and he sniggers. "Tell me why it bothers you, Sprinkles."

"It doesn't," I bark out in a mild but completely obvious panic while shrugging. He's not buying my pathetic act.

"My parents had mentioned him and his wife having an adorable son Drew's age. I didn't think it was a big deal," Ace says. "Do you hate him?"

"Howard?" I ask as if I am just catching up to the conversation. "Or his kid?" I almost choke on my own words. *His kid? Why on earth would I even mention his kid?*

"I'm getting this strange feeling that you're hiding something," he says, waggling his finger at me. "An affair?"

"I would never," I scoff as I roll the charm on my necklace back and forth. "I hope you were kidding?"

"You're so cute." I roll my eyes. "Of course I'm kidding, he's not your type anyhow." He shrugs.

Except he is...

CHAPTER 17

❝Is it normal for Boo to take this long of a nap? She didn't nap this long in Yosemite," Ace asks as he turns off the engine in Tater's driveway.

"No. She slept horribly last night on that crap mattress you bought her." His contagious laugh fills the car and my soul. There isn't much negative things to think of him, is there? "I'm kidding. I think I should move it in my bedroom because I loved it."

"I'll send you a king and I can set it up Monday after the reunion." He shrugs.

"Ace, stop buying us mattresses." I burst out laughing and he easily joins.

"I'll carry her in. Where should I lay her?" His gentle assistance is refreshing and quite welcomed.

"She sleeps in Uncle Tater's bed."

He's so careful and gentle as he pulls her limp limbs out of the buckles. He carries her up the front porch, and I'm overwhelmed with emotion. She looks so miniature in his giant arms. He smiles at me while he carefully opens the door to Tater's house.

"What?" he asks softly.

"You're just very good at this."

"This," he says and points to Drew, "is easy." Then he points to me and adds, "You, however, are not."

"That's good. No woman wants to be called easy," I quip and

he shakes his head in amusement.

"I'll be right back to help with the booze and the thousand dollars' worth of meat," he says as I watch his high and tight booty.

"A thousand dollars? Good thing you got that huge signing bonus the whole country was talking about," I tease.

He looks happy and triumphant. "So you do follow me?"

Hard not to but I don't point it out. Instead, I busy myself with the full car as he shuts the door behind him. I take a deep breath and wish I could turn off my emotions, but his cute tushy makes it near impossible.

"Hey gorgeous," a familiar voice rings out. I peek my head around the car and see Justin walking down the front porch. His smile is suggestive as always, dark hair coiffed to perfection with his smoldering eyes taking in every inch of me, making me feel small and exposed. He's not extremely tall. For someone of my stature, though, he would be considered the perfect size. About the size of Dexter. He for sure works out, as his fitted polo and nicely tailored chinos showcase his definition. He walks toward me with smoothness and swagger. Does he stand in the mirror and practice that seductive strut? When he is standing right in front of me, his arms snake around my waist. My toes lift off the dirt as he spins me around. "Lily, you look amazing."

"Hi Justin," I say, melting into him and the intoxicating animal magnetism he exudes all the time. "You look good."

"Not as good as you. Please tell me Ace hasn't swept you off your feet yet," he says with a devious smile as he stretches his neck out to look me in the eyes.

"Well, he is pretty charming as you remember." I pause and stare in his eyes. "Could you set me down? This is getting uncomfortable."

"Aw, I'm sorry. I'm just stuck right in the middle of nostalgia seeing all of you at the same time." His eyes are shimmering with joy and his hearty chuckle is the same. "And you look so gorgeous. Every time I see you, I can't help but think you're the one that got away."

Still every bit as flirtatious. The comment makes me feel so uncomfortable. I feel weird about Kylie, his wife, and even Ace who is going to walk out any minute. I look away from him, waiting patiently for him to put me down.

"Now would be good," I say. A laugh escapes those perfect lips, and he sets me gently on the ground. He steps back and looks me up and down with a devious glint in his eyes. *He's so bad.*

"Dang, you haven't changed at all. Like I just let you out of a time capsule," he says with a hypnotic smile.

"I don't know if that is a compliment or not, but I feel older and less shiny."

"You're just as shiny." He reaches around me to grab an armful of booze. "Kylie and I figured the last time the five of us were all together was Christmas night when we were twenty-one. Don't remember the year but we all went to Willy's so we had to be twenty-one."

"Sounds right," I say nonchalantly.

I know for sure it's right. I will never forget that night. Ace and I had sex, despite both of us being attached to other people. I remember crying the next day because I didn't want to say goodbye to Ace. I was so conflicted with my feelings for Ace, and I was terribly ashamed of cheating. The mere memory makes me feel guilty.

"Well...." Justin trails off with a look of amusement on his face. "You even listening?" *Oops.* "Is the tree house still there?" Justin asks, referring to the one in Ace's parent's backyard.

"Oh, yeah...It's still there," I say and grab a bag of meat.

"We have to go get a picture of the five of us in there." We spent many days and nights in that tree house as kids.

"There has to be a weight limit. Have you seen Ace? No way we can all climb in there." Our harmonic amusement feels quite comforting.

Justin talks about his life with animated eyes, and I smile the whole time because he is adorable. He decided not to bring his kids last minute, thanks to a fight he had with his wife.

"Bummer!" I say. "I was looking forward to meeting them. And I'd love to meet your wife. She's gorgeous." I haven't heard the best things about her from Tater and Kylie but I'm all about being polite.

"I will bring the kids next time, but you had your chance to meet Maria on our wedding day," he says, annoyed. I shrug. I backed out last minute, telling Justin and everyone that I was sick. Truth is, I didn't want to see Ace.

Kylie comes bounding down the front step.

"Oh my god, doesn't he look so handsome?" she squeals as she cracks open a cold beer. Justin lunges for her and starts doing what he does best, flirt with a pretty woman. Kylie flirts back as always, and it's still hysterical to watch them both be perverts.

Ace walks out with a big smile. "She woke up. I cuddled her for a few minutes so she would go back to sleep. She told me she hates Tuft & Needle," Ace says to me, then grabs Justin in a big hug.

"Dude, what is happening? Are you getting Botox?" Ace asks Justin with a look of serious curiosity.

"Don't tell me you're not!" Justin exclaims.

"Nah, that's just weird. I'm not a fan of the way it looks." Ace grabs Justin's face and starts inspecting his forehead and instructing him to raise his brows. Justin eventually pushes Ace off, but it's too late; his secret and our amusement is evident.

"You are just trying to make me look bad in front of Lily," Justin says. I shake my head and walk away.

"What a fun weekend...Two married men pining over a celibate widow," Kylie says, following after me. I throw my head back and laugh.

"Idiot!" I exclaim.

"Who? You or them?"

"You!" I shout back and keep walking. She runs and jumps on my back and I fall forward. We both start cracking up while she rolls off me and I roll on my back, which means we can't get up.

"Oh brother, you two haven't changed one bit. Still sound like hyenas," Justin says, reaching two hands down and pulling us up. "Although, Lily looks smaller, if that's possible."

"That's what I've been telling her." Ace's eyes pop out in relief that he has someone to agree with him. Anybody will agree, so I'm not sure what the big deal is.

We all stand in the kitchen, catching up with Justin before other people from town start to file in for the big reunion. I drag Kylie into the bathroom.

"Ace and I kissed last night. Like a steamy, way-more-than-friends kind of kiss," I admit with big remorseful eyes.

"Whoa. When's the wedding?" she asks, completely serious.

"Stop, I feel guilty," I say and hold my wedding ring up to her face. "Plus, he's leaving and in the middle of a very public divorce. I have Drew to think about." My head involuntarily shakes back and forth.

She has a mischievous glint in her silver eyes. "How steamy was this kiss?"

"Pretty steamy. I can't go to Dallas with him Tuesday." The revelation is impactful for me.

"You can't back out! I got a bikini wax and let me remind you in case I wasn't clear about it on the phone, that shit hurt like you can't even imagine. I earned myself an NFL husband, dammit."

"I know...Drew is already so excited," I say and fluff my hair in the mirror. "How can I go, though? It's weird now. He's trying so hard to bring up our past. Have the talk about what went wrong but..." I look at her in the mirror, and she's beaming.

"It was bound to happen, don't you think?" She pushes me aside to wash her hands.

"No. It's in the past. I don't want to dig all that up. Makes me feel..." I pause, trying to find the right word.

"Lils, he arranged a private jet for us," Kylie begs. I laugh at her facial expression, which says to me she is solely going on this trip for the private jet. "Please don't make that painful bikini wax be for nothing."

I agree to go through with our plans and then follow her to the kitchen and find Drew, resting her cheek on Ace's shoulder. My heart melts at what he could be to her. I know Ace, and he would be the best role model she could ever ask for. He could be a daddy to her...She deserves a daddy.

GET A GRIP! I yell in my head. What on earth is wrong with me? He doesn't want to be her daddy.

"Thanks Ace," I say. "I can take her from you."

"She's fine...Just woke up a bit scared," he whispers.

I find her eyes and smile at her. "Hey Boo, your cousins are outside. Want to go chase some lizards with them?" She pops her head off his shoulder.

"Yeah." She reaches her tiny smooth arms for me. I grab her and place her on my hip. She used to be so light. I won't be able to carry her much longer. Makes me so sad every time I think about it. I'll likely never have any more kids, so her growing up fast makes me feel like doors are slamming in my face.

My parents are outside catching up with Justin. I set Drew down, and she scampers off with her cousins. I grab a seat next to Justin at the table and Ace does the same.

"Who would have thought Ace Lancaster would have a failed marriage?" Justin says.

I smack his arm. "If you can't say something nice Justin...." I say, reminding him to keep his manners.

"I'm not trying to be a jerk. Just, come on, she must be the biggest bitch ever," Justin says. "Who would ever let him go?"

"Oh, I know. I can't agree more," my mom, Ace's biggest fan, says. "I won't even sell a magazine in the liquor store anymore if it has her name or her face on the cover."

"You are so sweet, Maggie, but make a profit though. Please. At the very least, something good should come of this mess I've created," Ace says, taking full responsibility for his disaster of a marriage.

"You didn't create it," my mom says like a super protective

lioness. I internally roll my eyes.

"I married her. It was all wrong from the start. I got caught up in the power of fame. We had just won the Superbowl, and I was getting a lot of attention. Meeting celebrities and such. Trina is the center of Hollywood. She can't even set her big toe out the front door without being spotted. Truth be told, it was a little intoxicating at the time. I lost my head."

"Oh Ace, you have always been so grounded. I'm sure you were fine." My mom pats his hand. Oh Mom, let the man own his faults. It's okay to have them. My dad and I both smile at one another, exchanging our secret amusement.

At that moment, Devyn comes running up. "Auntie! Drew is hurt," she yells with fear and concern etched all over her face. Panic wraps me up like a tight burrito. I fly up and run behind Devyn as she leads the way to the back of the house. Drew is laying on the ground crying. She has scrapes on her legs.

"Boo, what happened?" I am surprised by how calm I am.

"She fell from that tree," Devyn says and points to the limb above my head. *It's so high.* "I told her not to move like Daddy taught me."

Stay calm.

"That was quite a fall. Where does it hurt?" I ask her, quietly praying she didn't break anything.

"My arm hurts." My parents, Ace, and Justin all bend down.

"Devyn, how did she land?" I ask her.

"On her side and then she rolled over on her back."

"Drew, how does your neck feel?" my dad asks.

"Fine. Just my arm hurts." Her crying has stopped.

"Can you move it?" Ace asks.

She smiles at him and picks her arm up and moves it. "Yep." She's pleased with herself. My dad sits her up, and my brother comes running out to check on his niece. He looks her over and gives her the clean bill of health with strict orders to eat as many Popsicles as her tummy can handle, which makes her laugh.

"No more climbing trees," I say and squeeze her tight.

"Mommy, I'm really good at it though." I try not to roll my eyes at her sweet face.

"Boo, go get a Popsicle before I wring your little neck." She laughs like she always does when I say it to her. Her and Devyn grab hands and walk into Tater's house while I try to release the tension. I look into my dad's calm eyes for reassurance. "Man...I almost had a full heart attack." A small strained giggle escapes me.

"Couldn't tell you were in that state. You seemed calm."

"I don't feel so calm...I just want to cry." I bury my face in my hands to push the emotion away. "I thought she broke something or was paralyzed for life. That tree is so high! Being a freaking parent is so stressful. How did you have three of us?"

My dad puts his arm around me. "When you were nine, we took a pontoon boat out with the Millers. I had only driven a pontoon once before and the propeller was a bit tricky. I thought it was off and you were the first to jump in the water from the back of the pontoon. The propeller sucked you underneath and your mom screamed that you had vanished, and I hit the emergency button. You used your instincts and grabbed on to the side of the boat and hung on for dear life. When the propeller stopped, you surfaced, and I broke down in tears. Sometimes, after all these years, I still have nightmares about what could have happened. What would my life be like without you? As parents we worry and we protect, but sometimes we are the ones that fail and we can only hope by the grace of God that you are protected. Sometimes I lay awake and think, what if he spared you for me in trade for Dexter? Sometimes I wonder if it was one of the other kids there that day, would they have had those instincts or...would we have had a more devastating outcome? It was and remains a reminder of how precious you are to me." His eyes are shining with emotion. "We're all just reminders of how precious life is."

"Dad, why have you never told me this?" I ask with tears pouring down my face. "I do like to be reassured that I'm not completely crazy. This story lets me know I'm not the only parent who is terrified I'm doing everything wrong."

"I don't know...It never felt right till now."

"It's the perfect story! So, I'm not crazy being so scared with her?" I ask him.

He pats his heart and smiles. "No, being a parent isn't easy and sometimes scary as hell! I had a moment like that with all three of my kids. Something scary that I still carry around. Cam almost fell out of a two-story window by balancing on the ledge on his stomach, legs and arms stretched out because he thought he was Superman. I didn't see Rose when she was two standing at my feet when I was moving a pot of boiling noodles to the sink to drain. I tripped on her and the scalding pot and all its contents fell to the floor, miraculously missing her."

I wrap my arms around my dear sweet dad and hug him tightly and then realize everyone is still standing around. Cameron, my mom, Ace, and Justin all stare at us. I do remember that day, but I never knew it haunted my dad. I never thought much of it. I guess that is his point; my fears are not hers at this young age. Never knowing about my dad's fear was a good thing. Children are meant to be fearless and confident.

"Okay, enough of these pussy stories," my brother shouts out in mock annoyance, lightening the mood like only he can.

"I can't believe you're a doctor," I say as he helps me to my feet. "You are heartless."

"You don't need a conscience to be in medicine, only a degree!" he says. "You did good, sis! Your husband is still dead, but you did great."

"You're insane." I hit him in the stomach. "Always a joker."

"Let's get you a drink!" Justin says and puts his arm around me. "I can see after all these years I had you on a pedestal...but you're way too crazy for me." I throw my head back and laugh.

"And whatever pedestal I had you on burned when you cheated on your wife." He rubs his face and grimaces under what appears to be a cloud of regret hanging over his head.

"We can't all be the Ace Lancaster's of the world," Justin says, looking up at Ace. I give Ace a big smile. He is one in a billion for sure. I wonder if that is why Ace is taller than all of us because, metaphorically, we all look up to him. His high achievements, morals, and of course his finely sculpted tushy.

"Lily." I turn around and see a nervous Kylie and Tater.

"What?" I ask, preparing myself for the worst. My heart can't take anymore today. First I wake to my dead husband hating me, the guilt of that amazing kiss, running into Howard, Ace and I having a sort-of fight, Drew getting hurt and now...

"Howard," Kylie says, and Cameron bursts out laughing.

"Is he here?" Cam asks with that amused glint he gets in his eyes whenever Howard and I are around each other. Kylie and a scared Tater both nod. "This night just got fucking awesome!" He throws his head back.

"Cam," I whine and he ruffles my hair as if I'm still six. "Please...don't do this."

"Okay, what's with Howard?" Ace asks, looking around to everyone's faces for an answer.

"Lily thinks he looks like Dexter," Cam says through cruel laughter.

I fold my arms under my chest and glare at him. "He does."

"Not even a tiny bit. I love you, but you're nuts when it comes to your dead husband."

Jerk!

"Never mind them," my dad says and puts his arm over my shoulder, turning me away from Cam, who is only poking fun of me at this point.

"Nobody, not one person, even sees it, but Lily thinks he's been sent here to haunt her," I hear Cam say as we walk away.

"Cam...he reminds her of him for some reason. Stop being a jackass or I'll make it so you can never have that fourth baby," Kylie threatens. I feel a swell of pride for my amazing best friend. To me, Howard embodies Dexter. I think they look alike. Same voice, same sense of humor. It's annoying Cameron makes fun of me for this. I was Dexter's wife and I knew him better than anyone.

When my dad and I sit back down, I watch Cameron, Tater, Justin, and Ace all in a deep conversation where we left them. Maybe it's self-centered, but I know that deep talk is about me.

And Dexter...and maybe Howard...

CHAPTER 18

~

At about 9 PM, my parents take all the grandkids home. More people from high school keep showing up until the wee hours of the morning. Howard's haunting stares throughout the evening keep me from relaxing until he leaves with his family. I can finally breathe again.

People I haven't seen in years came into town for this, even May Appleton, which is bizarre. She keeps cornering me with stories of success, and I get the feeling she's happy that my life sucks.

Justin, Tater, and Ace tell story after story and keep us all laughing. Kylie and I stumble to the guest room at about 2 AM, laughing hysterically, and she insists on showing me her vagina after her "botched wax job."

I throw myself on the bed in a fit of laughter and wait for her to get her old 501 cutoffs, from middle school, off. She put them on wet because they were tight, and she wanted them to stretch. They are still tight. She looks adorable and was flirting with all her old high school flames in front of Stan, who left hours ago in a rage. He doesn't want her going to Dallas. For someone like Stan who isn't willing to put her first, he still knows he will never get better than her. Losing her is scary for him. Must be hard being that stubborn and selfish.

She finally gets the shorts off her hips and my jaw drops. "They took *all* the hair?" I ask, gobsmacked.

"Everything is gone," she says, clearly upset, which kills me. "I had to strip down and then she made me throw my knees up to my ears so she could get my crack." She looks mortified and I scream in laughter. "Did I mention she was training a girl so I had an onlooker watching the whole show?"

"What a show!" I manage to say as tears stroll down my cheeks.

"Yeah...what a show is right. I'm not sure who to feel more sorry for, her or me." She pulls her small cutoffs back up and winces. She decides against wearing them to bed and grabs a pair of shorts Tater put on the dresser for me to sleep in.

"Kylie, will it ever heal?" I ask. It's red. Really red. It looks so angry about its bald life. *Is it swollen?*

"Probably not! How will it even be possible for me to land an NFL husband with this poor puffed-up puss?" she says with a fake cry.

"It looks like it got beat with a sock full of nails and rocks. I'm going to get you some ice. We need to heal it up so you can land your man," I say with compassion. She lays on the bed, nodding, like she really needs this attention. I walk out into the kitchen and fill a Ziploc bag with ice. When I close the freezer, I turn around to a smiling drunk Ace leaning against the wall.

"You two sneaking off?" he accuses in a playful tone.

"Yep," I admit with an exaggerated giggle. *I'm drunk.*

"What is the ice for?" he asks.

I look around, making sure there is nobody around to hear, and then I tell him about Kylie and her puffed-up puss. We laugh so hard. When we stop, we land in an awkward silence that is totally unlike us. I look away. He wraps a hair tendril around his finger.

"All week I have been crazy jealous of Justin coming back. I should've gone home last week, but I stayed to come between you two. I was so happy when you told him cheating on his wife scared you off," he says with serious eyes.

"He's a dog. I guess he always was, and I was just blinded

by years of friendship and love." I sigh. "It was always you...not Justin. I'm sorry for never telling you that. I think I enjoyed the drama a little bit back then. Two hot guys *fighting* over me." His eyebrows raise in amusement. "I know, not as sweet as most people think."

"You're pretty sweet, Sprinkles. As near perfect as any woman could ever be." His eager eyes look me up and down, sending an almost painful surge of electricity through me. His hand finds its way down to my arm, leaving a trail of blazing heat in its wake. My head is swimming with thoughts of the last time we were intimate. How on earth can I resist him?

Don't.

I spring up and kiss him. His arms go around me and pull me closer. He's so tall I'm having a hard time kissing him with my short stature, which was always an obstacle with him. He lifts me off the ground still kissing me, igniting an inferno in me. My heart is pounding out of my chest as he peppers kisses down my neck. My head is flooded with memories of the last time we had sex and how amazing it was. Christmas night...in the bushes...in his room. I feel faint at the idea of sex with him. I want him so bad it hurts.

Kylie screams my name, and I quickly push him away. Despite how good it feels, guilt and shame about so many things plague me. When our eyes meet, I glance away before that look in his eyes kills me. I need to get out of here before we end up in a bush. I'm a mother now. I shouldn't have sex with anybody in a bush, especially someone that lives the famous life so far away and going through a divorce.

"Okay, friend. Remember your promise," I say as I pick the ice pack off the ground that I dropped in the heat of the moment.

"You kissed me," he says with a big cocky smile.

My mouth drops. *Damn, he's right.*

He looks so arrogant that it gets under my skin. "You did and you know it." I squint at him and he smugly chortles. I did kiss him, but he started it by talking about his feelings.

Kylie yells for me again. "Coming!" I shout back.

"None of this anymore," I say as I walk away with my heart pounding out of my chest.

He rolls his eyes and it's just about the sexiest thing I've ever seen. "Sprinkles, come back. I want to kiss you again." I hear him say as I shut the door.

I jump in bed and tell Kylie about the steamy second kiss, while she ices her botched wax job.

"Oh my god...You need to bone him!" she yells. I cover her mouth and shush her.

"Kylie, there are still like twenty dudes sitting around that fire right outside this window. Not to mention May Appleton, who has been obnoxiously overjoyed all night at how bad my life turned out."

"Just bone him," she yells again. "Screw May! I hate her dumb hair. Did she walk into the salon with a bowl and say take me back to the days when this shit was cool and E.T. had just gone home?"

We both laugh so hard she falls off the bed and then I run out into the hall to pee because my bladder can't take it. When I come out of the bathroom, I bump right into Ace. I look up at his face, and it's our undoing. He grabs me and places his warm lips onto mine. We breathlessly make out like we're fifteen again.

"That was you that time," I say as I push him away, coming to the revelation that this needs to come to an end.

"Lily, you are just way too cute for me to resist. I still have *big* feelings for you after all these years." He pushes me against the wall and tries to kiss me again, but I move my head.

"Ace, we are just drunk and caught up in old feelings." I duck under his arm, but he grabs me and puts me back, smiling irresistibly.

"These are not old feelings," he proclaims. "I'm even crazier about you than I was."

"Ace, I don't know what this is, but you and I are both drunk," I say and pat his chest. He lets me escape from his giant arm trap.

I shut the guest room door and I hear him yell on the other side, "These are new feelings!" I smile as little *new feelings* of butterflies swarm my belly.

Kylie and I talk for several minutes about Ace and his *new, big* feelings for me. Then we erupt into a raucous of laughter as always before falling asleep with *big* smiles on our faces.

~

I wake up early to the sound of boats and like fifty motorcycles driving around in my brain. I roll over and look at Kylie and start laughing. All it ever takes with the two of us is one look. Just the one reveals everything. She's hungover, last night was hilarious, she iced her puss, and I made out with Ace Lancaster, who has *new, big* feelings for me. Oh, and Justin gets Botox. And she hates May's E.T. hairdo.

"I swear you two laugh in your sleep." I hear a familiar muffled voice and hang my head over the edge of the bed to see Ace and Justin on the floor.

"You two look so cute cuddled up," I say and pat Ace's head. He is right up against the bed.

"We were afraid Stan was gonna write on us if we slept on the couch," Ace says, smiling up at me. "Needed to take refuge behind a locked door."

"Stan came back?" Kylie asks with an eagerness in her voice. "Did he ask for me?"

"Not to me he didn't," Ace says. "He was probably giving you space so your poor puffed-up puss would heal!"

Kylie hits me. "I can't believe you told him!"

"Then he told Tater and I," Justin says.

"I hate you all," she says, standing off the bed.

"How is it this morning, Love?" Justin asks. Kylie jumps on him and tickles him until he pins her on the ground and makes her scream uncle.

"I think we should be more concerned that these two keep

kissing." Kylie points to Ace and I. I throw my empty water bottle at her head for bringing it up.

"It never used to concern us," Justin says. "I think we should marry them off this weekend and be done with it."

"The only problem, genius, is his wife," I look away from them feeling incredibly regretful and stupid.

I lay and stare at the ceiling and listen to these three giggle and recap our reunion night. Tater pops his head in with a huge smile. "I have breakfast burritos being delivered from the restaurant. Mimosas and Bloody Marys are set out. Come join me." He starts to shut the door but peaks his head back in. "Oh and Kylie, I have a big bag of ice for you."

Kylie throws a shoe at Tater and we all die of laughter. I can see this joke will be one that we tell and say for the rest of our lives. Kylie turns to me. "I hope you're proud of yourself," she says, but I know she really isn't mad.

"Kylie, it's adorable. You tried something new. How does it feel today?" I ask seriously.

"Much better, and I'm gonna rock my bikini today."

Justin tickles her. "Yeah, you will. Still hot, Kylie."

I return my gaze to the ceiling, even though I can feel Ace staring up at me. I am trying to avoid him because I want to make out with a married man and that makes me feel so evil.

"Let's go eat," Ace says to me. I give in and roll on my side and look down at his cute face. "Come on, Sprinkles."

"I'm not hungry," I say.

"I am. I'm done trying to fit in my junior high clothes," Kylie says. I crack up at her attempt.

"Why would you even want to look like you did in eighth grade?" Ace asks in disbelief. "You weren't cute then." *I can't breathe.*

"I just want my eighth grade body back," Kylie says in utter shock that Ace can't understand that. They have never understood one another. They get along and love each other, but it stops there. "I'm gonna get high before breakfast. Lily, you want to join?" she asks in a super condescending way.

"I'm off weed," I remind her.

"What?" Justin shouts at me. "Lils, you're the best *on weed*." Kylie beams with what can only be validation.

"That's what I said! Mr. Perfection here and Daddy Tater told her she was no good on it. Ace threw all kinds of money at the problem and put her in weed rehab and, well, my heart is broken," Kylie says, straddling Justin's waist like they're a couple.

"Dummies!" Justin yells. Ace rolls his eyes and laughs. "What about the time she was *soooo* high she convinced me she was having a heart attack? I almost called 911 but you stopped me and had to basically give her mouth to mouth because she was yelling, 'My body is shutting down.'"

"Dude...it wasn't cool. She freaked me out and ruined my high. I was so worried about her." *Aw, I love him.* I flip my lower lip at his sweet confession. "Last time she was high, Cam had to give her a Heimlich because she was laughing like a hyena and choked on a grape."

"What about when she—"

"Decided that crayons were yummy...or the time I tried to confess my crush on Mr. Appleton? I wanted to drive to his house and tell him that I was in love with him and he was my one and only soulmate." I rub my face. "I told you guys I was going to slice Mrs. Appleton's throat if I had to. I'm aggressive *on weed*."

"Yeah." Justin stretches his smile into an awkward angle, finally coming to terms with the severity of my actions. Kylie swats his chest while snorting gently.

"Don't jump ship, Justin. She's hysterical. In her defense, Mr. Appleton was so hot," Kylie says.

"Not that hot," I say.

"Still likely hotter than Kylie in eighth grade," Ace sniggers.

"Ace." Kylie rolls her eyes as she looks at the ceiling. "Can I please have a piggyback ride to the kitchen?" Ace stands and offers her his hand for assistance while Justin and I watch in adoring amusement.

They leave the room bickering about her hair in eighth grade. Ace points out her blunt bangs, asking where they went terribly wrong and arguing they made her look like Frankenstein. Justin turns and looks at me after they make their exit.

"You okay? You freaked about Ace?" He lays by me on his stomach with his chin in his hands. There has always been something so mysterious about Justin. Sure, he's a devious sex hound, but he is one of the best listeners. He always gives really sound advice.

"Totally. He's married and technically I am too. I was ready to die an old maid and now I kind of want him, but he is an NFL star always traveling. He's going through a disaster of a divorce and I have Drew to think about. I feel guilty about Dexter. I should be with him and Drew should have a daddy."

"Lils, you need to get out of that pretty head of yours. I'm sorry your husband died." His words are gentle. "He is gone, and it is sad and horrific. But you have your health, an adorable daughter, and he'd love you both forever. You are the kind of girl that makes all of us guys want to be a better man."

"Okay Jack Nicholson," I say with a smile.

"It's a good line and so true when you meet a girl you want to be with. You still motivate me to be a better man. Only, I love you enough to know I could never do it. Not all guys can. Ace, though...Well, you can always trust him. He's a huge NFL star and still so down to earth."

I sigh because that's a good point. So famous but still just as humble as our years in high school. He truly is one in a billion.

"I know this goes against all of our codes of conduct, but do you think we could work?" I ask. We all made a pact a long time ago not to talk about each other with others in our group. None of us abide by it, clearly.

"You and I? I have always wanted it to work," he teases. I swat his arm. "You and Ace have that special thing. Why did you talk to me after Dexter died but not Ace?" Justin pinches my arm. "And admit you didn't come to my wedding because of him."

I take a deep breath and grab his cheeks in my hands. "I miss you. Why did you cheat on your wife?"

"Changing the subject? Still a coward," he says with his bad boy smile and bedroom eyes that always make women lose their minds. "Same reason I cheat on everyone...I get bored. I want to be the good guy but deep down, I'm just a bad guy." His eyes squint, putting emphasis on just how bad he can be. "She wants a divorce and I'm not going to fight her. I don't think I can do the whole dad thing."

"Who's the coward now?" He nods. "Maybe you should change your vocabulary and say you don't want to do the whole dad thing." His bedroom eyes reveal sadness. It makes me realize Justin is kind of a closed book when it comes to emotion. It's not easy for him to be vulnerable.

"I don't want to be a dad," he says and then sits up to grab his chest. "Oh, that hurt...That really hurts."

"Sometimes I wish I wasn't a mom, and every day I wish I wasn't a single mom," I admit. "Not because I don't love her, but it's isolating at times and I'm for sure over my head. I battle myself internally with guilt over not being good enough for her."

"Thanks for trying to sink to my level, but I think we know it isn't possible." He grabs my hand, pulling me out of the comfy bed. "Let's go eat, gorgeous." He stops me as I'm about to walk out and grabs both my hands gently and takes a deep breath. "You can have him if you want. Everything else will work itself out." He looks so sincere, almost as though he wants to cry. "When we were younger, I caused a lot of drama for the both of you. I know I adored you but more than that, I wanted to beat him at something. He's too perfect and it bothered me. I'm sorry for always being such a jackass."

"Aw, what is this?" I ask. "We were all young and caused drama. All I know is that when Kylie and I had that huge fight over who was going to be the announcer for the boys' softball game, I couldn't stop crying. You were so devoted to cheering me up that day. We ditched fourth hour and you took me to Ma's and made me laugh for hours. You were and still are so much fun. All I ever will remember is the good times. You're my bestest friend!"

"I want you to know I won't do that this time around," he says and looks so remorseful. "I was such a shit back then when it came to you two."

He hugs me quickly, which makes me think of how I hug Ace forever. I want to hug him now. It feels like what I need. Not just a want, but a need for that kind of intimacy.

CHAPTER 19

~

Boating was fun and Drew had a blast. I went on the boat with my parents, Cameron, and his family. I stepped on the reunion party boat a few times and laughed with them, but I was happy to get a little distance between Ace and I. So many people were out on the lake, and it was a little stressful. I went tubing with Drew though and she loved it. She also went with my brother, Ace, Tater, and Kylie. It was like Drew day on the tube. We got a million pictures of her and Jeanie is getting one framed for her as promised.

After my parents took the kids home, Ace made a couple pitchers of Moscow mules and we watched the sunset over the lake. Many people came and went throughout the night. I stuck like glue to Cameron and Jeanie until they walked home to go to bed. I tried to go with them, but Kylie dragged me into the bathroom and I got a ten-minute lecture on being a wimp and running from my feelings.

On Sunday, just the five best friends went boating. We all agreed to make this a yearly reunion, no matter what is happening in our lives.

I drive Justin to the Whimsy airport so he can head home.

"I will text you when I land safely," he says while hugging me on the curb. "Have fun in Dallas."

"I will, and I'll give you a full update on how Kylie's poor puffed-up puss does with the Dallas Cowboys." We both laugh at our favorite joke of the weekend. "Hey, so you guys went to bone town once."

He nods his head, looking a little sheepish. "Secrets don't work in this group."

"I guess I just never knew you saw her that way."

"Lily, I see everyone that way," he admits. "I'm a pig."

"So, she was just some random hookup for you?" I ask in complete disbelief. There is no way I can see him using Kylie.

"Kylie is like..." He looks lost in thought. "You know, this isn't a conversation for outside the airport."

"What kind is it then?" I ask with my hands on my hips. He looks deep in contemplation. "Don't even admit that you used her. I may never talk to you again."

"Lily...I..." He smiles slowly. "I promise I didn't. Can we leave it at that?"

I squint my eyes. "You are dismissed, but this conversation isn't over. Something feels very off about this *vibe* you're putting out right now."

"Okay, Lils. A raincheck for sure. Maybe over a candlelit dinner and wine?" he teases. Such a relentless flirt.

I drive to my parents to pick up Drew. My mom is on me like white on rice as soon as I walk through the door.

"Did anything happen between you and Ace this weekend?" Her pretty green eyes are going to pop out of her skull if she doesn't chill.

I roll my eyes and my dad does the same.

"Mom, we kissed a couple of times and honestly, I feel so guilty about it I want to just crawl into bed and skip Dallas," I say.

"You have nothing to feel guilty about. I am so tired of this... Dexter..."

"Let her be! Don't tell her how to feel," my dad says, folding up the *Whimsy Gazette* and slamming it on the table. "Honestly Maggie!"

They start bickering while I yawn for a solid five minutes before I walk down the hall and crawl into bed with Drew and Devyn to cuddle. I spend the day eating Goldfish and watching kids shows. When Drew and I get in the car to go home, it's almost dinner time.

When I pull in the driveway, Ace is sitting on my front porch. He looks as gorgeous as ever. Drew squeals in excitement and despite the little flurry of desire I always feel upon seeing him, I'm anxious about this impromptu visit.

"Hey, how are you?" I ask while Drew runs and hugs him.

"Good. Can we talk?" Ace asks with a cautious smile.

"Sure," I say, trying to sound casual, but my palms are sweating. I kept my space from him the rest of the weekend. "Come on in. I thought you came to set up my mattress." My Tuft & Needle arrived and is sitting on the front doorstep, along with several other packages.

"I'll take care of that, then we can talk." His smile could melt the damn polar ice cap.

I put the key in the front door. "Mommy, I want to unlock the door," Drew whines and my head pounds a little harder. Kids and hangovers don't mix.

"Just let me do it," I whine back.

"No, you told me this was my job from now on," she pouts with a petulance that could never be rivaled. The thing is, it takes three minutes for her to do it because it's a tricky lock that needs to be fixed. My dad and Cam always forget, even when they come over to specifically fix it. I'm just about to lose it when Drew puts her hands on the keys to take over.

"Sprinkles." Ace lightly brushes my hand away from the keys. "Give her a minute."

The sigh that I release could never be rivaled as Drew flashes me an irritated smile.

Tell me about it, girl!

I'm tired, hungover, my front door lock sucks, she's a handful, and I'm sexually frustrated because Mr. Big Shot has a cute tushy. That's what I'd love to explain to her. After a solid three minutes that almost bring me to my knees to pray to God to help guide her tiny hands, she finally unlocks it.

"Good job, Boo. I'm going to fix this thing real quick," Ace says as he twists and turns the handle, trying to figure out what's wrong with it. "Can I go through the garage to find what I need?" I watch Drew do a quick somersault in the entryway before she runs to her room. She missed her American Girl dolls. I missed my house, my bed, and my sobriety.

"You don't need to fix it," I say and yawn. "You've already got a long list of chores to do now that you're here." He laughs and despite my better judgment, I turn my face to take in his warm smile. *Big mistake!* He's just so sexy and a physical yearning envelopes my entire being.

I plop down on the couch and pat the open spot by me for Ace to join.

"I don't ever want to drink again. Maybe at the next reunion, but Drew is in a foul mood and I have so much to do. I wish I had Harry Potter here to wave his wand and tidy it up." I sigh as I look at the dusty coffee table. "What's up?" I force a smile while I rest my tired head back and momentarily close my eyes. It feels so good. I need to go to sleep at 7 PM when Drew goes down. That's what I always say, but then I get sucked into my freedom and stay up way too late.

"You've been ignoring me after you kissed me. I hate it." He looks distraught as he runs his hands through his hair. Like it was hard for him to say.

"You kissed me in the hall," I say defensively.

"Yeah, but you kissed me first." I shake my head in amusement. "Why are you ignoring me, Sprinkles?"

"I haven't been ignoring you," I say. He laughs at my blatant lie. "Okay, I have been avoiding you, not ignoring you."

"Call it what you want, but I can't spend a week in Dallas with you avoiding me in my house," he says. "What is going on?"

"I just feel guilty and confused," I take a deep breath. "I don't want to say goodbye or get my hopes up."

"Our goodbye is far away and when we do, it will now remain a temporary goodbye. We can still talk after I go home. We can plan visits. Let's just have fun while we're in Dallas." He squeezes my hand gently. "Why are you stressed out about something that hasn't happened yet?"

Because I love you, dummy.

"You're right. Let's just have fun. Now let's set up my mattress. I won't lie, I'm excited to sleep on it tonight." I wish I didn't have feelings for him. "Also, what are all these?" I walk to the entryway where Ace set all the packages.

"Just some other things I thought you might like," he says.

"For me?" I'm a little blown away. Ace has always been a very generous person, but his status has catapulted that into a new level. He's too cute.

"Yeah, and Drew." He helps me carry them to the couch. I open two Echo Shows. One for Drew's room and one for me. I can talk to Drew and watch her sleep.

"Oh my gosh that is creepy but so thoughtful and I love it!" Next I open a small pink hydro flask for Drew and several bigger ones for me. He brought one to Yosemite and I loved it. "Ace, you're way too kind! I love you!"

We both flinch at the words and then pretend it didn't happen. Being in a relationship in the past makes the word *love* such a loaded word for us.

"I sent a Tuft & Needle to Kylie and Tater too."

I raise an eyebrow. "Not Justin?"

"He has one. Otherwise I would have." He runs his hand through his hair with a cheeky smile. "I did send him something though."

"What?" I hum as I watch his muscles twitch under his Tater's tee. Man, he makes it look like a million bucks. I've never seen a Tater's tee look so good on anyone.

"A Botox package." He smiles so widely I can't help but laugh.

"Come on Big Shot," I say playfully and try to pull him off the sofa. "Set my bed up." I pull with all my might but he doesn't budge. He gently tugs my arm and I fly onto his lap. We have a fleeting gaze that makes my pulse race. I fight the powerful urge to kiss him. It's damn near impossible when his warm hand slides across my lower back. I stand up quickly, even though I want to rip all his clothes off.

After my new bed is made, I throw myself on it. He falls on it next to me and we talk about our fun reunion weekend while Drew sets up a fort out of my dirty sheets in the corner of my room.

"Mommy, can we have a pizza delivered tonight?" she asks in her messy tent.

I smile at Ace. "It's like she's reading my mind," I say. "Or she knows it's the only way she's getting food tonight."

"Why don't you take a shower and start packing? I'll order a pizza and watch Drew." My heart is doing funny things because I am such a mom.

"Now I really don't want to say goodbye to you. You are way too good to me." He grabs me and kisses my cheek, causing warm butterflies to swarm my belly. I don't want him to let go of me, so I let him hold me for a little while before Drew begs him to come in her tent.

I shower, then decide to draw a bath and take advantage of my hot friend. I can't stop thinking about him, which only makes me feel more guilty and anxious about my feelings for him. I always knew deep down inside if I saw him all my feelings would resurface. Not only that, but is it possible he is even better looking and sweeter now? I'm sure he doesn't feel for me what I am feeling for him. Everything is magnified because of Drew. He thinks we had a nice kiss and I'm pondering if I would want him to adopt her one day after we get married. I'm also very aware that some part of me has already let Dexter go, and I feel awful about that.

When the water is room temp and I'm pruned, I climb out and wrap myself in my robe and sit in the big comfy chair in my closet that Dexter bought me. I look at his empty side of the closet, his dresser that is now filled with pictures and remnants I couldn't say goodbye to. I pull out the shirt he wore to work that day and I push it up to my nose and try my hardest to imagine what he felt like in my arms, how he kissed, and what he would say about my feelings for Ace. Since I never washed it, the shirt still smells a little like him. Would we be happy now if he were alive? Would he have enjoyed fatherhood? Not everyone does. Look at Justin.

I walk across to my side of the closet and open my dresser. I pull out a picture that I have had of Ace and I since I moved to college. I kept it at the bottom of my sock drawer since I was eighteen. The smiles on our faces are the ones that make people envious. The happy times we shared seem to always flood my mind and heart when I see this. I set it down because this is not why I opened the drawer. I take a deep breath and grab the picture of Dex and I on our wedding day. I compare my smile and the men. Dexter was spontaneous and exciting. Ace is thoughtful and loyal. I remember walking down the aisle and Dexter not meeting my eyes right away. After a beat he did, but, in those seconds, I was doubtful of his love for me.

Kylie and I slept here the night before our wedding. I couldn't sleep from anticipation. I also couldn't sleep because Ace had called me every day that week leading up to my wedding. I still don't know what he was calling for and I never asked. I bolt up, stuffing the picture back in the sock drawer and put everything else away. In my bedroom, Drew and Ace are on the bed with a half-eaten pizza and she's asleep. It's so cute I can't resist grabbing my phone to snap a picture. Then I sit down and face him.

"Can I ask you a question?" I nervously ask him.

"Anything." He smiles.

"The week before I got married, you called me every day. Why?" He shrugs while looking sheepish. I raise my eyebrows, pressing the matter further. "Are we going to keep doing this, or shall we talk about it?" we both laugh.

"I want to, but then again I don't." He rubs his chin and

wears a mischievous smirk that drives me crazy.

"I get it—"

"I wanted to try and stop you from marrying him. I was devastated and always thought we would end up together." He looks almost relieved at his admission. I feel shook, almost like my body is in a blender. "Why didn't you call me back?"

Ugh...my turn already?

There's a long silence as I steady myself but I think if I want to remain sane, this all needs to be said.

"In my heart, I knew that's why you were calling. Flowers had been bought, dinners reserved, Lucille was running amuck, bossing everyone in town around, and she honestly scared me." His blank stare makes me aware that I am not answering his question. "If I took your call...if I had talked to you." I feel annoying pricks in the back of my eyes and take a deep breath while he patiently waits for me to answer his question. "I almost didn't marry him because of you." It's almost a whisper because I don't want anyone to hear. Especially Drew or Dexter. "I think this is playing a big part in my guilt because on my honeymoon, all I did was think about the mistake I made marrying him. Do you remember the promise you and I made to each other?"

"I do. We agreed to meet back here after college graduation," he says. "That last Christmas before you graduated college, we had that one night together. That is when we made the promise."

"When Tater came back from visiting you soon after I got home from college, he said you moved in with some girl named Yvonne." I roll my eyes like a jealous teenager and he bites his lower lip to stifle his amusement. I shake my head, so he knows I don't find it funny at all and he better bite that lip harder. "That truly broke my heart." He nods like he understands. "I was so sad because I always thought you'd choose me the way I always knew I'd choose you." I sigh. "Why didn't you come like you promised?"

His face falls. "I didn't come for many reasons." He sits up and lays Drew gently on the bed. He scrunches his nose so I know he's deep in thought. "I was already living the high life of going pro. I was arrogant and I thought you'd hold me back."

Ouch.

"And now? Why on earth would I get involved with you if you think I *hold you back*?" I bite. I take a deep breath to steady myself before he responds. I'm stung but deep down, I knew this is what he would always say.

"I wasn't in a very humble mind frame at that time. I told myself you'd hold me back, but I was really enjoying the stardom, the girls, the parties, and the money. When I heard you got engaged, I went into a deep spiral of depression. Then the week before you got married, I rallied myself and was determined to win you back. Only, my courage was diminished when I came home the day of your wedding. I snuck into the church, and I saw Dexter and your dad. I listened to their conversation. He loved you so much. The things he was telling your dad were so beautiful. I related so much. It was like our feelings for you were mirrored. But he was willing to give you everything I couldn't. Normalcy and Whimsy. Your two greatest loves. He seemed to be the better man."

I stopped breathing in there somewhere. *Oh...my heart.*

"You were here on my wedding day?" Hot tears slide down my cheek before I even recognize the emotion behind them. *He didn't ever stop loving me like I thought all these years.*

"Yes." He nods. "Broke my heart to walk away, but I did. For you."

"I wouldn't have married him if I had caught one glimpse of you, Ace. I wouldn't have been able to go through with it. I had all these doubts and anxiety about Dex." I stop there, feeling a little overwhelmed with these confessions. I also wouldn't have Drew, so to say more on this subject would be such a betrayal to my soul. A betrayal to her and to Dexter.

He came to stop my wedding.

Ace looks confused. "I thought you were in love with him?"

"I was...I mean, I am." I grab a tissue from my nightstand and sit back down. I think before speaking. "With you, it always felt meant to be and with Dexter everything felt..."—*forced*—"different."

His eyes flicker with what I can only guess is joy. "What are you saying?" he asks with a hopeful smile.

"I don't exactly know." I stand back up, full of so many conflicting emotions. He did come back. Late, but he did. "I don't see how we could ever make this work. But the timing feels right... No, not at all really." I laugh. "But like it was always going to happen. Am I crazy?"

"No...." he starts, but I cut him off.

"You are here, and we are both kind of single-ish. Those kisses were so...Well, I don't know the words, but I know they are somehow better than our last ones," I say while pacing my room. He laughs and then I laugh. "Are you making fun of me?" I do sound like a mad woman, speaking in half sentences and stringing many thoughts together, trying to make sense of it all.

He nods to confirm, and we continue giggling while he gently slides off the bed, careful not to disturb Drew. He stands in front of me. "We could try," he says eagerly. "I won't let you down."

"I know you would never mean to, Ace, but it's a lot to ask of you. Do you understand what she is?" He looks at Drew and then back at me. "She is my heart, and there is no way I could put her through losing you. She already loves you. With everything you have going on, I can't expect you to take on my messy life. You are..." He interrupts me and grabs me in a warm embrace. I know this is a kissing moment, but I need to make sure he gets it. "Ace, this isn't something I can just jump into. Anything we share affects a tiny little life who is already growing up missing something huge." His thumb traces the outline of my jaw as his eyes bore into mine. "My heart can't take losing you again." I gulp back the pesky tears trying to break through my eyes.

"I don't think you understand, Sprinkles," he says gently. "When I saw you at the liquor store, I knew why I came home. It wasn't to escape the media; it was to get you. Lily, I love you." I jump at his words. In what way does he mean? I stare at him. "I'm not sure if I fell in love with you again the minute I saw you or if I was always in love with you." He pauses and grabs my hand. "I think both are true. In these last ten years, I have loved other women and they have all been disasters. Makes me appreciate you even more. Makes me appreciate and miss what we had...a simple and honest love."

"We did some pretty low things to some pretty good people when we were in college." I have always felt so guilty about the times we cheated on others. We were so selfish to do that.

"Trina publicly cheating on me is my karma, I guess." He kind of laughs. "That is even more evidence we should be together. We can stop hurting others and just be the way we're meant to be. Sprinkles, I have thought about you every day since we said goodbye at that bus station. I keep a picture of you inside my nightside table, and I look at it every day." My heart races, he's done the same thing?

"Which picture?" I ask.

"The one of us at the parade on Fourth of July when we were sixteen..." he says. I abruptly pull him into my closet, I'm stunned at this revelation.

"Is it this one?" I pull out the picture of us in a foldout chair on the sidewalk with huge smiles. It was right after we had sex for the first time and this picture has always been such a huge treasure to me.

He looks amazed. "Yeah."

"I have had this picture in my sock drawer since I left for college. I stare at it all the time."

He smiles and looks so happy. "Lily, this means something. *We* can't ignore this. Out of all the pictures we took over the years we both stare at this one? Can we please try?" He pleads with his pretty eyes that are swirling with love for me.

"To ignore it?" I quip. He shakes his head, letting out a sigh of annoyance. "We probably should ignore all of this."

"Sprinkles, don't be cute right now," he teases.

"Ace, you're married. I know she is horrible and you can't wait for your marriage to be over, but I don't want to be some rebound chick."

He laughs. "Sprinkles, how can you even think that? I just confessed that I came here to stop your wedding. I'm so in love with you. I could never use you. I want this more than anything in the world. I know I will regret this moment for the rest of my life if we don't at least try." He is so sweet and sincere. I want to try too. My heart wants it so bad, but my head is shouting out many reasons this won't work. But his smile and his hand placed so perfectly around mine drowns out all those reasons.

"Okay, let's try," I say and throw my arms around him. He pulls me onto his lap as he plops into the chair. "We have to tread lightly with Drew. I don't want her hurt." His nod and soft kiss seals the deal that he understands.

Ace helps me get packed and then I carry Drew to her bed, singing to her when she starts to stir. I tiptoe out of the room and smile brightly at Ace, who is outstretched on my bed and watching baseball on the TV.

"You want to watch a movie?" he asks. I shake my head, a huge smile curving onto my lips. "Baseball?" I shake my head again. "What do you want to do then?" His smile is playful and hopeful.

I slide my robe off and slowly walk to the bed. I feel somewhat self-conscious because I'm sure my thirty-one-year-old, post-baby body isn't as awesome as my twenty-one-year-old, pre-baby body. He grabs my hand and pulls me on top of him and we make love. I push through the guilt and the heavy emotions because I want him so bad. I want this to work, and it feels refreshing to want something and someone.

We're both tangled up in my bed, completely satiated by one another's passion. The long stretch of silence isn't uncomfortable but it does leave room for my mind to wander.

"Lily, you are so beautiful. Thank you for trusting me with your heart and Drew's," he says gently letting me know that he completely understands how much her happiness means to me.

It's so sweet but gosh, I am so emotional right now. I cover my face to push back my tears. "The guilt may take a little while for me to get used to. Please don't take it personally." He grabs me tighter and kisses my cheek.

"I won't. Man, your body is incredible!"

"Really?" I ask while I roll over to face him. "I felt very self-conscious. I've had a baby and it's been ten years."

He rubs my side with his fingers. "Better than ever. It was truly amazing!" he says with sincerity.

"Ace, I haven't done that in years! I almost died it was so good." I laugh in complete glee.

CHAPTER 20

~

I'm so happy and content tangled up with Ace in this bed. Well, despite the anvil of guilt sitting on my chest right now. I'm trying to ignore it and think of how people can move on after their husbands die. I'm not a horrible person. And how can I not be happy right now? Ace is absolutely amazing and seems so sincere about loving my little Drew, too. How could he not? She's darling.

"You want anything from the kitchen? I'm gonna grab some ice cream." He kisses my cheek before standing, letting me admire his great form and bare tushy.

I shake my head and then sit back and enjoy watching him walk out of my room in just his underwear. I'm internally squealing. I get a text from Lucille telling me to repaint my white picket fence because it looks "dingy and abandoned." Also, she demands I bring Drew over tomorrow to say goodbye.

"Who you texting?" Ace asks when he sits down with a big bowl of chocolate ice cream.

"Lucille. I have to bring Drew over tomorrow morning to say goodbye." My face might split open from my smile seeing him half naked in my bed. "Also, she'd like me to paint my picket fence because, according to her, it looks awful." I roll my eyes and set my phone down. I sit up and he puts a tiny bite of ice cream in my mouth and I happily accept it.

"Fence looked fine to me," Ace says with a shrug.

"Oh, it was painted less than a year ago at her firm request. Cost me five hundred dollars. I'd like to get at least two years from it."

"Wow. She really tries to control so much." *Tell me about it.*

We eat ice cream and talk until we can't keep our eyes open. I fall asleep with a buzz of euphoria mixed with a little bit of guilt.

I'm dancing at my wedding. I can see my mom and dad at their table holding hands, adoringly watching their oldest daughter dance to her first wedding song. My brother and Tater both look so happy. I look up and see Ace's face instead of Dexter. It all feels so wrong. It's not "Unchained Melody" playing. It's something else. My mind is screaming. Where is Dexter?

I start shouting for him and punching Ace in the chest while Tater and Cameron pull me away. Kylie is in my face, saying gently, "He's dead." I'm screaming and flailing my limbs and Ace is begging me to calm down. I can't calm down...I'm supposed to marry Dexter. I ask for Drew and nobody knows who I'm talking about. "She's my daughter!" I yell over and over and over again. Then in a quick puff, everyone disappears, leaving me running around frantic in a dark void yelling out for Drew.

My body lurches forward and my eyes shoot open while I scream for Drew.

It was just a dream.

"Go back to sleep...You're fine," Ace whispers.

"I gotta get to her," I say hysterically as fresh warm tears stream down my face. My body withers against his. "I have to save her."

I'm crying? Was I crying in my sleep?

"Okay...let's go see her," Ace says calmly as he pulls the covers off himself.

I jump out of bed, nearly running down the hallway to her room. I carefully open the door and see her tiny body tangled in her blankets. As a relieved sigh hisses out of my body, the tension leaves. I cross the room and tuck her back up under the covers and kiss her soft cheek. I want to crawl into bed with her, but Ace is standing in the doorway in his black boxer briefs, concern etched on his face. He motions for me to come back. I reluctantly leave my sweet baby and take his hand.

That was my guilty conscious showing me all I would have lost if I had never been with Dexter. She is my reason for living, my reason for everything. I owe him a world of gratitude, not to talk about how I pined for someone else on our wedding day.

Betrayal...That is what I did last night. Betrayed Dexter and Drew.

"Come here, Sprinkles," Ace says once he is back in bed. I realize I'm absently standing in my room. I feel hollow. His eyes bore into me. "Was it the same dream? Was she drowning?"

"Pretty much," I say and crawl next to him. He wraps his arm around me, pulling me flush up against his chest. "Sorry I woke you."

"Don't be silly. You okay? Can you go back to sleep?"

"Yes. I'm fine." I pat his hand, reassuring him that I'm okay. He nuzzles into my hair and then I hear his soft, airy snore. Eventually after I stop beating myself up, I find a dreamless sleep.

In the morning I wake alone and notice it's 8 AM. I bolt up and run into Drew's room. She isn't there. I dash into the living room, yelling Drew's name.

"Mommy, we want to bring you chocolate chip pancakes in bed!" Drew pouts while she stirs a wooden spoon around a big bowl on the island. She's standing on a chair next to a sexy shirtless Ace.

I smile at them both before turning to grab my camera and get pictures of her messy flour-covered face and clothes. I forgot he was here. I don't mind waking up to his bare chiseled chest. *Thank you muscle gods for creating this perfection of a creature and planting him in my kitchen this morning.*

"Oh, you're cute, but I want to eat with you at the table," I say and kiss her cheek while still taking in Ace in my kitchen without a shirt on, making pancakes with my daughter. *Too good to be true.*

"Ace says I get ice cream on the plane and I get a surprise," Drew says looking truly excited for our big adventure.

"That's so fun!" I beam at her and then stand on my tippy toes to kiss Ace on the cheek. "She never sleeps this late so I was scared."

She does. I'm just a spaz.

He laughs. *Probably because he knows I'm a spaz.*

"She came out this morning while I was cleaning up your living room and wanted to surprise you with breakfast in bed," he says and then kisses me on the lips in a secret way behind her back. This is all so surreal having him here. I set the kettle on the stove to make a cup of tea feeling very dazed. When I turn around, he is staring at me, looking lovestruck. Which is what I feel. I putz around the kitchen grabbing a teabag, and when I look back at him, he's still staring with the same look on his adorable face.

"*Despacito*," I remind him. We agreed to be cool around Drew and still act like friends. I place the teabag in my favorite mug. It has a picture of Drew and I on a sled when she was two, all smiles and rosy cheeks for the both of us.

"Alexa, play 'Despacito,'" Ace says and seconds later, I've got Bieber fever.

"That's awesome! Totally creepy, but super awesome. Kind of sums up everything about you, Big Shot." I wink, grazing my eyes over his entire body.

"That wounds me." Ace feigns being offended and then taps my butt.

After a super fun breakfast, Ace goes to his parents to say goodbye, and I take Drew over to my parents to say goodbye. We walk into their house and yell for them both. They don't answer, and I finally spot them out their sliding glass door, down by the lake, sharing a sandwich. They pass it back and forth, and then my mom rests her cheek on his shoulder. That is true love right there. They don't always agree, but they sure do love each other.

I thought I was going to grow old alone. But I feel like Ace and I could have what my parents have.

Drew is becoming impatient, so I let her down and open the slider and she screams for them. My mom stands and opens her arms for her. My dad struggles to get off the ground and it breaks my heart. For me, watching my strong dad age is very unsettling. We enjoy a nice game of Go Fish at their table before our time runs out. Drew also has to say goodbye to Lucille. I buckle Drew in the car and then face my parents.

"So, I decided to give it a shot with Ace." My silly mom grasps her cheeks in her hands while her pretty eyes pool with tears. My dad grabs me in a big hug.

"Sweetheart. I'm so happy," my mom says softly. "You two have never stopped loving each other."

"Please use discretion with Drew. I don't want her to get hurt. She's my first priority. So maybe hold off on telling Darla." My dad laughs while my mom looks wounded. It's unthinkable for her to keep something this juicy from Darla. "Call Bernie, Mom. I'm sure she has been pestering Ace as much as you have been pestering me."

This seems to pacify her. "Oh, good idea. Nobody will be happier."

"I know you two worked closely to arrange the liquor store reunion," I say to her.

"No...that was all fate." She swats the idea away with her slender fingers and my dad rolls his eyes.

"Maggie, the jig is up!" I can't help but bark out a laugh.

"I'm not mad," I say and hug her. "I think I love you just a little bit more if that's even possible."

"Aw." She squeezes me firmly and kisses my cheek. "I love you, Lily." She has the most radiant smile on her face. "I hate to say I told you so, but I did," she hums and bobs her head as if she is listening to music. She nudges my dad while they both laugh. "Have fun in Dallas. If anyone deserves it, it's you."

I give my dad a big squeeze and then drive away. I can see

them waving in the rearview mirror with their arms around each other. I am one lucky girl to have them as parents.

"I already miss them," Drew says.

"Me too, Boo, but we are going to have so much fun." I smile so she can see it in the mirror.

We walk through Lucille's door and Drew runs in her arms. "How long will you be gone?" Lucille asks after they have a few moments together.

"At least a week," I say with no smile because I hate feeling like I have to tell her every single detail about my life.

"Can you call when you know?" she asks in a rather sour tone that makes my blood start to boil.

"Drew will call every morning." Drew nods in agreement.

"Every morning because I will miss you, Mimi."

They have a sweet goodbye and Lucille buckles her in the car seat. When she shuts the door, she stares at me. "You are going to keep her away from the media, right?" she asks with a heck of a lot of unnecessary attitude.

"Yes, we aren't going to be out with him at all. We will only see him at night at his house. He has a pool with a slide, a creek so we can fish, and he has quads and horses. If we take her out, it will only be with Kylie and I." I hug her because I don't want to be angry with her for loving my daughter. "Thank you for all you do."

"Just keep her safe and make sure she takes her vitamins." Lucille waves her finger at me as if I'm a toddler myself. "Changes in weather and altitude can wreak havoc on an immune system."

Really? Is she just making shit up?

I nod and smile anyway.

"If Kylie decides to use social media, then tell her to only post pictures of Drew in matching clothes." She rolls her eyes and I bite the bottom of my lip to stifle a laugh. "I don't want to see documentation of her being *paraded* all over Dallas looking like a little hobo."

That's my cue to leave. That word...

"I'll deliver the message. I've been meaning to talk to her about it anyway," I say with a huge sarcastic smile.

"Oh good. Sounds like we're finally on the same page." She almost smiles. "Lily, do you need some money? Those shorts look dingy. You have got to have something better in that closet of yours." I might as well be a stinky rotten fish with the way her face is pinched up in disgust.

I'm wearing brand new white 501 cutoff shorts and an olive long-sleeve blouse tucked in with the sleeves rolled up, paired with a beautiful Chanel belt that Lucille gave me for Christmas one year. I have on cute gladiator sandals and pretty jewelry to polish it up. I just ripped the tags off everything I have on with the exception of the belt. Mom specifically bought me this stuff for the plane ride. I look nice and I felt super good about myself until now.

"No Lucille." I'm trying to keep the irritation out of my voice. "I have money."

"Oh, how can I forget?" A very exaggerated and annoyingly musical laugh escapes her hot pink lips. As if she found the last spotted Dalmatian to make her jacket. "You have Dexter's money, which as you know used to be my money," she bites before looking me up and down as though I am her worst enemy. Like I'm a monster she has to slay to save her kingdom. "Go shopping while you're in Dallas. Dexter wouldn't approve of the way you two look like you just crawled out of trash bins. Use the money to take care of your daughter, Lily."

I have no words.

She turns on her heels and walks back to the house, leaving me frozen in shock. She glares back at me and after she shuts the door, I let out the tense breath I was holding onto. *Why is she so awful?*

I get in the car and look down at my hands in my lap that are shaking like tiny baby leaves in a hurricane. I feel insignificant under her words. *Should I give her the money back?*

I drive absently to Tater's restaurant to grab Kylie, trying to absorb Lucille's tone and her words. It was legally his, and it was in his will to give it to me. I also was on the life insurance policy. I paid on that too. That is what we did together. Should I give her Dexter's trust fund instead of it being in Drew's name? My mind is fried when I pull into the parking lot. My mood instantly lifts when I see Kylie sitting on the bench with her brand new pink suitcase, waving like a lunatic. Kylie hasn't been on a vacation in a long time and she does work really hard. She's past excited. I'd say it's more like a psychotic state of euphoria.

She jumps in the car and starts squealing and tickling Drew and I. "Girls' trip!" she keeps yelling, which makes Drew giggle.

"Ace isn't a girl," Drew says.

"Forget him!" Kylie says in a playful way. "We are just using him for his private jet."

I turn and look at Drew. "Aunt Kylie is teasing. She loves Uncle Ace."

"How'd it go with Bitch-ille?" Kylie asks under her breath so Drew doesn't hear. I look in the rearview mirror and see her with her headphones on, singing softly to *The Little Mermaid* soundtrack.

"I think she wants me to either buy a shit ton of clothes while in Dallas or give her Dexter's money back." When she gives me a perplexed look, I tell her the whole conversation.

"If I would've been there, I would have thrown a handful of dirt in her face!" Kylie whisper-yells. "That piece of poop." She is really trying not to swear in front of the swearing police in the back seat. "That money is Drew's. Not to mention you earned that shit."

"Auntie, that is a *not nice* word. Mommy tell her. Ace also doesn't like that word. He'll kick you out of his house if he hears you say that," Drew says with squinted eyes and a scrunched nose. Kylie and I look away so she can't see us laughing. "Don't laugh at me!" she yells and that really gets us going.

I barely get out of downtown Whimsy before I have to pull

the car over. We both get out of the car so we can stop laughing. When I try to get in the back seat to apologize to her, she screams in my face like a little banshee. She really hates it when we laugh at her and I wish I could stop, but this makes it even funnier.

After a few minutes, we get her in a better mood and Kylie apologizes for using a *not nice* word.

"Hey girls!" Ace beams when we pull up. He opens the back door and immediately pulls Drew out. "Boo have you been crying?" His sensitive voice makes her little lip fold over. She rests her cheek on his chest.

"Kylie said a *not nice* word," she whines and rubs her little eyes, fighting off another round of tears. She's tired after the long weekend.

"Oh no," Ace says while he winks at Kylie and I. When he turns to walk her to the plane, Kylie and I let a loud laugh rip out of us.

"Kylie, did you see her red face? It was like an exorcism." She slaps my knee. "Oh my gosh we're awful. She is sad and puffy-eyed and we almost peed our pants."

"Please, she needs to loosen up," Kylie blurts out and I grip the steering wheel for support. *Loosen up?* "Look at her, she's fine now. Mr. Congeniality smoothed it all out. Now she's gonna go meet some hot pilot and you know what Auntie Kylie is going to do?" She raises her eyebrows while using a baby voice.

"What?" I ask.

"First I'm gonna smoke this joint behind your car, and then I'm gonna get white girl wasted on the bottomless mimosas Ace promised. Maybe I'll press my tits up against the jet window and give the birds a good show." She winks and I shake my head in amusement.

CHAPTER 21

~

I climb out of my car and approach the sleek white jet. A plush red carpet pours down them from the top of the stairs, dramatically beckoning me up into the opulent aircraft. A wave of excitement pulses through my veins at this ultimate first-class experience. A polished flight attendant greets me, extending a glass of champagne out for me.

"Thank you," I say, smiling sweetly at the pretty flight attendant.

"You are very welcome, Mrs. Moore. Please let me know if you need anything at all while on board." How does she know my name? What kind of witchery magic is this? Is she a Wiccan? I look for a nametag, trying to reciprocate a pleasantry with this mystifying creature before me. "I'm Crystal," she says coolly as if her sorcery has read my mind. *Interesting.*

I walk up the steps to see the cutest thing of my life. Drew is in Ace's arms while they talk to the pilot, who puts a captain hat on her head. I pull my phone out and start taking pictures. She is beaming and all traces of Kylie saying a *not nice* word have disappeared. *Thank goodness.* I introduce myself to the pilot while Drew takes a tour of the cockpit.

The plane is gorgeous inside. There is a white leather couch and several plush chairs that recline, much better than the ones in coach. Man, they really treat us terribly in commercial coach. I'm at a loss for words as I sit down and watch a super high Kylie stumble through the door with a mimosa in her hands. I immediately laugh.

"Well, this doesn't suck," Kylie says and Drew scowls at her. Suck is a *not good* word, though not as terrible as *not nice*. I pat her leg and she looks at me suspiciously like she thinks I may laugh. When she sees I'm not, she climbs on my lap, still shooting daggers at Kylie. "Oh Boo. I'm so sorry. I have candy." Kylie pulls a lollipop out of her back pocket from Tater's restaurant as a bribery. Always a good thing to have in your arsenal with toddlers. Drew takes it and then lets Kylie hug her.

Kylie widens her eyes into saucers as she plops down in the chair across from Drew and I. "Tough crowd today."

"Just don't upset her again!" Ace snaps at Kylie in sarcasm. We all laugh, even Drew, who thinks Ace is her hero for standing up for her. "I'll kick you off this plane if you use that language here." He wags his finger at Kylie and she snorts, which pushes Drew into a fit of adorable giggles.

"Come color with me, Boo?" Kylie asks, pulling out a brand new coloring book and crayons from her backpack. Drew jumps off me and runs onto Kylie's lap, full of excitement. Kylie squeezes her again and kisses her cheek. "Love you, baby girl."

"Love you too, Auntie." Drew pulls out a crayon, gasping when she discovers they're glitter. "Beautiful." She inspects it so closely I can't help but giggle.

~

The flight is super comfy and about halfway through, Drew fell asleep and wound up taking a decent nap. Kylie was chatting on the phone with Tater, so Ace and I slipped into the bathroom and joined the mile-high club. I couldn't resist asking him if he had ever done that before with anyone else and he said he hadn't, so that's super exciting. Right now, Ace, Kylie, and I are sitting on the floor with a pile of candy in the center talking about *Game of Thrones*.

Drew wakes up and slides off the couch, her rosy cheeks

bright. "Mommy, can I eat some?" she asks sweetly.

"Yes, Boo. Pick one," I say to her. She grabs a Crunch bar and goes and sits on Ace's lap. He opens the candy for her. She eats it quietly while we all vent about *GOT*. Every few minutes, I pinch myself that she is on his lap and not mine. Does she prefer him over me? Drew never picks anyone over me. When she is covered in chocolate, he reaches for my package of wet wipes and handles it like he's been cleaning messy toddler cheeks his whole life.

"Whoa…whoa," Kylie shouts with her hand outstretched in his face. "Did you just clean her cheeks with a wet wipe without World War Three starting?"

Ace looks down at Drew, who smiles up at him. "Yeah, I guess."

Kylie looks at me with wide eyes as her head cocks in disbelief, letting me know she is offended and in complete shock. Ace stares at me expectantly. "There was an incident. Boo, you tell Ace the story." She frowns and shakes her head, but we beg and then she turns and faces him with her big intent eyes and baby teeth poking through her perfect pink lips. *Perfection.*

"Auntie Kylie tried to clean my face and I didn't like it, so I bit her like a T-rex." Drew lets out a tiny roar and Ace laughs. "She wouldn't listen to me when I said stop, so I bit her hand."

"Is biting nice?" I ask her and Drew shakes her head.

"No, but neither is using *not nice* words." Her teenage sassy voice she likes to use is loud and proud right now. She gives Kylie a serious look.

The pilot announces we are landing, so I get Drew buckled into her seat. She stares out the window, focusing on all the pools she can see. Ace points out landmarks while Kylie and I look at her fashion magazine. The landing is smooth, and Ace closes all the blinds as soon as we touch down when he sees a mob of paparazzi waiting for him to exit the plane.

"Such a celebrity," Kylie teases. "Or is just cause your wife is playing hide the sausage with an even bigger celebrity?"

"You're a real smart donkey," Ace snaps back under Drew's

intent watch from her car seat.

"I wanna play hide the sausage too. Sounds fun," Drew says innocently.

"It is, Boo!" Kylie looks oddly proud. "Auntie is very fond of it." I clap my hand over my mouth to control my hyena laugh while Ace stands, ignoring all of this inappropriate behavior amongst the toddler.

"I'm going to go talk to the press and then get in the limo. You guys stay in here and after I leave, another limo will pick you girls up and take you wherever you want," Ace says.

I smile at him. "Thank you, Ace." A swarm of butterflies whiz around in my stomach, and I want to attack him so badly. He bags up his laptop and then kisses us all on the cheek. I squeeze his hand and whisper, "I miss you already." He steps away and smiles, and I can't remove my eyes from him because he is so stunning. I want to give him a real kiss, but Drew is here.

We stay hidden on the plane and play Old Maid until our car shows up.

"Where to?" the driver asks when we get in the car.

Kylie and I stare at each other. We have no idea where we are. Neither of us have ever been to Dallas, nor are we accustomed to private jets or limos.

"What would be fun for her?" Kylie asks the driver and points to Drew.

"There is a zoo, a museum, an aquarium…" the driver recommends in a strict professional manner, ticking the options off on his fingers.

"What will it be, Boo?" I ask her, but I have a feeling she will say zoo because it's all she has talked about since Lucille took her.

"Zoo," she says without hesitation. *Knew it!*

~

Kylie is absolutely thrilled they have alcohol at the zoo for her. After we have seen as many animals as I can bare being caged up, we sit at a play area for Drew. I remember going to the zoo, Sea World, and Marine World Africa USA and loving them as kids, but now all I think about is how the animals could be missing their family. It's like an innocent man being locked in prison. Some of these places say they're rescuing them or conserving them. I wish I could believe them, but I don't. We wouldn't have to intervene if we hadn't started messing with their lives to begin with. Man fixing man's mistakes seems to be a vicious cycle. Kylie is sitting next to me in a quiet drunken state while Drew climbs the stairs to the slide.

"I had sex with Ace last night, he told me he loved me, and I agreed to give it a try." She spits out her beer. "Shocked?"

"YEAH! I want to cry I'm so happy," she says. "Does Drew know?"

I throw my head back and laugh. "You are so special." I pet her head.

"I mean, does she know you two are dating?" she asks, annoyed. "I know you didn't tell her you boned. Duh!"

I roll my eyes with my face-splitting grin. "No, we should tread lightly. Plus, what would I even say to a toddler? I think it's more of a gradual display of affection to introduce her to the idea."

"Seems logical." I nod. "Oh my word! How do you feel?" she asks while she shakes my knee with her hand. "Was it amazing?"

"It was. I have guilt about Dexter and Trina, *his wife*," I say. "I never thought I would be the other woman."

"They're getting a divorce." She snorts, showing her amusement. "And she is totally hiding the sausage with someone else."

I know she's right but technically, she is still his wife and I'm the other woman.

Kylie grabs my hand and looks at my wedding ring. *Here we go.* I pull my hand away and slide it under my thighs.

She squints at me in disapproval. "Did you say it back to him?"

"No, because what if this is just some rebound? Are we hanging on to old feelings that won't last?"

"Does it feel the same as it did in high school?"

"Yes in the safe way, but no in the passion area. I mean, he was fabulous to me before, but he has learned a few things. On the plane he—" She spits more beer out. I should probably wait for her to swallow before dropping more bombshells.

"The plane? When?" she asks, stunned that she missed it.

"When you were on the phone with Tater." I grab her beer and take a sip. She grabs the cup back out of my hand, staring pointedly at my wedding ring.

"Take it off," Kylie barks. "Dexter was—"

"Don't push me Kylie," I say in a warning tone.

"Fine, I'm getting another beer." She stumbles to the beer window while I watch Drew. She's talking to some boy with big blonde curls on his angelic head. He is darling. His mom is decked out in makeup and cheetah print pumps with her tiny shorts. *I am not that kind of mom,* I think as I look down at my jean shorts and gladiator sandals. I feel like a sad little turd next to this lady. She pulls her phone out and starts scrolling with her giant purple nails. I decide I need to quit watching her toss her silky dark hair off her tanned and sculpted shoulder and turn back to Drew.

She's sitting in the sand with the blonde boy. He hands her his sand shovel. She aggressively yanks it out of his hand before swatting him on the cheek with her free hand. No reason that should have happened. Cheetah Pumps hasn't even noticed that her poor son is getting lynched by my not-so-angelic daughter. *Loosen up, Drew!* Kylie's words ring in my ears.

"Drew, we don't hit," I say. "How would you feel if he hit you?" She glares at me with her clear eyes. "Do you think you'd be sad?" She nods and starts to fake cry. I want to laugh. "Do you think you would want an apology?"

She wipes her fake tears and hands the shovel back to the boy. "Sorry," she says. He opens his little mouth and lets out an earth-shattering scream and runs to his mom.

She glares at Drew and I like we're pig shit. I flinch, feeling like I want to pounce her. I can handle her judgment of me. Judging my pride and joy? *I'll cut her!* I grab Drew's hand and as we walk by the lady, I smile as sincerely as possible and say, "Sorry, she is learning."

She smirks. Oh, I hate her. What kind of woman wears pumps to the zoo? I redirect Drew to the slide. She has been hitting kids lately. Everyone says it's a phase, but it's tiresome. I'm always overloaded with a whirlwind of tiring emotions when she does it. *I'm a failure, she's a jerk, the other kid is a jerk, she needs a dad, maybe I should brush her hair more.* Kylie said the other night, "Trying to land a man is a mind fuck." No, parenting is a true mind fuck. My phone rings and I answer it when I see that it's Ace.

"Where are you guys?" he asks, excited.

"The zoo. Kylie is drunk and Drew keeps hitting boys. I'm ready to go before I start fighting moms," I say and giggle.

He laughs that little lovestruck laugh and my heart soars.

"I'm about done and can bring dinner home to y'all. Maybe in about an hour?"

"Great, I'll rally the troops and meet you there," I say and then we both pause. "I miss you."

"I can't stop thinking about you," he says and my smile spreads. "I love you, Sprinkles."

"I can't wait to see you." Kylie sticks her finger down her throat as she takes her seat next to me. "Kylie is gagging. I told her about us trying again. One less person we need to hide it from." I'm giddy.

"Please hide it," she slurs and I nudge her leg in amusement.

"We are gonna do more than try, Sprinkles."

By the time we hang up, I am in a trance. God, I hope this isn't a rebound. My mind keeps shifting to Drew on his lap on the plane instead of mine. She is already in love with him. It makes me happy but also nervous as hell. It's not only my heart on the line. I already know I love him, so how can my mind be saying one thing and my heart be saying something completely different? My mind is saying to go slow, be careful, don't rush into anything. My heart is a complete mess because of the conflict with Dexter, so it's hard to even make sense of it. Not to mention my intuition which is saying he's *the one*. Which one do I listen to?

I think they have all steered me wrong at one time or another.

CHAPTER 22

~

I suggest to the girls that we leave, but Drew begs to go see the otters and tigers one more time. After that, we get sucked into the souvenir shop where Kylie and I lose our heads and buy her everything, which is so stupid since she isn't even asking for half of it. It's just all so cute, and I want her to have everything in the whole world.

By the time we get to Ace's house, it's 8 PM and Drew has fallen asleep. I carry her out of the car and up to his front door. "Wow...this house," I say to Kylie.

"Marry him. Put that baby down and marry him. If you don't, I am." We both laugh as she rings the doorbell. "This could be your new home. You know he has a chef?"

"Hi." I beam when Ace opens his giant door, the biggest one I've ever seen. His smile awakens my butterflies and a giddy feeling spreads through me like fire in dry brush. He bends down and plants a soft kiss on my eager lips.

I love him.

I feel like a horny teenager. He kisses me again, but I want more. I'm like a crack fiend.

He grabs Drew which I appreciate because she is heavy and breaking my back. My jaw drops at the opulence when we walk inside. The ceilings arch high overhead. Parallel dramatic staircases frame each side of the entryway, one for the husband and one for the wife. The white marble floors look freshly shined, and I quickly kick my shoes off. Who has the job of keeping this house immaculate?

We follow Ace behind the staircase and into the huge living room with gigantic windows that look polished as well. Outside them, I can see his expansive yard and the biggest pool ever. Each piece of furniture appears custom made. No doubt this was professionally decorated. I spin around, and Kylie and I exchange knowing glances. Knowing he's rich is one thing, but seeing it right in front of me is a little different. I can see the huge dramatic kitchen from here, complete with white cabinets that extend to the ceiling and beautiful stone countertops that gleam under the huge pendant lights. This looks like Chip and Joanna got a hold of this house. Very stylish.

"Holy bat testicles, Ace!" Kylie exclaims, and we both turn to look at her overwhelmed face. "You have shiplap! I didn't think anybody actually did this!" Her face is absolutely mystified. "Man, this solidifies how bad my life sucks."

"Please don't say that word even when she's sleeping. Keep it clean," Ace warns. Our laughter echoes through the expansive home. *Mansion.*

"Ace, what did this place cost?" she asks bluntly as she spins around, taking everything in.

"More than your bikini wax," he points out.

He takes us on the tour while still holding Drew. He doesn't want to lay her down and then leave her. If she wakes up, she would most likely be scared in this giant unfamiliar place, which would be my fear. He came to that conclusion on his own. Again, my heart, my head, and my intuition are all at odds.

He leads us through the backyard after showing us every room on the main floor. His pool has three water slides, a small one and then two that mimic something straight out of a water park. It also has a zero entry, a swim-up bar, and a jacuzzi. His pool house has to be the size of my house. Maybe even bigger. It has a state-of-the-art home gym with equipment I have never seen. He leads us back to the main house to show us the base-ment, which of course has a movie theater and a bar with a mini kitchen for entertaining.

"Do you entertain a lot?" Kylie asks.

"Nope, never even come down here. I'm thinking of selling, but the location is perfect," he says. "We can watch a movie to-morrow night. I will invite some guys from the team. Some single guys."

Kylie looks elated.

Our last stop on the tour is the master bedroom that is the whole top floor. It's insane.

"A double staircase for one room?" I ask, trying to take it all in.

"This room is bigger than Whimsy," Kylie says with her jaw dragging behind her.

"That bitch took my Tuft & Needle," Ace spits as we notice an empty place where only a pile of bedding is left. "I loved that bed." I rub his back to try and comfort him.

"Just pull out your phone and pay the overnight shipping," I suggest, which earns me a warm smile and a sneak peak of his small dimple.

"I will." He bends down to kiss me while still holding Drew. I can see Kylie stick her finger down her throat out of the corner of my eye.

"I need wine." She dramatically rubs her temples.

Ace laughs. "You sure about that?"

"Where are the presents, Lancaster?" She starts down the steps.

"Not that you deserve anything...but there's several boxes on the ottoman in the living room," he says and smiles at me. "You deserve stuff though." I scrunch my nose and welcome his warm soft lips on mine. *He's so cute!*

He got many floaties and pool toys for us to enjoy while we're here, including matching flamingo floaties for Kylie and I.

He bought Drew many toys, which will make her light up in the morning. And he bought me a pillow like the one I have at home. "You were bummed you forgot yours." I can't help but kiss him.

"I love it! That is so sweet," I exclaim. "Kylie, isn't that the sweetest?"

"Honestly, I'm not that impressed. I remember reading you bought Trina some million-dollar horse when you guys started dating," Kylie says with a look of boredom on her face.

"I can't ride a horse," I say to Ace. "Plus, this is the best pillow in the whole world." I mean it too. When I travel, I bring my memory foam pillow that has cooling gel in it. I hate to sleep without it.

Ace finally lays Drew on the couch after holding her while we opened the boxes. It's hard to pinpoint all of my emotions.

I grab her favorite blanket out of her Snoopy backpack and cover her up. I bend down and kiss her, tucking her worn-out stuffed bunny in her arm. Kylie's already in the kitchen plating herself some pasta that Ace got on his way home.

"You hungry, Sprinkles?" Ace asks.

I turn and smile up at him. "Yeah."

"I'll bring you a plate so you can stay in here with her," he says gently before giving me a kiss that sends warmth through my whole body. He's very cognizant of leaving her unattended in a house she doesn't know and I love that about him.

"How was the press?" I ask Ace once we're all seated on his comfy sectional with Drew sleeping beside the three of us.

"Super annoying and intrusive. Like I would tell them how I feel about her. I'm glad I didn't know about the Tuft & Needle when they interviewed me. I may have snapped. I just bought it after she left, so it wasn't like it was hers. And the headboard was new too."

"Is she gonna take you to the cleaners?" Kylie asks.

"Nah, she is doing fine financially and we both signed prenups." Ace shrugs.

"How romantic! The stuff true love is made of." Ace rolls his eyes.

"I know...The whole thing was a joke to begin with, including the million-dollar Thoroughbred. I hope she trips and breaks a tooth at her big concert next week in front of all her fans. I hope it costs at least ten Tuft & Needles to fix." His frustration has made his eyebrows furrow.

"So brutal," Kylie teases.

When we all decide at 10:00 to go to bed, I feel sad because no way Ace and I can sleep together. If Drew does wake up alone in this big house, it could traumatize her forever. I don't know if I am ready for the three of us to sleep together.

Kylie reads my mind the way only she can. "Let me sleep with Drew and you two lovebirds can sleep together."

"You sure?" I ask with hope.

She nods. "Yep! Have fun. Do good and maybe he will Amazon Prime you a Shetland pony tomorrow."

Ace and I crack up.

Ace picks up Drew and leads us back to a guest room big enough for many Shetland ponies. Kylie's suitcase is already in here. He lays Drew on the bed and she starts to stir. I interject myself to lay almost on top of her while I shush her until her body and breathing return to a rhythmic pattern. We take the room across the hall from them. This guest room is as big as my whole house.

"Ace, this house is amazing. I can't believe you own it and are in the NFL. I'm so proud of you," I say.

"Does it scare you some?" he asks with a small nervous smile.

"YES!"

"Why?" he asks gently.

"This house...your money...your fans. And of course your biceps are way better than mine," I say and flex my tiny bicep. He laughs, gently tossing me on the bed before removing his shirt and exposing his gorgeous form.

"All I did today when I was away from you was miss you and

think about you," he admits while climbing on top of me.

"Me too." I ruffle his hair with my fingers as he plays with the end of my hair. This intimacy is very fulfilling.

"I know we need to go slow, but would you consider moving here with me when football starts?" Ace says and I flinch because that is not *despacito* at all. I can't even imagine moving here. This house is huge and a little cold. His ex-wife lived here. He has a chef. How weird is that?

My eyes are focused on the art hanging across the room, a huge painting of a cow's face. It's staring right at me, its round brown eyes filled with understanding and compassion. I wonder often if we should be eating cows or cuddling them. They're so cute and this one seems to be boring its eyes into my soul. I wonder what this cow's intuition says about Ace asking me this question so soon.

"Sorry...too fast. I just can't help it. I feel like we have so much lost time to make up for," he says while turning my face back toward his, away from the solace of the cow's eyes. His eyes are filled with a love that I have missed over the years. It's so easy to love Ace, despite him putting me and this sweet cow on the spot right now. "Do you feel like we have lost time?" It's a rather romantic question, and the answer requires too many swirling emotions for me. His eyes are pursuing my intuition to take the lead here, which is shouting, "Don't ever let him go!" My heart is pleading to go slow as it processes everything. All that dissipates when he smiles at me and his little dimple catches my attention. I grab his face and kiss him with great passion. Words may not be in my best interest right now. I can just show him how my heart feels.

In the morning, I wake to him showering and whistling. I replay all that has happened in the last thirty-six hours. He is not moving slowly asking me to move here. I don't think I want to lose him, and I know I'm about to burst by not telling him or screaming from the top of some high-rise building that I love him like crazy. When he comes out wrapped in a towel smiling ear to ear, my heart skips a beat. His body is one that should be taped up on a wall or gracing the cover of a fitness magazine.

"Come here," I say and throw his side's bedcovers back. He crawls into bed, both of us giddy, faces inches apart and staring at each other with happy eyes. "Hey Ace."

"What?" He looks and smells so good.

"I love you too," I whisper. His eyes light up even more, which seems impossible since they were already so bright with happiness.

"I know," he says with arrogance. "I can see it in your eyes, and I love you more."

"On one hand I am scared, but on the other I don't know how much longer I can*not* kiss you in front of Drew." I trace a line on his defined chest.

"Affection isn't bad. You have been affectionate with me ever since the first day at the liquor store," he says. "Maybe don't stick your tongue down my throat."

"Okay...PG affection around Drew is allowed." We are incapsulated in euphoria. He pulls me to him and covers us with the sheets and starts kissing my belly. Then we do more things that are so *not* PG.

~

I head out of the room to go see Drew and Kylie, who are laying in bed watching TV. Drew sits up and reaches her arms out for me. "Auntie Kylie is sick," she whispers. "No yelling."

I stare at Kylie with a huge grin. "I bet she is," I say and then laugh at her.

"Is his chef here? I need like a trough of grease. Did I finish a bottle of wine by myself when we got here?" She looks rough. I nod to confirm. "Ouch."

"The chef is here and making you blueberry pancakes," I tell Drew as I carry her out of the room, leaving Kylie to pull her hungover self together.

The four of us have a great made-to-order breakfast by Ace's wonderful chef, Pierre. Pierre is making us a French dinner to-night, so Drew is probably getting a Happy Meal before we come home. Ace is inviting a couple NFL players back tonight to meet Kylie. She is beyond excited and doesn't even remember saying last night that her vagina is crack-a-lackin, which made Pierre howl in laughter when it was brought up.

We're heading out for a day of shopping and mani-pedis while Ace trains and does some other work. We head to the mall and stare in awe at the size of this sucker.

"Everything is bigger in Texas," I say, taking it all in.

"Is Ace's penis bigger in Texas?" Kylie whispers with a waggle of her eyebrows and a sarcastic evil smile. I giggle at her immaturity.

First place we head to is a lingerie store so I can buy new pajamas and other intimates. Since I've had no interest in the opposite sex in the past five years, everything in that area of my life is awful. His favorite color on me is green, so I find such joy in buying an emerald green bra and underwear. *I can't stop smiling.*

When Drew falls asleep in the stroller after our late lunch in the food court, I tell Kylie, "Ace asked me to move in with him."

"Holy bat balls, Lils! I hope you said yes. But...you didn't," she adds, exhausted and annoyed.

"What's the rush?" I ask.

"Uh...he's hot and wanted by most females in the world," she says. "He held your not-so-tiny daughter for thirty minutes while he gave us a tour of his *mansion*. And I heard your orgasm last night...quite impressive."

"Stop," I say, but her eyes pop open. "Really, were we that loud?"

"Yeah...it was crazy. Although it has been five years for you. Or maybe it really is bigger in Texas?"

I laugh. "Seriously though, I can't live in his house he lived in with his wife."

"Could you live with him at your house that you lived in with Dex?"

"Yeah...I think so," I admit, shocked by how easily I answered that without even a second of hesitation.

"No difference. You could fly home a lot and when he is on break, you could both be in Whimsy. Tell him to buy you a more modest and boring house and accept your happily ever after already," she says with no patience as she slips on a pair of clearance sandals.

"How much money did Tater drop in your account for this trip?" I ask.

"None," she says.

"Guess he doesn't want to fund your landing-a-NFL-player trip."

"I have no money and I need to look like one of these fancy-schmancy Dallas women tonight. I need to look like somebody fierce to land my man," Kylie says with defeat as she eyes a high falootin' slender woman holding up a pair of designer boots.

"I'll buy you a fancy outfit," I say.

She looks skeptical. "You will?"

"I mean, you will be sleeping with Drew during this whole trip." I bite my lip as I look out the corner of my eye at her amused expression.

"True...Let's get out of this sad pathetic clearance section then," she teases.

After several hours, we decide for a house movie night to get her new sexy cutoff shorts that cost more than any pair of shorts I have ever bought myself and a sexy black plain tank top that fits her perfectly everywhere. She got some nice sandals and great jewelry. I had to get a new outfit too. I'm wearing adorable dark blue shorts with a striped blouse that ties at the belly.

"You sure it doesn't show too much of my belly?" I ask as we walk out of the department store in our new outfits.

"No. You look great. Ace will love it."

We walk to the salon to get nails, makeup, and a blow-out. I talk on the phone with Ace while getting my toes done.

"You're a goner. What did he say?" Kylie asks when I hang up and I register the dopey smile spread on my face.

"That he missed me...I got butterflies," I say. "I can't even remember the last time I got those."

"Mommy, can I have butterflies too?" Drew asks while she climbs up on my lap after her manicure.

"Yes, I saw that we can actually start a butterfly garden. Should we do that?" I ask Drew.

"Yes," she says with no enthusiasm so I will probably run home and order it online for her like I do everything else. I'm much more excited about things for her than she is. She did love the cowgirl outfit I bought for her while she was asleep. She stripped down before her manicure and put it on. Kylie and I broke our phones taking so many pictures of her in *The Little Mermaid* underwear in the nail salon.

Kylie posted a picture of Drew in her hot pink glitzy cowgirl outfit on Facebook. Within minutes, Lucille called me. "Lily, we talked about this. She looks like trailer park trash. Tell Kylie to remove it now."

"Actually, we talked about her matching. It's a set and she matches. It's like Halloween came early this year. Drew loves it. Here Drew, tell Mimi how much you love your outfit." I pass the phone so Drew can tell her how happy she is in the outfit. *Get a grip, woman. She's four and rocking a hot pink sequin cowgirl outfit with enough sass to fill this mall. Not everyone can pull this look off.*

Kylie and I both roll our eyes, exhausted by Lucille policing everything about this trip. She made Drew pass the phone to me after they talked this morning and told me she was getting quotes on my *ramshackle* fence and, within the last twenty-four hours, she decided my whole house needs to be repainted. She hates the white paint with bright blue trim. Wants me to paint it gray with black trim. She also said she hired somebody to remove my grass and put in turf because my yard looks like a nesting ground for hobos. I don't want fake grass! I like real grass!

"Lily, how will you survive the next fourteen years with this irrational woman? I would've already shanked her. You're so good and poised all the time," Kylie whispers as Drew twirls with the phone on her ear, demonstrating to Lucille, who can't see, the way the skirt was made for spinning.

"Thanks for the compliment. I have no idea how I will survive. A gray house in Whimsy? No, we all use cheerful colors." I shake my head at her. I'm so frustrated.

CHAPTER 23

～

Within a minute of standing in Ace's expansive foyer, we are bombarded with five of the cutest football players I have ever seen, besides Ace. We follow them into the bar area while we wait for Pierre to finish dinner. Kylie is in heaven with the stunning men before us. When your major love interest for most of your life is Stan, the man who has no job and makes money from selling prescription pills and unemployment checks, this attention from accomplished men has to feel amazing. Spencer, the most charismatic of the four men, pours Kylie and I each a glass of wine. He has rich velvet skin with hazel green eyes that, in contrast to his dark complexion, look like liquid gold. Kylie looks pleased with her stunning set-up. The other four he invited are just here to hang.

"Boo, did you eat dinner?" Ace asks Drew, who nods. He looks at me for confirmation.

"Happy Meal while we had our hair done." I smile widely, feeling weak in the knees when his eyes do a slow scan of my body. His look lets me know he approves of my new sexy outfit.

"Then come here and let me make you a Shirley Temple." Ace hoists her up onto the bar and starts making the drink while she excitedly shows him her new purse filled with L.O.L. dolls from our shopping spree today. She asks for extra cherries, which he happily gives her. My heart is soaring at the sweet interaction before me.

"There's more new toys for you in the living room," Ace says and her little face lights up. Okay, he spoils her. *Should he be doing that?*

"Mommy, can I play with my new toys by that TV?" Drew asks and points to the TV in his giant living room.

"Yes, what can I put on for you?" Ace asks her while I rummage through the bags finding all the new toys I bought her. I set them all out and laugh like a psycho. *I spoil her too.*

I run my hand through my hair. "It looks like Christmas morning in here," I say and smile at Ace. "Let's not buy her any more stuff while we're here." He laughs and puts his arm around me. I look up at his amused face. "Is there more coming?"

"Just a few more things, but I'll stop if it makes you uncomfortable. I just want her to have fun here. How much fun can a four-year-old have in this house if there aren't any toys?" Gah... that's cute, true, and sweet! "We can leave them here so she has stuff next time."

Next time? My heart is thudding in my ears listening to him think ahead to our future trip.

"I swear that's the sweetest thing you've ever said to me." I stand on my tiptoes and gently kiss his soft lips then glance around, making sure none of the house guests saw. I'm not sure how to act since he is still married.

"These guys are all cool. Wouldn't have invited them if they weren't. So just relax." He must be a mind-reading Wiccan like Crystal, the flight attendant.

We open toys for her while she plays until Pierre announces dinner is ready. We all make our way to Ace's massive dining table that can seat twenty people. We sit at one end where the gorgeous place settings are laid out. Drew's plate is covered by a cloche and when Ace lifts it, there's a coloring book and a new L.O.L. doll beneath it. *Over the top.*

Pierre begins serving us food by setting down a beautiful Lyonnaise salad, which I have never had because Whimsy doesn't have French cuisine, nor am I fancy. For Drew, he serves her a scoop of rainbow sherbet with a cute heart-shaped butter cookie placed on top. Her eyes light up before she digs in. Upon my first bite, I almost whimper. Okay, so maybe I could get used to a chef. Drew eventually climbs on my lap and falls asleep.

"Sprinkles, let me go put her in the bed," Ace says as he positions himself to take her.

"If she wakes you have to shush her—"

"I watched you last night. I know what to do," he says with his magnificent and charming smile.

When he comes back from tucking her in without incident, Ace grabs my hand and leads me and the others down to his basement.

He has three rows of reclining movie chairs in the front and a soft sectional sofa that is more like a bed in the back of the room. The couch is raised, and he motions for me to sit there while he starts the film and gets the popcorn ready. It's *Jurassic World*, which I've never seen, so I am excited to watch it. The minute he sits, we wrap ourselves around one another, unable to keep our hands off each other. He keeps kissing my neck and whispering in my ears, distracting me from the film.

"Stop," I say with a smile. "I don't want these guys to get the wrong impression."

"They can't see us," he says. "Remember what we use to do at the drive-in?"

"That is not happening." I laugh and spend the rest of the movie canoodling with him.

When the movie is over, we walk his teammates to the door and watch them leave. Kylie is on cloud nine and starts gushing about her attraction to Spencer. "Lancaster, you know me well. He's perfect."

"He better treat you well or I'll kill him." His protectiveness on this matter is just too cute. He knows she deserves better than Stan. Everyone does.

"Oh Ace, I love you and I want at least half your money in this divorce settlement." She winks at me before she gives us both goodnight hugs.

Ace grabs my hand and starts pulling me to the stairs. "Where are we going?"

"My room. The Tuft & Needle was set up today. I'm excited." He lifts me in his arms and I squeal.

"I like the other room," I say right before his lips land on mine.

"You like the guest room better than mine?" he asks, amused, while he rubs the tip of his nose lightly over mine. Almost like he thinks I'm crazy because the master is very nice. It's totally exquisite, and maybe under other circumstances I would feel comfortable in there.

"That's where you slept with your wife," I say and shrug, wiggling my shoulders like I have the heebie-jeebies.

"Good point. I'll drag it down while you put that new lingerie on you told me about in the movie theater."

"Hurry," I say as he sets me down. After all that heavy petting in the theater, I feel like I could explode.

~

The rest of our stay, we swim with Boo, who has become insanely good. Ace has taught her to dive and go all the way to the bottom of the pool to get the rings. Watching their relationship grow has become my favorite pastime. Seeing Drew so proud of her accomplishment is a joy that is hard to put into words.

Kylie, Boo, and I have spent so much time at that amazing mall, buying way too many things. I never shop so it has been nice and according to Lucille, it was much needed.

Tonight is our eleventh night here. Kylie has to go back tomorrow, but Ace is taking Drew and I to Corpus Christi to his beach house.

Tonight, Spencer's daughter Megan, who we have already met and spent a good amount of time with, is going to watch Drew while the four of us go to dinner. Drew thinks Megan is the coolest thing in this town. She is fifteen and has a lot of experience with four younger siblings from her mom and stepdad. When we leave, we set the security alarm and that makes me feel better about leaving them in this giant house.

"They'll be fine," Ace says in the car. "She's in good hands."

I smile wanly and cuddle into him a little deeper. "I know...I'm just a nervous nelly. Be thankful I got *off weed* or this would be really bad." His bright eyes dance in amusement before he bends his head and kisses me.

"I can pull them up on my phone while they watch TV in the living room. She is exhausted from all the swimming we did today." He shows me a picture of her cuddled on the couch with the big stuffed animal Ace had ordered for her the other day.

"Amazing." I grab his phone, completely blown away by technology. "Yet so creepy."

I stare at them for a long time and when Ace tries to gently pry the phone from my hand, I look into his eyes. "Have you ever heard of dry drowning? That's where my mom fear has taken me right now."

"Sprinkles!" he exclaims and takes his phone back, sliding it into his jacket pocket. "That's too dark. She will be fine."

I nod, but dry drowning is a real thing and I'm terrified of it.

"So, you and Drew must be excited for Corpus?" Spencer asks after we get our drinks at this gorgeous upscale restaurant.

"I can take Boo home." Kylie surprises me before I can even respond. "Give you two lovebirds a romantic weekend getaway."

I scrunch my face. "Isn't that extra crappy Mommy material?"

"No, your parents will be thrilled to have her. I know Maggie will do anything to give you two time alone to bone," Kylie says. I bury my face in my hands, embarrassed in front of Spencer.

"That is just wrong, Kylie." I pull the menu up to shield my face from Spencer.

"Their moms have been trying to get them back together for years...the whole town really. You are looking at Whimsy's sweethearts," Kylie tells Spencer, motioning to us like we're a brand new shiny car on the showcase showdown. Spencer raises his eyebrows as if he is impressed.

"Were you in on it?" I ask Kylie.

"Eh, no, but I knew about their years of plotting and when Trina showed up in Maui, it got intense. Bernie was trying so hard to get you home." Her intensity clarifies how much our moms plotted.

"That is an understatement," Ace says, amused. "My mom came and got me."

Didn't know that part.

Kylie laughs. "She stormed out of Tater's after she saw it on the news and told me, 'I'm bringing my boy home and getting Drew a daddy.'" My mouth drops and I shoot my hands over my stunned face.

A daddy? Oh boy.

An awkward laugh escapes me. "Crazy ladies." I look at Ace to see how he is handling this information. His smile is broad as he leans in to kiss me.

"I'm super grateful for those two crazy ladies," he whispers, making me feel giddy as always.

Spencer is so wonderful and witty, making this dinner enjoyable. I can tell he is smitten with my snorty best friend and that makes me thrilled. We spend a great deal talking about Corpus. When we get in the car, I call my mom to see if she would want to keep Drew for the weekend. She is thrilled at the idea, just as Kylie had predicted. I feel excited but also guilty, like I'm abandoning her. I'm sure everyone in this car won't understand and will tell me I'm being dramatic, so I text my mom.

Me: *How am I supposed to put my baby on a plane without me?*

Mom: *She is going to be flying without you in a few weeks to go to New York with Lucille. Think of it as practice.*

Me: *UGH!*

Mom: *It will be fine. I know it's hard, but you have got to trust me on this. Everything will be fine.*

"Is that Lucille again?" Kylie looks like she is ready to kill someone.

"No. Thank god." I put my phone away.

"Good! I've had enough of her! The call yesterday about the picture I posted of you and I floating on the double floaty together..." She clenches her jaw in frustration.

"Lily you look like a *slut* in that suit," Lucille had said. "Kylie is an awful friend for portraying you in such a bad light." I think if Lucille would've said that in front of Kylie, Kylie would be behind bars on death row after murdering her. The picture was adorable, and we looked anything but slutty.

The mention of her name makes me aware that she won't like this little impromptu trip Ace and I are planning, which makes me want to start biting my nails or pulling my own hair out. Something to help ebb out the torturous nagging voice and her disapproval about everything. It's exhausting but if I'm being honest, I guess I'm a bit afraid of the confrontation she always throws at me.

CHAPTER 24

~

The next day I wake with a little apprehension about leaving Drew. I want to bring her with us, but I don't want to upset anyone, meaning Ace. He was so excited to have me all to himself. Last night, Kylie went home with Spencer, so Drew slept with Ace and I, which was fine. She did another night too when Kylie was with Spencer.

"Mommy, when I get to Grandma's, can Devyn come to sleep with me?" Drew asks. I look over, startled to see her awake. I thought I was alone in my thoughts.

"Sure, Boo. My guess is Grandma and Grandad will let you do whatever you want." I open my arm for her to come cuddle. "You okay with me leaving you for a few days?"

Drew was still awake when we got home and we told her the plan. She seemed excited at the time.

"Yes. I love it when I get to sleep with Devyn," she says, making me feel a little stung.

"But I'll be far away," I remind her.

"I also want Grandma to make me her cookies," she says, ignoring my cry for help.

"I can make those. I know the recipe."

"They're not as good as when Grandma makes them." *She's right!*

"Sprinkles, you trying to back out?" Ace asks while he stretches his giant form and yawns. Drew rolls to him, turning her attention away from my broken heart.

"No." *Yes!*

He laughs, catching my lie. His giant paw reaches over Drew and grabs my hand. It's warm and strong and damn it, I love it!

"Your mommy is going to miss you," Ace says to Drew. "So will I."

Drew shrugs. "Is Pierre going to make me pancakes before Auntie and I leave?"

Ace and I both laugh. Clearly she's fine with this. I climb out of bed to go start packing up her things. I find Kylie in the room already stuffing her suitcase. "How was your goodbye with Spencer?"

She flips her lips. "I'm bummed, but he already called after he dropped me off and said he'll come see me."

"Your snorts have charmed him…and maybe that shiny new vagina of yours."

"He's for sure worth a sore crotch." I laugh softly as I fold Drew's little clothes. "How'd Lucille take the news of Drew coming home with me so you can go bang at the beach?" Kylie asks.

"My dad said she took it well." I bob my head in sarcasm.

She shoves my shoulder. "Scaredy cat! Your dad told her?"

"Yes! I'm sick of her yelling at me. She doesn't yell at my dad," I defend myself against her mockery.

"I get it. I probably would've done the same." Kylie shrugs before she heads to the bathroom to start packing her toiletries. I help her before I move into my room and throw the last few things in my luggage that I missed last night.

We have a nice breakfast of blueberry pancakes and sausage. I had to fight back the tears the whole time. I can't believe I am sending her home without me. In the limo on the way to the airport, I keep hugging Drew while I continue to fight the impending tears. When Kylie boards the private jet with her, I start sobbing. My mind is racing with all the things that can go wrong. A tsunami hits Corpus Christi and I get stranded for months.

She forgets me over the next three days because she loves Devyn and my mom's cookies. The plane crashes and my whole world ends. What would I even do? The dark and dangerous thoughts that enter my brain as a mother have the power to annihilate me.

"Ace, this is so unlike me," I say once the plane is a tiny blip in my vision.

"Lily, you are a great mom and we are going to have a blast," he says and then kisses me quickly before throwing me over his shoulder and carrying me onto the second private jet he has waiting for us to board. My spirits lift the minute he does.

Ace has access to all these private jets because he invested in a start-up company several years ago, and now they're huge. They have many jets and since he's a majority shareholder, he uses them all the time. He won't even fly commercial now. *Snob.* Although, I wouldn't either if I had this option. If he can't get access to any of the company's private jets, he charters a small plane.

He sets me down. This plane looks exactly the same as the one we arrived in, even though it's not. I start fidgeting with my hands and searching through my bag for gum or something to take my mind off Drew. I feel like a crazy lady as the feeling of doom wraps around my lungs, threatening to steal my breath and my sanity. *She's too little.*

"Okay Sprinkles, let's have a drink to calm those nerves." He rubs his hands together as he starts rummaging through the fridge.

"Where's the red carpet and pretty flight attendant?" I ask as I look around and down the airplane stairs.

"Cost cuts apparently. I'll be your flight attendant today." I laugh at his suggestive eyebrow waggle.

"I'm high maintenance," I say as I take an empty glass off the rack and hold it out to him as he pulls a cork off a bottle of pinot. "Also, I may have a full- blown panic attack with my baby on another plane."

"I'll distract you." Again, his tone and eyebrows are suggestive, making my stomach flutter. The pilot steps out of the cockpit and introduces himself to me. He already knows Ace. By the time we get clearance to take off, I'm half a glass in and feeling much less anxious about Drew. Not to mention there is so much kissing and giggling. After we are in a "free to move about the cabin" altitude, we go back into the mile-high club. By the time we land, I'm smiling ear to ear.

There is a car waiting for us that takes us to his adorable beach house. As soon as we walk in, I see a line of Christmas photos down the entryway of his family. I knew they always spend Christmas here, but to see it all documented is sweet.

"Why are there no pictures of Trina?" I ask, inspecting all his pictures on the wall. There was none in Dallas either. Like she never existed.

"I took it down last time I was here, about three months ago," he says. "I had one with her on the wall. She only came here once. Not a big family gal. Plus she considered this a dump." I turn around, looking for any traces of leftover love for his ex-wife on his face. He smiles at me with so much adoration I quickly abandon that insecurity. Honestly, I don't have any insecurity about Trina. I think that is what makes me look even harder. Am I just being naïve to believe he has no unresolved feelings for her?

He puts his hands on my hips and presses the front side of his body into my backside. "Should we take our clothes off right here or do you want a tour?"

"I want the full tour first." He sighs, which makes me laugh. He grabs my hand and shows me the whole house and his private view of the beach off his balcony in the master. This place feels like him, and I like it much better than his giant mansion back in Dallas. This has four bedrooms all with multiple beds, except for the one giant king-sized bed in the master. He stands behind me and starts guiding me toward it.

"Is it a Tuft & Needle?" I ask.

"It was delivered yesterday. I had the housekeeper make it before we came." His voice is husky and the warmth of his breath on the back of my neck sends a tingle down my spine.

"Any more Amazon purchases made today? I think you may have a shopping addiction, Ace," I tease.

He spins me around before gently pushing me back on the bed.

"I feel like I have an addiction to you, Lily." His smile is intoxicating. I think I have an addiction to him, too. I have never been this in love before. My head is constantly spinning, and I feel like the only thing that matters is him. When he is not with me, I can't focus on anything because I am too busy missing him and when he's with me, I can't focus on anything because I'm too busy staring at him.

He slides my tank top strap over my shoulder and plants his lips on my collarbone, flooding me with yearning and lust.

Later in the afternoon, after I talk to a safely-landed Drew, we head down to the beach with a bottle of white wine and some cheese and crackers. We lay in the sun and enjoy our romantic little picnic. Every time he kisses me, I push him away. "I don't want to push you away, but I feel panicked about the media," I say as I check our surroundings.

"Never seen one here." With an award-winning grin, Ace pins me on the ground and kisses me. "I can't keep my hands off you...It's a problem."

I don't ever want his hands off me. I am completely gone.

·

CHAPTER 25

~

We spend the whole three nights being beach bums at his house. We haven't left once. I wake up the morning we are supposed to leave feeling sad it's ending. I sneak out of the room to call Drew, who talks my ear off and asks if she can spend the night at Uncle Cameron's tonight. "Boo, don't you want to come home?" I ask.

"Yes, but I also want to sleep in the tent in Uncle's living room with Devyn and Oscar. We are getting pizza and drinking root beer floats. Uncle even said we could do smores outside and he'd tell us ghost stories." She's so excited it comes out almost in one breath.

By the time we hang up, I have agreed she can sleep over. She doesn't seem to be missing me at all. It makes me feel less guilty, but is this normal?

Me: *Mom, is it normal that Drew doesn't miss me?*

Mom: *We are keeping her very entertained. You know how much she admires her cousins.*

I jump in the shower while Ace is still sleeping, pondering my independent daughter. I decide after going back and forth that this is a good thing. I have such an amazing family that I can trust to keep her safe, happy, and loved.

A few moments later, my thoughts snap away when Ace steps in. "Morning, Sprinkles," he says with a mischievous smile on his face. He hasn't shaved in a few days and he looks yummy.

"Morning, Big Shot. How'd you sleep?" His arms shoot around me.

"Good, I like how you hold me so tight in the middle of the night." His sincere smile sends a wave of heat through my core. His soft hungry lips claim mine with unparalleled heat and passion, leaving me breathless when he pulls away. "Call your parents and see if we can stay another night?" he asks with eager eyes.

"No," I say between kisses that quickly escalate into more.

~

Today is Friday, and we have stayed six nights. The plan is to leave Sunday. I really miss Drew, but Ace and I are in heaven here. Every time I feel guilty, he reminds me she is with my parents and that I deserve this time away to relax. Or I just pick up the phone and call her and she talks my ear off with all the fun things she is doing.

Ace and I have a beach day planned. We are heading out with a picnic and then going out on a jet ski later this afternoon.

"You look gorgeous in that suit," Ace says, staring at me like he would rather have me than the turkey sandwiches I packed. I bought it yesterday at a shop and I do really like it. I'm so tan at this point so the hot pink looks great on my skin.

"Behave out here," I remind him while he keeps touching me everywhere. "I'm serious."

He doesn't stop at all and when we head back up to the house, I see a guy on his balcony taking pictures with a huge camera.

"Oh my god...is he taking pictures of us?" I ask.

"Shit!" Ace exclaims and starts walking toward the guy. I reluctantly follow behind him. "Are those of me?" he yells to the guy up on the balcony.

"Yep," the guy says with so much arrogance. Ace looks pissed.

"Who you work for?" Ace asks. His jaw tightens like somebody is twisting a wrench at the joints.

"Myself...I'll sell them for a lot of money. Talk about being in the right place at the right time." His smug cavalier attitude doesn't do much to relieve the tension in Ace's jaw. I walk away because I want to cry. My racing heart is thumping in my hollow chest, and I swear I can hear it. Ace starts to negotiate money with this lunatic, and I almost fold over and barf when he offers him twenty thousand dollars for the camera and everything on it.

I get in the house and busy myself by putting everything away. I wash the few dishes in the sink, call Drew to say hello, and then clean the fridge, taking the shelves out and scrubbing them in warm soapy water.

Forty-five minutes later, his refrigerator and kitchen cabinets are sparkling. I am freaking out. His kitchen looks great though. Ace finally walks through the door with the camera. "We should be good," he says.

"Oh my god! Ace, how much did that cost you?"

"Doesn't matter," he says casually. *It does.*

"Ace..." I start but he cuts me off.

"Lily, let's not talk about it. It's water under the bridge." He tucks a stray hair behind my ear. "I have never had so much fun in my life as I have here with you. I don't want that scumbag worrying you. Let's enjoy our last two nights."

I take a deep breath and look up at him and smile. "Can we take a bath and order from that Chinese restaurant again?" *I'm addicted to Chinese food.*

He nods with a big greedy smile and I laugh when he throws me over his shoulder and bounds up the stairs. We cancel the jet skiing because we have only had sex once today and that is just dull. While in the bath, sitting between his legs with my head resting on his chest, he asks, "Lily, am I sleeping through it or are you not having the dreams anymore?" I tilt my head up to stare in his eyes, still pressed against his chest.

"Not since the first night in Dallas...I haven't even thought about it." I pause. "That is the longest I have ever gone without one."

"Why do you think that is?" Ace asks, running the soapy loofah over my arm.

"I'm happy, relaxed, and did you notice I ate my whole sandwich today?" I ask. "I usually feel tied up in knots and stressed."

He kisses the top of my head. "I love you," he whispers and I spin all the way around to climb on his lap.

"I think it's you that is doing all this good for me. The way you love me. I feel so safe and happy all the time." I never ever thought I could be this happy.

"See, I told you. You needed a man," he teases. I tug at his chest hairs playfully and he winces.

"Well, if any man will do, then I should find one who is already divorced," I tease and push away from him to the other side of his giant tub.

"No other man," he says. "Just me. I know this is silly, but I'm old fashioned. Will you be my girlfriend?"

I laugh until he leans forward and grabs my waist, pulling me back on top of him. "Good thing I'm old fashioned, too. Yes, I will be your girlfriend."

"Why did you never change your name after you married Dexter?" he asks, amused. "Being old fashioned and all."

"Lily Drew sounded weird and there is so much paperwork. Not to mention you have to go to the social security office. It's a pain. It's a needless tradition." I hold my breath, trying to think of a way to change the subject.

"I like the way Lily Lancaster sounds." He pulls me flush against his chest. "One day?" he asks gently and sincerely while my eyes study his. A wave of nausea flows through me...or maybe that was just butterflies. I smile and kiss his neck, which leads to other things. When we are both breathless and exhausted, I bury my face in his neck.

Marriage? I'm not sure I want that again...I'm positive I don't.

We get out when Ace's stomach growls and order an insane amount of Chinese food. We watch a movie and fall asleep entwined around one another.

The next morning, we wake and go to breakfast, then walk around and do more shopping. We end up on some beach later in the afternoon, sand squishing between our toes as we meander along the shoreline, flip flops in our hands. He kisses me, and then we hear his name and turn around to a few people with cameras asking who I am. I feel sick. We decide we better rush home.

We are about a mile away on the beach while being followed by three men with cameras. Ace calls a driver, who picks us up and takes us on a tour so we can lose the men before he drops us off at home. When we walk in, stress has tangled every one of my facial features. He takes one look at my face and says, "Let's go home now instead of tomorrow."

Yep!

I pack so fast while he calls for a car and arranges our escape. We can't get a private flight, so he thinks it's best we drive to Dallas and fly to Whimsy from there.

"You mad at me, Sprinkles?" he asks when we get on the road.

"No. I just keep thinking about all that money you spent yesterday to get rid of that picture and now we still got caught." It's disheartening.

"Don't worry about any of it. Before this divorce, nobody ever really noticed me. I wasn't on tabloids," he says. "I promise it will go back that way."

"I guess the divorce from a big-time country singer doesn't help," I say as I pull my knees to my chest. I don't even know how to process this. I knew he was famous, but understanding his reality is out of my grasp. How can he live under this scrutiny all the time? I feel bad for him. I reach over and grab his hand. "Man, that one guy was very aggressive." At one point I thought he might grab me, and Ace got very protective and shoved him away with his arm. It wasn't hard, but it did put things into perspective for me.

"I'm so sorry. It's my fault. I just love you so much I never wanted it to end." Ace looks so sad and broken, making my heart hurt. "Please understand it will go away soon." Does he think he will lose me over this?

"I didn't want it to end either. It's not your fault. We were just walking down the beach." I push my lips on his cheek. "I love you more."

Several hours into our long drive back to Dallas, Kylie calls. "Lily, you are all over the internet. You look so tan."

"Did my suit look good?" I ask, full of anxiety.

"So good! Way better than that fat Trina looked," Kylie says like a tried and true best friend, bashing another woman to make me feel better. "That is what a couple comments say on a Facebook thread I was reading. A lot of people hate her."

"What else are they saying?" I hate this anxiety.

"That you're pretty and you two have been seen by locals all week. Picnics on the beach, late night walks. Everyone wants to know who you are," she says. "You are a mystery."

"Who said I was pretty?" I ask frantically, and Ace laughs at my sudden vanity. This is a lot for a small-town girl to feel watched by America. Not only that, but Ace is like a living legend. He has fans that think he can do no wrong, so of course they may hate me from just one look.

"Here...I'll read one." I put her on speaker phone so Ace can hear. "Ace Lancaster has been spotted all over Corpus Christi with a beautiful young woman. Nobody knows who she is, but several locals have confirmed they have seen them all over town kissing, holding hands, and looking very much in love," Kylie says in a regal southern accent for theatrics.

"Oh my heavens," I say and lean back in my seat.

"A few weeks hiding in Whimsy and this will all blow over." Ace seems to believe it as he squeezes my hand as if it is the pep talk of my life.

"Ace, this stresses me out," I say after hanging up with Kylie.

"Sprinkles, it will be okay," he says gently.

"Ace, we are having an affair! I'm so worried about your image," I whine as I rub my sweaty palms over my leggings.

He shrugs it off. "I'm more worried about your image."

What image? "I don't have one. I live in Whimsy where everyone probably knows my blood type and my social security number. The garbage man and the gate guard both have keys to my house."

"I love how cute you are." I can't help but smile at his sweet compliment. His warm palm rubs my upper thigh.

"Should we get a room halfway? I'm tired," I say with a raised brow and he smirks as he catches my meaning.

"We are about an hour away."

"Too long," I tease. We don't stop because we don't want to get spotted.

Once back at his house, I log into Kylie's Facebook and feel the pit in my stomach take over my whole body. There I am everywhere I look in her newsfeed.

"I actually think I may faint," I say to Ace. "I look like a slob!"

"Lily, close that laptop. Let's take a shower and order in. I have a movie we can watch in the theater. Let it go. Please," he begs and puts his hands on my hips. When he does this, it always makes me forget everything. The way his giant hands feel on my tiny hips is such a turn on.

"Can we get Chinese food?" Chinese food always perks me up.

"You are a Chinese food addict."

"I lived on it in college...Whimsy doesn't have Chinese."

We have a good night, and I forget all about the pictures and everything else. That is the effect Ace Lancaster has on me. When it is just us, all my troubles, fears, and insecurities melt away under his attention and affection. I am so in love with him. It's almost impossible for even me to understand.

CHAPTER 26

~

Once back in Whimsy first thing Sunday morning, we are all the buzz. Nobody can stop talking about our 'hot week on the beach.' That is what Bernie is telling us as we pull out of the tiny airport.

"Now kids, I gotta run into the store and get dinner. Drew requested mashed potatoes and I thought what better to pair it with than Ace's favorite meatloaf. A welcome home dinner," she says while patting Ace's knee. Every time Bernie makes meatloaf, she makes enough to feed a small country so I'm sure many people are coming to dinner.

"I'll run in...Just text me a list," Ace insists because he is a complete and total gentleman.

"Oh honey, if you go in, you'll be accosted by the whole town. I think it's best I drop you both at Lily's. Drew is going to meet you there," she says to me by turning around to make eye contact. "Like I said you two are the toast and the talk of the town right now." She looks almost scared which confuses me. We're at the one stoplight in Whimsy, and I see Mr. Mackabee approach Bernie's window. She unrolls it after he taps on the glass.

"Hey guys, I can see you two are an item now. Don't worry about me confirming that with any media. You're safe here." He obnoxiously clears his throat. "That is what Reverend Weathers said in church today. We needed to provide a safe and secure place for this to die down," he says, adding mocking tones to imitate

Reverend Weathers, the sweetest man alive.

Bernie changes the subject. "We sure would appreciate that. Can I stop by in about thirty minutes and get four loaves of that noble bread you make?"

"I will make sure it's fresh if you give me forty-five." Mr. Mackabee beams with pride and then glances back at me. "Pink is for sure your color, Lily." Gross. He's referring to my bikini in the pictures. The light turns green and Bernie accelerates, waving goodbye.

"What a jerk!" Ace belts out. "He can't talk about my girlfriend that way." I can't help but laugh at his bruised ego.

"Girlfriend." Bernie coos. "I'm so happy to hear this. All I have ever wanted was for you two to be together," Bernie interjects as she waves to Tony. He opens the gate when he sees her car.

I smile and roll down my window and yell out, "Hi Tony!"

He waves. "Glad you're back safe. That sunshine did you good, sweetie."

"You coming to Bernie's tonight?" I ask and he nods. I wave goodbye as Bernie drives into the subdivision.

When we pull up at my house, a couple of my neighbors come out to *help* with our luggage.

Bernie doesn't even get out of the car because she wants to go to the grocery store, the hardware store, and Mr. Mackabee's bakery. It's about fifteen minutes of Ace signing autographs, and the crowd is getting bigger. My parents pull up and look mystified at the crowd of locals on my lawn, which I notice is now turf. *I never approved that, Lucille.* I make a beeline for their parked car, almost running over Mr. Buckets, who is driving me crazy anyhow.

"BOO!" I yell when I open the door. "I missed you like crazy."

"Mommy, why are all these people here?" she asks with big saucer eyes.

"Just out for a walk and stopped to say hi. Let's get inside," I say as I release her from her car seat restraints and pull her into my arms. I glance back at Ace who has a smile on his face, but I can tell his patience is fading.

My parents make themselves at home after my dad helps with the luggage. Drew and I are on the couch catching up when Ace finally walks in with a solemn look on his face. He shuts the door and locks it, which makes my dad laugh. Nobody in this neighborhood locks their doors. We do when we're gone for a long time, but I would typically keep it unlocked in case my brother wanted to stop by or for Kylie, who is supposed to pop in after her shift.

The five of us play a few games of UNO before we head to Bernie's for dinner. Normally, I would walk there, but that welcome home party on my brand new turf was more than I wanted to see of the town today. The three of us drive over with my parents.

Everyone that comes to dinner tells us how crazy everyone in town is acting now that we're dating. It's sorta funny, I guess. First this small town gets a big-time football star they get to say they all know, and now one of the small-town gals gets to date him. And our relationship was just plastered all over the place.

Humor will get me through this, I think the following morning when I take Drew to the club for her swim lesson and a Pilates class for myself. I smile the whole time I'm in the grocery store with Drew, even though it took four times as long. I smiled at everyone on my lawn—*turf*—when I got home. I even chatted with them all for a few minutes.

By Tuesday afternoon, my sense of humor is starting to fade. I can't be in the spotlight like this. If he wasn't married, maybe I wouldn't feel so weird. When I ran into Mr. Buckets at the grocery store yesterday, he said, "Do you really think he'll leave Trina for you? She is lovely and her voice is gorgeous." He is clearly unaware that she steals Tuft & Needles from unsuspecting men.

When I came home and told Ace, he was furious. He kept apologizing and I kept reassuring him that I was fine. That's when we both decided we felt exposed and could do with a lockdown at my house for a few days.

Today is Friday, and I haven't gone into the store in weeks

to work. Yesterday, I could've worked at home, but Drew and I built a whole world out of Legos and then made my mom's famous cookies that she told me weren't as good as my mom's. If you're ever having a really high moment in life, feeling so good about yourself, hang out with a toddler and they'll set you straight with any false hope you have about your life. I decide I must rid myself of the distractions and work from home. I've arranged for Drew to go over to Lucille's. I wrestle my especially rambunctious daughter in her car seat after Ace sets out to go to the gym at the club. "Boo, are you hyped up or what?"

"Ace gave me sugar when you were in the shower!" she yells and sticks out her bright purple tongue. "NERDS!"

"Oh boy," I say before kissing her on her forehead as she wiggles away from my lips. I squeeze her tiny cheeks in my palms to keep her still so I can properly love her. She rubs her forehead with her palm as if I passed on a radioactive disease to her. "You don't like kisses anymore?"

"Not when I don't want to hold still. Mimi and I are going to have fun today." *Don't count on that.*

I smile at her perky disposition and then put my face right in front of hers. "Can I please have a kiss?" She nods and giggles before kissing me. Then she wraps her arms around me and squeezes me almost to death. As we pull out, I notice nobody is lingering around my *turf.* I hate that Lucille changed my front yard without my agreement, but damn it, it looks so good! Every time I look out my window, I have to admire how amazing and real it looks.

I walk Drew into Lucille's house and watch Lucille's face pinch up in complete disgust when she sees her outfit. She's wearing some purple shorts and a Dallas Cowboys t-shirt that she has proclaimed to be her favorite shirt, obviously because Ace gave it to her. I brace myself for a lecture but instead she stands and smooths her immaculate long-sleeved gray blouse. *God forbid she get wrinkled by hugging her granddaughter.* She flashes me a seemingly sincere smile. *What is happening?*

"Can she sleep over? John is gone for the night and we can

get pizza," Lucille asks. Her warm tone takes me by surprise.

"Sure," I say with a hesitant smile. "I can get her in the morning."

Drew scampers off to her overfilled toy bin when she sees new stuff without so much of a look my way. "Bye Boo, have fun. I love you," I say with a giggle. She turns around and runs back to give me a hug. I squeeze her extra tight.

Lucille walks me to the door. "The pool repairs will be done in the next week or so. We will install a fence and just do her lessons here."

"Okay...I'm sure she will love that." Her eyes flash from her normal icy blue to a fathomless dark gray. *Is she a Wiccan? What in the hell was that?*

"So, how serious are you with Ace?" All traces of the warmth she had radiated not even a minute ago have been replaced with a nasty tone that doesn't sit well with me.

"Pretty serious," I say. "I know how you feel, Lucille, and I will be very careful."

"Your picture was everywhere. What kind of a life is that for Drew?"

"He is very good to her, Lucille," I say, annoyed. "He would never hurt her."

"I think you two are only thinking about yourselves and Drew is just along for the ride. You left her for three nights and then stayed an extra four to parade all over Corpus Christi, half naked with a married man." My face warms while my eyes sting with tears. There's that word again. And half naked? We were on a beach in one-hundred-degree weather.

"My parents were thrilled to have her," I say defensively but truth be told, I do feel guilty about the whole trip. Her scathing assessment is like a cloak of shame being draped over my slouched shoulders.

"Maybe she should stay here until you figure it out," Lucille says.

How dare she! Figure what out?

"I'll be back at 10 AM tomorrow to get her," I say and storm out. *She is insane!*

CHAPTER 27

~

I drive back home seething. I slam my front door and the cabinets while cleaning up our breakfast dishes. When my heart rate regulates to a normal pattern, I open my laptop and start working. Ace walks through the front door, back from his morning workout. I start right in venting about Lucille while I pace the living room and toss a few throw pillows around. He grabs me by the shoulders.

"Just breathe. Sit right here and breathe," he says with a calmness I love. "You both need to remember you want the same things for Drew." I sit down...I take a breath...

"It's hard when she is always telling me what to do. Why does she think she has a right to tell me who I can and can't see? '*Maybe she should stay here till you figure it out,*'" I say, mimicking her nagging voice. "What does she suggest I figure out?" I take another deep breath to steady my thoughts. "Does she want me to admit I love the turf? Because I don't want to...but she was right. I love that fake wannabe grass more than I ever loved the old lawn." I rub my face. I hate it when Lucille is right. I must admit, she is right about a lot of things, but she's also crazy as they come.

"I love you," he says with the most adoring smile. "When you get mad, you're even cuter."

"I want to punch her." I hold up my fists. He laughs and kisses me, which leads to a shower and no work finished for the liquor store because we can't keep our hands off each other.

"I can't work from home if you are going to be here. Next Thursday, you need to make yourself scarce."

"Then we may need a date night here and there with a sitter because that was the best day of my life," he says. "You wanna go dancing at Willy's tonight? Dinner at Tater's?"

"Okay. It's a date." I beam like he just asked me to prom.

"Wear that blue dress I bought you in Corpus," he says with devious eyes that scorch my core with desire.

"Is that appropriate for our bush?" I tease, thinking about the time we had sex there.

He laughs. "The great thing about bushes is there is no dress code." He looks a little sinister right now, and I feel flushed thinking about it.

People in town seem to have gotten over our relationship. At Tater's, nobody comes over to have Ace sign an autograph. Tater and Kylie meet us there to tag along on our date. I order the Tater chili, a dinner special, consisting of ground filet and chunks of potatoes in three-bean chili. They topped it with fresh jalapeno, white onion, and a little dollop of sour cream.

"Tater, you are a *tater* genius!" I says after a few bites.

"This brisket hash is insane," Ace sings. I rub his leg because I could die from his cuteness.

"Let me taste it." He puts a tiny bite up to my mouth and when I open, he kisses me instead.

"Get a room. You two aren't even fun to be around," Kylie says while she takes a bite of Tater's famous scalloped potatoes.

"Okay, we will cool it," I say.

"No we won't," Ace says, pulling my face to him and kissing me. I laugh and push him away. Kylie rolls her eyes.

"I'm happy you two are together again." Tater looks sincere.

"Me too...I don't know why Kylie can't be happy," Ace says with feigned sadness.

"Oh whatever. I'm thrilled like everyone else in town. It would just be nice to have a conversation with the two of you instead of watching your little PDA show." Tater tickles her side, introducing cute snorts.

Darla is at Willy's when we walk in and just about glowing like the sun when she spots Ace and I.

"You both are a gorgeous couple and I'm thrilled. This is what was always supposed to happen. Dexter—"

"Was a good husband and would have been a great dad," I say, warning her not to say another word because I'm done with everyone and their opinions.

She squints her eyes. "It's just..."

"Darla, let's do a shot of Fireball." Her eyes light up at the mention of her favorite drink.

"I thought you hated shots?" she asks suspiciously.

"I do, but I would like to celebrate tonight. I haven't had a nightmare since my first night in Dallas...the longest I have gone without one. I feel really good." This graces my ears with an enthusiastic squeal.

When Stan shows up, it's not long before he and Kylie start fighting. He's being such a baby and having a public fit about her breaking up with him before heading to Dallas. Kylie has broken it off with Stan a hundred times, and every time she gets back together with him.

He thinks it'll work out like every other time and take her home with him, but I think he's wrong.

"No, it's over. For real this time," she says firmly.

"BITCH!" he spits. Faster than lightning, Tater's fist lands right on his jaw, making him stumble back onto the bar. Stan picks up the empty barstool and chucks it at Tater. Tater ducks and it hits me instead, which gets Ace riled up. He punches Stan before Willy's nephew, Ted, escorts Stan out and the whole bar carries on.

Ace and Tater are still pissed and acting all manly dumb right now. "Come on Big Shot, let's go home," I say, pulling his arm.

The four of us walk out and I gasp when I see the whole side of my car looks like Freddy Krueger annihilated it.

"I'll kill him," Ace says, looking murderous. "He still does this kind of shit?"

"Yep, I'm issuing a lifetime ban on that jackass at Tater's," Tater says.

I have never done anything to Stan. Why did he key my car? They both beg me to press charges against Stan but no way. This town is so small and, in a few months, Stan's lifetime ban will be lifted like it always is and he'll be at Tater's, drinking beer and making things awkward. Drama is always forgotten in small towns and then blamed on one sole person, and it won't be me on this one.

~

I wake the next day late at 10 AM to the phone ringing.

"Hi, Lucille," I say, trying to sound awake and peppy after our late night.

"So, John is in Yosemite and wants Drew and I to come for the weekend."

"Oh...I guess that's fine. Can you stop on your way out so I can say goodbye?" I ask.

"Uh...we are halfway there," she says. *What?* "I thought it would make you understand that I am serious about Ace being in her life."

I see stars. My jaw hurts from gritting my teeth. "Lucille, you can't just take her without asking." I'm shaking as I choke back tears. "I can't believe you!"

"You can talk to her, but we won't be back until Sunday night," she says as though she is being so generous letting me talk to *my* daughter.

Drew gets on the phone. "Boo," I say while still holding back tears. "Two Yosemite trips in one summer...Who is the luckiest girl in Whimsy?"

She giggles and we chat for a few minutes before she hands the phone to Lucille.

"I can't believe you," I spit. I want to scream and yell and call her every name in the book. "Call me when you check into your hotel."

"We will. I'm sure you've had enough time to figure out what the right thing is." She pauses and I hold my breath. "While we're gone, you can let Ace down gently." *That is what she wanted me to figure out?* My boiling point with her has been reached.

I hang up on her because what I am about to say won't be good for anyone. What I need to figure out is how to get her off my back about everything I do. She was right about the turf; what if she's right about this?

"BITCH!" I scream out as I fly out of bed. The rage coursing through me is unfamiliar, nothing I have ever experienced. It's as though I am floating above, watching myself pace my room like a freaking lunatic. I'm having a hard time processing that this is actually happening right now.

Ace's billion questions flying out of his mouth feels like an interrogation and I'm not even able to hear them. I reach for my phone and call the only person who can fix this.

"Just stay calm and when she calls, ask her what she means by letting Ace down gently," my dad says. "Maybe you are just upset and blowing it out of proportion?"

"Okay. I will. Answer if I call," I demand in a not-cute way. She brings out the absolute worst in me.

"Of course, Lily. Just stay calm," he repeats. "She is not in danger from Lucille."

I don't know how much better he made me feel, but at least I think I'm breathing again.

"Lily, why can't you talk to me about it?" Ace snaps me out of it and I notice how sad he looks. I try not to let it annoy me but everything is annoying right now because of Lucille trying to rule my life by holding Drew over my head.

"Because that crazy bitch only listens to my dad. Not even her own husband can talk her down. He'll fix it…he always does." I am giving myself a pep talk more than anything because I wonder when my dad's charms will not affect her anymore.

"Has something like this happened before?" he asks.

I sigh. "When Drew was one, she threatened to try and get custody if I didn't stop nursing her. She felt if I nursed her for any longer, Drew would grow up too dependent on me." I run my hands over my face. "I wanted to keep nursing. I wasn't ready to give it up, and she made me feel like I was some kind of freak or something. Like it was gross. Anyways, my dad talked to her and I nursed Drew until she was almost two. I had weaned her down to like twice a day by the time she was eighteen months old. We tapered so slowly that she stopped nursing on her own. It was a perfect relationship we shared, and Lucille almost ruined it by getting in my head and making hideous threats." Rage courses through my veins. "I can't do it anymore with her. I'm going to lose it." I have now surrendered to the tears.

"She would never be able to get custody," Ace says, annoying me to no end. I shake my head, trying to dislodge his cavalier attitude about child custody laws.

"Ace, I don't even want to find out if she could. I don't want to know how far she'd go. The woman has deep, *deep* pockets," I point out with an unsavory taste in my mouth. He starts rubbing my back, but I don't want to be touched. I hate the world right now.

"I think maybe you should just go to your mom's and give me the day to figure this out," I say cruelly.

"No way." He pulls me into his chest. "We can figure it out together. I love you and this is my problem, too."

Only it's not.

As if he's reading my mind like that Wiccan flight attendant, he says, "Lily, it is my problem because I can't do what I have to do in life if your world is torn apart. We're a team." He directs my face to look into his eyes and I take a deep breath. He's too good for me but, regardless of my anger and feeling insecure about how he doesn't need to be in the middle of my messy life, I let him kiss me, which leads to amazing sex.

"I can't believe the amount of sex we have," I say and giggle, laying my head on his glistening chest. It rumbles with laughter beneath my cheek. "I'm not trying to shut you out. I just don't want to push you out of my life with all my chaos."

"You can't get rid of me. I'm never letting you go again."

"I like the sound of that," I whisper, drawing circles with my finger on his sculpted abs.

Later in the morning when Lucille calls, I take a huge breath before answering.

"Hi," I say, trying to be calm like my dad suggested.

"We made it. She is napping so I don't want to wake her," Lucille bites. Like she is holding all the cards. Makes my stomach turn.

"Tell me, what do you mean by breaking it to Ace gently?" I ask just like my dad suggested.

"I don't want you seeing him anymore. It's a selfish decision on your part," she says, making the angry stars swirl in my vision again. "Good moms put their kids first."

"You can't tell me who to date Lucille." My voice cracks. My calm façade wavers from the burning fury beneath.

"I can and I am. You're raising my son's daughter. I have a say in every single choice you make in regards to her," she says like a raving lunatic. "Parading around with Ace is not in her best interest. You let her eat what she likes and she looks like some kind of hobo all the time. You're unfit."

"I disagree, and I'm not going to stop seeing him because you said so. You aren't the boss of me." I fight back angry tears.

"If you don't, I will file for emergency custody. Just remember, he is married and you are a cheater," Lucille shouts. "It will be very easy to prove how unfit you are."

"Custody!" I exclaim. "You want to take her away from me? You're unfit and cruel and, trust me, there's a whole town that would love to testify against your crazy ass."

We fight back and forth until we hang up. I throw my phone on the floor, when I notice the shattered screen I finally break down. Ace comforts me while I sob in my hands.

My pounding heart starts to calm as he rubs my back. "Will my phone still work?" Broken phone...broken car...broken home. He inspects it.

"It's just the screen. Very impressive with this toddler proof case, though." He kisses my cheek and hugs me. I grab my phone and cry harder at Drew's shattered face on my screensaver.

"We'll get it fixed after breakfast, no need to cry about it," he says gently as he puts my shoes in front of me. "Let's get out of the house for a bit."

"I don't want breakfast. I think I should go to Yosemite and fight Lucille. I can't imagine what's going through that woman's head."

"Do you really think Drew is in danger? I'm sure Lucille just needs to calm down," Ace says rationally like my dad also mentioned many times on the phone.

"She's not in danger but my sanity is," I say as I wipe away my tears. "There's a crazy rich woman who wants to take my daughter from me."

I call Kylie in the car and ask her to meet at Ma's for breakfast because Ace is right that I need a distraction. We sit in the parking lot after putting our names on the wait list from all the tourists today. I immediately start ranting and raving the minute Kylie and Tater show up.

"I am really starting to hate her!" Kylie exclaims. "I want to drive to Yosemite and drag her around the trails by her hair until we find a big angry bear."

"Call the cops! That bitch kidnapped your daughter," Tater shouts.

"Oooohhh she did!" Kylie says. "Fat cow."

Ace's phone rings and he passes it straight to me when he sees it's my dad. I tell him all about my latest screaming match with that nut job.

"Unfit, Dad!" I'm yelling and getting stares from all the tourists.

"She will call me, or she will answer eventually, and I promise you this will go no further," my dad says. "Lily, you are not unfit. You're the most loving mother in the world." I smile. My dad always believes in me and I know he will fix this. Lucille is intimidated by him for some reason.

"I don't think she is intimidated. I think she has a lot of respect for him," Tater says after I share my hypothesis on why only Earl Moore can get through to her.

"Yeah, nobody is afraid of your dad," Ace says once we get seated in a cozy booth. I slide as close to Ace as I can get.

"How's he gonna eat?" Tater looks wildly amused.

"He loves me. Plus the closer I am, the closer he will be to my food and he is a total fat ass."

"Match made in heaven. I eat everything and she barely eats," Ace says while rubbing my arm.

"You'll have to stop stealing her food when you knock her up because she put some shit *down* when she was pregnant," Tater teases and looks a little disgusted.

"I was a whale!" I exclaim and Kylie chokes on her coffee.

"She ripped my quarter-pounder out of my hand after she inhaled hers," Kylie says.

"I was hungry...almost possessed," I say to Ace. The laughter with these three was exactly what I needed, and I am so grateful for Ace getting me out of the house.

After our meal and many cups of coffee, we get my phone fixed and then head to Red's to drop my car off. Bernie picks us up and lets us know we are going to her house because she is making her famous meatloaf again, listing off a slew of people who plan on attending. Word has spread about what Lucille has done, and it's now a witch hunt. Everyone wants to be here for me.

"I love seeing you two together. Makes my heart happy. What will you do during football season?" Bernie asks while the three of us peel potatoes at her kitchen table. She's making twenty pounds tonight, so it's going to be a pretty big affair.

"I hope she can tag along for most of it with Drew," Ace says proudly while I focus intently on my russet potato. As lovely as it sounds, it is quite unrealistic for a single mom to uproot her kid for a game of pigskin. Then there's Lucille demanding I dump him.

"Well, Lily, Tim and I go to most games so we can always help with Drew. We could even fly together."

"Thanks Bernie," I say with a big phony smile. They don't seem to sense my tension on the topic. My phone rings. It's my dad so I excuse myself so I can give him my full attention.

"She still isn't answering," he says and panic surrounds me. It's four in the afternoon and I'm losing hope.

"Should I just make the drive to Yosemite?" I ask with a lump in my throat.

"No. You at Bernie's?" he asks.

"Yes...pretending to be thrilled to go on the road with Ace while he plays football. My stomach is in knots, Dad. When will you guys be home? I want to come over." I need my parents and my old bed.

"Your mom and I will be there in a little bit so stay put. We will sort this out. She is not going to try and get custody. Just stay calm and enjoy your good company." We hang up and even though I know he's right and Drew is not in harm's way, I still don't like this at all. I walk back to the table and tell them the news about Lucille.

My parents come with Cameron, Jeanie, and their kids. Tony and his wife file in later, along with Sammy and his wife, Tater, Kylie, Darla, and so many more. It's a great time and a welcomed distraction to my frantic mind. Ace and I walk home together after it dwindles down. It's a warm night and we hold hands and keep stopping to kiss. We are so in love it could make anybody sick with envy.

"Thank you for making today fun," I say and smile up at him.

"I love you," he says. My heart is the lightest it's been all day.

I have texted Lucille a dozen times asking to speak with Drew before bed so when my phone rings with her name on the screen,

I almost have a litter of puppies from excitement. Drew and I talk for several minutes before Lucille tells her it's bedtime.

"Drew, can you put Mimi on the phone?" I ask Drew sweetly so she doesn't suspect her grandmother, who she adores, is a grade-A prick.

"Mimi, Mommy wants to talk to you," Drew says on the other end. I can hear Lucille tell her that she will call me back. *I know she's lying!*

"Love you, Mommy. I miss you."

"Boo, I miss you more…" I say and suck in the warm night air, hoping it will stop the impending tears. Once she hangs up, they come in full force.

"Listen, if she's not back with her tomorrow by one o'clock, then we call the cops. You're her mom. Without consent, this is kidnapping," Ace says as he wraps me in a hug.

I feel happy at the thought of that horrible woman behind bars.

CHAPTER 28

~

My dad smoothed it all over with Lucille, making her see that taking her mom out of the equation after already being fatherless was not in Drew's best interest. We both apologized for the things we said while fighting, and she admitted she didn't have a say in my personal life. I don't know if she really believes that last part, but I've decided for my own sanity to just go with it. The past five weeks we have coexisted in a somewhat peaceful nature.

She had my house painted behind my back when Ace and I took Drew to San Francisco last weekend, but Ace had it painted to better suit my style. The look on Lucille's face when she pulled up to my house to get Drew for swim yesterday was one I hope to always remember. I don't want a gray house with a black door. I loved my bright turquoise trim, but now it's white with gray trim, with bright yellow shutters and front door. It looks gorgeous.

Ace has basically moved into my happy yellow house. It feels like a family, I'm in heaven and a pure state of bliss with Ace here. I wish it could go on forever like this. We cook dinner together and take Drew on walks down to the pier for ice cream. The other day was her first time on the golf course, and we fished a whole day away in a canoe out on the lake. Drew asks for Ace to put her to bed most nights. I almost feel like she prefers his bedtime stories to mine. He makes pancakes and swims with her at the club almost every day. On the Fourth of July, we watched the parade and fireworks with our parents. This feels like the most perfect life, and I think it was always supposed to be this way.

We had a deep talk about our future yesterday over a nice lunch in Davenridge. I agreed to travel with Drew during football season and then when football is over, we will all be here. It sounds chaotic. But I couldn't let him down when he asked because of that irresistible look in his eyes. Then he ate the rest of my food as I thought of all the negatives of Drew and I traveling for sixteen weeks out of the year.

I came to the realization I can do anything so long as I have him in my life. He makes everything better. He feels like the completion to my soul.

Drew leaves for nine nights in New York with Lucille tomorrow. Part of me feels like she is gonna try something sneaky while she has her, like flee to Canada, dye her hair, and change her name. I have no choice but to trust her, and I must keep my promise to let her take her if I want to maintain this peaceful coexistence.

Ace and I are going to take a little vacation together before pre-season training. We are going to Dallas first, and Kylie is tagging along so she can see Spencer. Then Ace and I are traveling to Corpus Christi again for a few nights before we have to say goodbye for three weeks. We both are sick about it. It gives me anxiety to think about being without him. I'm so used to being spoiled by him. I can imagine my house descending into chaos without his help. Dirty laundry and dishes piling up while I run around in dirty socks looking for bandages and clean underwear.

Spencer has made two trips to Whimsy to see Kylie. She has also gone out for a long weekend with him. They're officially official, and she is going to stay with him while we are in Dallas. I finally talked to Tater about his feelings for Kylie and cried because boy, he sure loves her.

"Yeah…it's true," he said and looked ashamed of himself. "Do you hate me?"

"What? Why would I hate you?" I asked, amazed at his insecurity.

"For never telling you. It's just…I love her so much. In every way possible I love her. I love her humor, her heart, and all her weird quirky flaws. Like, you know when you go to the movies with her and she gets nachos? I love that she bites into those chips with so much excitement everyone in the whole cinema can hear. I can't even hear the movie most of the time when she's eating them." He looked like a sad puppy in an ASPCA commercial.

"Yeah, but what about how she leaves all her food wrappers in her bed and never cleans anything?"

"Love it," he said. "Even picking up her pieces of chewed gum she sticks all over the furniture, how she never screws the lid on anything all the way. I just love it."

"Aw, Tater." I hugged him and wiped my tears. "Tell her. You are clearly in pain over this. For years you have been in pain. I'm sorry for never noticing. Do you hate me?"

He laughed, though his weepy eyes revealed everything. "I could never hate you. I can never tell her because she deserves better than me."

"So, you let her *parade* around with the likes of Stan?" I asked.

He didn't even smile, which made me even more sad since saying the word always makes us smile.

"I don't want to tell her because I know she doesn't feel the same and I don't want to lose her. Now she has a real shot with Spencer. Ace says he's a good guy."

"There is no one better than you. You have to tell her what you just told me."

He shrugged in defeat. "Another lifetime, perhaps."

I haven't been able to stop thinking about him ever since. I promised and swore I wouldn't tell her about our conversation, but it's going to be hard. She should be with him, or at the very least see his face when he tells her. Words are one thing, but to feel the emotions behind them is an entirely different ballgame. She may feel the same but not know it, which is totally possible. He is her everything. She can barely make her own pot of coffee without calling him. Ace is telling me to butt out, but I am having a hard time biting my tongue.

"Maybe if I let it slip to Darla..." He holds his hand up in protest.

"Tater would never forgive you," he says while I pack Drew's suitcase and she practices somersaults next to me.

"Yes, he would," I say with a smile so full of my own ego he has no choice but to point it out.

After Drew falls asleep, Ace and I clean up the dishes from dinner in a perfectly synced routine.

"I don't want this to end," I say as he grabs the trash bag out of the bin.

"We have many days together before we say goodbye." I give him the puppy dog eyes. "Sprinkles, it will only be goodbye for a very short period of time." We have been over all this a million times, so he actually looks a little annoyed that I'm bringing it up again. When he sees my face fall, he sets the trash down and puts his giant hands on my hips. My heart starts to race and my head starts to spin the way it always does when he does this.

"I can get you a little place to stay while I'm at pre-season training so you're close. Maybe sneak you in at night," he teases.

"Who is going to take out the trash? Plus, when you do the laundry, it is always so much better than when I do it. What if my nightmares start back up? I need you." He smiles like his head is about to explode from me feeding his ego.

"I thought you didn't need a man."

"I guess you're right." I start to let go of him but he kisses me, reminding me of another reason I need him.

I let him go so he can take out the trash and I can wipe the counters.

After everything is in its proper place, we climb into bed and make love. It is just as fantastic as ever. He grabs my hand and spins my wedding ring around my finger. The tightening in my chest makes me pull my hand away and put it under the covers out of sight.

"Do you still feel guilty?" he asks gently.

I stare at him. I don't want to talk about it, so I need to change the subject.

"What time are we leaving tomorrow?" I ask while I rub his back under the covers.

"Noon," he says. "Is that okay?"

"Yes, I'm so excited to be distracted while Boo is gone," I say. "I love you."

~

When we land in Dallas Sunday night, we do the same thing as last time. He gets off the plane and talks to the press while we stay aboard and sip champagne, waiting for the second car. The car drops Kylie off at Spencer's on my way to Ace's. I go in and say hi and check out his high-rise penthouse in the city with his magnificent view. I'm more envious of the Chinese food restaurant in the lobby.

When I get to Ace's, I ring the doorbell with excitement. I missed him and I can't wait for this time together before we have to say goodbye. He answers the door without so much of a hello, his phone pressed into his ear. His glum expression is not what I was expecting on our first night here. He turns away and walks back in the house with my luggage. It doesn't take me long to realize his cold greeting is because he is in a tizzy as he talks to his lawyer about his divorce.

"I bought it way before she was ever in the picture...She can't have it! Tell her to buy her own beach house. She has her own money. She publicly humiliated me, and I don't feel like being very generous with her," he yells and again walks away from me, out of the room and up the stairs to the master bedroom. I wheel my suitcase back to "our" room that we used last time. I unpack it to busy myself because his divorce makes me uncomfortable. I decide to shower and drown out the uncomfortable situation since Ace is still on the phone and yelling in the living room now.

When I get out, he's in the room sitting on the bed. "She wants both my houses...both of them!" he yells and I jump. I have never seen Ace so angry and it feels wrong on his sweet face.

"Can she do that?" I ask, cautiously making my way to the bed to sit beside him.

"My lawyer is saying to play nice because technically I'm having an affair, too. She has pictures of your picture in my drawer and says I was in love with you the whole time." Ace runs his hands through his already disheveled hair.

"Maybe we should stop seeing each other until your divorce is final?" I ask with sad eyes. It's not what I want but it sounds selfless, which is what love should be about. Makes me think of Tater and how he has selflessly put Kylie's happiness before his.

"What? No! She is already engaged and parading all over the media with a giant pink diamond," Ace bites.

Parading...I hate that word even when he says it. The moment is so tense that not even the word can make either of us smile. He takes several deep inhales and exhales, trying to steady his temper.

"He says to give her the Corpus house because this one is worth way more. Says it will look good and chivalrous." He smiles at me through his frustration. I grab his hand in mine. "I love that house, this one not so much. I bought that one with my first big check for my parents and our family. We have spent Christmases there. I pictured you and I taking our kids there one day." I, too, have had the same thoughts. I loved that house and all his family pictures there. It felt more like him than this place.

"Give her this place?" I say and shrug my shoulders.

"This place is appraised at eighteen million and the beach house is appraised at 2.2 million."

"Whoa...can't you just give her 2.2 million?" I ask with big eyes.

"Maybe." He perks up. "I will offer her 2.5 million and see what happens." He stands.

Before he walks out of the room, I ask, "Ace, were you in love with me the whole time?" I keep thinking of Trina saying that.

"Yes," he says with his giant irresistible smile and my eyes light up to match. "I never stopped and never will."

"I love you." A beam of light might explode out of my body at the sheer delight at what it feels like to be loved by such an amazing man.

"Let me make this quick call and I will be right back to show you how much I love you," he says and I giggle.

"Hurry," I say with excitement.

I read a couple chapters of my new book. He is taking forever, and I'm restless. I turn on the TV, and it's Ace's interview after the flight. "So, who is she?" the reporter asks.

"Nobody, just a girl I had a little fling with while on vacation," he says. Pictures of us in Corpus flash over the screen. They are far away, so it isn't a great shot of my face. I am burning that sun dress when I get home. No way I looked like that in it when I left the house. Like a beached whale. Kylie is a liar by saying I looked good. Now there is one of me in a bikini and if I had a revolver, I would use it. *I'm hitting the gym!*

"Looked like more than a fling," the nosey Lady presses.

"No more than a fun week with a pretty girl."

Wow, that really hurts me. I know why he said it, but he sounded so convincing. Maybe it's irrational, but I feel my heart break into a million pieces. I fall asleep waiting for him and in the morning when I wake, he is already gone. He left me a note.

There will be a car here to pick you up at noon. We are going to celebrate with a nice lunch. We finalized our terms for the divorce, and it should move quickly now. I love you and you are a beautiful genius. Love, Ace.

I smile and feel happy it is almost over. One obstacle getting out of the way for us to be together.

I call Kylie and see how her night went.

"Great! He wants me to move here," she says. "He told me he loves me last night."

"Wow! Do you feel the same?" I ask.

"Heck yeah...What's not to love? He is handsome, a great

dad, he treats me like a princess...I'm going to marry him and have cute NFL kids!" I laugh lightly for her benefit but my heart aches for Tater. *I want to tell her!*

"Good for you, but before you say 'I do' you have to keep your promise to me."

"What?" she asks.

"Kiss Tater...just once," I say and giggle with her.

"I will. I had forgotten about that, but a promise is a promise." Never one to back out of a promise. One of the many reasons I love her so much.

At noon on the dot, I am dressed in a black sheath dress and beautiful black wedges I bought last time I was here. I have some jewelry on, and my hair is straightened to a sleek perfection. I climb into the limo that is dropping me off at the fancy restaurant. He is outside waiting for me when we pull up, and he escorts me out of the limo himself with an enthusiastic kiss. We get seated right away with his reservation. He gets a bottle of champagne and after we order, I ask, "So, she accepted? You get to keep the house?"

"She gets it the whole month of August to say *goodbye*." He air quotes the word with an eye roll. "I'm giving her 3.2 million because her emotional attachment to the house is *killing her*," he says, again accompanied with air quotes an eye roll. "I have to pay her ten-thousand dollars in monthly spousal support for the first year. I was ready to agree to fifty thousand to stop the back and forth...I just hope it goes fast now."

"Oh my god, ten thousand!" I exclaim. "3.2 million? And you are happy about all this?"

"The sooner this is over, the sooner the media will be off my back and then Lucille will be off yours," he says.

"Oh Ace, I feel awful and sad. I'm not worth that," I say. "Maybe we should just cool it and you give her nothing. She doesn't deserve any of it."

"No she doesn't, but I don't want to cool it. I love you and want to move forward. Do you?"

I grab both of his hands. "Of course..." I feel him spinning my wedding ring. I flinch and pull my hand away, putting it under the table. "You are giving up so much."

"So, I retire a year later...or they name a football cleat after me. It's just money," he says.

We have a lovely lunch and walk out hand in hand with big smiles. The smiles quickly fade when we discover two men with cameras waiting outside, yelling for Ace and asking for my name. It's so aggressive I can't help but want to run. Instead, I climb in Ace's car as the valet guy holds the door open for me and Ace possessively delivers me safely in the seat. "I'm so sorry," he whispers before walking around to his side. "Sprinkles, I'm so sorry," he repeats with complete remorse when we drive away.

"It's okay," I say, but my chest tightens when I think of Lucille. "Maybe they will realize I'm nobody and think it's not worth talking about."

"No," he says as we drive down the road. Luckily they don't follow us, probably because they want to catch the big country music star in there.

That night, Spencer calls and lets us know we are on this tabloid show called *XYZ*. Ace reluctantly puts it on so we can assess the damage.

"She's pretty, but who is she?" the host asks. I gulp loudly enough for Ace to turn his attention to me. "Nobody knows. Let's be the first to find out."

Shit!

CHAPTER 29

~

We immediately agreed to cancel the Corpus trip as to not be seen in public together after the *XYZ* airing. We hunkered down in his house the rest of the time. When he had work stuff during the day, Kylie and I hung by his pool soaking up the sunrays or went shopping with our NFL boyfriends' credit cards. Well, technically, Ace gave me a card with my name on it, but I felt weird about using it.

Me: *Do you want to buy me a $300 purse?*

Ace: *Yes, you can buy whatever you like today. Just have fun and quit texting me every time you want to buy something.*

Me: *I feel guilty.*

Ace: *Just please me tonight, woman.*

I laughed and swiped that card with zero remorse, bringing home my beautiful purse from the high-end boutique. I did please Ace many times that night and many more times since then.

Today is my last day here. Kylie and I had another lazy day by the pool before she heads out in the afternoon to go have dinner with Spencer and his daughter. I get in one of Ace's many cars, a beautiful creamy white Porsche, and zip to the grocery store to get stuff for dinner. When I'm in the checkout line, I see my face on a magazine with Ace from when we went to lunch. I pick it up and can't help but buy it. I have to know what it says.

It is surreal to see myself on the cover. It's a side by side of me with Ace and an old picture of Trina with Ace. It says "Then and Now." I look terrible in comparison to his ex. I have minimal makeup and that simple dress. My hair looks great so I should celebrate that for a minute. She is made up with big Texas hair, makeup, and cleavage. I look like a dumpster in comparison, even now, wearing a pair of cutoffs and a tank top over my bikini. I also have a Cowboys baseball hat on that I grabbed out of Ace's closet. They look happy together, though, and she is pressed up against his side, holding a music award in one arm, while they both smile at the camera. Ace has a genuinely warm smile on his face with her. In the one of us, he looks a little mad.

Don't do this. He loves you and you know it.

"I look like a plain Jane next to her," I say to Kylie on my cell as I drive back to Ace's house.

"Forget that fake cow. You're a real woman," she spits.

"What about how happy he looked with her?" I ask, trying to gulp down my insecurity.

"They were posing for a picture that they consented taking. You were ambushed for your picture. He also knew Lucille would freak…which she did."

Boy did she…

She refused to let me talk to Drew when I called to tell her goodnight. I had to beg and remind her that she agreed she doesn't have a say in my personal life. It took a good hour of back-and-forth texts and my dad talking her off her crazy train.

"I need to hit the makeup counter if this is my new life," I say while I stare at my face on the magazine and it hits me. This could be my new life, and I don't think I want any kind of fame for Drew or myself. If I am judging my appearance, so are many others.

"Lily, this is your new life." *Damn it, she's right.* "If you want him, you have to ride out this storm." I sigh on my end, making her sigh as well. "You do want him, right?"

"Yes. I want this to be my happily ever after. Drew getting a daddy and me getting…*him*." It's what I've always wanted.

A few hours later, I have a meatloaf in the oven and freshly whipped potatoes in the crockpot keeping warm just like Bernie does. It's Ace's favorite, so she gave the recipe to me before we left. I made it for him a few nights ago, and he said that I did it just like Bernie. I think he was lying, but I can't expect to ever come close to filling her shoes with her signature dish. I can't wait for him to walk through that front door. I showered and put on a cute outfit with a very sexy bra and underwear set underneath. I want our last night together to be perfect.

I see his headlights pull into his driveway, and I run in the kitchen to check the meatloaf. Maybe five more minutes left. He walks up to the front door and fumbles with his keys. He is such a glorious specimen. Today he did a photo shoot for a fitness magazine and texted me pics all throughout. I have been waiting to rip his clothes off for hours. I plan on attacking him as soon as he walks in. I fluff my hair in the window and ready myself. He walks through the door with a solemn look on his pretty face.

"What's wrong?" I ask as my smile drops. I can tell something bad has happened.

"This." He walks past me into the living room, I follow him with a lump of stress in my throat. He turns on the TV and I sit and watch. Within a minute, tears stream down my face. *This is awful.* Pictures of Dexter and I from our wedding plaster the screen, and they are talking about his death. The pictures switch to him with *Elle.* Then she's bragging to *XYZ* about their love. *I'm going to be sick.*

"Is it true?" he asks, flicking the TV off.

"Yeah...Dexter died," I say with the attitude of a hormonal teenager.

"The part about him cheating on you with that awful woman," Ace says. His jaw clenches and he looks tense.

"No," I say and keep my gaze on him steady. *This is not going to be easy.*

"Lily, I know you're lying! Was Dexter cheating on you?" His booming voice takes me off guard and my resolve vanishes.

Warm guilty tears stream down my face. "Yes."

"Why? You have got to explain this to me. All I can hear is you telling me how much he loved you, and you being his everything. Sounds more like *she* was his everything." The sympathy and concern are etched all over his stressed-out face.

"Ace...there is a lot they blew out of proportion." I stand, retreating toward the kitchen. "I have to pull the meatloaf out." I don't want to do this. Anxiety is wrapping itself around me yet again, threatening to steal my ability to breathe. My hands are shaking as I grab the oven handle.

"Lily, you have to tell me." His anger radiates off him as he stands behind me. He puts his hands on my shoulders. "You can trust me, Sprinkles."

He takes over, grabbing the oven mitts and pulling the meatloaf out for me, which is great because my hands are unstable and I can barely keep it together. He sets the meatloaf on the stove. I hang my head and weep. I'm so ashamed and never wanted this to be known. For the last five years, all I have done is try to forget this part of my life.

"He was having an affair with Elle for the last year of our marriage. She worked with him, and his trips to San Francisco were becoming longer and longer. He denied it at first and then promised to stop, but he didn't. She was calling the house and begging me to divorce him. It was *awful*. I was pregnant at the time. It was supposed to be the greatest joy, but all I wanted was to be divorced and *not* pregnant.

"He called her in front of me and broke it off, or so I hoped. Three days later, the day he was killed, he came home reeking of her and I lost it. I threw a vase at him, called him every name in the book, said I wished I'd never met him, punched him in the face."

I pause, trying to compose myself.

"He said he was going to go for a run so I could cool down and when he got back, he was going to change our phone number and would never see her again. I didn't believe him...I wanted to because I was pregnant with his child. As he was walking out, my only certainty was that we were done and I hated everything about him."

I close my eyes and take a deep breath so I can get this last part out and be done with this. Only, what will Ace think of me? My greatest shame revealed.

"I yelled out to him, 'I hate you and I hope you get hit by a car.' Those were my last words to him. That is the last thing I ever said to the man who gave me Drew. Dexter had his flaws like everyone, but to die that way and for me to have wished it…Ace, it killed me. My guilt is so deep that sometimes I can't breathe.

"The dreams…You and Kylie could analyze them all day long, but it's simply my guilt. I don't deserve Drew. How can somebody that wishes death on someone deserve her? That is why I'm so afraid of losing her. And I owe it to Dexter to paint a true picture of him than what he showed me in the end." My body trembles as guilt and sobs sweep through me. I didn't want this to ever come out. The silence in the room is deafening as I wait for Ace to reply.

"You were understandably hurt, Sprinkles. You didn't really mean it, did you?" he finally asks.

"Oh, I've asked myself that question millions of times before. In that precise moment, after months of his lies, I just wanted him out of my life forever." I know he can see the shame I carry like a hidden badge. "Obviously now…" I take a huge breath as he cuts me off.

"Oh, Lily. I know nobody speaks poorly of the dead but… what a jerk," Ace says and I flinch at his words. "I now see why Cameron doesn't like him."

"He wasn't a jerk!" I yell at him. There is a long silence. "Did Cameron really tell you he didn't like him?"

"Yeah, told me he hated him and that it felt good to say," Ace says, repeating Cameron's words that I too have heard him say many times. "But why all the talk about you being his every-thing?"

"I was," I say, half believing it myself. "That is what he always said…It is what I have been saying to myself since he died. It's easier and less painful to believe that than the messy days leading up to his death." He grabs my hand and I can see his anger tapering off. This is not how I wanted to spend our last night together.

"Lily, why do you still wear the wedding ring?" Ace asks, spinning my ring in his fingers again. I pull my hand away and tuck it behind my back. *I don't know the answer to this.* "Take it off. It bothers me and now it really bothers me. He didn't love you. You weren't his everything."

I sigh and walk away. This is for sure not his business.

"Lily, seriously, take it off!" His voice is raised and my blood boils to the point of having a near heart attack. *I am so angry.* I spin around and face him.

"Ace, don't tell me what to do! I will take it off when I'm ready. I may never be ready," I scream and almost flinch at the shrill tone I barely recognize. I hold up the magazine I bought earlier. "I look awful in this pic in comparison to your glitzy ex. I never want to see Drew on one of these. You quit football." I step closer into his face—well, his chest.

"What? I can't," he says, annoyed. "That isn't even the same."

"It's me telling you what to do. Doesn't feel good, does it?" I throw the magazine down on the table. "Plus, I'm not going to take my ring off for a man who is just having a *fling* with me."

"What?"

"I saw your interview when you got off the plane," I scream and walk back toward the bedroom.

"That was to protect you." He tries to grab my hands but I throw them off.

"I'm sure it was to save face that you fell for a woman that is not from this world. This isn't me." I motion to his giant house. "I look like a pathetic nobody on that magazine next to you and her. It's a lowly feeling."

"Lily, you are not lowly! You're the most stunning woman in the room wherever we are. Dallas, Corpus, Hollywood, Whimsy. I love you." He puts his hands on my hips. I close my eyes so I don't have to see that warm look in his eyes. I'm not falling for it this time. Good sex is not love. I throw his hands off and continue into the room, frantically stuffing clothes into my suitcase.

"What are you doing?" His voice etched in panic. He takes a stack of clothes out of the suitcase. It's no matter. I don't need them anyway.

"Going home! It's over. We will never work. I'm forever a small-town girl. Your millions and millions of dollars and your fame are way too much for me and my daughter," I say while I grab all my toiletries. I click the Lyft button on my phone. He watches in silence while I pack.

"Lily, take a breath," he says gently.

I flinch and push him out of the doorway. "You take a breath. I just want to go home and pretend none of this ever happened. I can't believe all that is on the news. Have you even begun to think of Drew?" I stare at his face.

"Well...I had just found out before I walked through the door so not yet. She is four though. We can fix this." *He has no idea his world will kill Drew and I.*

"No, we can't! Nobody in town knew about her lying cheating daddy. Even blubber mouth Darla hadn't let it slip. My parents, Darla, Tater, and Kylie are the only ones that knew, but now they all know! Her whole life they will all know and think poorly of her dad. Can you imagine what that will be like for her? He was more than that! Not to mention that Lucille is probably halfway to Canada with her by now!" I yell and make my way to the front door. *I have got to get home! I have got to get to her!*

"Please, just sit for a minute," he begs. "I love you. Or let me leave and you stay here. Maybe a few hours and we can talk again. Just please, whatever you do, don't leave angry." I look away from his broken face. His heart is not the most important thing here.

"I have to get to Drew." I pause. I feel so exposed and vulnerable. "She is the most important part of this messy equation."

"Sprinkles, please...I love you." His sad tone doesn't even reach my heart strings.

I shake my head in disbelief that he thinks catering to his needs is even an option right now. "Maybe you do love me…but you don't love Drew," I yell and point my finger in his face. "Begging me to stay in Corpus those extra nights, saying how excited you were for this alone time with me…You wish I didn't have her." I grab the door handle.

He shoves it shut and steps between me and the door. "That is *not* true. How can you even say that? I love her…I love you. You two are my everything." Tears glisten in his blue eyes.

"The last man that said that to me was lying too," I spit while I glare at him.

My eyes are so full of hate. His gaze is steady as if he is not planning on backing down. He finally moves out of my way so I can open the door. I get in the Lyft and never look back. I cry quietly in the back seat the whole way to the airport. No flights to New York until tomorrow night and they leave tomorrow morning and there are no flights to Whimsy since it's so tiny, so I fly to San Francisco. I land at 3:00 AM, rent a car, and make the rest of the drive home.

The whole time Ace keeps calling but I don't pick up. There is nothing more to say on this matter. He needs to go do what he does, and I need to focus on Drew. When it's 9 AM New York time, I call Lucille to talk to Drew. I take a cleansing breath while it rings. *Maybe she hasn't seen it?*

"Are you happy?" Lucille screams at me the minute she picks up. "My son's name drug through the mud while you look innocent and abused. Poor Drew will never truly know what a good man her dad was because this will always come back to haunt her!"

It's my fear too.

"Lucille, I'm truly sorry that they dug all that up, but it's not my fault. Can I talk to Drew?" I ask.

"No, you may not. And Lily, it is your fault!" she screeches before she hangs up on me.

For the rest of the day, she ignores my calls. They were supposed to land in Whimsy at 8 PM, but they didn't come home. I'm losing my mind.

CHAPTER 30

~

I stayed up all night crying about Drew. My brother came over before he had to head to work. Lucille answered the phone when he called, but she said she wasn't bringing Drew back and that I'm an *unfit* mother. My brother is pacing the living room as their screaming match continues. My dad was unsuccessful when he spoke to her this morning; she hung up on him.

"Listen asshole, I already called a lawyer. This is kidnapping. I suggest you get your disgusting ass on a plane now before they arrest you," Cameron screams. His swearing has escalated to weird proportions. It's safe to say Lucille and Cameron will never be *cool* again after this. She was supposed to be home with Drew eleven hours ago. I want to get on a plane and get her, but I also don't want to scare Drew. Lucille hangs up on Cameron and then he calls my dad. He comes over and we try all day to get a hold of her with no success. I'm a wreck!

The next day, we got Betsy McDonald, an attorney from Davenridge and a friend of the family, to call Lucille. She agreed to get on a plane and come home. So after her holding my daughter from me for three terrifying days, I am now waiting anxiously for her to be safely in my arms where she belongs.

The day is long and I'm a mess. I haven't slept more than an hour at a time since I left Dallas. My mom hasn't left my side. Cameron and my dad worked tirelessly to get her home. Tater kept bringing food and helped my parents with the liquor store when Darla was unable to. It's been a stressful time for all of us.

Lucille pulls up in my driveway at 9 PM and I run outside. I get Drew out of the car with a giant smile. "Boo! I missed you!" I hold her tighter than I ever have, shaking slightly from the biggest scare in my life.

"Mommy, I was so ready to come home. I cried so many times." I look at her with sympathy as anger surges through me. *Was she as terrified as me? I want to kill Lucille. She will never be able to see her again.*

"Boo, we will never be apart this long ever again," I reassure her before I kiss her cheek. "I love you more than Red Vines." Her tiny musical giggle fills my heart. "Go inside with Grandma so I can speak to Mimi." I hand her to my mom, who takes her inside with Tater and a very angry Cameron. He wasn't allowed to come outside, though boy did he want to. After the front door shuts, I look at Lucille in the front seat of the car.

"You bitch! How dare you keep my daughter from me. I have played by your rules for far too long. It is over between Ace and I. Not because of you, though. If I wanted to date him, I would. You will never tell me how to dress, feed, or bathe my child ever again," I snap.

"How dare you! She is my granddaughter," Lucille says, nerved.

"And she is my daughter!" I spit. "You are twisted if you think I will ever trust you with her again! She was crying? She wanted to come home so bad? You are a horrible person! She needs me, Lucille! Why do you want to take the most important person away from the person you claim to love most in this world?" Something shifts, and I see a small trace of remorse swirl in her cold eyes before she switches back to looking beyond furious.

"Listen here you little gold-digging *bitch*!" My jaw drops and I'm about to lunge for her throat, but my dad's voice cuts through.

"Lucille, you crossed a major line. Respect my daughter or I will call the police. And don't you ever call her a gold-digging bitch again. You know that is the farthest thing from the truth."

His calm and cool tone is impressive after everything she has put us all through.

"Earl, excuse me, but this isn't your business." Her snide tone makes my blood boil further.

"Lucille, it is just as much my business as yours. We're both the grandparents after all." His steady gaze makes her look away.

"I'll see you Thursday, Lily. Have her dressed in a pretty dress and matching shoes." I laugh maniacally.

"Lucille, get the fuck off my property!" She jumps back, startled by my hostility, and here I thought I was being so calm.

John puts his hand on her knee. "Let's go home." She turns to him and nods.

You will be lucky if you ever see her again, and it's for sure not going to be Thursday!

For the next three days, Drew and I stay in the house under a tight lock and my newly installed security system. I have never felt so vulnerable in my life. After the whole world finding out about my secret and Lucille traumatizing Drew, I don't ever want to leave the sanctuary of our little home again. Wednesday morning, I drive into Whimsy and get a new phone number so Ace will stop calling me. After we run a few more errands, we drive over to see Tater.

Drew runs right up to him and squeezes him tight. "I missed you," she says to Tater, who lights up. She just saw him last night when he put her to bed.

"I missed you!" he exclaims back to her.

"Where is Aunt Kylie?" Drew says, looking around.

"Dallas," Tater says and looks heartbroken. My heart aches for him.

"With Ace?" Drew asks with excitement. "I miss him." She looks up at me. "We gonna go back to see him?"

"No, we are staying home for a while. Let's all get milkshakes," I say, trying to sidetrack her. We sit at a booth and she quietly draws while Tater and I talk behind Drew's back about Lucille, referring to her as Mrs. B, short for bitch. A name my brother gave her the other day when he was talking in front of Drew.

"Mr. Brandon has called several times looking to talk to you," Tater says, Brandon is Ace's middle name so it's a clever code to not set off Drew. "And poor puffed-up p-u-s-s is fuming you haven't called her back."

I smile at his name for her. "I will call her back when I put Boo to bed. I changed my number. I will text you so you have it. Please do not give it to Mr. Brandon," I plead as I push my milkshake around.

He starts to say something, but I cut him off, holding up my hand in protest. "I tried. It didn't work, so I need to move on." I'm very ready to put Ace Lancaster behind me. Drew asks if she can go play in Tater's free arcade.

"Lily...." He pauses, and I know he doesn't want to say what he wants to say. I wait patiently. "He didn't do anything...and you with that ring...Please just go be happy. Move there with him. Boo will be happy as long as she has you."

"Tater, I know you love us both. We won't work." I shake my head in determination not to break my heart at the mere mention of him.

"But this charade you have going on in Whimsy will?"

"Charade?" I ask, baffled.

"He was a grade-A d-i-c-k," Tater says, spelling even though Drew is gone. "But you act like he was sainted, a prince charming."

I shake my head. "I am to blame too—"

"Yeah, yeah, I've heard it all. For years I have listened to you spin this horrible story in his favor. He was a putz and he cheated, then he kept doing it right in front of you, driving the dagger in a little more each and every time. You snapped, finally you snapped, and he deserved to have been told a lot worse. You didn't actually kill him, you know? Fritz Montgomery did, and he is in prison for at least two more years. Fritz was always gonna end up killing someone with his daily drunk driving. I'm just glad it wasn't anyone I love. You never should have married him, and you almost didn't. I had the getaway car at the ready. You wanted to bolt, remember?"

"Yeah, but I didn't. I made a choice and I said the vows. I let him live in this small town that he hated. I never even considered moving to San Francisco when he asked. Shut him down every time he mentioned it," I say. "I wasn't innocent in our awful relationship."

"No, but you didn't cheat or lie," Tater says. He is wrong there. I slept with Ace when I was home for Christmas that one time. We weren't married but still…

"I told some lies…"

"Lily, just stop. I'm tired of it and so is everybody. He was a snobby jerk. Nobody liked him." I glare at him. "He cheated on you and no matter what you did, you didn't deserve that. Man Lily, do you remember the time she came to Whimsy and slashed your tires and he still defended her? She was threatening to beat you up. Like I said before, he was an asshole."

"Tater, he wasn't. He was human…He made a mistake. At least he went after what he wanted," I say to him, taking a dig about Kylie. He sighs and looks away. An awkward silence stretches between us, which is not usual at all. Tater is my brother from another mother. He has never ever hit on me or had feelings for me. He is just a rock to Drew and I.

"I love you but I should go. Don't give my number out." My stern voice doesn't even sound like me.

"Okay," he says, annoyed and still not looking at me. I stand and call for Drew. I let her hug Tater and then I hug him, but it isn't a good one. When I get in the car, I angrily text Tater.

Me: *I didn't get mad at you about Kylie, so you can't get mad at me about Ace.*

When I get home, I pull my phone out so I can add people to my contact list and see two new text messages from Tater. The first is the picture Drew was drawing at the restaurant. It's of me, her, and somebody else.

Tater: *Who do you think that is?*

I zoom in on the picture and realize it's Ace. She has him wearing cowboy boots and holding a football. My eyes pool with tears. I set my phone down and walk away from it. It beeps again.

Tater: *That little girl thinks Ace Lancaster is her daddy. You said you didn't want to hurt her.*

I turn off my phone, and Drew and I play with Barbies. She asks about Ace all night.

~

A week passes, and Drew has asked about Ace every day, multiple times a day. She isn't the only one that misses him. There is a hole in my heart. The phone rings and I pick it up when I see it's Kylie. I miss her too.

"Hey girl, how's Dallas?"

"We are in Southern California now for the pre-season training, remember?" she says with an edge.

"I forgot. You okay?" Her voice is about ten octaves too low for her chipper self.

"I'm bored outta my mind. I think I'm coming back for a bit. I'm just in some crappy apartment all by myself."

The next day, Drew and I pile in the car and drive to San Francisco to bring our girl home. We are going to stay two nights in the city before coming back, though.

"Mommy, I miss Ace," Drew says about an hour into the car ride. "Can I call him?"

"He is working right now...Maybe tonight," I say, which is what I have been saying every day to her.

"Promise me." I look at her in the mirror. She is angry with me and I can't say I blame her.

"I promise, Boo." Lying to my sweet baby girl.

I wait anxiously for Kylie to get in the car at the airport. Drew is sleeping and I'm a rattled mess. When she gets in, I cry upon seeing her because I can't do life without her right now.

Tater is mad at me. Justin is team Ace, and so is my mom. My dad yells at her for butting in. I have no one except my brother, who is always on my side.

"Oh...why are you crying?" Kylie asks with a flipped lip.

"I just feel so alone, and everyone hates me. I need you," I say through an onslaught of rapid tears. She gently snorts.

"Nobody hates you. Let me drive." I hop out of the car so she can get in the driver's seat. When our paths cross at the back of the car, we hug for a long time and I cry until we get yelled at by some angry airport guy for taking too long. Everybody is so rushed these days! Once back in the car I start venting about Boo and her attachment to Ace.

"If you promised, you have to keep it!" Kylie scolds me.

"You can call him with her. I'll sneak away." She sighs but agrees to it.

That night I leave the hotel to pick up takeout from across the street while Kylie and Drew call Ace. I do the same the next night and it rips my heart out that I can't call myself, but there is no way we can be together.

When we get back to Whimsy, I drop Kylie off at Tater's restaurant for a work shift.

"Why are you working if you plan on leaving in two days? Is this fair to Tater?" I ask.

"Why wouldn't it be?" Wow, she is clueless. I give her a look and she sighs.

"I think everyone is exaggerating his feelings for me." She looks annoyed. I want to tell her so bad that he is madly in love with her.

"Aren't you stealing some poor employee's shift?" I ask.

"I have no money," she blurts out.

"You have Spencer's money, and you sure did swipe that Amex in San Francisco," I point out. She throws her head back in exhaustion. "You plan on marrying him?"

"I pretty much have to marry him even if I don't want to,"

she says as she climbs out of my car. That's not a good way to enter a marriage.

"Did something happen?" I ask.

"No, he is just boring and so into football. I feel like a trophy wife. Go get your nails done...here's money for a new cocktail dress," she says, mimicking him. "When I mentioned getting a job, he said it would look bad if he had a girlfriend who was a waitress. Well, fuck you Spencer, I like waiting tables!" Drew sucks in a deep breath. Kylie apologizes for saying a not nice word and Drew scolds her, which makes us both laugh.

When I get home, I play the answering machine. Ace left five messages.

"I miss you. Please call me," he says on the last one, making my heart break. My hands are shaking. I never wanted anything to work so badly.

"Mommy, why does he sound sad? Call him. He misses us." Drew's sweet voice makes me even sadder.

"Is that what he said to you last night when I had to go to the lobby?" I ask, kneeling down to meet her angelic eyes.

"Yes, he said he loves us both and misses us. He is coming to visit soon," she says with a big smile before bouncing to her room to go play.

I grab the phone to call him. Only I don't. I just hold it, wondering how I can make it work with Lucille's disapproval. The phone rings and I answer, hoping it's Ace. "Hello?"

"Hey Lily!" It's my dad. I close my eyes when the disappointment washes over me. He's saying he's bringing dinner. I start cleaning up my kitchen when I realize it's still messy from when we left the other morning in a frenzy to pick up Kylie. There is pancake batter stuck on the counter that requires an aggressive scrape with a butter knife. I cry while I do it. I was so used to having Ace help with all this daunting house stuff, leaving me more time to focus on being a better mom to my sweet Drew. I felt so happy and energetic all the time. Every time she asks for a glass of water or anything, I'm overwhelmed by this feeling of being the worst parent. I don't want to do it all on my own. I miss him so much it's killing my soul.

My dad walks through the door with a bag full of tacos and chips and salsa from Francisco's, the only Mexican restaurant in Whimsy. They have the best tacos in the world.

"Where's Mom?" I ask, exhausted from my day and these past few weeks. The dreams are back. They are different but still nightmares. Me losing Drew in a big crowd. My mom getting cancer. My brother losing his legs.

"She went for drinks and a movie with Darla. Now, tell me all about your trip," he says to Drew. She jumps on his lap and spins her little web. She is slow and deliberate, making no mistakes when she talks. It's like watching a piece of finely crafted technology. How can she be this well-spoken at this age? I love her. Maybe I am doing something right.

I start to relax and get out some paper plates because I don't need more dirty dishes.

My dad puts Drew to bed while I shower and unpack my suitcase. When I'm done, I sit next to him on the couch and grab his hand.

"Do you think I should call Ace?" I ask him.

"Only if you want to," he says gently.

"I want to but...there is so much stuff." I flail my arms so he knows just how much stuff there is.

"There is always stuff." He flails his arms back. I giggle at him.

"Did you and mom ever have stuff?"

"Still do," he casually admits and laughs. "Your mom is the love of my life, but I could kill her daily. The woman drives me nuts." I squeeze his hand tighter.

"I love you so much. How did I get so lucky to have you as a dad?"

"I'm the lucky one," he says with his hand on his heart. "I would love to see you take off that ring. Why do you keep it on after all this time?"

I arch my back and realize this question makes me very un-comfortable, even coming from him. I know he will never judge or criticize, so why do I feel this way? I ponder this for some time while my dad sits in silence.

"I don't know," I say and start crying. "I used to think it was the guilt, but now I don't even know why. We had a terrible mar-riage. He was having an affair. I almost didn't marry him. I kept a picture of Ace Lancaster in my sock drawer since college."

"Yes, so why keep it on?" my dad asks gently.

"Way back when, I did love him. He was so full of sponta-neity and charisma." I pause and ponder my next question to make sure I want to know the answer to it. "Did you like him?" He sits quietly. I guess he wants to answer this carefully.

"Yes, I did like Dexter. He was head over heels for you, but I never bought your love for him." I flinch at his observation. We both stay silent for a long time, my hand in his. "When he showed up after he quit his job in New York to live with you here, I saw regret and despair in that pretty but fake smile you put on your face. Broke my heart. For you and for him. He was *lovesick*."

I look in his gentle blue eyes. "And that isn't good?"

"Depends. In Dexter's case, I would say no. You did tell him no when he first proposed...something you never talk about. You told him no over and over again. I can't even remember how many times he proposed to you." He shakes his head in disbelief with a small smile curving his lips. "When he proposed at Willy's in front of the whole town, he finally had you. He knew you wouldn't say no and humiliate him in front of everyone. He knew you would never betray him. That desperation that he felt for you made him lovesick. He was just as sick as a terminal patient in the cancer wing. He didn't stand a chance," he says with a gentle squeeze of my hand as tears roll down my cheeks.

"Oh Dad, I feel so guilty that I let it all happen." I reach for-ward and grab a tissue off the coffee table.

"Don't feel guilty. He was a determined man and couldn't keep his wits about him. In the end when he finally saw he would never be to you what you were to him, he made choices that humiliated the both of you."

I look down at my ring and think for a long time. "Everyone will know I didn't love him. Drew will know I didn't love him," I say. "It's like the one thing still protecting his name. I wear the ring so they all think his wife adored him."

"Drew is four and probably won't notice or care. Everyone knows the truth about your marriage now. You can stop hiding behind that ring. Anyone that matters to you knows that you loved him and would never say a bad thing about him."

"I did love him once. We just were never meant to be," I say and wipe my tears. Deep down, I knew it was a temporary love, never meant to be forever.

"Take it off sweetie," he says in such a soft whisper I almost don't hear it.

"Okay." I slide the ring off my finger and set it on the coffee table. "It feels good." I stare at my emaciated finger where the giant diamond signifying our giant lie of a marriage sat and then smile brightly. "Am I the craziest person in the world?"

My dad laughs. "You are human. You just needed time. Now as for Ace...He may not wait forever. He may get tired of waiting for even you, sweetie."

"So, I should call him?" I ask, hoping he will tell me exactly what to do.

He studies my face with a big smile. "I think you want to. If I'm right, then you should call him. Block out all the noise and listen to *your* heart. Not your mom's, or Tater's...just yours."

I rest my head on his shoulder. "What about Lucille?"

"You let me handle her," he says like the protective dad he is. "Just for once, Lily, do what is best for your heart. If you follow your heart, then Drew will see how important that is."

I sigh. I know he's right. "Can we watch a movie together?"

"I'd love that." He kisses my forehead before I sit up to grab the remote.

I choose the original *Vacation* because I know it's his favorite movie. We have watched it hundreds of times, and it never gets old.

After it's over, we talk late until my mom calls looking for him.

"I better go. Thanks for entertaining me," he says.

"I'm so glad you came tonight, Dad. I really needed you today."

"I could feel you did." He pats his heart the way he always does with me, and I wrap my arms around him, squeezing tight.

I inhale his warm spicy scent. "I love you."

"Sweetie, you have no idea how much I love you. The minute you were born, you had me wrapped around your finger. It will always be that way." I giggle and hug him one more time before I let go. He always lets me end the hug. He never pulls away first. I beam up at his warm face etched in adoration. "Kiss that perfect human one more time for me before you go to bed."

I nod before he opens the door to leave. Once he's gone, I turn off the TV and all the lights thinking about Ace the whole time. I want to call him but it's so late and I know he has a long day at practice tomorrow. I really don't want to bother him. He mentioned that training camp is brutal and they are treated like prisoners. Last thing I want to do is get the boy in trouble.

I cuddle with Drew in her room, unable to fall asleep while Ace and Lucille tangle my thoughts. This could be a huge battle with her, and I don't know if anything in this world is worth possibly losing my sweet Drew. I know my heart will never heal if I don't get him back, though.

Sometime around 4 AM, I fall into a restless sleep, caught between a half-asleep and half-awake state. I still have a nightmare. This time, Drew and Devyn are in the box and Cameron is blaming me. "It's all your fault, Lily!" His torturous screams wake me.

At least I don't scream, so Drew is still sound asleep. I sigh, trying to find sleep again...

I miss Ace.

CHAPTER 31

~

I wake the next day to Kylie calling in tears.

"Come get me," she whispers. "I'm at Tater's house. Don't bring Boo." I glance at the clock and read 6 AM. Two hours of sleep are what I get to function on today. Should be fun. I don't hesitate for one second, though. I need to get to Kylie right away.

We hang up and I run Boo to Jeanie so I can go get Kylie. I find her walking down the road away from Tater's house. She climbs in my car and looks distraught. I haven't seen her this broken up since her mom passed away.

"What happened?" I ask in a gentle tone.

"I kissed Tater last night as I promised," she manages to get out through sobs.

My eyes widen. "How was it?"

"At first weird...so I tried it again and it felt really weird so I kept doing it till it felt right. By that time we had already had sex." I cover my mouth to hide my smile. "Oh stop. I know everything, including what you didn't tell me," she says. "I know you wanted this."

"Not if it breaks your heart I don't. I just wanted it to work because I love you both so much," I say. "Did you spend the night?"

"Yes, and we had sex three times, by the way, and when I woke this morning I felt so...." She sighs and flails her arms.

I am hanging on to every wild flail, waiting for her next word. "Felt so what?"

"Happy, okay? I felt happy," she blurts out. She doesn't look happy though.

"That's good." I rub her arm. "Why are you in tears then?"

"It's not good! I'm supposed to board a plane in thirty minutes to go see Spencer," she says. "Drop me off there on your way to get Boo."

"*What?*" I ask, shocked and a little angry that she's abandoning Tater while he still sleeps, thinking he just landed the girl.

"He's rich and handsome and doesn't live in Whimsy. I could go to school and become a masseuse or something, maybe open a waxing place here in Whimsy. There isn't one, ya know," she says like a crazed lunatic. "He could make all my dreams come true."

"Are you going to name this waxing studio Puffed-Up Puss?" I ask. I wait over a minute for her to laugh.

"Smart ass. Take me to the airport...I can't be late," she says. "There is a dinner tonight that Spencer wants me to attend with all the wives."

"Okay," I say with reluctance. "You know, Tater would make all your dreams come true, too. He could afford to put you through school, and he would. He may not be as rich as Spencer, but he is very successful."

"I can't take his money. He works too hard."

"I thought you were gonna stay here all week?"

"Spencer told me this dinner is important, and did I mention he won't even be there? Just a bunch of spoiled NFL wives," she yells and looks at me with swollen eyes.

"Please stay. We can hide in my house and smoke weed. I'll get back *on weed* for you. Drew can stay at Cameron's tonight and we could drink wine," I beg. After many failed attempts, she boards that dumb private jet out of Whimsy. I feel so helpless. My best friends need a happily ever after together, damn it!

I call Jeanie to see if she can keep Drew for a few more hours while I run some errands. I drive home, grab my wedding ring and engagement ring, and head to the jewelers. The jeweler is in Davenridge. I drive without thinking how they won't open until much later since it's so early. I find a little diner in Davenridge and am greeted by a perky hostess who says, "Party of one?"

This really hits a nerve. I don't want to be a party of one. I want to be a party of two with Ace.

"I'll be right back," I say and run back into the parking lot and pull my phone out. I dial Ace's number and it goes straight to voicemail. I anxiously hang up, then pace around the parking lot trying to think of what to say. I owe him so many apologies, but where do I start? After taking a deep breathe, I dial his number again.

"Hi." I say after the voicemail beep rings in my ear. My voice is small and feeble. "This is Lily. This is my new number. I know you are busy but when you get a few minutes, well, more like a free hour, can you please call me back?" I pause. How do I sign off? "I miss you." Then I hang up and feel stupid. What a pathetic voicemail. I should have said I loved him and that I am the biggest fool ever.

The hostess seats me and I chug so much coffee while reading the newspaper. I am going to pop. I keep staring at my phone hoping to receive something from Ace. It doesn't happen. At 10 AM, I get back in my car and drive to the jewelers down the road. This is it. This is where Dexter bought the giant ring. Oddly enough, I remember the name: Ace's Fine Jewels. Talk about a sign.

"Hello," I hear as soon as I walk through the door. I smile at an older gentleman standing behind a row of sparkling glass cases filled with beautiful jewels.

"Hi. Are you the owner?" I ask.

"Yep, been here forty years," he says with pride. "Joseph." He sticks his hand out.

"Lily," I say while we shake. "I was expecting to meet an Ace."

"The store was named after my dad, who was the original owner. My mom's name was Lily." I laugh. If that's not a sign, I don't know what is. "They were married fifty years when my dad passed. She passed three short years later. They had a beautiful love. Been searching for the same all my life. Thought I had it once, but I was stubborn and let her get away."

"I am sorry to hear that," I say. *Alright, alright. I won't let him get away.*

"It's not all bad. I help make rings that have started so many beautiful love stories."

"Yes, I believe you made mine." I set it down on the polished glass case.

"Why yes...this is my work," he says while carefully studying it under his magnifying glass. "Sold it about seven...maybe eight years ago to an excited young man named...." He pauses and thinks for a minute. "Dexter."

"Wow. That is impressive," I admit.

"Where is he?"

"He passed away five years ago," I say and his face falls.

"Well, that is terrible. He was very in love with you. Said you were his *everything*," he says. "I will never forget the look in his eyes. I have done this for so many years. People get married for so many reasons...He was marrying you because of love. The kind of love—"

"That falls apart," I finish, and I'm stunned I say it out loud, but it's true. It feels good to speak the truth. Something I haven't done about us since he died.

"Oh...well, shoot. Tell me what brings you in Lily?" he says, wounded by his mistake in thinking we had some great love story.

"I want to put the wedding band on a chain for our daughter. This I want to sell back to you." I hold up the huge engagement ring and he raises his eyebrows.

"This is a twenty-four-thousand-dollar engagement ring."

"Perfect amount to start a new love story that I would bet my life on," I say. He smiles and asks what I mean. I giggle at his nosy face full of excitement and spill the beans.

Four hours later, I'm back in Whimsy at Kylie's bank making a sizable deposit after calling a very heartbroken Tater who gave me her account number. I call her as soon as I get in my car.

"Check your checking account," I say as soon as she answers.

"Why?"

"Just check it." I stay on the phone while she pulls it up.

"There was a huge deposit made...Why?"

"You know that ring you have been begging me to burn? Well, I sold it and I want you to have the money from it," I say.

"Uh, hey crazy, you have a daughter!" she yells.

"I put the wedding band on a chain for her. I will give it to her later...Dexter and I had a great young romance that ended terribly. I want that money to be redirected to a new love story that I know will stand the test of time. Plus Whimsy *needs* a waxer," I say.

"Lily Moore! I can't accept this." Then I hear her little laugh and a tiny snort. "God, I love you though."

"Sure you can. I don't need the money and I owe you a lifetime of happiness. You have always been here for me and you are my whole heart, Kylie. Please let me do this. That atrocity of a ring needs to do some good."

"I can't—"

"Kylie, you have had so many tough breaks in your life. First your baby sister died, then your dad died, then you dropped everything and took care of me after Dexter died. Then you took care of your mom when she was dying. You put everyone before yourself. Let me put you first just this once. Please let me do this for you," I plead. We always planned go to college together, but she felt guilty leaving her bereaved mother.

She is silent for some time. "I'm coming home." We both scream and I cry happy tears for her and Tater.

"You accept it?" I scream.

"*Yes!*" she screams back. My whole body is buzzing with excitement.

"Call Tater, he's a wreck," I say and she agrees to call him.

"Lily, you are my best friend forever," she says. "Call Ace, he's a wreck."

"I did. I left a pathetic message that is haunting me. He hasn't called back."

"Their coach isn't messing around at that training prison. He'll call as soon as he checks his phone. Most likely soon."

"I love you!" I scream. "Hurry home!"

She squeals and we yell we love each other for several minutes before we hang up. I'm so excited for them. I adore Spencer, but Tater and Kylie are like the ultimate duo.

I drive to my brother's with a giant smile on my face. I love *love*. I am going to call Ace again when I get home. I need to apologize for the things I said that last day in Dallas. He loves Drew and I so much. We can make this work. I could live in Dallas part of the year. Maybe not once Drew starts school but that isn't for a year, so I could cross that bridge when I get there. I pull in Cameron's driveway and float through the front door.

"Hello," I say to my brother, who is on the couch staring down at his phone. "I just had the best day!" He lifts his face and my heart instantly sinks when I see tears on his broken face.

"What?" I ask, knowing it's awful. "Where is she?" I notice the house is completely still.

"Lily, I've been calling you." He gets to his feet in such a broken manner. I just start crying. My young vibrant brother looks as though he can barely stand. Like he has no strength.

"What?" I yell again. He walks to me and puts his hands on my shoulders. Tears stream down his crestfallen face. *Oh god.*

"Where is Drew?"

"She's fine, it's Dad," he says and starts sobbing. "I can't even say the words."

"You're scaring me," I say and push his hands off my shoulders. "Where is he?"

"He died," he says and covers his face. He clutches his chest as though he's going to collapse.

There's a loud ringing in my ears, a tingling in my fingertips. Is my heart still beating? I don't think it is.

"NO!" I hear myself yell. Everything is distant. "What do you mean?"

"He had a massive heart attack and was gone before the paramedics even arrived at the store," he says through sobs. "He's gone, Lily."

I feel actual physical pain when he says it. Pain I have never felt. Not even with Dexter. Cameron hugs me and we both weep endlessly.

"Cameron, he can't be dead," I say. "Not Dad."

"I know...I feel like it has to be a nightmare," he says. "Rose is going to come back."

"Cameron, how can you even make a joke right now?"

"Oh, I'm not joking. Can you just imagine what she'll be like?" he says as tears fall down his face. It makes me laugh even though I'm crying. A surge of confused emotions rolls through me.

"Where is Drew?" I ask through sobs.

"Jeanie ran them down to the pier to get ice cream, so they don't know yet. How do we tell them?" He starts pacing. "Their little faces...their little hearts..."

"Who is with Mom?" I ask as the panic sets in and the pain spreads.

"Darla and Bernie." He wipes his face with his hands. "They were there when it happened." He sighs. "We were going camping this weekend, just the two of us and Oscar. He planned it all. It was supposed to be a weekend of male bonding and fishing."

I grab him in a tight embrace while we both sob into one another. "I just saw him last night. He brought me tacos and convinced me to take off my wedding ring." Cam's shirt is wet with my tears as I think of his gentle and encouraging words, his warm smile, how he'd pat his heart for me. *I can't ever accept this.*

We both sit down and cry our hearts out, tangled in a web of denial and grief. When my mom walks through the door, the pain tightens. How will she live without him? He was still so young, only fifty-eight. I grab her in a hug and Cameron wraps his arms around the both of us.

"He was acting totally normal and then, bam, it just happened while he was ringing up Mr. Wilson," she blubbers through her sobs and hiccups. "I tried…"

"Mom, you couldn't have done anything," Cameron says. We all weep in disbelief at this sudden and horrific loss.

"Cameron, can you buy Rose a plane ticket? Call her and arrange it for me."

"She's coming so soon?" Cameron looks beyond bewildered at this request. "Damn you, Dad!" He looks up to heaven and shakes a clenched fist. It makes me laugh so hard that even my mom can't resist. The laughter is short lived as the reality keeps settling in with every phone call my mom gets. Tater calls crying and says he's coming over.

A minute after I hang up, Ace calls me.

"Hi," I say with a watery smile.

"Are you crying?" he asks.

I pause and take a deep breath. "My dad just died," I say out loud for the first time. My brother is right; it's like my whole body is rejecting the sentence. It was one of the hardest things I've ever had to say. Now, I'm really crying.

"How? When?" he asks. I sob out the details as best I can. "Lily, I'm so sorry." His voice is broken.

"When will you be here?" I ask. I need him here with me. I can't do this alone. "Can you even come?"

"I don't know," he says. "Do you know when the funeral will be?"

The word stabs me right in my lungs and takes my breath away. *I have to plan my dad's funeral.* We end the conversation when a somber Tater walks through the door.

I walk right into Tater's arms. All of the women take turns

crying in his chest. Then my brother steps into his embrace, his sniffles muffled against Tater's shirt. I hate to see them both so upset, it's heart wrenching to say the least.

More crying ensues as calls stream in. My mom and Darla are drinking whiskey and Cameron has joined them. It took him thirty minutes on the phone with Rose to get her a flight and he is beyond stressed now. I should have done it for him.

"Jeanie just pulled up," Bernie says. I can't believe any of this is happening and now we have to tell the kids.

When they all walk through the door with their angelic smiles, the air leaves the room as we all prepare for the heart-breaking news we must hand them.

"What's wrong?" Jeanie asks, but she already looks like she knows. Cameron whispers in her ear and she hides her face in his chest.

Devyn starts panicking. She's like me. She senses something wrong and then crumbles the way I did.

"Kids, let's have a seat," my brother says. We sit them all down and I put Drew on my lap.

"Grandpa got really sick today and he died," Cameron says. The words beat me down like a sucker punch to the gut you never saw coming. I squeeze Drew tighter. "He is in heaven now with Buster." Buster was my brother's cat that got hit by a car earlier this year. The kids were devastated.

Devyn screams and starts crying immediately, Oscar reaches for his mom, Delilah drinks her bottle and plays with a book, and Drew looks at me. Heartbreak etched all over her angelic features.

"That is where Dexter is?" Drew asks. I flinch at her calling him Dexter. When did that start?

"Yes, Boo. He is with your daddy in heaven," I say.

"We won't see him anymore?" Tears brim at the edges of her eyes.

"Only in our dreams," I say and hope that it's true.

"And when we go to heaven," Cameron says to all the kids. I hold Drew and cry with her.

CHAPTER 32

~

The next five days inch by. I moved in with my mom. She's a wreck. She hasn't showered or even got out of bed. She doesn't eat or sleep or even talk. Rose is home and, of course, making everything worse. Talking about his *will* and how much money we'll get. I snapped last night and almost punched her.

"If you don't shut your mouth, I will kill you! We are getting nothing! Mom gets it...Mom has it!" I yelled. She finally shut up.

Cameron had already thrown in the towel and gone home before he murdered her. She is leaving Sunday after the funeral and I can't wait. It's horrible I have a sister I loathe so much. The whole town is in a state of despair at this news. My dad was loved by everyone. Not one dry eye shows up on our porch to drop off food for us. We have had more food delivered than we could ever eat, but it is what people do in these times. At least in Whimsy.

Kylie and Tater have been running the store for my mom. We made one of the employees a manager and increased his pay, but Kylie and Tater are still handling everything so we don't have to worry. It's nice having such great support right now. Our hearts are so broken by the soul of our family leaving too soon.

Ace will be here this evening. I have talked to him every day but not about us. There probably can't be an us now. My mom needs me too much. Cameron is amazing but I'm her daughter. Plus, Cameron is a doctor and has three kids and a wife. Drew and I are alone, so it makes sense it should be me. I make her a coffee, and Drew and I carry it to her. We do this every morning, but she doesn't speak, just weeps and drinks her coffee in silence. I completely understand, but I'm so worried about her. We all are. Drew climbs up onto the bed.

"Grandma, I made you something," she says softly and hands my mom her drawing she has been working on since yesterday. My mom finally smiles. *Thank god!* She sits up and hugs Drew.

"Tell me about it," my mom says while wiping her red nose with a tissue. My broken heart finds a little relief. I sit on the other side and wrap my arms around my mom.

"This is Grandpa and Dexter holding Buster. These are their angel wings and halos, and this is God," Drew says in her slow, precise way. "He is happy, Grandma. Can you please be happy too?"

Oh my heart. Last night when I was tucking her up with Bernie, she told us that she had dreamt of Grandpa the night before and that he was smiling and wearing a gold crown. Then this morning she woke and said he got his wings.

"Oh Drew...I just miss him," she says and weeps with her whole body while I hold her. She's crying so hard Drew looks a little frightened.

"Drew, go ask Darla to make us breakfast. I'm starved," I say, reassuring her with a smile.

"Okay Mommy. You stay here and hold Grandma...I'll help Darla," she says like a little angel.

She floats out of the room, her blonde curls bouncing.

"She is so cute, Mom. I can't believe he won't get to see her grow up."

She turns to me and puts her hand on my cheek. "I'm so sorry I haven't been here for you," she says. "I thought we had years left. It was so sudden and I just can't..." Her sobs are killing me.

"Mom, I'm sorry for your loss. You were married for thirty-six years," I whisper once she calms down.

"Thirty-six incredible years. I can't believe he's gone. Every time I open my eyes, I feel all this pain come crashing down on me. How do I live without him?"

"I don't know, but we will figure it out. I know that we all need you. We need your love and we need to hear your voice. All the kids miss you so much," I say. "Can we get you in a shower and then we can all eat breakfast together?"

She takes a deep breath. "Yes...I can do that. I feel so awful I haven't been here for any of you." She looks ashamed of herself.

"Please don't feel bad, Mom. We're all just doing the best we can. I understand. If I didn't have Drew, I would have been in this bed with you." She laughs a tiny, tired, heartbroken laugh. When she gets in the shower, I call Cameron.

"Mom is taking a shower and has agreed to breakfast with all of us so come over *stat*," I say.

"Thank god, I was starting to unravel with her checked out."

"I know. She feels bad, so don't say anything. Just be happy. We all need to be a little happy even if it's only for just a few minutes."

I make her bed and almost change the sheets but think better of it. That was a process for me, losing his scent. I put a load of laundry in. I don't wash any of Dad's things. It breaks my heart to see his bright blue polo that made his incredible eyes pop in the hamper. He had it on when he came over the other night. I pick it up and hold it to my nose and weep. Smells like his soap, his aftershave, like all my happy childhood memories. I can never wrap my arms around him, hear his laugh, or ask him for advice again. He was the greatest dad.

When I get out to the kitchen, Bernie and Tim are at the table with Drew while she draws. She tells them about how her drawing got her grandma up and she knew it would.

"I put my whole heart into it," she says. "Now I'm putting my whole heart into this one for Ace."

Bernie hugs me and I smile at her. "He says he will come straight here to see both of his best girls," she says and brushes my long hair over my shoulders. "Why don't you let me braid your hair, sweetie?"

"Okay," I say as I choke back more tears. "That would be nice."

"Yes, sweetie, you have been taking care of everyone. Let me take care of you for a little bit."

"I really appreciate everything you both have been doing," I say to Bernie after we move to the couch, leaving Tim with a drawing-obsessed Drew.

She braids my hair and sings while she does so. Bernie performs at Willy's two times a week.

"That was beautiful," I say. "What was it?"

"Something I wrote yesterday. I was hoping to sing it Saturday at the funeral."

"You wrote it? For him?" I ask.

"No baby, I wrote it for you."

I turn around with tears and a smile. "For me?"

"It's about letting go of pain through love and carrying on for all the good you still have. For me, thinking of all of you without Earl is heartbreaking, but you without him is the hardest for me to imagine." I start sobbing and let her hold me. She talks about my childhood and how she has always loved me. She reminds me of our matching bulldog puppies Ace and I had. Chuck and Lola were littermates and after he got Chuck, I threw a tantrum that prompted my parents to get me Lola. After a decent stretch of time, I fall asleep on her lap.

I wake when Cameron and his rowdy bunch burst through the doors, excited to see Mom. I smile up at Bernie, who is still stroking my hair.

"Will you sing that song Saturday?" I ask and she nods, a comforting smile gracing her face.

At breakfast, the kids are so silly and make us all laugh. Even my mom. While Cameron and I are cleaning up the dishes, Drew runs in the kitchen crying.

"Mommy, my tummy hurts," Drew says.

I pick her up and check her head and notice she feels warm.

Doctor Cameron steps in and checks her out.

"Let's go pee in a cup," he says to me and I think the color drains from my face. It sounds so ominous for a healthy toddler to pee in a cup.

"Gross," Drew says with a pouty pinched-up face. I laugh, making the color return. I'm so worried about everything right now.

Once we arrive at his office, she is scared to pee in the cup and causing quite the scene. Cameron looks baffled and stunned by her reaction.

"I will pee in the cup too," I say and walk her back to the bathroom.

I show her how and she laughs when I get pee on my hand. I set her on the toilet and put the cup in, and she cheers that she didn't pee on me. We get cleaned up and I pass the cup off to my brother.

"I'm positive with her symptoms it's a bladder infection so let's do antibiotics, but I will run the full panel on her pee to be safe," he says while he fills out a form. He keeps rubbing his face and tired eyes.

"What's a full panel?" Drew asks him.

"They are going to test your pee to make sure it's healthy pee," he says and rubs her cute head.

"Can you test Mommy's to make sure hers is healthy too?"

"Sure," he says. When she looks away to grab a present from the treasure box, he shakes his head and rolls his eyes, making it perfectly clear he is not going to honor her silly request to test my pee. He's funny and I'm so grateful for him I can't resist wrapping my arms around him.

"I love you so much, Cameron. Please never leave me," I say.

"Where would I go?"

"Don't ever die...I just keep thinking Mom is next..."

"She is healthy as a horse," he says. "Dad always struggled with blood pressure. You know that."

"I know...How's your ticker?" I ask.

"Strong," he says. "Let's go buy a kiddie pool and pizza for the kiddos and keep this laughing going."

"Good idea."

The afternoon drags by while we wait for Ace. My palms have been sweating the last thirty minutes. I keep checking my face in the mirror and my clothes...It's so silly. Rose looks like a total slut and I hate her because I know she got dolled up for Ace. Cameron is on the edge with Rose and it's beginning to show. It's really taking a toll on my mom. It's like the whole room is one giant ticking time bomb.

Cameron yells to the kids, "Aunt Rose is taking you all to get ice cream!" She glares at him. She's aware how badly he wants her gone.

"Fine, but I'm not paying," she says like a sixteen-year-old.

"And I'm not going!" Drew says and glares at Cameron.

"Drew, you don't want ice cream?" he asks, amused.

"No, Ace is coming. I'm getting ice cream with him later," she says matter of factually. "Just us, like we used to, Mommy."

She has a plan, and nobody is getting in her way.

"Boo, we will go, just us three," I say and she relaxes.

When Ace gets to the house, Drew runs outside and jumps in his arms. I watch them out the window. She is talking nonstop and hands him the picture that she worked on all day and wouldn't let anybody see. Everyone else joins me at the window. Nobody speaks while we watch them play in the front yard. He is teaching her to throw and catch the mini Nerf football he brought her. I just start crying. I want to be a family with him. How can it ever work though? My mom will be a full-time job. She will need me. She's barely hanging on as it is. My mom puts her arm around me and cries with me.

Don't forget about Lucille...

When he walks through the door, I almost run to him but subdue myself. I hug him so tight. "I'm so sorry, Sprinkles. So so so sorry about your dad." His voice catches and I just cry in his arms while he holds me. I have missed him so much and this is what I need...I need him. I let him go so he can say hi to everyone else. It's another big cry fest.

"I got here as soon as I could," he says to my mom and I. "I feel so awful I couldn't come right away."

"You're fine, Ace. We are just happy you're here," my mom says tenderly.

Tater and Kylie show up with Justin a few minutes after Ace and bring us an early dinner.

"Okay...new rule. Stop bringing food. There is no more room," I say. "My freezer is full, Cameron's freezer is full, and so are Darla's and Bernie's."

"More is coming," Darla says, amused. "This town is in a cooking frenzy."

"This town is so predictable. I won't be moving back after college," Rose snaps.

"Finally! Some good news!" Cameron says with a huge smile. I look away to hide my amusement.

"Should have been you that died," Rose barks at Cameron.

"Ew," I say and walk away before I punch her stupid face and maybe bust her filled lips.

"Mommy, let's get ice cream now. I want to walk there," Drew says, running after me into the kitchen.

"You ready?" I ask Ace.

"Yeah! Been looking forward to it all week."

I smile at him with all I have. I guess I have been looking forward to this little ice cream date as well.

Drew talks the whole way and asks a million questions about everything. She stands in the middle holding our hands so we can swing her. We eat our ice creams while we sit on the shore of the lake. Drew asks Ace, "Are you my daddy?"

Whoa! I don't know what to say to her.

"Drew, your daddy is in heaven with Grandpa," I remind her as I smooth her hair down.

"I never get one then?" My heart shatters at her loss and even worse she looks so confused.

"Come here, Boo," I say and pat my lap. She curls in and rests her cheek on my chest. Ace stares at me with sad eyes, they trigger this avalanche of guilt and I look away. *Why do I feel guilty all the dang time?* I can still feel his eyes boring into the side of my face, begging for me to look at him, as he sighs and walks away. My body is frozen. Drew slumps her body up against mine and I snap out of it.

"Do you feel okay?" I press my palm to her forehead. "Oh Boo! You're burning up...Let's get you home."

I stand and motion for Ace, who is staring at us from a bench. "She has a fever," I yell to him. He runs over while I grab her shoes and her L.O.L. dolls that she brought along.

"Let me carry her." She goes right in his arms and cries.

"I don't feel good. My tummy hurts worse now." He rubs her head and kisses her cheek.

"You'll be okay. I'll read you a book when we get home," he says gently.

The whole ten-minute walk is silent, and he takes her straight to my old room. I get her some water and medicine. He has her in her pajamas and is cuddled next to her reading *Goodnight Moon* when I come in. I give her the medicine and water and lay beside her. She falls asleep quickly.

"I could be her daddy, you know?" Ace says to me. I roll over and face him.

"I know Ace. Lucille would try and take her away from me if we started dating again," I say, beaten and defeated.

"She can't afford or beat my lawyers."

"The only one that could ever talk her down was my dad and he's gone. I'm terrified of what she will do now." The tears come on so fast. He grabs my hand. "I'm still just a girl who needs her daddy."

"Come here," he says and pulls my hand. I climb over Drew and lay on him while he hugs me, comforting me with his warmth and love. Eventually we fall asleep in my childhood room, sleeping next to my sick baby girl.

CHAPTER 33

~

I wake the next morning with a pain in my heart and a queasy stomach. Today is my dad's funeral. I handled almost everything about today and still I don't want to go.

Drew is up and feeling better. Her fever is gone. She is making pancakes with Ace when I finally gather enough courage to face the day and come out of my room. I see her on a stool in my mom's pink apron, holding a spatula with Ace guiding her hands to help her flip. Makes my heart so happy to see them doing this again.

My head snaps toward the familiar sound of crying. Darla is on the couch with my mom looking through my parents' wedding photo album.

I'm so tired of all the sadness. I turn right around and crawl back into bed. The guilt of my insensitivity washes over me and within one minute I'm sobbing relentlessly. A few minutes pass before Kylie walks in. She lays beside me and cries with me.

"I hate today," she says. "Funeral, Ace leaves, Justin leaves... What do we have to look forward to?"

"Rose leaves tomorrow," I say.

She throws her arms above her head. "Yay!"

"With my dad..." I pause because I still have a hard time saying it. She pats my hand as if she understands. "You haven't told me about what happened with Tater when you got back," I say, welcoming the distraction.

"Well, I called him after we hung up and told him I loved him and was moving home, never leaving, and opening up a waxing joint here and calling it Kylie's Poor Puffed-Up Puss. He was waiting for me at the airport with flowers and a hot kiss. We are madly, grossly in love and I'm never ever letting him go." She beams. "Thank you for making me feel like I didn't need a man to be successful. I just need you." I laugh at her silliness. I rest my hand on her arm and pat it.

"I love you so much. Don't ever leave me! How's your ticker?" I ask.

"Good...I think," she says. "Yours?"

"Cameron says it's good." I suck in a huge breath. "I'm dreading today. Complete dread."

"I know." She squeezes my hand and we both lay silently in bed. It's a silence that makes me start to calm down. Kylie is just what I needed this morning.

Ace and Drew bring us breakfast in bed, but Kylie leaves and says, "See ya soon. Call me if you need anything at all!"

The three of us sit in bed and eat the pancakes and bacon. Drew scampers off to make a fort in Grandma's bed to "make her feel better."

"How are you, Lily? You didn't eat much," Ace says.

"Honestly, I feel like barfing," I say and lay back. "I can't believe today we put him in the ground. I can't believe I never get to look in those eyes again. I'm mad that he didn't take better care of himself and I'm mad he died. I'm mad at him! He's dead and I'm mad at him...I'm an awful person. Selfish!"

He moves the tray and grabs me in a nice hug. "You're allowed to be mad at him. Heck, I'm mad at him." I smile at his teasing.

"How's your heart?" I ask.

"Good. I'm very healthy," he says. "You?"

"Good, but I should probably have Cameron look me over again. It's been over a year."

"I wish I didn't have a game tomorrow. I'll come back Monday to help you."

"You don't have to, Ace. Let's not drag this out and make it more painful than it already is. I can't be with you. I can't lose Drew and I can't leave my mom right now and probably never again," I say. "As much as I love you, it will never be."

I cry while he holds me and says nothing. Not one word.

~

The church is packed. Ace has taken Drew to a room with the Sunday school teacher to sit with the other kids. Devyn insisted on sitting with Cameron in the church. Oscar didn't want to come, and I didn't give Drew the choice. Sitting in a room with hundreds of crying adults dressed in black is no good for her innocent heart. I grab a seat next to my mom, who is already blubbering uncontrollably. *I'm in hell.* Ace comes and sits next to me and grabs my hand. I try to pull it away, but he firmly holds it in place.

"Lily, don't be stubborn," he says, annoyed.

My mom starts laughing hard and making a scene. After a minute of her hysterics, I lean toward her and ask, "You okay?" She's wavering between the extremes.

"You are so damn stubborn. Just like your dad. You're so much like him," she says and continues to laugh like a maniac.

"Okay?" I catch Cameron's eyes, who looks like he is about to lose his lunch. I scan the pews, not surprised to see the church so packed, but touched. Whoa, I spot Lucille sitting a few rows back and she smiles at me, but I turn around abruptly. "Damn it!" I say.

"What?" Ace asks.

"Lucille is here, and she just smiled at me. I don't want to deal with her today of all days. I hate her," I say. "Why did she smile? She doesn't smile...It's likely a trap." I'm rambling now.

He puts his arm around me, and I try to resist because Lucille is watching. I don't want to set her off today. "Sprinkles, just relax please." His calm voice and his warm breath on the top of my head after he kisses it make me give in. I sink into him and grab my mom's hand with my free one.

The funeral is so long. We opened it so anybody could get up and say a few words about him, and fifty percent of the church jumped on the opportunity. What people said about my amazing, gentle dad will stay with me forever, and I can only hope that I'm half as adored as he was in his life. I have never cried so hard or loud, and I kept going through tissues. My poor mom was an even bigger mess. By the time I stand to exit the church, I'm so dizzy I plop right back down.

"You okay?" Ace asks me, bending his face to mine.

"I just got dizzy. I'm okay." He helps me up and intensely looks me over.

"You're pale." Then he places his hand on my forehead.

"What's going on?" my mom asks distantly, like she really doesn't care.

"Lily is dizzy."

My mom yawns like this is really boring. "She doesn't eat. Of course she's dizzy."

"You should eat something, Sprinkles," Ace says, still inspecting me.

"I'm a veteran at starving to death. That dizzy spell was probably from grief," I say absently. Man, this headache is brutal.

I'm so cried out. Drew is on my lap in the big limo and my mom is drinking bourbon while Rose bitches about the lengthy service. Cameron didn't want to ride with Rose. His dislike for her is at an all-time high. Ace is in the car with us and says, "I have never seen such a turn out. Boy was he loved."

"I hate that," I say while looking out the window.

"What do you hate?"

"Hearing about him in the past tense."

Get used to it.

"He *is* so loved," Ace says. "Very, very loved."

More tears come. "How is there anything left?!" I yell while dabbing my face with my soggy Kleenex. My mom laughs hysterically. I hand Drew to Ace and go sit by her across the limo, snuggling into her.

"You did good on the flowers you chose," my mom says while she wipes my tears away. I shrug. "The casket you chose was so beautiful, too. You've been such a wonderful blessing through all of this."

"Thanks, Mom," I say.

"Your eulogy was so well said. He would have been so proud of you," she says. "I'm proud of you."

"I would have done it but nobody asked me," Rose says like a bratty teenager, her arms folded under her hard boobs and plumped lips pursed out. Her makeup still looks flawless. Did she even cry?

"Nobody asked Lily. She just did it," Ace says with such pride it warms my heart. Rose rolls her eyes.

I needed to address all the heartfelt condolences this town has bestowed to us. Cameron also spoke, it was amazing and so funny. I don't know how he does it. How can he always add humor? "Cameron…" I look at my mom with watery eyes.

"That boy is a godsend with his wit," she says and we both laugh.

"Did he call dad a dimwit?" I ask, feeling a bit lighter thinking about his humor.

Ace nods. "And he called you a dumb blonde."

After they lower the casket into the ground and everyone clears out, I stay. I stand over his coffin alone and weep. I can't believe he is in there. Part of me wants to jump in and look at him one last time, no matter how creepy that sounds. I close my eyes and try to feel him, picturing him with his hand on his heart the way he always did. His silent way of telling me how much I meant to him. I never saw him do it to anyone else.

I put my hand on my heart so he can feel how much I love

him, how much I still need him. Nobody loves us the way our parents do, and now I only have one left. It's daunting and lonely. "Can you hear me?" I ask my dead dad softly. "Send me a sign if you can."

"I believe he can," Lucille says behind me, and I flinch when her arm goes around my shoulder. "I know you hate me...but I had to come." She starts sobbing. I say nothing, but I'm shocked at her emotion. I barely saw her cry over Dexter. She pulls a big stack of folded papers out of her purse and hands them to me.

"What's this?" I ask. *Is she serving me with custody papers at my father's funeral?*

"A family," she says. "At least, that's what I see."

I open the papers and see so many of Drew's drawings. All of Ace and I with her.

"She drew these nonstop when we took her to New York. When I asked her about them, she said, 'It's me with Mommy and Daddy,' only she wasn't talking about Dexter. She was talking about Ace. I almost had a heart attack when she started calling her daddy *Dexter* instead," she says. "I felt like my son was being erased. I overreacted and overstepped my boundaries. I have made so many mistakes with you and her. I won't stand in your way or her way of having what you want ever again."

"Oh Lucille, I just heard her call him Dexter too. I have never encouraged that," I say as tears slide down my face. Seriously, where is it all coming from? I have a splitting headache, probably from dehydrating myself. "I did love him. Please know that," I add with sincerity.

"He was hard to love sometimes, but I know you did." Tears pour down her face. "I knew he was cheating on you."

My eyes get big and my crying stops. I have always wondered if she did, but we don't talk about him.

"I met her," she says, ashamed.

"When?"

"John and I flew to San Francisco and we met him for dinner. He brought her, acted like she was just a colleague, but John and I knew better. I asked him to breakfast the next day alone. We both let him have it, and he admitted he was in love with her." She's crying so hard and I can see she feels awfully guilty about this.

"Thank you," I say softly.

She lifts her gaze toward mine and looks stunned. "For what?"

"For having my back and for telling me now."

"Lily, I know he was in the wrong, but to have the whole world know...It just turned me into a mama bear. I want him to be remembered for his quick wit, his romantic nature, his big heart..."

"He will be. I don't hate him. I tell Drew all the funny and sweet things he used to do for me all the time. I have pictures of him we look at together. He would have been a wonderful father, and it pains me every day that she doesn't get to know him," I say. "Never see him sing karaoke, to tell one of his exaggerated stories, to feel his passion about life. I wish he was still here every minute of every day. I'm just as much to blame for his infidelity. I was in love with someone else too."

"Ace?" she asks as she reaches in her purse to get us both tissues.

"Yes," I admit. "Dexter was so amazing, though, and he loved me so greatly. I wanted it to work and I did love him." I really want her to feel safe that I am doing right by him with Drew. I want her to know he was of great importance in my life. He gave me the greatest gift of all—Drew. He will always be my hero for that reason alone. If he died and there was no Drew, my life would have been a darkness I don't think I would've survived.

She turns and smiles at me. All the anger and resentment we have both felt these past few months is gone. I can see it in her eyes, and I can feel it in my heart. It feels so good to let that go.

"Can you forgive me?" she asks.

"Yes, I love you, Lucille. I really do. I know we don't see eye to eye on most things, but you are so important to me. I miss you. We miss you."

"I miss you both so much, Lily!" she cries and hugs me. "I

want to fix all of my mistakes. If you want Ace, I will not stand in your way...You have my word."

I shrug. "He travels a lot, and I need to be here with my family. I've not changed my mind about being with him."

She looks confused. "You sure, Lily?"

"Positive. I belong here with my mom," I say and feel my heart break into a million pieces.

"You are overwhelmed with grief...You may change your mind, and I will be your biggest supporter. You can move. We can move. We are flexible and Dallas has great shopping," she says.

I smile wanly because it can never be.

~

That night when I go to sleep, I cry about my goodbye with Ace earlier. I was awful and barely said anything to him. I just couldn't do it. When he hugged me, I patted his back and stepped away. There was no long embrace like we usually have.

"Thanks for coming," I said without much interest. He was visibly heartbroken. Then I turned and walked back into my room and shut the door behind me, leaving him to the rest of his goodbyes. He knocked on my bedroom door, but I didn't answer. I couldn't face him again.

When I heard his car start, it took everything in me not to run out and beg him to stay. I sat on my floor and cried, ashamed of the awful thoughts that ran through my head. That he would get injured, and the career that he loves would be over. That if he really loved me, he would quit football and move home here where we all belong.

CHAPTER 34

~

The next morning, my stomach is so tied up in knots for think-ing such horrible thoughts I can't eat. I am barely functioning by the time Kylie comes over with fried chicken.

"Oh thank god!" I yell when she walks through the door. "What took you so long?"

"I had to wait for Mr. Buckets to open up," she says, re-minding me it's Sunday and Mr. Buckets opens late. "Now tell me what's going on. You were blubbering so hard on the phone I couldn't understand you."

I start pacing and telling her what I was thinking when Ace left, and I slam the rosé she hands me while the adrenaline of being a terrible human courses through my evil veins.

"Oh Lils...you were a dick but you're grieving and he knows that. We all do. You're not an evil villain." Kylie hugs me tightly.

"But you admit I was a dick?" I ask.

"For sure," she says, rubbing soothing circles on my back before Drew comes out in a fancy twirly dress. Her hands are adorned with sparkly white gloves and a shimmering wand. Mimi is taking her for the day and night. They are driving to Yosemite to have tea at the resort and driving back here before the day is over. This is the first time I have agreed to Mimi seeing Drew since the sort-of abduction. We need to start somewhere, and Drew has missed her.

"Oh Boo! You look enchanting! Can I fix your hair in a smooth bun so your tiara will be showcased more?" I wipe my tears.

"Yes please, and put in that sparkly hairspray Ace bought me." She smiles, looking very proud of her outfit. I think even Mimi will approve...aside from the wand and tiara that is, but she did say yesterday she wasn't going to slam her outfits anymore. We'll see...

When Mimi shows up fifteen minutes later, she praises Drew's appearance while she spins around. Kylie's jaw hit the floor and it even took me by surprise. I give Mimi a huge hug in front of Drew and tell them both I love them. I want to have a united front with her from now on. We're a team. Team Drew. When I tell Kylie this, she points out that Ace is one of those players.

"Okay, let's not talk about him or the funeral for the rest of the day. I've been so bogged down I need distractions today," I beg with pleading eyes. Instead, I listen to her gloat about her and Tater. How her classes in Davenridge for esthetician school start in two weeks. She has a lot of great things to look forward to, and she is most excited that Tater bought them a Caribbean cruise package. They leave over her Christmas break.

"Justin is filing for divorce," she says as she grabs another piece of chicken from the bucket. I catch her eyes as something flickers through them.

"Hey Kylie?" She looks at me as she wipes a streak of grease off her cheek. "Does Tater know about you and Justin?"

"Nothing to tell, and why create the weird tension?" she asks.

"I partly agree. Like the past is better left in the past." She nods while she sinks her teeth into a drumstick. "But...I have this nagging suspicion that it wasn't nothing."

She shifts and then sets her drumstick down on her plate of empty bones. She looks deep in thought. Man, she can eat for such a slender girl. "It was nothing. You know how Justin is. He's impossible to keep still." She shrugs before taking a sip of her rosé.

"You sure you two aren't harboring some kind of explosive love for one another?" My eyes are squinted. Why do I have such a nagging suspicion about them?

"Nope." The pop in the *p* echoes around the room as if it's saying, "Back off Lily."

"You know you can tell me anything, right?"

She beams at me with a genuine smile. "Of course, silly."

My mom and Darla walk in with a few TJ Maxx bags. They must keep that store in business.

"Hey girls, Rose left okay from the Davenridge airport," my mom says, setting her bags on the table. "Oh that looks good. I have never needed a drink more than today." She grabs two wine glasses for her and Darla before making herself comfortable on the sofa with Kylie and I. She turns toward me. "Lily, you okay?"

"She feels like shit about Ace." Kylie says and I slap her leg.

"Tell me why." Concern is etched all over my mom's grieving face.

I roll my eyes and then tell her and Darla everything. They both agree I'm a dick.

"Okay, I'm a dick, but can we please not talk about him today? I want to just sit with you three and enjoy something…anything. I'm tired of crying and I want to laugh." I catch my mom's sad eyes. "Mom is that bad? Am I being a dick again?"

"No, sweetie, I agree. Let's just have a girls' night. Kylie and Darla, make us laugh," she demands of them as she leans back, slides her shoes off, and parks her dainty feet on the coffee table. I do the same as I smile around at my three best gal pals.

"Well…Maggie, when was the last time you got high?" Kylie whispers, as though she is eight and inviting us into a secret society of an underground magical world filled with bunnies.

My mom laughs. "Probably high school. Why? Is that what you have planned for me today? I'll do anything you suggest to make me laugh and release this tension." Kylie and Darla both squeal in excitement.

Before I know it, I have agreed to get *on weed* one more time, just to say I got high with my mom once. Honestly, my life is such a disaster that it doesn't matter anymore. The grief is too much. I need a reprieve.

Before we know it, the four of us are laughing so hard when Kylie tells them about opening her own waxing studio and calling it Poor Puffed-Up Puss. The story behind the name sends my mom over the edge and she pees her pants at fifty-eight years old. Smoking a joint with my mom is surreal. We are both widows, now stoner widows, who apparently need Depends instead of underwear.

We stay up late. Tears mingle with laughter, lessening the powerful grief that could swallow me whole if I let it. My mom too...

~

What do we do now? No one is bringing food or calling to check on us. It feels like everyone has moved on, except us. I don't know what my next move should be. Do I move in with my mom? Should I sell my house?

I decide to go home and get all of our clothes first. Drew and I make several trips while my mom is out with Darla. They went to Davenridge to go shopping and have lunch at Olive Garden. When my mom and Darla come home, I'm in my old room putting away our clothes.

"What's all this?" my mom asks, looking around at the big mess.

"Just went and got more stuff so we can stay here. I could just move in...sell my house," I say with a smile. "Roomie?"

She laughs awkwardly. "Uh, no. I don't want to live with you."

What?

"Hey," I say, stung by her appalled facial expression.

"Sweetie, I love you so much. You are the most loving and amazing daughter anyone could ever ask for, but go home. Better yet, go to Dallas and get your man."

"Mom, I'm not leaving you or Cameron right now," I say and shake my head.

"Sweetie, Darla and I are going to take some of his life insurance policy and go to Europe for three months," she says.

Three months? Is she on weed again?

"What? You're leaving us? Dad just died, Mom!" I exclaim. My throat starts to tighten at her bizarre behavior. Is she cracking up, losing her mind? Darla grabs Drew and leaves the room. "Are you high again? What the fuck, Maggie?"

She cocks her head. "Lily—"

"You get high once and now you're backpacking through Europe and having unprotected sex with European men who probably smell like smoke?" I ask in disgust.

"Sit down with me," she says while patting the space next to her on my bed. I do as she asks. "Your dad used to say, 'If I die, I want you to take that money and do something bold and adventurous.' So I'm going to do it! It was something we always talked about doing together. This will be good for all of us. Your brother knows and so does Rose...I have been dreading telling you because you think I need you to take care of me and I don't. Part of me thinks you want to take care of me just to hide from Ace." I stare at her in absolute awe. She hands me the phone. "Call your brother. He got Drew's urine test results and needs to talk to you. I just left his house."

"Mom, you can't go to Europe like some horny teenager! We need to stay close. Dad would want us together," I say, dumbfounded by her bombshell.

"I'm going. My flight is booked. Call your brother," she says and shuts my door as she walks out.

What? I absently dial Cameron's number, feeling scorned and abandoned.

"Did our irresponsible mom tell you she got high the other night and is going to Europe for three months? Like she has no family or little grandkids? W-T-F?" I bark out.

"Yeah. So, I wanted to talk to you about Drew," he says with seriousness, completely skipping over Mom.

"Was it a bladder infection?" I ask, still marveling at my mom abandoning me. *Dad just died!*

"No! This is so crazy. Drew is either a medical marvel or she is aging miraculously," he says and laughs. Now he sounds like himself.

"Why?"

"She's pregnant!"

The words take a minute to process. "What?"

"Hey dingbat...you turned in your pee instead of Drew's. Congratulations, it's an NFL baby!" he exclaims. "Should I tell him, or will you?"

"Why would you give her a pregnancy test?" I ask, flummoxed.

"I'm also a dingbat and filled out the wrong form. Apparently, grief is a *real* doozy for us Moore's."

After going back and forth, with me in denial and him repeating that I'm indeed pregnant, I start crying.

"I smoked weed the other day." I gulp back the reality that I may be building a crack baby.

"Don't worry about that," Cameron sighs as if I'm silly for even bringing it up.

"I can't be pregnant...two kids and no dads. This is not the way it's supposed to be. I will be like the town slut and talked about forever with my two bastard kids *parading* all over town without *grandparents!*" I yell at my mom, who is peeking her head through the doorway, watching me come unglued. "Will their last name be Snow like on *Game of Thrones*? Oh god, that is a horrible fate. They don't stand a chance," I say and Cameron, another huge *GOT* fan, laughs.

"Lily, Ace is not going to let his kid be a bastard. You'll only have Drew Snow to worry about...but she is a very cute and smart little bastard."

I'm on the verge of sobbing. "That is *not* funny!" I say and throw myself on the bed. "How did this happen?"

"Oh sweetie, you're too old for this talk." My mom dismissively swats the air.

"Get out! You're abandoning me! Drew and this bastard baby aren't even going to have grandparents!" I say and feel hopeless, suffering enclosing all around me. "I miss Dad."

"Tim and Bernie are excellent grandparents. She wants a girl, and yes she knows because I told her!" Her smile is annoyingly bright. She waves her hand as she leaves the room. "I miss your Dad too," she yells.

"What ever happened to doctor-patient confidentiality?" I ask Cameron, stunned that he already told people.

"Doesn't exist in this town. Jeanie knows and so does Kylie. Jeanie couldn't resist telling her when she ran into her at the store. Everyone is thrilled! We really needed some good news."

"I'm hanging up on you," I say and throw myself back on the bed again and wail. "Why?"

I spend the rest of the evening in denial and don't take any calls, three of which were Ace. God, if he knows already, I will come undone. He has a game in San Francisco Sunday against the 49ers. I can tell him after if I'm still pregnant. People have miscarriages all the time. All the time.

"Sweetie, you do not want a miscarriage," my mom says, ashamed of me when I say this thought out loud.

"You have never been abandoned by both your parents in such a short time frame or been a single mom!" I shout.

"Come here." She beckons me to her as she holds her arm out for me to come sit on her side. She holds me on the couch while Darla rubs my feet and we watch chick flicks. "I don't want a miscarriage," I weep halfway through *Clueless*. "Please don't ever tell either of my kids I ever said that." Darla throws her head back in a giant laugh while I wipe yet more tears off my face with my nine billionth tissue this week.

"Lily, we know that. It's okay, sweetie, this is a lot to take in.

You're overwhelmed," Darla says and my mom kisses my head.

"Thank you, Darla!" It feels good to have some understanding with this overwhelming news.

Pregnant? What will Ace think of me getting back on weed while building his NFL baby?

CHAPTER 35

～

Saturday comes, I'm crying nonstop, and I'm still at my mom's because I need her. She is taking care of me. She says I need to go home in a few days, and I feel wholly heartbroken by her cruel dismissal.

"Did you guys tell Ace?" I ask after Drew goes to bed.

"Sweetie, no, we won't do that to you. He is going to be so overjoyed and when you see his face, you will know why this all happened," she says. "Now, come sleep with me tonight."

I light up. "Okay. I love you...Don't go to Europe. What if something bad happens? I need you."

"Sweetie, all your life your dad and I wondered, will she ever *go away?*" I cock my head. What does she mean? "GO AWAY!" she yells at me and I flinch.

"Mom, Dad didn't want me to go away," I say, wounded.

"No sweetie, it's an exaggeration. You have always needed us more than the other two. You relied on your dad to fix everything for you and he did because you were his baby. Maybe even his favorite. We parents aren't supposed to have favorites, but you two had a very special bond and he loved you like you wouldn't even believe," she says with tears in her eyes.

"Do we have a special bond? Because right now, I am feeling very *un*loved by you."

"Sweetie, yes! You are my whole world and my best friend! I

couldn't have gotten through these last two weeks without you." The sincerity swirling around her misty eyes lets me know she means it.

"Okay," I say, still unconvinced. *Why is she leaving me then, and why doesn't she want to live with me?*

"Do you need to hear that you're my favorite?" she asks, amused.

"I mean, it would be nice..." I say and she hugs me.

"You are my favorite. How's that?" I know I'm likely not her favorite but it feels great to hear the words.

We cuddle and talk for hours in her bed. I'm so lucky to have transitioned my relationship with my mom into a friendship that means the world to me. I miss my dad and always will, but at least I still have my mom. Death is monumental, but it also highlights what we still have. That is what my mom and I have been trying to focus on as life moves forward.

"Lily, your dad wanted you to be with Ace. He never said it because he didn't like to pressure you the way I do, but he would want you to call him and make this work."

I sigh as I think back to our last conversation as he gently coaxed me out of the ring and told me to call Ace. "Mom, I just need time to process all this."

"Time is precious...Do you see that?"

I know what she means. We never know what each day will bring and how much time we have here in this life. We fall asleep hand in hand. I wake screaming in a sweaty mess. My mom bolts up with me.

"Sweetie, I thought they had stopped?"

"No," I admit. "It was different though, Ace and Drew together in the glass box. I could hear them, and they were begging for me to get them out. To save them, but I couldn't."

It's a sign. I've never had a nightmare about Ace being in the box.

"Lay back down," she says while she pets my head. I cuddle up close to her. She goes back to sleep quickly, but I lay awake lost in my thoughts about my new baby. Drew will be thrilled to be a big sister. Ace may be shocked but after it wears off, he will be thrilled. We both had talked about wanting this. He wants to have kids with me, and I said I wanted it too. Lucille gave me her blessing and my mom is kicking me to the curb, so what is holding me back now?

Dexter.

Not my love for him, but how our relationship just fizzled and died. When we started dating, I fell hard. I would call it a whirlwind romance. We were so consumed with each other I couldn't think straight. We moved fast and, in the end, our love was not strong enough to make it through life. I don't want that again, especially with Ace. I just need time, that's all.

At 6 AM, I finally get out of bed and decide to go for a walk. I find myself at Tater's for breakfast. Tater is here, but Kylie isn't.

"So, pregnant?" he asks, amused.

"Good grief, is there anybody in this town that doesn't know?"

"Just the daddy! Speaking of Ace, Kylie and I are leaving in about an hour to go watch his game. Going to get a room. You want to tag along? He gave me tickets for you and Drew," he says. "Ya know, get your little family back together."

"No, my mom and I have plans." *What a lie.* My mom has plans with Darla and some other ladies to go to Davenridge and get their nails done. She didn't even invite me and when I asked to tag along, she told me no. This was for her and her friends. At the same time, she told me this is the last week I can stay at her house. I don't want to go home, though. "Maybe next week Drew and I could come stay with you and Kylie for a few weeks."

"No...you can't. We like to walk around naked." He waggles his eyebrows suggestively.

"Gross," I say. "I'll go stay with Cameron then."

"Why not just go home? Or better yet, go see Ace."

"I think I will take my breakfast to go," I say. "You're annoying and I'm trying to grow a bastard."

"Do you even understand the true meaning of a bastard?"

I shrug. *Does it even matter?*

I smile at the young cook, David. "Hey David, can you box it up for me?" I yell to him. Tater waves him away.

"No...I'll eat with you," he says and sits. "Why don't you want to go home?"

"Because my dad died and I'm sad. I just want to be with my mom. She is being so mean about it. My dad would let me stay with him if it had been her," I say and my eyes fill with tears. "Sometimes it feels like he was the only one who ever understood me."

Tater laughs. "He was a sucker for sure, with your big green eyes. You are what I like to call a radioactive clinger. Your mom knows if she lets you stay, you will never leave. Life is happening all around you. Before you know it there will be another baby and Drew will be in kindergarten. Don't you want a partner to share it all with?" he asks. "Someone to hold your hand through it all, someone to laugh with?"

"Radioactive clinger?" I ask, the title a wound in my gut. He nods. "I do want someone to share it with, but what if I call Ace and we get back together and I move my daughter and it doesn't work?"

"It will work. Ace isn't Dexter...Ace is the best guy I know. He loves you like crazy, Lils." He slaps his hands together and aggressively rubs them back and forth. "But, let's play your little game. It doesn't work so you come home and raise two babies on your own and move in with your mom and get a shit ton of cats, get fat, and never try anything ever again."

I laugh. "Tater, I get your point, but I am so overwhelmed. My dad..." I say and the tears start.

"I know Lily, he was your rock, your best friend, and he will be missed forever. You are so much like him though...I know you think you can't do any of this without his protection, but you can. Who did everyone turn to when he died? Who kept the family going? It's you. Believe in yourself." I smile. "When you spoke at his funeral about him, all I thought was that you are him. The way everyone confides in you, the way everyone adores you. You need to channel his love for you and *sprinkle* it around," he adds.

"Tell me, what is really going on? Either you don't know yet or something is freaking you out about Ace."

I flinch as something clicks. I shift uncomfortably, trying not to meet his eyes.

"Lily Marie Moore, spit it out," he barks.

I sigh, a tidal wave of emotions flooding over me. "When we started dating again, he mentioned why he never came back for me."

"Tell me what he said." His gentle voice and kind eyes pull me in.

"That he thought I'd hold him back. Me and my two bastard kids would for sure hold him back, don't you think?"

"Oh Lils. You both were young and things have changed. He was stupid back then. Don't you see how much stronger that makes your relationship? That he felt safe enough to tell you his truth?" He grabs my hand. "He was such a dick!"

It's not true, but the fact he's saying it to make me feel better means the world to me. "You're the sweetest guy. Is your heart doing okay?" I ask, concerned.

"Well, I did just get on blood pressure meds. Cameron says I need to cut back on the booze and the fried foods. I hate getting old. All I wanna do is hook myself up to an IV of beer so I have two free hands to rotate French fries and corn dogs into my mouth," he teases.

I laugh. "Please take care of yourself." I grab him in a hug. "I love you."

We eat breakfast and then I walk home with pancakes and bacon for my mom and Drew. I drift off, deep in thought about Dexter and my dad. *Are they hanging out?*

What would Dexter think of Ace being a part of Drew's life? Before I know it, I've walked all the way around to the one-lane bridge that Dexter died on. I haven't been here since he died, skirting around and taking the new bridge to Tater's. A little breeze stirs behind me, as if it's encouraging me to step onto the bridge. A little magic force pushing me forward. I walk slowly and when

I get a quarter of the way down it, I notice two people fishing, a young boy and a man. The closer I get, the more intrigued I am by their exchange. He's teaching the little boy to cast. Is it a father and son? They both have caps on so I can't see them, but when the man looks at me, I freeze. It's Howard. My palms start sweating and I turn to go.

"Hey Lily!" he yells. "Good morning!"

Crap!

I turn back to face him and wave. "Hi Howard," I reply. "I'm on the wrong bridge. See you both later."

"But if you go all the way back around to the new bridge, then it will take you twice as long to get home. It's pretty warm. Do you need a water if you're going all the way back around?"

It is warm.

"You okay, Lily? You look white as a ghost," he says. My lip starts quivering. Cameron is right; he doesn't much look like Dexter, but something about his mannerisms really remind me of Dexter. Before I know it, he's leading me to his little chair next to his tackle box. "I think you should sit down."

"I'm sorry," I whimper out as the floodgates open.

"Don't be. We have been thinking about your family. The day of the service, we couldn't get through the long line of people waiting to pay their respects. I'm so sorry for such a huge loss. I absolutely adored your dad." He leans down to look in my eyes, then hands me a cold bottle of water from his cooler.

"I mean, I'm sorry I'm always so rude to you. You remind me of my husband, Dexter. This is where he died...so I came here to talk to him for the first time ever and see you?" I take a small sip of water. *Signs everywhere, but what do they all mean?*

Relief washes over his face. "Really? I'm flattered. So my mug reminds you of someone you loved, made a baby with." He laughs to himself and I can't help but watch him as he brushes his hair off his forehead. He looks truly amused and deep off in another world as he looks around the bridge. It's almost a visible thing, his racing mind. Like Dexter's. "I'm married," he says with a warm sarcasm that makes me laugh. As if he's warning me off. As if he's worried I have feelings for him. He's joking, of course. "Well, we love it here so I guess to make this work between the two of us, I'll have to get facial reconstruction." I giggle. That's exactly what Dexter would've said. Like he's flirting but not really, wanting to solve my problem by doing something grand. He always did huge grand gestures for everyone.

Howard and I chat about nothing for a few minutes before he and his charming, goofy son decide to give me a few minutes to myself by taking an "adventure down to the shore to skim rocks."

I stand out of the chair as I take a deep breath. I look down the bridge and see the vase that the community had mounted for people to fill for Dexter. They built a little memorial for him here. I slowly walk down to it. This is where it happened. This is where my life changed forever. There's a little vortex of wind that I swear circles only around me. "Hey Dex. How ya doing?"

I feel so weird. This is weird. I'm just talking to myself.

The wind picks up, blowing leaves and tiny twigs all over the place. I take it as a sign to say more to him. "I'm sorry about never coming here before. I was very angry about Elle and the whole affair, plus you made me a widow at twenty-six. Not cool." I shake my head so he knows I mean it. "Now I just wish you were still here to hug me and tell me everything is going to be okay. I always think about when you first moved here. I think about how excited you were."

I laugh to myself. The words flow easier now. "I mean, you were such a good sport. You decide you love a crazy girl who loves nothing more than her family and this small town. You tried to devote yourself to them as much as I did. Only, neither one of them ever loved you back, did they? My family, my friends, all of Whimsy never really let you in." I pause, thinking deeply about his predicament. He loved someone else but got me pregnant. "It must have been a lot for you too at the time. I know before you loved her you tried to love me enough for the both of us. I think if I wouldn't have met Ace Lancaster before you, then I could've loved you the same. I wasn't able to give you all you deserved because my heart belonged to him.

"But do I leap again? What if he really would be held back by me and my insane chaotic life?" I sigh and take another deep breath back in. "Surely me and two kids are overwhelming, and he's such a good football player. A chance of a lifetime I'd hate to ruin for him. What about Drew? Do you approve of how I'm raising her? Do you mind if another man raises her?" I bend down and pick up a little white flower that has blown by my feet. I inspect it and smell it.

"I hope you know that I miss you every day. I also want you to know that because of you, I have the most beautiful little girl in the world." I take a minute to weep. "I'm sorry for everything." I drop the little flower over the bridge walls and watch as it floats down to the water.

~

My mom leaves a few hours after I get home with their cold breakfast. I pathetically begged her not to go, but she did. It's just Drew here, and I feel so lonely. I call my brother.

"Do you guys want to barbecue or something? I'm going crazy here," I say while pacing the living room.

"Well, sure. We can come over around five?" he says absently. I don't think he wants to come over. I think of my mom saying to go away and Tater calling me a radioactive clinger. *I can't be that bad. Radioactive? Criminy, it sure sounds bad.* Lawrence's words replay in my head, "You're so fucking clingy."

"No, come now and we can go walk down to the beach and let the kids play. Maybe grab a bite to eat and some ice cream," I say, radioactive clinger style, because five is too far away and I'll lose my mind.

"Uh...okay. I'll get everyone in the car." *He doesn't sound thrilled.*

"Hurry!" I say with an edge that shocks me. "Sorry, I'm just going crazy here."

We hang up and I get Drew dressed. She is so excited to see her cousins and I'm happy not to be alone.

My phone rings and I see it's Justin calling.

"Hey," I say with excitement to have someone to talk to. "Whatcha doin'?"

"I know I'm supposed to stay out of this stuff, but I can't on this one," he says.

"What?" I ask, intrigued and excited for a distraction. Hopefully it's some kind of juicy gossip.

"I just talked to Ace and he's going to announce his early retirement today after the game on national TV. This will be his final season because he is moving back to Whimsy so he can be with you," Justin says.

"Wait...what?" I ask as my heart pounds out of my chest. "Why wouldn't he ask if that is what I wanted?"

"You aren't taking his calls and he thinks if football is out of the equation, then you will be with him. Is he wrong, Lily? This is huge. He is a football star and adored by his fans. He wants to give that up to go play house with you. Do you want that?" he says with an edge. Clearly team Ace.

"*No!*" I exclaim. "He can't quit. I'll call him."

"He is probably too busy getting ready. I will try to stop him, but I can't make any guarantees I can get to him before he does it. He is in a contract and paying a shit ton in legal fees to break it."

"Do you think I'm a radioactive clinger?" I ask, not even knowing what it for sure means.

"Yes, Lily, and you just blew up Ace's life."

Damn it!

I feel like the biggest asshole. I call Ace straight away, but he doesn't answer. This was one of my wishes I made the other night when he left and now he wants to do it. I wished Dexter would get hit by a car and it happened. And then that weird wind on the bridge, circulating around me as though Dexter was there. Am I some kind of Wiccan? I get goosebumps and call Kylie on her cell.

"What the fruit loops is a Wiccan?" she asks. Tater laughs in the background.

"It's like a half witch or something."

"You're not Wiccan. You're tired because you don't ever follow your heart and you're starving to death...That shit will make anyone crazy. Grab some saltines or something." I start babbling about the wind and talking to Dexter and seeing Howard while she keeps snorting.

They convince me I'm not Wiccan, but we get cut off and I realize I never told them about Ace, my purpose for calling in the first place. That seems totally Wiccan to me, and now I'm even more convinced.

My brother and his rowdy family walk through the door. I tell the kids to go play dress-up in Grandma's closet, and then I launch into my story about being Wiccan, sending both Cam and Jeanie into a fit of laughter.

"All I keep thinking about is Dexter. He moved here for me... He gave up his dreams for me. I ruined our love by my love for this town and you guys." I'm totally rambling and frantic.

"Or it was ruined because a Wiccan and a human could never work," Jeanie teases. I glare at them for not taking this seriously.

"Dexter was a dick!" Cameron exclaims. "I guarantee it won't be like that with Ace."

"Still, he loves football...He can't quit," I say.

"I agree! You need to quit this Wiccan shit and go to him! Call Rocky and charter a plane and go!" he says while looking at the clock. "Or maybe you could ride a broomstick? Could be quicker."

"Hagrid rides a motorcycle. Bewitch your dad's in the garage and land right on the football field, put a love spell on Ace, and carry him off into the sunset," Jeanie says and Cameron adoringly laughs with his wife.

"Okay," I say, ignoring their jabs at my expense. "I'm going to call Rocky." Rocky is my dad's friend who has many little planes as a hobby. But he has been known to give lifts to his friends.

"Yelllo!" Rocky's gruff but chipper voice greets me.

"Hey Rocky. It's Lily. Can you fly me to San Francisco like now?" I ask and hold my breath.

"You bet! Congrats on the baby, by the way."

Oh geez, this town is unreal.

Cameron drives me to the airport to meet Rocky, who is elated to help Ace and I.

"I was going to watch the game, but this is better," Rocky says as he starts the loud plane engine. I instantly look for something to grab onto as he taxis the runway, and I realize I can feel every tiny pebble he drives over. Plus, Rocky has always been a little weird. Not in the way that he'd ever hurt me, but he might feel compelled to do some Blue Angels stunts on the way there.

Please Wiccan magic, keep this plane and my NFL baby safe.

CHAPTER 36

~

The ride was bumpy and rough in that miniature contraption. I want the engineers' name and address so I can give them a piece of my mind. I barfed twice in the forty-five-minute flight, and I don't know if it was turbulence. For all I know, it was a mid-flight collision with another plane that sent us catapulting through the sky to where we plopped on the ground in San Francisco. I finally breath when we come to a complete stop. "Thank god," I manage to say as the tears of impending death fight to release out of my eyes.

"Great flight, kiddo!" Rocky beams like a lunatic. He starts whistling "Zip-A-Dee-Doo-Dah."

Really?

"What's your plan now? You going to tell him about that kid you're cooking and get him back?"

"I don't know," I say as I glance down at my shaking hands and wonder if I can even walk.

Rocky shrugs. "Common sense is a flower that doesn't bloom in everyone's garden." I grab another barf bag and vomit not so quietly. *What does that even mean?* He laughs while shaking his head. "Your dad couldn't fly with me either. You Moore's are too queasy."

Or you're insane...

"Can I get out?" I ask with a shaky voice because to be honest, I don't know if I'll ever recover from this flight. Or if I want to continue to have strange small talk with Rocky.

"Sure can. I'm just turning right around and heading out once I get the clearance," Rocky says as he pushes gadgets on the plane that look as though they have been tacked on with Elmer's glue. "Sure was great to catch up Lily!"

I don't believe I did anything but scream and barf for forty-five minutes.

I get off the plane after reluctantly thanking him. I have to hold onto the outside of the plane to catch my bearings before walking away. I rent a car and turn on my GPS to find Levi's Stadium. I call Ace, Kylie, Justin, and Tater over and over, but nobody is answering. It's 3 PM and there is a lot of traffic. I'm stressed out and still reeling from that joke of a plane ride.

Finally, Kylie answers.

"I'm almost there. Can you get Ace? How can I get to him?" I ask with adrenaline pumping through my veins.

"No, I'm trying, we all are, but he can't see us...or he isn't looking. He is playing an intense game right now," she says. "Use your Wiccan powers and summon him!"

"How can I get in?" I ask, ignoring her lame joke. I'm certain the only reason that plane, Rocky, the NFL baby, and myself are still intact is because of my new Wiccan powers.

"I'll meet you at the entrance. Text after you park," she says. "Or summon me—" I hang up on her. Simple folks never understand gifted people.

I park and run like never before despite my exhaustion and nervousness tugging down my limbs.

Kylie is at the entrance and gives me a big hug. "Slow down... It will all work out."

"I'm freaking out!" I say. She ushers me to our seats. "He is on the other side!" I exclaim and start flailing my arms. "These seats are crap! I may as well be home!"

"Well, we are in the first row," Justin says and laughs. "Sit down...let's think."

"No, I'm just gonna go," I say and before anyone can say anything, I jump over the wall and run. I run for my life as people chase me, so I'm bobbing and weaving and yelling for Ace. This is a really big field. I feel like I'm slowing down.

I can see him, and he finally sees me, and he starts running to me. He is yelling at the security to back off. A few coaches get involved, and I try to catch my breath while they all scream and stare at me like I'm the devil. Like I have ruined something very sacred. When the security guard tries to put cuffs on me, Ace goes crazy. More official people finally step back and give us a second. Everything keeps fading in and out because I can't breathe. I'm out of shape!

"Lily, what are you doing?" he asks as he looks around at the crowd. I follow his eyes and see us on the giant screen and notice all the fans are quiet. You could hear a pin drop for sure.

"I missed you," I say and turn and smile at him. He looks so cute with his rumpled sweaty hair in his football uniform. With all those pads, he almost seems heroic, unreal in some way. Like Iron Man, larger than life. This man loves me enough to give up his passion.

"I miss you too. Let's get you to your seat and we can talk about this after the game," he says with a sweet smile. He also thinks I'm crazy.

I grab his hands instead. "I'm so sorry about our goodbye the other day. I was so cruel."

"Sprinkles, I'm not mad at you even a little bit. I do have to get you off this field, though." He tries to lead me, but I pull my hands out of his.

"I *was* Dexter's everything!" I yell, making him pay attention. "I wasn't lying to you about that. I could see it in his eyes. When college ended, he got a big fancy job in New York and asked me to move there. I was supposed to stay for two weeks to see if I liked it but on the third day, I told him there was no way I could live there. I broke up with him. I went to Whimsy and a week later, he was there and said he quit his job and would work a blue-collar job as long as it meant having me. I wasn't happy.

I didn't want to be with him anymore, but I felt bad, so I went with it. And it just kept going until he asked me to marry him. I originally said no, but eventually after many proposals I said yes.

"When we were married, he begged me almost daily to move to San Francisco because the commute was killing him. I couldn't even entertain the idea; he wasn't my everything. He finally saw it. I hurt him and he started cheating. I don't blame him. These past five years, I was trying to protect his name for Drew, for Lucille, but mostly for him. I should have told him I didn't love him anymore. I let him give up too much for me. That is why you can't quit football," I say with tears in my eyes. "Not for me or anyone. This is your dream and you have worked hard your entire life for this. I can't let you quit."

"Sprinkles, I love you. My life is miserable without you and Drew. I can't sleep or eat. I'm lovesick without you two."

No!

"I never want you to be lovesick for me or anyone," I say and pause as I think of my dad saying Dexter was lovesick. I realize now that lovesick is when you can't have who you love. Ace can have me. "I'll move with you. After this game, we will go get Drew and we can go with you. Because I know that you, Ace Lancaster, are my everything. Your love fuels me and makes me feel complete in a way I never knew existed. I don't want to spend one more day not being yours. Everyone keeps telling me to follow my heart, and my heart is you...I'm supposed to follow you."

"I won't use his words, but I do know that you and Drew are my whole world. I can walk away from this for us," he says, motioning to the team intently watching us.

"No, I want to move with you. I want us to be a family. I want you to look at me for the rest of my life the way you are looking at me right now."

His face lights up, and he grabs my hips and pulls me to him. "Lily, I love you more than anything." He lifts me to him and kisses me. Good thing he is holding me so tightly as I am feeling weak in the knees and a little dizzy from all that running. The crowd is going crazy. I laugh when I remember where we are.

My head is spinning, and it dawns on me that it's because of the pregnancy. I pull away and smile at him.

"I'm pregnant," I say with big eyes while I scan his face. At first, he looks so overwhelmed with emotion, but then a huge sappy smile spreads across his face.

"A baby? Our baby?" he says with tears in his eyes. I know what my mom meant when she said I would know why this pregnancy happened the moment I saw his reaction. This was how it was always meant to be. We belong together. He is looking at me like I am about to give him the world. We really can have it all, our own little fairy tale.

"Well, I wasn't sure if it was yours but..." He kisses me again before I can finish teasing him. The crowd erupts into a huge applause.

He sets me down and gets on one knee, grabbing my hand, "Lily Moore, I have loved you since the day I met you. I don't care whose baby that is. I want to spend the rest of my life with you. Will you marry me?"

I throw my head back and laugh. "Yes!" I exclaim. He pulls me on his knee and kisses me again. When we stand, he throws his arms up to the crowd and they all go berserk. The wild emotion and elated feelings from the overwhelming amount of people is a buzz I never expected. I cover my face; this is so crazy. He scoops me up and carries me across the field, then introduces me to a guy that will help me find my seat. Ace grabs me one last time. "I love you. Thank you for making my day."

"I love you more," I say.

"Give her my hotel info so she can go there after the game," he says while smiling at me.

"I'll go straight there" I say and kiss him one last time.

My head is swimming. Did I just agree to marry him in a football stadium on camera? Is he even divorced yet? I decide to skip the analysis and just be happy. I sit back down with Kylie, Tater, and Justin, who are all ecstatic and drunk.

"So, what happened? Did you tell him about the baby?" Kylie asks.

"Uh...yeah. I just baby trapped him on national TV," I say with sarcasm.

"Does he know you're Wiccan?" Tater asks.

"I'll tell him after our warlock son is born," I say with a huge smile that I imagine will never leave my face again.

"Good! I'm so proud of you! Are you going home with him?" Tater asks.

"Where he goes, I go. My head is spinning," I say.

"I'm sure, but you are glowing, Lily, and so is he. Best day ever!" Tater yells. Everyone in the near vicinity is congratulating me and it feels surreal.

The overwhelming sense of joy feels somewhat foreign after the last few weeks of hell. When the game is over, I drive to his hotel and give my name to the concierge. They immediately hand me the key. I open the door and find it filled with beautiful lillies and chocolate-covered strawberries. He is so sweet. After all this running, I'm taking a shower, climbing into a fluffy robe, and sending my clothes down to be laundered.

It's a couple of hours before he shows. When he walks in, I smile brightly and jump into his arms, wrapping my legs around his waist. We hug in silence for a very long time. "I love you," I whisper in his neck.

"I'm so sorry I said you were a fling. I thought I was protecting you." I raise my face to look into his beautiful eyes. I'm so happy I get to see them until the day I die.

"I was being silly. I know how much you love Drew and I, Ace. I'm so sorry for the things I said to you in Dallas. I was so cruel."

"It's okay, I understand. I'm sorry I told you to take off the ring...I had no right," he says. "I didn't handle my insecurity well."

"You did, though. It wasn't fair to you and I'm sorry for that."

"I'm just glad it's all behind us now." He looks so relieved.

"Only moving forward now...no more looking back," I say

gently and flutter my empty ring finger at him so he can see it's gone. He smiles and rubs his thumb over it. "I took it off the day before my dad died, and then I pawned it and gave Kylie the money so she can become Whimsy's premier bikini waxer," I say and he laughs. "I did it for me. I'm sorry I wasn't honest with you from the beginning. I felt responsible for keeping his honor intact. He wasn't a bad guy and I know a lot of people dislike him, but it is very important for me never to hate him. For Drew, for Lucille, and for myself." His thumb brushes my jawline as his eyes swirl with understanding. "As for my cold feet recently, it was a culmination of many things. One in particular was brought to light just this morning by that genius Tater. I didn't want me or either one of my kids to hold you back."

"Sprinkles." His voice sounds so remorseful as he registers that I am repeating his words. "Really?"

I shrug. "I know you don't feel that way, but sometimes the ghosts of our pasts can't help but hold us back." He sits on the couch still holding me around his waist, his eyes penetrating deep into mine. His nose scrunches.

"I can't have my fiancée thinking that she's holding me back." His little smile is adorable. "Did you know that after you left Dallas, there was this giant pain in my chest? Like a stabbing pain. For a minute, I thought I was having a heart attack. I have no idea what it was, but I know I don't ever want to lose you again. You don't hold me back; you propel me forward. I am a dad now because of you, and of course I mean our baby in here"—he places his warm hand on my belly, stirring a great deal of emotion in me—"but I also mean Drew. When I first came back and landed my eyes on your gorgeous face, I wanted you back. There was this voice in my head repeating that you had a kid, almost like a warning. The minute I met her, though, that voice shut up because she is perfect, and I think she and I are meant to be together, too. She's my daughter, Lily, my baby girl. You three will never hold me back. Do you understand?"

"I know. I just had to face the insecurity. Also, there's something else I have to tell you that may make you mad." I place my hands on his shoulders and take a deep breath. "I smoked pot with my mom before I knew I was pregnant." I close my eyes so he knows how terrible I feel.

His hearty laugh makes my smile widen and I open my eyes. "Come here." He places his warm hands on either side of my cheeks and gently pulls my eager lips onto his. His hands trail down to my hips, and he nudges me off his lap. "Stand up." His excitement makes me giddy.

He gets off the couch in a swift and rather energetic motion for somebody who just finished an intense game of pig skin. He grabs my hands in his, all while looking down at me with the most gorgeous of smiles. He drops on one knee and pulls out a beautiful ring from his pocket. I cover my mouth in complete shock. It's from Tiffany's, and it's exactly what I have always wanted. Well, I don't know for sure if it's from Tiffany's, but the box looks like their signature Tiffany Blue, and he is an NFL star. This is my dream ring coming from my dream man.

"Lily, I was going to do this tonight when I landed in Whimsy, but then you ran on my football field. Not how I planned it, but I think this is better. I had this ring made last time you were in Dallas." My eyes brighten. "Will you finally get *off weed?*"

I can't stifle my laugh.

"I'm serious, Sprinkles...I'll only marry you if you give it up." I plop down on his knee and wrap my arms around his neck, his laugh mingling and flirting with mine. It's intoxicating to love someone this much, feeling the air between us crackle with our own electricity. Like his mere presence turns me on. His eyes soften into something a little more serious but still swirl with excitement, humor, and the love he has for me. All the things I love most about him. "Lily, will you marry me?"

"Yes!" I almost scream. "How many more times will you ask me today?" I feign being annoyed and he laughs before kissing me with great passion. His mouth begs mine to be his forever. The slow and deliberate movements he makes to remove my robe, the gentleness in which he moves me to the couch, is as though he is handling his greatest treasure...a value insurmountable to him.

CHAPTER 37

~

We are both wrapped around one another, naked and satiated from something we both greatly missed.

"So how do you feel? You're okay?" Ace asks, referring to my pregnancy. How do I know this? Because I'm Wiccan, that's why.

"Good. I was so consumed with Lucille and then my dad. I can't believe I didn't know sooner. All the symptoms are here. Sore boobs and fatigue." I yawn just mentioning it.

"You know, I'm going to fuss over you this whole time. Starting with making you eat dinner because if I know you, you haven't eaten today."

"I tried eating pancakes this morning, but I was too stressed about telling you I was pregnant and ruining your life." He tugs me in even tighter and laughs with me.

He orders room service and we lay in bed talking about nothing and everything all at the same time. We get interrupted when there is a knock on the door. Ace throws a robe on while I pull the covers over my head, like a kid trying to be invisible. I don't know why. His fame is something I may never get used to.

"You're safe now, Sprinkles," he says. My phone rings and Ace hands it to me, smirking. "She can't even let us have this night?" I know immediately it's Kylie.

"Hey girl!"

"Lils, you're on TV!" she screams. It sounds like she's at a bar. "I mean, you look so cute."

"Oh god," I gulp while a flush creeps up my cheeks. "The proposal?"

He grabs the remote as Kylie drones on and on about how excited she is. It's hard to hear her.

"Call me tomorrow!" I yell. I hang up and watch the video of me running and almost getting arrested. *Oh boy...*

"Here's my interview after the game." He shoves a piece of watermelon in his mouth. I sit up as he invites me into his side.

On the screen, Ace is grinning ear to ear. They lost but he doesn't seem to care nor does the press, who is only asking about me. "Lily Moore is her name then?"

"Yes," Ace says coolly.

"How did you meet? Who is she?" another asks.

"We met in preschool. She was my high school sweetheart and the love of my life and today she agreed to marry me." His smile is ridiculous. I laugh and he tickles me for making fun of him.

"You are so newly divorced. Is this a good idea?" I scrunch my nose in distaste at the rude comment.

"Yes, best idea I have ever had. Plus, I've thought about it since I was a kid. Life took us down different roads. They eventually crossed again and the moment I laid eyes on her, I knew we would be together forever." I grab his face and kiss him. He clicks off the TV.

I tell him how I found out about the pregnancy and how the whole town already knew before me or him. He tells me he put his Dallas house on the market.

"So we can go house hunting together," he says.

"That's fun. How much can we spend?" I shamelessly inquire.

"As much as you want. I think we should sell your house and build a new one in Whimsy, one down by the lake," Ace says. "Start completely fresh."

My smile is blinding. "Oh my gosh...I've always wanted to *build* a big ol' house down by the lake!"

"I know, Lily. We used to say we were going to do it together, and now we are," he says. "Tomorrow when we go home, I am going to show you the two lots I love in the country club on the lake. I can just buy the lot and then we can build when we're ready." I kiss him with passion, and he laughs between each hot press of my lips. "Buying real estate really turns you on, doesn't it?"

"Sure does. Also, I know where I want to live in Dallas." I nod my head in excitement.

"Where?" He's amused. "The mall?" *I do love that mall.*

"In Spencer's building. We can have the charm of the country in Whimsy and the luxury of the city in Dallas."

"Is this solely because they have an amazing Chinese food restaurant in the lobby?"

"Likely!" It totally is, but I think it would be fun to live in a place like that for part of the year. Like we're staying in a swanky hotel.

The next day we fly home to Whimsy on another tiny chartered plane, and I barf the whole time, though the plane wasn't quite as bad as Rocky's. Ace doesn't seem to mind.

"Is that morning sickness?" Ace asks when we get in the car.

"I guess," I say with tired eyes. We stop at the store and Ace gets me a ginger ale and saltines. I throw up in the parking lot again before he comes back.

"What took so long? I'm dying," I say.

"The whole store wanted to congratulate us, and I relived the proposal forty times before I could get out of there." He opens the ginger ale for me. I smile and take a small sip.

"No more tiny planes," I say and then immediately barf the tiny bit of ginger ale out the car door.

"That's really sexy," he teases while I laugh through dry heaves. I start feeling better after a stretch, and he drives me off to his dream properties.

He takes me to the two lots, and I choose the bigger one, which is about a ten-minute walk to my mom's house and eight minutes to his parent's. He calls Vina, a trusted and experienced Whimsy realtor, and she takes care of it. We walk the property several times and imagine our big two-story house with a basement. "How many kids do you want?" he asks, excited.

"Two more?" I say, not totally convinced.

"Or three?" he asks with a head tilt.

We're both giddy the drive to my mom's to get Drew. She saw the proposal on TV with Cameron and Jeanie who were cheering and crying, so she kind of understands. She runs over to me and I pick her up in a tight hug.

"You are going to marry him?" she asks with a big smile.

"Yes," I say.

"Will he be my daddy?" She looks so hopeful I can barely stand it.

"Yes."

Ace grabs her from me, hugging her firmly. "Only if you want that?"

"Yes!" she exclaims. "And a puppy."

"One day, Boo," I say between giggles. "Right now we have to pack so tomorrow we can get on the plane. Ace needs to get back to work. We will be gone for a while. What do you want to pack?"

"Toys," she says. "And my tutus."

That night, everyone came to my mom's to send us off. Vina also stopped by to tell us the offer was accepted. The house guests stayed late, and even people not invited caught wind of us leaving and wanted to come congratulate us. Some brought gifts. Drew stayed close by us, smiling the whole time. She slept in bed with Ace and I in my double bed with a mattress from the eighties. It wasn't a great night's sleep.

"I'm getting a Tuft & Needle delivered if we have to stay here again," Ace says the next morning. Drew rolls her eyes, which cracks us both up.

I cry when I say goodbye to everyone at the airport, even though my mom is flying out next week to watch a game with Bernie, Darla, Tim, John, and Lucille. Cameron, Jeanie, and the kids are coming out the day they leave for a family vacation. Kylie and Tater are visiting in three weeks. I am going to see everyone soon, but I'll still miss them so much until then.

When we are on the plane and Drew is tuned into *Trolls,* I cuddle up to Ace and rest my head on his shoulder. The day I saw Ace again was a day that focused on all my painful scars left behind from Dexter's death. They had been throbbing for years, threatening to rip open. They oozed at a rapid rate, paralyzing me from such a huge trauma. Ace, slowly and with much tenderness, helped me to close those wounds. It was painful to stitch them up but worth me facing the ghosts. Behind them all, he was standing there, willing to accept me and all my scars.

"Hey Sprinkles, when we come back in a few weeks, Rocky offered to come get us. I thought that would be fun," Ace says. Of course he would say that. He hasn't flown with him before.

"As Rocky would say, common sense isn't a flower that blooms in everyone's garden." No way I am ever flying anywhere with that man again.

"That bad?" He smirks. "He was pretty pumped, which made me pretty pumped."

"You know who else was pretty pumped? Oberyn Martell before he fought The Mountain," I quip and then we both laugh at my *GOT* reference.

My life will never be more perfect than it is right now. A handsome soon-to-be husband, a perfect little girl, and a baby on the way. After years of nightmares and ghosts, it's finally a dream come true.

THE END

ACKNOWLEDGEMENTS

~

This book was written quickly and passionately at a time when I needed an escape. Kylie and Finn thanks for making me want to escape! You are my greatest joys in life but sometimes mommy just needs to retreat into an alternate world…to hide…from you.

There's so many people that helped me along the way with this book. My editor Makenna Albert was a complete joy. She respected my work and taught me so much.

My cover designer Anna Volkin was such a great match for me. She walked me through the entire process of book design and formatting with so much patience. Seriously, she's a saint with dumb blondes (me) and a genius with digital butts.

Terra without your love and adoration of these characters, they'd still be living silently in my head, heart and my laptop.

My mom and dad raised me in a loving happy home where daily I witnessed their love for one another. It was a great example to live up to. Proof that settling, would never yield that kind of expert level happiness. The kind of happiness that makes you laugh at nonsense. I grew up laughing at nonsense and still today I laugh heartily at nonsense.

Joey, my pint- sized pup sat with me all those long hours it took to build Lily, Ace, Whimsy and a darling little girl that embodies all my favorite toddlers through the years.

And finally, thank you to my husband and children for having dinners without me. You three make up all three chambers of my heart. Sorry I ignored you for so long while working on this project.

ABOUT THE AUTHOR

~

Born and raised in California, Montra is a small-town girl with a wild imagination. She loves living in fictional lands, either writing them, reading them or telling a tall tale in person. She's extremely indecisive and loves landing herself in awkward, chatty encounters with strangers. Maybe not in the moment, but she will laugh heartily about it afterwards. She wanted to write on and off throughout her life, but she also wanted to be a celebrity chef, a motivational speaker, a pottery teacher, a fashion designer and a professional tap dancer. She's a dreamer, who one day fell into an open Microsoft Word and just started typing. She hopes to one day publish all the stories she has written and maybe breed pugs for extra cuddles.

Follow Montra on
Facebook & Instagram

or find out more at **www.montraaldridge.com**

Made in the USA
Las Vegas, NV
05 November 2021